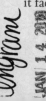
"So," Uhura finally said. "What are we going to do?"

Scott shook his head. "There's nothing we can do. We don't have any proof Spock's been compromised, and Starfleet hasn't ordered us to take action."

"Maybe I could declare him mentally unfit," McCoy said. "I could say his brokering a peace treaty was irrational, and—"

"And he'd give you a half-dozen reasons why it's completely logical," Scott cut in. "You should know by now not to argue logic with Spock. It's a losing proposition."

Uhura's temper flared higher by the moment. "Listen to the two of you!" she hissed. Backpedaling away from them, she continued. " 'Nothing we can do.' 'Losing proposition.' You're not men. Men would stand and fight! Men would eliminate Spock now, before his brand of appeasement spreads. But since neither of you seems willing to act like a man"—she drew her dagger from her boot—"I guess I'll have to do it for you."

Scott tried to interpose himself between Uhura and the door, but he wasn't quick enough. She cut him off and started backing out of the room. "Where do you think you're going, lass? What do you think you're going to do?"

"What you should have done, Mister Scott," she replied. "I'm going to kill Captain Spock before he—"

An incandescent flash of light and a lilting, almost musical ringing filled the air around Uhura—and when it faded she was gone.

STAR TREK®
MIRROR UNIVERSE

The Sorrows of Empire

DAVID MACK

Based on *Star Trek*
created by Gene Roddenberry

Star Trek: Deep Space Nine®
created by Rick Berman & Michael Piller

and *Star Trek: Enterprise*®
created by Rick Berman & Brannon Braga

POCKET BOOKS

New York London Toronto Sydney Memory Omega

Pocket Books
A Division of Simon & Schuster, Inc.
1230 Avenue of the Americas
New York, NY 10020

First Pocket Books paperback edition January 2010

POCKET and colophon are registered trademarks of Simon & Schuster, Inc.

For information about special discounts for bulk purchases, please contact Simon & Schuster Special Sales at 1-866-506-1949 or business@simonandschuster.com.

Cover art by Cliff Nielson; cover design by Alan Dingman

The Simon & Schuster Speakers Bureau can bring authors to your live event. For more information or to book an event, contact the Simon & Schuster Speakers Bureau at 1-866-248-3049 or visit our website at www.simonspeakers.com.

Manufactured in the United States of America

10 9 8 7 6 5 4 3 2 1

ISBN 978-1-4391-5516-5
ISBN 978-1-4391-6675-8 (ebook)

For what might yet be,
if we only have enough courage

Historian's Note

The Sorrows of Empire begins in mid-2267, shortly after the four crew members of the *U.S.S. Enterprise* crossed over to an alternate universe ("Mirror, Mirror"), and concludes in 2295, two years after the Khitomer Accords were signed by the United Federation of Planets and the Klingon Empire (*Star Trek VI: The Undiscovered Country*). All events occur in the mirror universe.

In every revolution, there is one man with a vision.
—Captain James T. Kirk

PART I

Sic Semper Tyrannis

2267

1

The Marriage of True Minds

Crushing Captain Kirk's windpipe was proving far easier than Spock had ever dared to imagine.

The captain of the *I.S.S. Enterprise* struggled futilely in the merciless grip of his half-Vulcan first officer. Kirk's fists struck at Spock's torso, ribs, groin. His fingers pried at Spock's hold, clawed the backs of the hands that were strangling him. Spock's grasp only closed tighter, condemning Kirk to a swift death by suffocation.

Killing such an accomplished officer as Kirk seemed a waste to Spock. And waste, as Kirk's alternate-universe counterpart had reminded Spock only a few days earlier, was illogical. Unfortunately, as Spock now realized, it was sometimes necessary.

Kirk's strength was fading, but his eyes were still bright with cunning. He twisted, reached forward to pluck Spock's agonizer from his belt—only to find the device absent. Removing it had been a grave breach of protocol, but Spock had decided that willfully surrendering to another the means to let himself be tortured was also fundamentally illogical. He would no longer accede to the Terrans' obsessive culture of self-inflicted suffering. It was time for a change.

Marlena Moreau stood in the entryway of Kirk's sleep alcove, sharp and silent while she watched Spock throttle Kirk to death in the middle of the captain's quarters. There was no bloodlust in her gaze, a crude affectation Spock had witnessed in many humans. Instead, she wore a dark expression, one of determination tinged with regret. Her sleepwear was delicate and diaphanous, but her countenance was hard and unyielding; she was like a steely blade in a silken sheath.

Still Kirk struggled. Again it struck Spock how great a waste this was, and the words of the other universe's Captain Kirk returned to his thoughts, the argument that had forced Spock to confront the futility of the imperial mission to which his civilization had been enthralled. The other Kirk had summed up the intrinsic flaw of the Empire with brevity and clarity.

The illogic of waste, Mister Spock, he had said. *Of lives, potential, resources . . .* time. *I submit to you that your empire is illogical, because it cannot endure. I submit that* you *are illogical, for being a willing part of it.*

And he had been unequivocally right.

Red stains swam across the eyes of this universe's Captain Kirk. Capillaries in the whites of his eyes had ruptured, hemorrhaging blood inside the eye sockets. Seconds more, and it would be over.

There had been no choice. No hope of altering this Kirk's philosophy of command or of politics. His doppelganger had urged Spock to seize command of the *I.S.S. Enterprise,* find a logical reason to spare the resistant Halkans, and convince the Empire it was the correct course.

Spock had hoped he could achieve such an aim without resorting to mutiny; he had never desired command, nor had he been interested in politics. Science, reason, research . . . these had always been Spock's core interests. They remained so now, but the circumstances had changed. Despite all of Spock's best-formulated arguments, Kirk had refused to consider mercy for the Halkans. Even when Spock had proved through logical argument that laying waste to the Halkans' cities would, in fact, only impede the Empire's efforts to mine the planet's dilithium, Kirk had not been dissuaded. And so had come Kirk's order to obliterate the planet's surface, to exterminate the Halkans and erase their civilization from the universe.

To speak out then would have been suicide, so Spock had stood mutely by while Kirk grinned and chuckled with malicious self-satisfaction, and watched a planet die.

Now it was Spock's turn to watch Kirk expire in his grip, but Spock took no pleasure in it. He felt no sense of satisfaction, nor did he permit himself the luxuries of guilt or regret. This was simply what needed to be done.

Kirk's pulse slowed and weakened. A dull film glazed the captain's eyes, which rolled slowly back into his skull. He went limp in Spock's grasp and his clutching, clawing hands fell to his sides. Dead weight now, he sagged halfway to his knees. Not wanting to fall victim to a ruse, Spock took the precaution of inflicting a final twist on Kirk's neck, snapping it with a quick turn. Then he let the body fall heavily to the deck, where it landed with a dull thud.

Marlena inched cautiously forward, taking Spock's measure. "We should get rid of his body," she said. Stepping gingerly in bare feet, she walked over Kirk's corpse. "And his loyalists—"

"Have been dealt with," Spock interjected. "Show me the device." He did not need to elaborate; she had been beside him in the transporter room when the other universe's Kirk had divulged to him the existence of a unique weapon, one Kirk had promised could make Spock "invincible." The device, which Marlena called the Tantalus field, had been the key to the swift rise of this universe's Kirk through the ranks of the Imperial Starfleet.

Marlena led Spock to a nearby wall, on which was mounted a trapezoidal panel. She touched it softly at its lower right corner, then at its upper right corner, and it slid soundlessly upward, revealing a small display screen flanked by a handful of buttons and dials.

"This is how you turn it on." With a single, delicate touch, Marlena activated the device. "These are the controls."

"Demonstrate it," Spock said. "On the captain's body."

He observed her actions carefully, memorizing patterns and deducing functions. With a few pushed buttons, she conjured an image of the room in which they stood. Some minor adjustments on the dials narrowed the image's focus to the body on the floor. Then she pressed a single button segregated from the others inside a teardrop-shaped mounting, and a blink of light filled the room behind them.

Marlena lifted her arm to shield her eyes, but Spock let his inner eyelids spare him from the flash. It was over in a fraction of a second, leaving him with a palpable tingle of electric potential and the lingering scent of ozone mingled with Marlena's delicately floral Deltan perfume. On the floor there was no trace of Kirk—no hair, no scorch marks, no blood . . . not a single bit of evidence a murder had occurred. Satisfied, he nodded at Marlena, who shut off the device. "Most impressive," he remarked.

"Yes," she replied. "He let me use it a few times. I only know how to target one person at a time, but he told me once it could do much more, in the right hands."

"Indubitably," Spock said. The communicator on his belt beeped twice. He lifted it from its half-pocket and flipped it open. "Spock here."

"This is Lieutenant D'Amato. The ship is secured, sir."

One detail loomed paramount in Spock's thoughts. "Have you dealt with Mister Sulu?"

"Aye, sir," D'Amato replied. *"He's been neutralized."*

"Well done, Mister D'Amato. Spock out."

Spock closed his communicator and put it back on his belt. He crossed the room to a wall-mounted comm panel and opened an intraship PA channel. "Attention, all decks. This is Captain Spock. As of fourteen twenty-six hours, I have relieved Captain Kirk and assumed command of this vessel. Continue on course for Gamma Hydra IV. That is all. Spock out." He thumbed the channel closed and turned to face Marlena. "It would seem, for now, that circumstances favor us."

"Not entirely," she said. "Last night, Kirk filed a report with Starfleet Command about the alternate universe. He called its people anarchistic and dangerous . . . and he told Starfleet he suspected you of helping breach the barrier between the universes."

Her news was not entirely unexpected, but it was still unfortunate. "Did the captain speculate why I might have done such a thing?"

"No," Marlena said. "But he made a point of mentioning your attempts to convince him to spare the Halkans."

He nodded once. "It would have been preferable for there to be no official record of the other universe's existence," he said. "But what has been done cannot be undone. We must proceed without concern for details beyond our control." Looking into her eyes, he knew that, for now, she was the only person on the ship—perhaps even in the universe—whom he could really trust, but even her motives were not entirely beyond suspicion . . . at least, not yet. But if the Terran Empire and its galactic neighbors were to be spared the ravages of a brutal social implosion followed by a devastating dark age unlike any in recorded history, he would have to learn to trust someone beyond himself—and teach others to do the same.

Picturing the shifting possibilities of the future, he knew he had already committed himself, and there was no turning back from the epic task he had just set for himself.

The great work begins.

"Congratulations, Captain," a passing junior officer said as he saluted Spock, who dutifully returned the gesture while continuing down the corridor to his new cabin.

Pomp and fanfare had never appealed to Spock. Pageantry had its uses in the affairs of the Empire, but aboard a starship it was a needless frivolity, a distraction ill afforded. He preferred to focus on tasks at hand, on the business of running the ship. The crew, sensing his mood, had obliged him. But the human compulsion to laud success was irrepressible, and he accepted it with stoic grace.

His ascendance to command, however, was only the second most compelling item of news aboard the *Enterprise*—the crew was buzzing with hearsay of the alternate universe. Chief Engineer Scott, Dr. McCoy, and Lieutenant Uhura, despite having been ordered to secrecy during their debriefings, apparently felt liberated to speak freely of it now that Kirk had been assassinated. Spock had made no effort to curtail the rumors or to interdict the crew's personal communications. The truth was out; attempting to rein it in would be futile. It had a life of its own now, and he decided to let it be.

He arrived at the captain's cabin, which he had claimed as his own. The door opened with a soft hiss. On the other side of the threshold he was met by the dry heat and dim reddish-amber glow that he preferred for his private quarters, a crude approximation of the light and climate of his homeworld of Vulcan. He was pleased to see the last of Captain Kirk's belongings had been removed from the compartment, and his own possessions had been moved in. On the far side of the room, Marlena was gently hanging his Vulcan lute on the wall.

Spock stepped farther into the room, clear of the door's sensor. The portal slid shut behind him. Marlena turned and folded her hands in front of her waist. "I assumed this was where you would want it displayed," she said.

"It is," Spock said. He had not expected her to still be there. She had been Kirk's woman for some time, and though she had sympathized with Spock's cause, he had anticipated little more from her than silent acquiescence. Apparently, she had taken it upon herself to supervise the transfer of his personal effects and to complete the preparation of his new quarters.

"You've received several personal transmissions in the past few hours," she said, moving to the cabinet where beverages were stored. "Some from other starship captains, some from the Admiralty . . . even one from Grand Admiral Garth himself."

"Yes," Spock replied. "I have already read them."

She opened the cabinet and took out a bottle of Vulcan port and two short, squarish glasses. "Missives of congratulation, no doubt." She glanced up at Spock, who nodded in confirmation, then she half-filled both glasses with the bright green liquor.

He accepted the glass she offered him. By reflex, he sniffed it once, to try to discern any telltale fragrance of toxins lurking in its tart, fruity bouquet.

Keen to his suspicion, Marlena smirked. "It's not poisoned. But if it will make you more comfortable, we can swap glasses."

"Unnecessary," Spock said, and he took a drink.

At that, she smiled. "Trust?"

His tone was calm and even. "A calculated risk."

With slow and languid grace, she reached up and stroked her fingertips across his bearded chin. "I've been a captain's woman, Spock. . . . Am I still?"

A stirring in the dark corners of his soul, the animal cry of his human half. It felt something for this woman—a hunger, a need. Dominated by his Vulcan discipline and his credo of unemotional logic, his human passions were deeply buried, strange and unfamiliar to him. But they paled in comparison to the savage desires of his ancient Vulcan heritage, whose lethal furies were the reason his people relied on the dictums of logic for their continued survival as a culture.

As if with a will of its own, his left hand rose and cupped Marlena's cheek, then traveled through her warm, dark hair. It was soft and fell over his fingers like a lover's breath. Her skin was warm. His fingertips rested on the side of her scalp, while she traced a line with her nails down his throat.

"You are still the captain's woman," he said.

Her hand moved along his clavicle, to his shoulder, down the length of his arm, until it came to rest atop his own hand, on the side of her face. "When I was a girl, I heard stories about Vulcans who could touch minds," she said. "Is it true?"

"Yes," he said, revealing his people's most closely guarded secret, one for which entire species—such as the Betazoids and the Ullians—had been all but exterminated. "We hide our powers from outsiders, and such a bond is never performed lightly. The melding of two minds is a *profound* experience."

She took a half step closer to him, all the while holding eye contact and keeping her hand pressed against his. "Do both people know it's happening?"

"They become as one," Spock said. "No secrets remain."

Resting her free hand against his chest, she whispered, "I wouldn't resist if . . . if you wanted to . . ."

It was subtle, nimble, and quick. His fingers changed position on the side of her face, spreading apart like the legs of an arachnid, seeking out the loci of neural pathways.

Marlena tensed and inhaled a short, sharp breath. Though she had said she wouldn't resist, she couldn't have known what the touch of a Vulcan mind-meld would really feel like. Nothing could have prepared her for the total loss of privacy, the ultimate exposure of her inner self to another consciousness. Even the most willing participants resisted their first time.

"My mind to your mind," Spock intoned, his rich baritone both soothing and authoritative. "Our thoughts are merging. I know what you know. Our minds become one. We become one."

The dark flower of her mind bloomed open in his thoughts, and the coldly rational structures of his logic gave form to her chaos of passions and appetites. Fears fell silent, motives were laid bare, and the union of their psyches was complete.

Years, days, and moments wove together into a shared tapestry of their past. The cold disapproval of Spock's father, Sarek, stood in sharp contrast to the volcanic fury of Marlena's father, François: an icy stare tore open a silent gulf between a father and son; a broad palm slapped a young girl's face again and again, leaving the hot sting of betrayal in its wake.

I have made my decision, Father.

I'm sorry, Daddy! Please stop! Don't!

Defenses took root, grew coarse, became permanent barriers. Marlena's weapon of choice was seduction; Spock's preferred implement was logic. He planned ahead, a master chess player thinking two dozen moves beyond his current position; she lived in the moment, moved with the shifting currents of power and popular opinion, never planning for tomorrow—because who knew what the universe would be like by then?

Yin and yang, they stood enmeshed in one another's thoughts. She, quick to anger, rash to act, desperately seeking one moment of tenderness, one solitary moment of affection, in a life that promised nothing but strife and loneliness. He, aloof and alone, desiring only knowledge and order, but watching the Empire begin an inexorable slide toward collapse and chaos.

All they had in common was the shared experience of meeting the humans from the other universe, the glimpse of a reality so much like theirs yet so different. He admired their discipline, their restraint, their stability. Marlena yearned to live among people of such nobility and compassion. Blending her memories with his own, Spock knew that the qualities he had so respected in the visitors, and the ones that Marlena envied, were inseparable. The others' self-control and focus in collective effort were made possible by the peaceful ethos they embraced.

Spock also had not forgotten that the visitors' merciful ways had saved his own life, when the alternate Dr. McCoy had risked being left behind in this cosmos in order to save Spock from what would have been a fatal subcranial hemorrhage. Marlena had witnessed that moment as well, with Kirk's alien assassination device. What she hadn't seen was that, after Spock had risen from the table, he had mind-melded with McCoy to force the truth from his weak human brain—and beheld a vision of the universe the visitors called home.

It was not without its conflicts, but the civilization to which the humans belonged was no empire; it was a federation, a democratic society, committed to peaceful exploration and coexistence, eschewing violence except in its own defense or that of others who ask for their aid.

That would be a society worth fighting for. Worth saving.

In every revolution . . . there is one man with a vision.

Marlena reached up and gently pressed her fingertips against the side of Spock's face. "I share your vision."

There were no lies in a mind-meld. Spock knew she spoke the truth; she knew his thoughts, understood

what he meant to do, though she likely did not realize all
the consequences of what would follow. But her sincerity was unimpeachable, and for the first time in his life,
he knew what it was to be simpatico with another being.
They were each the first person whom the other had
ever truly trusted. Though they knew the galaxy would
likely align itself against them and their goals, they were
not afraid, because at that moment, in that place, they
had one another, they were one another . . . they were
one.

He pulled back from her mind. Loath to be left
alone once more, she resisted his departure, clung to
his thoughts, pleaded without words for a few more
moments of silent intimacy. It was a labor to leave her
mind, and for a moment he hesitated. Then discipline
reasserted itself, and he gently removed her fingers from
his face as he severed their psychic link. Tears welled in
her eyes as she looked up at him. His mien, masklike
and vaguely sinister, did not betray the swell of new-
found feelings he had for her . . . but then, despite his
best intentions, a savage chord in his nature asserted its
primal desires. He pulled her close and kissed her with
a passion no Vulcan would admit to outside the sacred
rites of *Pon farr*.

She kissed him back, not with hunger or aims of seduction, but with devotion, with affection . . . with love.

Though he would never have imagined himself des-
tined for such a fate, he realized he might almost be able
to let himself reciprocate her feelings. *How ironic,* he
mused, *that after all the times I have chided Sarek for choosing
a human mate, I should now find myself emulating his behavior.*

Embracing Marlena, he knew he would never give
her up and she would never betray him. Whether that

would be a strong enough foundation upon which to erect a new future for the people of the Empire, he didn't know, but it was an ember of hope, one with which he planned to spark a blaze that would burn away a failed civilization already in its decline, and make way for a new galactic order that would rise from its ashes.

For the love of a woman, Spock would destroy the Empire.

He would ignite a revolution.

2

The Inevitability of Change

"*Main shuttlebay doors secure,*" intoned a masculine voice over the *Enterprise*'s intraship address system. "*Repressurizing shuttlebay. Stand by.*"

Captain Spock, Dr. Leonard McCoy, and the *Enterprise*'s newly promoted first officer, Commander Montgomery Scott, walked together down the corridor to the ship's main shuttlebay. The three men were attired in their dress uniforms, as were the members of the security detachment gathered at the shuttlebay door. As soon as the guards saw Spock, they snapped to attention, fists to their chests; then they extended their arms, palms forward, in unison. Spock returned the salute.

"*Shuttlebay repressurized,*" the voice announced.

With a nod, Spock said, "Positions, gentlemen."

The guards entered the shuttlebay single file, forming an unbroken line from the door of the shuttlebay to the hatch of the just-returned shuttlecraft *Galileo*. Phasers drawn and clutched reverently to their chests, they stood at attention, eyes front. A group of Vulcan delegates debarked from the shuttlecraft, boarding the *Enterprise* for transport to the imperial conference on the planet code-named Babel.

At the front of the procession, moving with confidence and radiating personal power, was the head of the Vulcan delegation: Ambassador Sarek of Vulcan, Spock's father. Trailing behind him was Amanda, his human wife, followed by the junior members of his diplomatic entourage. They all carried with them the spicy scents of the Vulcan homeworld. It had been four years since Spock had last been there, and eighteen years since he had last exchanged words with his father. It was likely, Spock knew, that Sarek would resist any overture of reconciliation he might offer, but he would not be able to avoid interacting with Spock now that he was the captain of the *Enterprise*. Under different circumstances, Spock might have found the necessity of contact to be distasteful, but as matters now stood it was a fortunate arrangement, and one he intended to exploit.

Sarek halted in front of Spock, eyed the gold tunic Spock wore, and made a silent note of the rank insignia. He looked Spock in the eye and said in a level voice, "Permission to come aboard, Captain."

Spock lifted his right hand in the Vulcan salute and waited until Sarek reciprocated the gesture before he replied, "Permission granted, Ambassador Sarek." He nodded at his two fellow officers. "Our chief medical officer, Doctor McCoy, and our first officer, Commander Scott." Scott and McCoy nodded curtly to Sarek, who returned the gesture.

Speaking more to Scott and McCoy than to Spock, Sarek motioned to the retinue that followed him. "My aides and attachés, and she who is my wife." He held up one hand and extended his index and middle fingers together. Amanda joined him directly and pressed her own fingertips to his. They both were stoic in their quiet companionship. It was a quality of their relationship Spock had always found admirable.

"Commander Scott will escort you and your wife to your quarters, Mister Ambassador," Spock said. "Once you are settled, I look forward to offering you a tour of the ship."

"Captain, I'm certain you must have more pressing matters to attend to," Sarek said, as verbally agile as ever. "Perhaps one of your junior officers could guide us." He clearly did not want to interact with Spock any more than was necessary to complete his assignment for the Vulcan government, but the protocols of military and diplomatic courtesy prevented him from saying so.

Spock intended to turn that limitation to his advantage. "It would be my privilege, Mister Ambassador," he said. "I insist."

Of course, Sarek could simply decline the invitation entirely, but Spock knew Sarek's devotion to the minutiae of decorum would prevent that. A subtle exhalation of breath signaled Sarek's grim acceptance of the inevitable. "Very well," he said. "My wife and I shall look forward to receiving you at your earliest convenience."

"Ambassador," Spock said with a half-nod, bringing the discussion to a close. Sarek looked at Commander Scott, who led the middle-aged Vulcan and his wife away, toward a turbolift that would take them to their quarters. The rest of the diplomatic team was escorted from the shuttlebay by the security team, as much for their own protection as that of the other Babel Conference delegates currently aboard the *Enterprise.*

McCoy turned and smirked at Spock. "Your father didn't look too happy to see you, Captain."

"My father is a Vulcan, Doctor. He feels neither happy nor unhappy."

The doctor snorted derisively. "You can tell yourself

that if you want, *sir,* but that man is *not* looking forward to seeing you later." He frowned. "Pure logic, my ass. I know a grudge when I see one."

"Perhaps," Spock said. "But be that as it may, I will not tolerate being interrogated on the subject by a subordinate—particularly not by one who tortured his own father to death."

McCoy bristled at the mention of his father. "Dammit, I was under orders! You know that. I was *under orders.*"

"Indeed, Doctor. As are we all."

The tour of the ship passed quickly. Spock escorted his parents from their quarters first to the bridge, and then through the various scientific and medical laboratories in the primary hull. Sarek made a point of limiting his remarks to no more than a few words—"I see," or "Sensible," or "Most logical"—never asking follow-up questions, and suppressing any attempt Amanda made to engage Spock in more than the most perfunctory manner.

After a brief visit to the astrophysics labs and sickbay, they arrived in main engineering, which was busy with activity, most of it directed from the bridge by Commander Scott, who still groused to anyone who would listen that he had been forced to leave his beloved engines in less capable hands.

Less than an hour later, the tour was finished, and Spock escorted his parents to his own quarters. He walked a step ahead of them, moving in long strides he knew his father would easily match. Stopping in front of his door, Spock turned and said curtly, "Mother, I wish to meet privately with Sarek. Please excuse us."

"Of course, Spock," she said, and started to step away.

Sarek caught her arm and stopped her, all the while keeping his hard, dark eyes fixed on Spock. "No, my wife. Stay with me."

Undeterred, Spock steeled his tone. "I must insist, Mister Ambassador. It is a matter of great urgency."

"I have nothing to say to you, Spock," Sarek declared. "You made your decision, and you must live with the consequences."

Amanda looked torn between them. "Sarek, please, listen . . ."

"Be silent, Amanda," Sarek said, his voice quiet but forceful. Returning his attention to Spock, he continued. "You could have been a leader on Vulcan, Spock. A man of power and influence. You rejected that for this? Most illogical."

Spock hardened his resolve. "I disagree."

"Naturally," Sarek said. He tried to walk away. "Let us pass. It has been a long day for my wife. We should retire."

"Ambassador," Spock said sharply, "I will speak my mind to you, and you will listen. As captain of this ship, I have the power to compel your audience—and much more, if I so desire. I respectfully suggest the wiser course of action would be not to force me to resort to such barbaric tactics."

For several seconds Sarek regarded Spock and took his measure. Spock waited while his father pondered his options. At last, Sarek folded his hands together and sighed. "As you wish, Captain. I am most interested to hear what you consider to be of such grave importance." He turned to Amanda. "I will rejoin you when my conversation with Spock is finished." She nodded her understanding and walked away.

Spock unlocked the door. It swished open, and he stepped aside to let Sarek pass. "After you, Mister Ambassador."

Inside Spock's cabin, the thermostat had been adjusted to a much warmer level than normal, and almost all traces of humidity had been extracted from its air—both changes being for Sarek's benefit. Seated across a small table from Spock, Sarek's face was steeped in long vertical shadows from the dim, crimson-hued overhead illumination. He shook his head.

"Your proposal is not logical, Spock," he said. "It is grounded in sentimental illusions."

"I assure you," Spock replied, "it is not." He picked up the ceramic urn of hot tea on the table between them and refilled their cups as he continued. "You yourself have admitted that conquering Coridan for its dilithium resources will inevitably consume more time, personnel, and resources than it can repay. Advocating a policy of waste is illogical." He set down the tea urn and looked Sarek in the eye. "However, enticing Coridan to join the Empire of its own volition, particularly if it can be accomplished without resorting to threats or force, would represent a significant and immediate gain for the Empire, at a relatively moderate long-term cost."

Sarek sipped his tea slowly, then set down his cup. "Even if I acknowledge the logic of your analysis, Spock, you must concede that negotiating such an agreement with a planet we could just as quickly invade would make the Empire appear weak. If our enemies come to believe we would rather talk than act, they will not hesitate to strike. Introducing supplication into our foreign policy will only invite attack."

"Your analysis is flawed, Sarek."

The accusation provoked a glare from the elder Vulcan. He reined in his temper, then said, "Explain."

"I agree that opening talks with Coridan will cause the Klingons and the Romulans to question our motives," Spock said. "But their scanners will still show our border defenses to be intact and our fleet vigilant. They will not attack."

Pensive now, Sarek folded his hands in front of his chest. "The other delegates will not be receptive to this idea."

"Then you must persuade them," Spock said. "It will cost the Empire less than conquest, and reap it greater benefit."

Spock thought he noticed a frown on Sarek's face as the older man rose from the table and paced across the cabin. Watching his father stroll the perimeter of the room as though it were an activity of great interest reminded Spock of his youth, growing up in Sarek's home on Vulcan. Whenever Sarek had become displeased with him, he'd paced like this. "As it ever was, so it remains," Sarek said, half under his breath. "You have served the ambitions of humans all your life—no doubt thanks to the influence of your mother and your own human DNA. Assuming command of a starship has only made your devotion to the Terrans' cause more strident."

"Why do you assume it is their interests I serve?"

Spreading his arms to gesture at the space around them, Sarek said, "You command one of their starships. You ask me to help increase their power and wealth by proposing we invite Coridan into the Empire. What other conclusion should I draw?"

"You have heard only the first step in my proposal,"

Spock pointed out. "I think you will find its later stages *intriguing* for their anticipated effect upon the status quo."

"I am well acquainted with how the Terrans adjust the status quo," Sarek replied. Many times had Spock listened patiently while Sarek recounted, with thinly veiled bitterness, the manner in which humans, immediately following their first contact with the crew of a Vulcan scout ship, had captured the scouts and tortured them into divulging the secrets of interstellar navigation. In short order, the Terrans had turned the Vulcans' knowledge to their own aims, laying the foundation for their nascent star empire.

"You assume facts not in evidence, Sarek." He waited until he once again commanded Sarek's full attention, and then he continued. "Strengthening the Empire is not my objective. In fact, I aim to do quite the opposite."

A twinge of emotion fluttered across Sarek's countenance. Fear, perhaps? He moved slowly, positioning the table between himself and his son. In a milder tone than he had used before, he said, "Speak plainly, Spock."

"Fact: The Empire's policies of preemptive warfare and civil oppression are not sustainable, and will soon collapse."

Cautiously, Sarek nodded. "Stipulated."

Emboldened, Spock pressed on. "Fact: Within approximately two hundred forty-three Earth years, uprisings will compromise the security of the Terran Empire from within, even as it wages a war against multiple external threats. The ensuing collapse will most probably destroy millennia of accumulated knowledge, triggering an interstellar dark age without precedent in the history of local space."

Sarek nodded gravely. "Vulcan's Council has reached the same conclusion. The Empire's collapse is inevitable."

"Agreed," Spock said. "The Empire cannot be saved. But the civilization it supports can be—with a different, more benign form of government."

The upward pitch of Sarek's tone would barely have been noted by a non-Vulcan, but to Spock it registered as indignation. "You speak of treason, Spock."

"I speak of the inevitability of change, Sarek." He picked up Sarek's half-full cup of tea from the table and held it before himself. "The Empire will fall. And when it does—" He let the cup fall to the deck. It broke into dozens of small jagged fragments, spilling tea in an irregular puddle across the carpet. "All within it will be lost. Unless—" He picked up his own cup from the table, opened the lid on the ceramic pot in the middle of the table, and poured his leftover tea back inside. Then he casually hurled the cup against the wall, where it shattered into countless earthen shards.

Several seconds passed while Sarek considered Spock's point. The metaphor had been obvious enough that Spock had not felt the need to elaborate after throwing the empty cup. He was certain Sarek understood he meant to transition the imperial civilization to a new form of government before making a sacrifice of the Empire itself, casting it aside after it had been gutted and reduced to a hollow shell of its former self.

"My son," Sarek began, sounding as though he were selecting each word with great care, "I ask this with genuine concern: Do you suffer from a mental infirmity?"

The question was not unexpected. Spock shook his head once. "I am in full possession of my faculties,

Father." He took one step toward Sarek. "It will take time for my plan to come to fruition. I must cultivate allies and fortify a power base. But it *can* be done—and if we wish to prevent the sum of all Vulcan thought and achievement from being erased less than three centuries from now, it *must* be done."

Sarek emerged from behind the table. He stepped slowly between the shards of the broken cups. "For the sake of our discussion, let us assume you can seize power over the Empire, and maintain your hold long enough to push it toward its own demise. What do you propose should replace it?"

"A constitutionally ordered, representative republic," Spock said. As he'd expected, Sarek recoiled from the notion.

"Most illogical," Sarek replied. "The Empire is too large to be governed in such a manner. It would fall into civil war."

Nodding, Spock said, "As an Empire, yes. But as a co-alition of sovereign worlds, united for their mutual benefit, much of its administration could be localized. Each planet would be responsible for its own governance and would contribute to the interstellar defenses of the re-public."

"Madness," Sarek retorted. "You would never be able to maintain control."

"Irrelevant," Spock said. "When it is in each world's best interest to remain united with the others, it will no longer be necessary to compel their loyalty. Self-interest will dictate that the good of the many also benefits the few—or the one."

The elder Vulcan stopped in front of the food slot and pushed a sequence of buttons to procure more tea.

High-pitched warbles of sound emanated from behind the device's closed panel. "The populace is not ready for self-rule, Spock. After centuries of dictatorship, the responsibilities of civic duty will be alien to them. They will reject it." The food-slot panel lifted, revealing a new ceramic pot and two empty cups on a tray. Sarek picked up the tray and moved it to the table. "And our enemies will capitalize on the chaos that follows from your reforms."

"I am not suggesting we dismantle Starfleet," Spock said. He moved to the table and stood opposite his father. "If reform is to have a chance to succeed, foreign interference must be prevented." He gestured for Sarek to be seated. As his father sat, so did Spock. He reached forward, lifted the teapot, and filled his father's cup with a slow, careful pour. "I do not propose to effect my changes all at once," Spock said. "Progress must come by degrees." Spock set down the teapot. "By the time our rivals are aware of the true scope of my intentions, they will be ill-prepared to act."

Leaning forward, Sarek said, "But when they do act, Spock, their reprisal will be catastrophic." He picked up the teapot and, with the measured motions of an old man in no hurry to reach the end of his life, poured tea into Spock's cup. "It is logical to conclude the Empire cannot endure, but to contend the solution to that problem is to prematurely destroy the Empire is . . . *counterintuitive,* at best."

"Indeed," Spock replied as he watched Sarek set down the teapot. Spock picked up his cup and savored the gentle aroma of the herbal elixir. "But to do nothing is more illogical still."

"True," Sarek replied. He breathed deep the perfume

of his own tea. They sipped their drinks together for several minutes, each contemplating what the other had said. It was Sarek who finally broke the silence. "I find much of what you propose troubling, Spock. However, given the inevitable decline and fall of the Empire, yours seems the most logical course."

"Most generous," Spock said.

"I offer you this caveat, however," Sarek added. "Even the most thoroughly logical agenda can be confounded by the actions of an irrational political actor—and humans are nothing if not irrational. They can be passionate, vindictive, sometimes even loyal . . . but more than any other species I have ever met, they are willing to kill and die for ideology. Most any species will fight for territory, resources, or survival. But Terrans, far beyond all the others, will readily slaughter billions and lay waste to entire worlds for the sake of an idea. Choosing the nobler of two paths will not come naturally to them. . . . They will have to be fooled into acting in their own best interest."

There was wisdom in Sarek's words, Spock knew. "Your point is well taken," he said. "Perhaps it is my own human ancestry that has spurred me on this admittedly ideological course of action. That, most of all, is why I humbly seek to enlist you as my chief political counsel."

"I would be honored."

Rising from his seat, Spock said, "There also is one other matter of importance." Gesturing toward the sleep nook in the back of the cabin, he called out, "Marlena. Join us."

Sarek also stood as Marlena appeared from the shadows. She was attired in her nightclothes, and her long, dark hair was tousled. She strode to Spock's side and clutched delicately at his arm. "You shouldn't have woken me," she said with a glare. "I was having a good dream for a change."

Spock ignored her complaint. "This is Lieutenant Marlena Moreau—my fiancée." Turning to her, he continued. "Marlena, this is Ambassador Sarek of Vulcan . . . my father."

She looked quickly from Spock to Sarek, then blushed with shame. "Forgive me, Ambassador. I didn't mean to . . . I mean, I wanted to make a better first impression than this. I . . ." She stammered for a few seconds more without forming any actual words. Spock and Sarek waited, each with one eyebrow raised.

"Emotional, isn't she?" Sarek noted.

"Indeed," Spock admitted.

"Why do you wish to marry her?"

With a tilt of his head, Spock gave the only honest answer. "It seems the logical thing to do."

Sarek nodded. "I understand." He took two short steps toward the door. "Rest tonight, Spock. We will speak again before the conference." He glanced once at Marlena, then, almost imperceptibly, signaled his approval to Spock with the barest hint of a nod. "The future awaits us; we have much to do."

2268

3

The Sleep of Reason

Death was close at hand; Empress Hoshi Sato II felt it. The shadows of her bedchamber vibrated with its icy promise.

Candles flickered on the periphery of the ornately appointed room. A haze of lavender incense smoke lingered like a gauzy blanket above her bed; her Andorian physician, Dr. th'Nellis, had chosen it for its cloying, quasi-medicinal sweetness, in a futile effort to mask the odors of the Empress's ancient, dying body.

Hoshi II found the fragrance repugnant, but after all Dr. th'Nellis had done to extend her life, she didn't wish to embarrass him by ordering it removed. The soft-spoken *thaan* had spent most of the past decade supervising the Empress's gene therapy, and transplanting vital organs and transfusing fresh blood from lobotomized clones of her predecessor, the original Empress Hoshi Sato. His efforts had verged on the heroic, but there was nothing more to be done.

Her body felt insubstantial, as if it were a feather on the wind. She was as weak as the winter sun, as tired as a dream that wanted to die.

Not yet, she thought, willing herself to live. She had words she needed to speak, a sacred charge she needed to impart.

She beckoned with one withered hand. "Come closer, sister."

Soft footfalls broke the silence as her teenage twin, Hoshi Sato III, stepped out of the gloom to stand by the bed. The youth caressed a strand of gray hair from her elderly sibling's cheek with one hand; in the other she held a wineglass filled with cabernet the color of blood. The young woman's touch was warm, but her expression was cold as she gazed down at the Empress. "I'm here," she said.

"I don't have much time left," the Empress said, her once-melodious voice reduced to a dry rasp.

The cloned echo of her youth replied without pity, "So I see."

The Empress summoned the last of her failing strength. "I never gave you a chance to know me."

"I know your reputation."

"Then you know only a fiction." A sharp pain in the Empress's chest stole her breath. When it passed, she continued. "Like the first Empress Sato, I wanted more for the Empire than war and slaughter. I wanted it to be secure. Stable."

Her heir-apparent let slip a soft snort of derision. "Forgive me for correcting your history, *Majesty,* but all your predecessor wanted was for her *dynasty* to be secure, and she saw the Empire as little more than a means to that end. That's why we exist—because she wanted to make sure *her* empire had *her* face forever. We're nothing more than copies of the biggest narcissist in galactic history."

"We bear her likeness, but that doesn't mean we're doomed to live in her shadow. We can chart our own path, sister."

The future sovereign smirked. "An ironic statement, coming from you."

"I ruled according to my conscience, not hers."

"Strange, then, that your actions and hers proved so similar. In fact, the only substantial difference I see in your respective reigns is that she had to conquer the Empire to became its tyrant. All you had to do was inherit it."

"A despot is what I became," the Empress said. "Not what I meant to be."

"Let me guess: you aspired to a *benevolent* dictatorship." She rolled her brown eyes and shook her head. "How banal."

The sovereign's voice faltered as she weakened. "I'd hoped to reform the Empire. Curb its excesses. Steer it toward a nobler path."

"A *reformer*? You?" Hoshi III laughed angrily. "The Murderess of Andoria? The woman who redefined 'ruthlessness' for a generation?"

The Empress exhaled heavily and squeezed shut her eyes in anger and shame. "I confess, I fell for the seductions of power. Couldn't resist serving my whims . . . my obsessions . . . my base desires. It was too much. I . . . I lost sight of myself."

Recoiling and adopting a suspicious mien, the younger Sato asked, "Why are you telling me this, Majesty?"

"So you can learn from my mistakes," the Empress said. "I no longer have the strength or time to chart a new course for the Empire. You do." She reached out and grasped her twin's hand, which was smooth and supple with youth. "You can steer the Terran Empire back toward honor."

Young Hoshi's brow knitted with confusion and amusement. "Why would I want to do that, Majesty? I've spent my whole life preparing to rule. And now, on the cusp of my coronation, you expect me to renounce the plenary power that's my birthright? To shoulder the burdens of a prince's throne while denying myself its most cherished perquisites?" She brusquely pulled her hand from the Empress's grasp. "Have you finally lost your mind?"

"No, I've finally found my reason."

The nineteen-year-old lunged forward as if to pounce on the bedridden sovereign. Perched on her fists, she hovered over her crone of a sister and let her lips curl into a menacing snarl. "You're just a confused old woman," she said, her voice freighted with contempt. "Honor? Nobility? You mewl like a coward fresh from a Klingon mind-sifter, or a child on her way to the agony booth."

Regret swelled in the heart of the Empress. There would be no counseling her successor, no mitigating the ferocity or terror of the reign to come. This new monarch was a child of raw power and old privilege, a twisted product of the corrupt imperial court, a scion of cruel ambition.

"Heed my words, or don't," said the Empress. "But do not mock me, child." She waved her hand dismissively. "I need to rest. Leave me."

"In a moment," the teen replied, locking eyes with the Empress.

Empress Sato II inhaled and savored one last breath tinged with lavender incense. She knew what was coming next.

The girl grabbed a pillow from the bed and pushed it

down on the Empress's face, leaning into it with all her weight and strength.

The Empress flailed feebly with her emaciated arms. Through the smothering mass of the pillow, she heard her successor pretend to comfort her.

"*Shhh.* Sleep, sister. It'll be over in a moment."

Within seconds the last spark of the Empress's will faded, taking with it her panic and fear. Her arms came to rest at her sides.

Poised on the edge of oblivion, she expected to hate her killer.

Instead she felt only gratitude—because the Empire had at last become someone else's problem.

4

The Fire of Sacrifice

The bridge of the *Enterprise* was a charred husk, a sparking shell resounding with the groans of the wounded. Thick, acrid smoke shrouded the overhead. The main viewscreen alternated between dull blackness and bursts of static.

Captain Spock pulled himself back into the command chair and sleeved a smear of green blood from the gash on his forehead. "Damage report."

Lieutenant Kevin Riley struggled to coax a response from the smoldering remains of the navigator's station. "*Excalibur*'s weapons fired at full power, sir. We've lost shields, and warp drive is offline."

"Casualties?"

Commander Scott looked up from the sensor display at his station. "Twelve dead, seventeen wounded. Daystrom's M-5 unit must've gone haywire," he said. "*Potemkin*'s been destroyed, and *Hood* and *Lexington* are in worse shape than we are."

"Analysis?"

Scott frowned. "One more hit and we're done for."

Lieutenant Nyota Uhura swiveled her chair from the communications console to face Spock. "Captain, Commodore Wesley is hailing *Excalibur*," reported the striking, brown-skinned human. "He's receiving no response."

"Helm," Spock said, "initiate evasive maneuvers."

Jabbing at his console with mounting frustration, Ensign Sean DePaul replied, "Helm's not responding, sir, and phasers have overloaded. Should I arm photon torpedoes?"

Scott protested, "Torpedoes? At this range, without shields? Are you mad?"

"*Excalibur*'s coming around for another pass," Riley declared.

Spock had anticipated a scenario such as this weeks earlier, when *Enterprise* had received its orders to participate in war games to test M-5—famed scientist Richard Daystrom's latest invention, a multitronic computer he claimed could run a starship not only by itself but also with greater speed and precision than with a living crew. Daystrom's boast had proved disastrously true. Granted control of one *Constitution*-class starship, M-5 had destroyed another and crippled three more in a single attack run. Its reaction times and ability to anticipate the responses of the four crewed vessels arrayed against it had been nothing less than superhuman.

Rising from his chair, Spock asked, "Mister Scott, do you have access to our library computer?"

"Aye, sir," Scott said as Spock joined him at the science station.

"Call up the data charts for *Lexington*'s and *Hood*'s command consoles," Spock ordered.

Keying in the request to the memory banks, Scott said, "Here they come." The classified schematics appeared on the screen in front of him. He aimed a questioning look at Spock. "Sir . . . are you doing what I think you're doing?"

"We have no hope of defeating M-5 by orthodox

means," Spock said. "Therefore, logic demands an *un-orthodox* response."

"But why not call up *Excalibur*'s console chart?"

Entering his command authorization into the system, Spock said, "Because M-5 has no doubt anticipated this response and changed *Excalibur*'s prefix codes."

The first officer's voice dropped to a fearful whisper. "And if Captain Martinez and Commodore Wesley have done the same . . . ?"

Arching one eyebrow, Spock replied, "In that case, Mister Scott, we are all about to die."

Commodore Robert Wesley waved away the smoke stinging his eyes and barked orders at the bridge crew of the *I.S.S. Lexington*.

"Get those fires out, dammit! Horst, get a fix on *Excalibur*'s position, now! Number One, tell engineering we need warp speed on the double!"

His crew seemed to be dazed; they responded to his commands as if trapped in slow motion. The commodore pushed his way to the upper deck of his bridge and shook the bloody-faced science officer until the man's eyes focused. "Snap out of it, Clayton! Get the sensors working and report!" Clayton nodded, turned, and hunched over the sensor console while he worked its controls.

Wesley hurried back to the helm. He pushed the dead woman slumped in the chair to the deck, and then he armed the main phaser bank.

I never should have trusted Daystrom or his crazy machine, he castigated himself. The scientist had seemed less than entirely stable, but his reputation as the genius who had unlocked the secrets of duotronic circuitry decades earlier had been enough to earn a measure of Wesley's trust.

Daystrom had assured Wesley that M-5 could destroy *Enterprise* during the war games and make it look like an accident, thereby ridding Starfleet of Captain Spock and his sympathizers. *Daystrom never said the multitronic system would try to kill the rest of us, too,* Wesley raged as he locked his ship's weapons on the approaching *I.S.S. Excalibur.*

His first officer, Commander Zeke Dowty, called out from an auxiliary tactical station, "Sir! *Enterprise* is falling back!"

"Hail them," Wesley snapped at his communications officer.

The slender Andorian *shen* frantically flipped switches on her console. "Comms are offline," she said, turning toward Wesley.

Lexington's helm went dark under Wesley's hands even as the ship accelerated into an attack maneuver against the fast-approaching *Excalibur.*

From the science station, Clayton shouted in alarm, "Our self-destruct package just armed!"

Scrambling to a command console, Dowty asked, "Is it the M-5?"

"Negative," Clayton said, eyeing a computer readout. "It's *Enterprise*!"

Dowty shouted, "Engage the override!"

Damn you, Spock, Wesley fumed.

He knew it would take his crew only moments to overcome the usurpation of their command console's prefix code. But as he watched *Excalibur* bear down on his ship and the *Hood,* he knew those were moments they would never have.

Spock sat facing *Enterprise*'s main viewscreen and watched *Excalibur* pummel *Hood* and *Lexington* with phaser beams. The two crewed vessels flanked *Excalibur* at point-blank range and returned fire, their phaser beams flaring impotently against the shields of the computer-driven starship passing between them.

"Now," Spock said.

Commander Scott pushed a button, and the viewscreen flared white as *Lexington* and *Hood* exploded—exactly as Spock had programmed them to do.

When the conflagration faded, only fragments remained of the three *Constitution*-class starships. The cloud of minuscule debris spread slowly against a cold backdrop of space and stars.

"All decks secure from Red Alert," Spock said.

The crimson lights on the bulkheads ceased flashing.

Moments later, Scott was at Spock's side with a data slate in hand. "Mister DeSalle says we'll have warp power restored in two hours, Captain."

"Very good, Mister Scott. Please continue supervising repairs."

"Aye, sir."

As Scott stepped away, Uhura swiveled her chair toward Spock. "Captain? Commodore Enwright is requesting an update on the war games." She glanced at the viewscreen. "Shall I tell him M-5 lost?"

Arching one eyebrow, Spock replied, "M-5 outfought us three-to-one, Lieutenant. It can hardly be said to have *lost*."

"Very well. Should I tell the commodore M-5 malfunctioned?"

"Yes," Spock said, though he did not believe the supercomputer's killing spree to have been the least bit accidental. "And you may add that M-5 has been decommissioned."

"Aye, sir." Uhura turned back to her station and re-layed Spock's message to the commander of Starbase 6, which had hosted the ill-fated combat exercise.

Spock steepled his fingers in front of him as he pondered the day's tragic events. *I seem to have underestimated the resentment my advancement has provoked,* he brooded. All at once it became clear to him the Tantalus field device would not be enough to guarantee his ascent to power.

He was going to need allies.

5

The Quality of Mercy

Elaan, the Dohlman of Elas, paced like a caged tiger. Spock watched the swarthy, lavishly bejeweled beauty prowl back and forth. She threw angry glances in his direction. They were alone together in Lieutenant Uhura's quarters, which Spock had designated as Elaan's cabin for the duration of this mission.

Grabbing a small statuette off a nearby shelf, she shouted, "You have no right to keep me here!" She hurled the figurine at Spock, who remained still and let it fly past, confident from the moment she'd thrown it that her hysteria had compromised her aim. "I am a dohlman! On my world, you would be—"

"We are not on your world," Spock corrected her. "We are aboard the *Enterprise*. And as a passenger on this ship, you are required to recognize my authority."

A fiery fit of temper propelled her across the cabin to confront him. Her eyes glistened with tears, and she looked on the verge of weeping. "Have you no mercy? No compassion? I am a dohlman, born to rule . . . to conquer." A single tear rolled down her left cheek to her jaw. Spock noted the subtle manner in which she lifted her chin, an invitation for him to wipe away her concocted grief.

He turned his back on her. "I am well acquainted

with the reputed properties of Elasian tears, Dohlman."
Spock stepped over to the small table that stood against
one wall and set the toppled teacups upright once more.
"Let us continue reviewing the protocol for your introduction to the Troyian Caliph."

Her footfalls were soft, the gentle pattering of bare
feet on the carpeted deck. She approached from behind him, and his keen Vulcan hearing was alert for
any warning of an attack. Elaan had already stabbed
and wounded Petri, the Troyian ambassador who was
originally given the task of educating her in Troyian
protocol. Because of Petri's subpar combat reflexes and
ensuing convalescence in sickbay, the only person from
whom Elaan would consent to receive further instruction in etiquette was the highest-ranking individual on
the ship: its captain.

She slipped past Spock, eyeing him first with suspicion, then with perverse amusement. "The Empire's
never taken an interest in our conflict before," she said,
dropping her voice into a slightly lower register, giving
her words a smoky, seductive quality. "Some of the Empress's envoys have even encouraged us to fight." Moving behind her seat at the table, she continued. "But now
you arrive and convince Caliph Hakil to accept a marriage as grounds for a truce and a treaty. Why?"

"A nonviolent resolution to the situation is the most
desirable outcome for all parties," Spock said.

"Not for me," Elaan shot back. "I'd much rather kill
the Troyians, down to their last infant. I've dreamed of
cleansing their world in fire and salting its ashes. How is
this outcome desirable for me?"

Spock pulled his communicator from his belt and
flipped it open. A triple chirp signaled his standby channel

was open. "Bring him in," he said into the device, and then he closed it and placed it back on his belt.

Moments later, the door to the corridor opened, and two security guards dragged in Elaan's bodyguard, Kryton. The young man's clothes were torn, and his face was bruised and bloody. He was barely conscious. "We caught him sending transmissions to a nearby Klingon cruiser," Spock said. "He has been conspiring with them to sabotage this mission, because he desires you for himself."

"Absurd!" Elaan cried. "I am a dohlman!" She stared in horror at Kryton, who hung limply in the hands of the two Starfleet guards. Disgust filled her voice with venom. "You're but a lowly soldier—you could never be my mate!"

Calmly, Spock explained, "Not as long as you remained Dohlman of Elas. However, once he had helped the Klingons conquer the Tellun system, you would be equals—as slaves of the Klingon Empire. A minor step down the social ladder for Kryton . . . but a significant demotion for you."

As she looked back at Kryton, her pity turned to fury. "You will pay dearly for this betrayal, Kryton."

The bodyguard's eyes were dull and half-glazed with pain. He lifted his head at the sound of her anger. "I did what my heart bade me, Dohlman," he croaked through bloody, swollen lips. "I love you. . . ."

"You are not permitted to love one such as me!" She whirled toward Spock. "Captain, please tell your men to remove this presumptuous worm from my chambers!"

The captain nodded at the guards, who pulled Kryton out of the cabin and took him back to the brig for his imminent execution, which Spock had postponed only until after this planned exhibition. For a change, Elaan was silent. Spock concluded she most likely was brooding over the sudden revelation that her staunchest defender had been about to sell her into slavery.

Finally, she broke her reverie. "Captain," she asked, "is that Klingon ship still nearby? Do they still plan to attack, to prevent my wedding to Hakil?"

"No," Spock said. "I have dealt with the Klingons."

Elaan looked quizzically at him. "I heard no alerts, no sounds of combat. Did they flee? Or did you strike your own bargain with them?"

"They are no longer part of the equation, Dohlman," he said. "I suggest you leave it at that."

The less said, Spock reasoned, the better. The Tantalus field device had enabled him to uncover Kryton's treachery; once the Klingon ship's precise coordinates had been locked in, Spock had found it remarkably easy with the Tantalus field to eliminate the Klingon crew en masse while leaving their vessel intact. He had already ordered Mister Scott to capture the Klingon cruiser and tow it back to Starbase 12 for a complete analysis, from its disruptors to its spaceframe. It was a fortuitous addendum to his growing list of accomplishments, but his principal objective for this mission remained incomplete.

"I have spared you from becoming a slave of the Klingons," Spock said. "And I would also spare you the indignity of being enslaved by the Empire. Marry the Caliph of Troyius and end the war between your worlds. United for your mutual defense, you will be able to negotiate from a position of strength for your worlds' immensely valuable commodity."

Perplexed, she tilted her head and squinted suspiciously. "What commodity, Captain?"

"This one," Spock said, reaching forward. He touched the long crystalline jewels that formed her ornate neckpiece, arcing down in a semicircle atop her chest. "Dilithium crystals, more abundant on your planet than on Halkan or even on Coridan. Elas and Troyius are in possession of the largest natural deposits of high-quality dilithium in all of known space."

"But the imperial engineers surveyed our planets decades ago," Elaan said, unable to hide her surprise. "They said they found nothing of value!"

"They lied," Spock said. "Because your two worlds are so well armed and well fortified, it would have been exceptionally costly for the Empire to conquer you in open combat. It was easier to provoke you into a prolonged war of attrition, so that when your worlds became so weakened they could no longer oppose an invasion, the Empire would eradicate you all."

The more he revealed, the sharper her focus became. "Why are you telling me this now?"

"Because the Klingons apparently are ready to conquer your worlds by force—an outcome Starfleet cannot permit. My orders are to halt your conflict by force of arms, and to subdue your worlds in preparation for an occupying force."

"Then the marriage . . . ?"

Spock nodded his affirmation. "A plan of my own making. If the Klingons attempt to annex your worlds, you will be better able to repel their attacks if your defenses are intact and united. This will also reduce the number of Starfleet vessels and personnel that must be committed to defending you, freeing our resources for other objectives—and preserving your autonomy from direct imperial oversight."

"Slaughter would have been quicker," Elaan said.

"But less effective," Spock replied. "And more costly. Better for all if peace can be achieved without impairing the value of either world to the Empire."

For the first time since he had met Elaan, she smiled. "You speak almost like a statesman, Captain Spock. And I say 'almost' only because I've never heard one sound quite so reasonable."

"Then you accept my proposal? You will wed Caliph Hakil?"

She gave an enthusiastic nod. "I will," she said with conviction. "And I shall do more besides. Once our worlds are united, I will see to it that the exclusive mining rights for our dilithium are not given to the Empire." Before Spock could counsel her that defying the Empire might undo all the benefits of uniting with Troyius, she added, "I will, instead, grant them directly to you, Spock." She strode to the bed and sprawled herself across it. "As a sign of my enduring gratitude."

"Most kind," he said, fully aware of the understatement. With control over such an enormous wealth of dilithium crystals, Spock's path to the Admiralty was all but assured. It was more than he had hoped for; he had intended only to cultivate a future ally in the person of Elaan. Instead, he had acquired himself a patroness— and a very generous one, at that.

Perhaps, he mused, *I have underestimated the persuasive value of fairness and mercy. If it can spur such generosity in one, how will it affect the many?*

He resolved to find out.

"First the Halkans, then that business with Coridan," whispered Montgomery Scott. "Now a peace treaty? It's damned peculiar, that's what it is."

Huddled with him were McCoy and Uhura. Their clandestine meeting was safe from eavesdropping in the dimly lit maintenance bay on one of the lowest decks in the secondary hull of the *Enterprise*. Scott himself had personally rid the compartment of listening devices and set up surveillance countermeasures in the bulkhead around it. There was no place on the ship more private than this.

"I agree," McCoy said, leaning forward over a scuffed workbench. "Spock's behaved oddly ever since the Halkan mission, when he asked Captain Kirk not to destroy the planet."

Uhura got a ferocious look in her eyes. "Our duplicates," she said. "From the other universe. You think they got to him."

"I don't know, lass," Scott said. "I can't prove it."

McCoy's tone was sharp. "You don't have to prove it. Starfleet ordered Spock to subdue Elas and Troyius, but he went and made them stronger than ever—then secured their dilithium rights for himself. He disobeyed fleet orders, Scotty—you can assassinate him for that."

"Not without orders from Starfleet Command," Scott said. "I keep filing reports, but nothing happens."

Pushing away from the workbench, Uhura sighed with anger and frustration. "It's as if he's protected by the gods," she said. "He disobeys Captain Kirk, and nothing. Seizes the ship, and nothing. Defies Starfleet Command, and nothing. It's like they're afraid of him!"

"Maybe they are," McCoy said. "After that business with the Klingon cruiser, I'm starting to fear him a little myself."

Scott nodded. "Aye. You didn't see it, lass. The whole ship was deserted, like the crew just up and vanished."

His stare became distant and creased with horror, and his voice, already quiet, hushed even lower. "Mess hall tables covered with plates of food half eaten, the gravy still fresh on the knives. A half-buffed pair of boots next to a bunk, the rag and the polish just lying on the deck. You could tell what every man on that ship was doing right before he vanished." He looked Uhura in the eye. "And not one bloodstain. Not a single phaser burn, no carbon scoring, no sign of a struggle. Just pieces of the lives they left behind. I've never seen a weapon that could do that."

She looked skeptical. "Then what did it, Mister Scott? Magic? Fairies and elves? A genie from a bottle?"

McCoy folded his arms and shrugged his shoulders. "Maybe the legends are true," he said. "Even in medical school I heard about Vulcan psionics. Some people think they're telepaths. Others say they can be clairvoyant or precognitive. Hell, I heard that in ancient times Vulcans could kill with a thought."

Uhura rolled her eyes. "And you really believe that?"

"I don't know what I believe," McCoy said. "But what I *know* is three days ago a Klingon ship was stalking us in the Tellun system. Then, less than an hour after Spock found it, it went adrift, and we boarded it to find every last member of its crew gone without a trace."

Scott looked from McCoy to Uhura and lifted his brow imploringly. "You have to admit, Uhura, it seems a bit too convenient to be mere coincidence."

"But we have no proof," she said. "We can't send a message to Starfleet Command that says we think Spock is using ancient telepathic powers to crush his enemies."

"You're telling me," McCoy grumbled. "They'd probably give him a medal and call him a hero of the Empire."

They wandered apart in the shadows and remained silent for a long moment. "So," Uhura finally said. "What are we going to do?"

Scott shook his head. "There's nothing we can do. We don't have any proof Spock's been compromised, and Starfleet hasn't ordered us to take action."

"Maybe I could declare him mentally unfit," McCoy said. "I could say his brokering a peace treaty was irrational, and—"

"And he'd give you a half-dozen reasons why it's completely logical," Scott cut in. "You should know by now not to argue logic with Spock. It's a losing proposition."

Uhura's temper flared higher by the moment. "Listen to the two of you!" she hissed. Backpedaling away from them, she continued. " 'Nothing we can do. Losing proposition.' You're not men. Men would stand and fight! Men would eliminate Spock now, before his brand of appeasement spreads. But since neither of you seems willing to act like a man"—she drew her dagger from her boot—"I guess I'll have to do it for you."

Scott tried to interpose himself between Uhura and the door, but he wasn't quick enough. She cut him off and started backing out of the room. "Where do you think you're going, lass? What do you think you're going to do?"

"What you should have done, Mister Scott," she replied. "I'm going to kill Captain Spock before he—"

An incandescent flash of light and a lilting, almost musical ringing filled the air around Uhura—and when it faded she was gone. No bloodstain. No phaser burns. No sign she'd ever been there at all.

All Scott could do was stare at the abruptly empty

space in the room where Uhura had stood. He tried to control his terror as he realized with a shudder the same fate might be about to befall him, as well.

A glance to his right confirmed McCoy was harboring the same brand of paranoid musing.

Their shared horror was interrupted by the shrill whistling note of the intraship comm, followed by Captain Spock's baritone voice. *"Spock to Mister Scott."*

Trading fearful looks with McCoy, Scott moved to a nearby panel and thumbed open a secure, encrypted channel that would mask his location if anyone happened to be monitoring for such information. "Scott here."

"Mister Scott," Spock said over the comm. *"Please meet me on the bridge at once. We need to discuss an adjustment to the bridge duty roster."*

A sick feeling churned in Scott's gut. He knew what was coming, but the protocol of the situation demanded he play along as if he didn't. "The duty roster, sir?"

Spock's voice was ominous. *"Indeed, Mister Scott. . . . We appear to have an opening for a senior communications officer."*

Rumors spread quickly on any starship, but some traveled faster than others. "I heard it directly from Doctor M'Benga," Lieutenant Robert D'Amato said in a nervous whisper across the mess hall table. "And he heard it from Doctor McCoy himself."

"It's just not possible," Lieutenant Winston Kyle said, hunched over his soup. "People don't just wink out of existence."

"Mister Scott saw it, too," D'Amato said. "Just zap— and she was gone. No blood, no ashes, nothing."

"Big deal," Kyle said. "A phaser on full power can do the same thing. Seen it a hundred times."

"But there weren't any phasers in the room," D'Amato said. "It's been torn apart three times, nothing."

Kyle swallowed a spoonful of his soup and shook his head. "You ask me, I think Scott and McCoy killed her, then they made up this stupid story to cover their tracks."

Lieutenant Michael DeSalle, who had taken over for Mister Scott as chief engineer, put down his tray next to Kyle's and joined the conversation. "Be careful what you say," he said, keeping his voice low. "Captain Spock hears everything."

Rolling his eyes, Kyle asked, "Now you're paranoid, too?"

DeSalle shrugged. "Caution pays dividends on this ship. Always has. You know that." He sliced through a rubbery-looking breast of chicken. "I heard Palmer got Uhura's job. She's keeping her distance from Mister Scott, though."

D'Amato shook his head. "I don't know. Way I heard it, Scotty's being set up."

"Forget 'set up,' he did it," Kyle said. "Don't you guys remember that flap on Argelius II? Three women dead, all evidence pointing at Scotty, then all the charges got dropped?"

"Thanks to Kirk," D'Amato said. "Like any of us would've gotten that kind of favor."

"That's what I'm saying," Kyle continued. "He has a history. And you know McCoy must have helped bury those forensic reports. So it's a lot easier to believe Scott sliced up Uhura and disintegrated the evidence than to pin it on some kind of crazy Vulcan psychic mumbo-jumbo."

DeSalle took a sip of his drink and raised his eyebrows at Kyle. "Don't be so quick to write off the Vulcans' psionic powers. If they can do half the things I've heard, we're lucky we outnumber them seven to one in the Empire."

"You ought to hear what M'Benga says about Vulcans," D'Amato said. "He interned on Vulcan. Saw things you wouldn't believe. He says they can read minds, plant delayed suggestions, even control weak minds from a distance. And in one of their oldest legends, the most powerful Vulcans used something called the Stone of Gol to kill people with just their thoughts—destroy people's minds, even erase them from reality."

"Sounds like someone's been hitting the Romulan ale again," Kyle quipped to DeSalle.

D'Amato's temper rose to the surface. "You don't believe me? Go ask M'Benga, he'll tell you."

"Proving what?" Kyle said. "That he's crazy, too?"

"I think you're forgetting something," DeSalle said.

Turning slowly to face DeSalle, Kyle asked, "What's that?"

A wan smile crept across DeSalle's face. "The Klingon cruiser," he said. "Its entire crew missing, like they'd been beamed out of their seats into space."

"Oh, you've got to be kidding me," Kyle said. "Can you really not think of a single way that could've been done without some kind of magical trick? Occam's razor, guys. What makes more sense—that cloaked Romulan ships used transporters to kidnap and dematerialize the Klingon crew, or that Captain Spock thought about it *really hard* and made all the Klingons go *poof*?"

"There's no evidence the Romulans were anywhere near here," D'Amato said.

DeSalle added, "Or that they can use transporters while cloaked."

Kyle nodded. "Exactly. And there's no evidence Vulcans have amazing psionic powers that can vaporize people. But which explanation sounds like it has a better chance of being true?" When neither DeSalle nor D'Amato replied after several seconds, Kyle shook his head in disgust, stood, and picked up his tray. "And you call yourselves men of science," he grumbled, stalking away to turn in his half-eaten lunch.

D'Amato and the chief engineer watched Kyle leave the mess hall, then they continued eating their own lunches. "Kyle's story does actually make more sense," D'Amato admitted.

"I know," DeSalle replied. He washed down another mouthful of chicken before he added, "But I still think M'Benga's right."

Checking to make sure no one was eavesdropping, D'Amato whispered back, "So do I."

It didn't take long for the stories to spread beyond the confines of the *Enterprise.* Missives sent via subspace radio carried word of Captain Spock's eldritch powers throughout the Empire. Tales traded during shore leaves and transfers from crewman to crewman, and from officer to officer, inflated the story with each re-telling. Within a few months, Spock's powers were said to be on a par with those of ancient Vulcan myths. His name became synonymous with power, and the terror he inspired made his growing reputation for mercy, compromise, and restraint all the more beguiling. *Why,* many wondered, *would a man who could destroy any foe choose to promote peace?*

That question now preoccupied Empress Hoshi Sato III. At the head of an oblong table, she presided over a meeting of her senior advisers in the war room of the imperial palace on Earth. Sheltered deep below the planet's surface, the vast, oval chamber was illuminated solely by the glow of its massive display screens, which ringed the walls.

"Grand Admiral Garth," she said, eyeing the notorious flag officer from Izar. "Where is Captain Spock now?"

Side conversations around the table fell away to silence as Grand Admiral Kelvar Leonard Garth straightened his posture and replied to the young monarch. "Your Majesty, Captain Spock and the *Enterprise* have just returned from their successful mission to the Romulan Neutral Zone. They are en route to Starbase 10 with a captured Romulan bird-of-prey in tow."

"And the disposition of the Romulan crew?" Sato asked.

Garth shifted slightly before he answered. "Eliminated, Your Majesty. The ship is empty."

A nervous murmur worked its way around the table. Empress Sato did not like the fearful tune this report was striking up among her cabinet. In a pointed manner she inquired, "By what means were they dispatched, Admiral?"

Garth cocked his head nervously. "The boarding party was not able to determine that, Your Majesty."

"But the ship was manned when *Enterprise* made contact with it, yes?"

The admiral nodded. "Yes, Majesty."

Sato nodded slowly. Pressing the question further

would serve no purpose but to embarrass Admiral Garth and make herself seem insecure or fearful. She had ascended to the throne less than nine months earlier and was determined not to be perceived as weak. *What would my first royal namesake have done?* She adjusted her tactics to turn this scenario to her advantage—or, at the very least, to postpone the crisis until she had amassed sufficient political capital to entertain greater risks.

"If memory serves, Admiral, similar circumstances attended Captain Spock's capture of a Klingon cruiser just a few months ago, correct?"

"Yes, Majesty," Garth said.

"And his family and heirs have secured the dilithium mining rights in the Tellun system?"

Again, Garth dipped his chin and confirmed, "Yes, Majesty."

"Then it seems to me that Captain Spock is an officer of greater resources than we thought," Sato proclaimed, projecting her voice to the far end of the table. "Admiral Garth, move Captain Spock to the top of the list for new Admiralty appointments."

"As you wish, Majesty," Garth replied, "but granting him that kind of power could be dangerous."

Sato frowned. "Clearly, Spock is already dangerous," she said. "Prudence would suggest we try to make an ally of him."

Apparently, Garth was unconvinced. "And if elevating his rank only fuels his ambition . . . ?"

"In that case," she said, her melodic voice laced with menace, "we shall make an example of him, instead."

2269

6

Vices of Authority

"Welcome to Elba II, Captain Spock," said Grand Admiral Garth, or, as he was more commonly known, Garth of Izar. The handsome, silver-haired flag officer gestured to his seductively attired female Orion companion. "This is my prime consort, Marta." The green-skinned woman curtsied to Spock and flashed a grin that hinted at the madness lurking behind her eyes.

Spock greeted Garth and his concubine with polite nods. "Thank you, Admiral. Allow me to introduce my wife, Lieutenant Commander Marlena Moreau." He gestured at Marlena, who bowed her head at Garth before shooting a quick but poisonous glance at Marta.

"A pleasure," Garth said, returning Marlena's slight bow. Gesturing at the dignitary-packed ballroom behind him, he said, "Your banquet awaits, Captain."

Garth and Marta led Spock and Marlena into the thick of the party. Among the guests crowded into the gilded room of the Elba II governor's mansion were many high-ranking members of the Starfleet Admiralty, as well as a dozen or so local planetary governors. All were accompanied by their spouses or lovers, and several also were attended by one or more aides-de-camp.

Marlena clutched Spock's arm excitedly as they

walked together. "Isn't it magnificent?" she asked, her eyes darting from one splendor to the next.

"Admiral," Spock said to Garth, "I wish to thank you for personally officiating at my advancement ceremony. It is a great honor to be so recognized."

The Grand Admiral of Starfleet gave Spock a cordial slap on the back. "The honor is all mine, Captain. Your defeat of M-5 is almost as famous as my victory at Axanar." Lowering his voice and cocking one eyebrow, he added with obvious admiration, "And might I say, your victory was *twice* as ruthless. Sacrificing *Hood* and *Lexington* was genius, Captain. If that oaf Wesley had thought of it, this would be *his* banquet instead of yours."

"Indeed," Spock said. He let the grand admiral make the introductions as they circuited the cavernous room. The socially mandated exchange of pleasantries took significantly longer than an hour. As they reached the end, Marlena's demeanor had devolved from weariness to boredom to outright surliness.

It seemed fortunate, then, that the ceremony itself was brief and perfunctory. Standing with Spock in the center of the room, Garth said only as much as Starfleet regulations required for the promotion to be official, and then he pinned Spock's new rank insignia on his uniform.

Garth beckoned a waiter, plucked two flutes of Deltan champagne from the Bolian's tray, and handed them to Spock and Marlena. Then he took two more for himself and Marta before shooing away the server. Raising his drink and his voice, he announced, "A toast to Starfleet's newest flag officer! Admiral Spock, may your record be one of strength and glory!"

In near unison the crowd echoed, "Strength and glory!"

Spock bowed his head in humble recognition of the accolade as the room's occupants sipped from their drinks in his honor.

The only VIP in the room to whom Spock and Marlena had not yet been introduced emerged from the crowd and smiled at them. "Admiral Spock, Commander Moreau," said the well-dressed human man with distinctly Asian features. "I'm Governor Donald Cory. I apologize for missing the ceremony, but I was occupied on official business." He offered his hand to Spock.

"No apology is necessary, Governor," Spock said, shaking the man's hand.

"Governor," Marlena said, holding out her hand to Cory, who lifted it and kissed the back of it lightly.

Cory's demeanor turned somber. "Let me also extend my condolences on the passing of Doctor McCoy. Xenopolycythemia is a terrible way to die."

"Indeed," Spock said. "It was unfortunate to lose such a skilled surgeon in his prime. Fortunately, Doctor M'Benga has proved an able successor."

"I'm glad to hear that," Cory said. He nodded at Garth. "At the grand admiral's request, I offer you both my suite for the night, as the first of your many rewards for ascending to the Admiralty."

"Too kind, Governor," Spock said. "We are honored to accept."

"Excellent. The room's prepared. You may retire at your leisure."

"Thank you, Governor," Spock said, adding with a nod at Garth, "Admiral."

Spock took Marlena's arm gently and guided her away from the duo and toward a nearby buffet table. As they crossed the room, Spock sensed Garth and Cory continuing to observe him and Marlena. As soon as they seemed to be out of earshot, Marlena whispered to Spock, "I don't trust them."

"Nor do I," Spock said. "The fact Admiral Garth arranged in advance for us to reside overnight on the planet's surface suggests he has an agenda that hinges on our continued presence."

Picking up a clean plate and wearing an insincere smile, Marlena said, "In other words, we're being led into a trap."

"Precisely," Spock said.

She grabbed a serving fork and speared a ring of pineapple from a platter of sliced fruit. "Then let's eliminate Garth and Cory now—a preemptive strike."

"No," Spock said. "Our actions must be circumspect and our reactions proportional. Until the grand admiral reveals his intentions, we will bide our time."

"So, we're to do nothing?" Marlena asked before taking a bite of pineapple.

Casting a subtle look back at Garth and Cory, Spock replied, "Biding our time does not mean lowering our guard." He met Marlena's conspiratorial stare. "The next move is Garth's. The *last* move will be ours."

Standing naked in the bedroom of his private suite inside the Elba II governor's mansion, Garth said to Marta, "It's time."

Using cellular-metamorphosis powers he had learned decades earlier from the Antosians, Garth changed his shape into a nearly identical likeness of Admiral Spock. Speaking with a pitch-perfect imitation of the Vulcan's baritone, he asked his Orion concubine, "How do I look, my love?"

She ran her hands over his chest and gazed lustfully up at him. "Good enough to eat," she said, her voice almost a growl. Pushing in a futile effort to force him onto the bed, she added, "I think I'm going to like this game."

Garth grabbed Marta by the shoulders and shoved her aside. "This isn't foreplay, darling. This is war."

"Spoilsport," she said, pouting as she sat on the bed, rebuffed and angry.

He turned and studied the fine details of his appearance in a mirror. "I spent years keeping an eye on Kirk," he said. "I never dreamed it would be his Vulcan first officer I'd have to worry about." Noting one of his eyebrows resting at too sharp an angle, he adjusted it with a thought. "Ever since Kirk deposed Pike, I've suspected he had some kind of secret weapon." Satisfied with his appearance, he turned toward Marta. "Judging from Kirk's service record, it was probably something he found in Doctor Adams's house of horrors on the Tantalus colony."

"And now you think Spock has it," Marta said, sounding pleased with her own meager powers of deduction.

Mimicking his subject, he raised one eyebrow. "Indeed." He picked up a communicator programmed to duplicate the signal encryption used on Spock's device. "If I'm right, and Spock captured some kind of superweapon from Kirk, then he's ten times more dangerous than Kirk ever was. Kirk was a thug; all he wanted was power and glory. But this Vulcan . . . he calls himself a reformer. Power won't satisfy him; he won't stop until he tears down the Empire."

Marta replied, "So? Kill him, then."

Garth-as-Spock smirked at his impetuous paramour. "Not until I find that weapon, my love." He gently pinched her chin and lifted it so she would look into his eyes. "I plan to beam up to the *Enterprise* as Spock, search his quarters, and find that device." Stroking her cheek, he added, "Once I have it, I'll terminate him, his wife, and his senior officers." He ran his fingers through Marta's hair, which was as black as a starless night. "And then, my flower, we'll pay a visit to Empress Sato III—and take her throne for ourselves."

He flipped up the communicator's grille and opened a channel. "Spock to *Enterprise*."

"Scott here," came the reply. *"Go ahead, Admiral."*

"One to beam up," Garth said.

"Aye, sir," Commander Scott said. *"Queen to queen's level three."*

In no mood to banter, Garth snapped, "Mister Scott, I said beam me aboard."

Unfazed, Scott answered, *"I said, 'Queen to queen's level three.' "*

Why was the *Enterprise*'s first officer being so obstinate? "We have no time for chess problems, Mister Scott. Beam me aboard."

"I'm following your orders, Admiral. Queen to queen's level three."

Garth struggled to suppress his rage. Spock had somehow learned of his shape-shifting ability and taken a precaution against its being used to impersonate him on his own ship. After a brief pause, Garth said, "Very good, Mister Scott. I will contact you later. Spock out." He flipped shut the communicator's cover, then pounded his empty fist against the wall and let out a roar of fury as he transmuted back to his own form. At last he bellowed, "Damn that half-Vulcan bastard! I might not be able to bluff my way onto the *Enterprise*, but I can still order it blown to pieces!" He flipped open the communicator and reset its frequency to hail his flagship. "Garth to *Imperious*."

They were the last words he ever spoke.

Before his XO could reply, a flash of light consumed him, and the last thing he heard was Marta's terrified scream.

Marlena brushed the tip of her index finger over the teardrop-shaped trigger of the Tantalus field device a second time and put an end to Marta's hysterical shrieking.

She returned the device to its standby mode. Its resonant hum filled her and Spock's quarters on the *Enterprise* until its concealing wall panel lowered into place. Then the only sound in the compartment was the low thrumming of the ship's impulse engines and the white noise of its ventilation system.

Her task completed, she took a communicator from her belt and flipped its cover open. "Marlena to Spock."

"Spock here."

"You're clear to return."

"Acknowledged. Stand by."

The channel clicked off, and Marlena closed her communicator. Seconds later, the room brightened as a swirling column of light shimmered into view a few meters from where she was standing. The air rang with the musical drone of the transporter effect as Spock materialized. As soon as the last sparkles faded from his person, he stepped toward Marlena. "Well done," he said.

He passed her and walked into their bedroom. She followed him. "How did you know about Garth's ability?"

"It was one of many secrets I found in Captain Kirk's logs after I killed him," Spock explained, removing the tunic of his dress uniform. "He had been researching Garth's history on Antos IV as a prelude to moving against him. Though I had not been able to confirm the grand admiral's shape-changing ability prior to this visit, it seemed prudent to safeguard against it."

Flush with adrenaline from the kill, Marlena pressed herself against Spock's back. "A wise decision, my love. Now that he's gone, the fleet can answer to you as its grand admiral."

Spock stepped away from her and turned about. "No," he said.

Marlena's brow creased with anger and confusion. "Why not?"

"It is too soon," Spock said. "I have been an admiral for less than five hours. If I lay claim to that title now, I will earn the contempt of every flag officer in Starfleet. Furthermore, the rank of grand admiral is bestowed only by imperial decree. If the Empress denies my claim to advancement, my own crew will be obligated to execute me for treason."

Slumping onto the bed, Marlena felt a tide of disappointment wash over her. "In other words, you'll *never* become grand admiral." Her remark drew a hard look from Spock. Feeling as if she needed to explain herself, she added, "You know the Empress will never permit it."

"Yes, she will," Spock said. "Because when the time comes for me to take control of Starfleet, I will make certain she has no other choice."

7

A Lamb to Slaughter

Dr. Carol Marcus had just spoken truth to power, and she expected to regret it.

Hidden within Starbase 47—also known as Vanguard—was a top-secret laboratory known as the Vault. The high-security facility had been designed as a repository for secrets Starfleet had unearthed in the Taurus Reach, but to Marcus it felt more like a prison. She and more than two dozen of the Terran Empire's greatest scientific minds, military and civilian alike, had been shanghaied into service a few years earlier aboard the enormous station, which was situated hundreds of light-years from Earth in a hotly contested sector of space. Her team members were the Empire's experts in a range of disciplines, but they shared one mission: Unlock the secrets of the Shedai, a precursor race that once had reigned supreme over a vast interstellar civilization in this region of the galaxy.

The process had started with a string of alien genetic information that had come to be known as the Taurus Meta-Genome. Later, Starfleet discovered a signal pulse they called the Shedai Carrier Wave and an energy wave known as the Jinoteur Pattern. All these breakthroughs were related to artifacts known as Conduits, which had been found on dozens of worlds across the sector.

It was a tantalizing mystery, but Carol Marcus was tired of it.

Defying orders, the advice of her peers, and her own better judgment, she had decided enough was enough. For spite's sake as much as for principle, she would not—could not—bring herself to continue applying her knowledge and insight to advance Starfleet's belligerent agenda and serve the barbaric whims of Vanguard's commanding officer. And she had said so. To the commodore.

That, she suspected in hindsight, had probably been a mistake.

The lab's secure inner door opened, and Commodore Diego "Red" Reyes stormed in. His fists and jaw were clenched, and dark veins throbbed on his shorn head. The garish collection of awards and insignia decorating his tunic jangled as he stomped across the Vault's open main compartment, and a long-barreled energy weapon bounced against his hip. He reached Marcus and bellowed, "Who the hell do you think you are?" She turned her head because looking at his right eye—a red-lensed, polished-steel cybernetic replacement—unnerved her.

Before she could reply, Reyes continued his harangue. "You think because you're the chief egghead down here, that gives you the authority to refuse my orders? I thought you were a genius, Doctor Marcus, but if you can't tell the difference between an empty title and real authority, you must be an idiot savant." Reyes looked past Marcus and saw the Vault's team of scientists trying to slink away. "All of you, get back here," he snapped. The others did as he commanded.

Turning back to Marcus, Reyes jabbed his finger at

her face. "I'm a busy man, Doctor. I can't have you shutting down my research division when there's work to be done."

"The reason I halted—"

"I don't *care* what your reason was," Reyes cut in.

"You should," Marcus said, her voice sharp and her gaze unyielding. "You've got us playing with fire, and we don't have enough safeguards."

Recoiling as if in disbelief, Reyes said, "*That's* what this is about? You shut down the most important classified laboratory in Starfleet because you're *scared*?"

"It's bigger than that," Marcus said. "The entity your people captured on Mirdonyae V is too powerful to be contained inside that experiment chamber. We need to think about how to dispose of it before it gets out."

Reyes stepped forward and backed Marcus against the circular, transparent-steel wall that encased the Vault's central experiment chamber. Behind her swirled an ever-changing mass of dark vapors and fluids—Vanguard's prisoner, the Shedai that called itself the Wanderer. "Dispose of it?" echoed Reyes. "Are you out of your goddamned mind, Doctor? That thing is the key to the Empire's future control of this sector, and maybe even the galaxy. We can use it to unlock every piece of Shedai technology in the Taurus Reach and bring the Klingons and Tholians to their knees—and you want to *get rid of it*?"

"We have to," Marcus said. "The longer we hold it, the higher the risk of its escape. And if it ever gets out of that chamber, it'll kill us all."

The commodore's smile was thin and humorless. "Then you'd better make damned sure it never gets out."

"You're not listening! You're courting disaster keeping that thing here!"

Locking one beefy hand around Marcus's throat, Reyes replied, "No, Doctor, you're the one courting disaster—by not following my orders." He closed his grip just tightly enough to restrict Marcus's breathing but not enough to stop it. "You don't seem to appreciate the big picture here, so permit me to explain it to you. We're in an arms race with the Klingons, the Tholians, and the Romulans. I don't have the luxury of playing it safe or catering to the fears of weak-kneed eggheads like you. The Empress gave me three things when she posted me here: a clearly defined mission, a deadline, and absolute authority in the Taurus Reach. Time is a factor, Doctor. I need results now, and I need you to deliver them."

Struggling for air, Marcus remained defiant. "I can't deliver anything if I'm dead," she said in a choked-off rasp. "And neither can you."

Reyes nodded. "I see. You need more encouragement. I figured you would." He released her throat, grabbed the lapel of her lab coat, and dragged her away from the experiment chamber to a nearby computer terminal. He jabbed at the console's keys and opened a channel. "Reyes to ops."

"Cooper here," answered the station's dark-haired executive officer as he appeared on-screen. *"Go ahead, sir."*

"Patch the feed from the brig to my screen, Commander."

"Aye, sir."

The image on the screen wavered and shifted to reveal an agony booth in Vanguard's brig. Locked inside was Marcus's eight-year-old son, David. The tow-headed boy was screaming to be set free, his palms pressed plaintively against the torture device's transparent-aluminum walls.

Marcus felt her stomach churn with fear. She wanted to lunge at Reyes and shout curses at the top of her lungs, but she felt paralyzed, as if she were made of stone and cemented to the floor.

"This is why you're going back to work," Reyes said. "One word from me and your son will experience more pain than anyone else in history." Jabbing his finger in Marcus's face, he added, "One more word out of *you*, and that's how he's going to die."

8

The Weight of Promises

Carol Marcus collapsed on top of Clark Terrell and relaxed into his thickly muscled brown arms. "Thank you," she said, aglow with postcoital perspiration.

"That's my line," he said, chortling softly and stroking her blond hair.

"I needed to get off the station for an hour," Marcus said. "I'm just glad your ship's in port for resupply."

Terrell smiled. "That makes two of us." He shifted the curtain of his bunk and checked the chrono on the bulkhead of his quarters. "You'll have to go soon. I have third-shift watch at zero-hundred."

"Just let me stay a little longer," she said, pleading softly. "I feel safe here."

He nuzzled the top of her head. "Don't get too comfortable," he said. "There are no safe places, here or anywhere else in the Empire."

She sighed. "I know."

While she appreciated Terrell's attempt to caution her, she wished he hadn't spoiled her illusion of privacy. He was easygoing, a trait he shared with most of his thirteen crewmates aboard the long-range Starfleet scout ship *I.S.S. Sagittarius*. His calm demeanor often put Marcus at ease in a way few other things ever could.

She whispered in his ear, "How can I ever be free of him?"

Hugging her closer, he said, "Free might be too much to hope for."

"I just can't understand why the Empress would give so much power to such a malignant sociopath," Marcus said. "He's a rank opportunist. As soon as he has enough power or leverage, he'll turn it against her."

Terrell shrugged one shoulder. "Of course he will."

"Then why give him the chance?"

"Because he's what she needs out here," Terrell said. "Hundreds of light-years from home, with little or no backup, it takes someone like Reyes to stand up to the Tholians and the Klingons at the same time. I don't like him any more than you do, but you have to admit, he's uniquely suited to this mission."

She shook her head. "He's a monster."

"Maybe. But he's Empress Sato's monster, and as long as he doesn't sink his fangs into her, she'll let him do as he likes."

No longer feeling safe or comforted, Marcus threw off the bedsheet and pulled aside the bunk's privacy curtain. "What he likes, Clark, is threatening my son." Tears of rage welled in her eyes as she looked back at Terrell. "As long as Reyes can hold David hostage, I can't risk defying him."

"If you ask me, you shouldn't have tried in the first place." Holding up his hands to ward off Marcus's rising tide of anger, he added, "What I mean is, you shouldn't have tipped your hand so soon. If you want to face off against a man like Reyes, you need to do it from a position of strength. Find your advantage first, *then* make your stand."

"Too late now," Marcus said, pulling on her shirt. Reaching down to pluck her trousers from the deck, she added, "Have you seen that green goon who parades around the station with Reyes? What the hell's up with that?"

Rolling his eyes, Terrell replied, "That's Ganz. Some kind of boss in a crime syndicate from the Orion colonies." He pushed a hand over his head of close-cropped, wiry black hair as he continued. "I wondered how long it'd take before someone like him started throwing his weight around."

"Why? What do you mean?"

He watched Marcus finish getting dressed while he spoke. "A lot of missions Reyes sends us on these days involve scouting safe routes for shipping. Courses that use stellar phenomena to scramble sensors, that kind of thing. Once we plot safe paths, we usually notice Orion smugglers using them within a few weeks. And the crew of the *Endeavour* says they've been ordered to run interference for Orion merchantmen that wandered too close to the Klingon border."

Marcus was hardly able to believe what Terrell was telling her. "Reyes is in league with the Orion pirates?" Flummoxed, she ran her hand through her hair. "That bastard's not just amassing power—he's lining his pockets." She turned toward Terrell. "If he hoards enough wealth and recruits enough Orion corsairs, he could set up Vanguard as his own personal fiefdom."

"I think that's the idea," Terrell said, nodding grimly.

Unable to stop herself, Marcus began pacing inside Terrell's quarters. "This far from the Empire, with that kind of power, there's no telling what Reyes might be capable of." She kneeled beside Terrell's bunk. "Promise me something."

"If I can," he said, taken aback.

"Promise if Reyes goes renegade, you'll get my son off this station and back to the Empire, no matter what happens to me."

Dismayed, Terrell said, "I can't promise that, Carol."

"Please, Clark. You're the only one I'd trust. At least tell me you'll try."

He pushed back the bedsheet and reached out for her hand as he sat up on the edge of his bunk. "Look, let's just hope it *doesn't* come to that, okay?"

Marcus was having none of her lover's artful evasions. "So you won't even try to help my son?"

Terrell sighed. "I'm sorry," he said. "Reyes is just too strong. The more power he grabs, the more the Admiralty pats him on the back for it." Giving her hand a gentle squeeze, he added, "It's not that I don't *want* to help your boy; I do. I just don't know how much I can do against a man like Reyes. If he decides to secede, I'll be lucky to survive with my skin."

She pulled her hand free of his grasp. "I understand."

He got out of bed as she walked to the door, which hushed open ahead of her. "I promise I'll do what I can," he said. "I just can't say what that'll be."

Standing in the open doorway, Marcus looked back at her naked lover, who had the body of a boxer and the mind of a scientist. "That's all any of us can say," she said, regretting the impossible position in which she'd placed him. She stepped into the corridor and added guiltily as the door shut, "Thank you, Clark."

2270

9

A Discovered Attack

"*Welcome home,* Enterprise. *Stand by for final approach vector.*"

Admiral Spock watched the superstructure of the San Francisco Orbital Yards loom large ahead of his ship on the main viewer. A spacedock control officer relayed flight-path corrections to *Enterprise*'s senior helm officer, Lieutenant DePaul. Seated beside the young helmsman, navigator Kevin Riley divided his attention between preparing the ship to make port and gazing wistfully at the blue orb of Earth growing larger on-screen.

After more than twenty-five years of active service, *Enterprise* was putting into spacedock for a bow-to-stern refit. Apparently unwilling to entrust the ship's future to its current chief engineer, Commander Scott had coordinated the planning of most of the ship's upgrades—especially those to its impulse engines and warp drive—in addition to carrying out his duties as the ship's executive officer. Scott had spent the past few weeks roaming the ship's halls in a maudlin fashion. More than once Spock had overheard his first officer lamenting "the end of an era."

On an intellectual level, Spock understood that humans sometimes formed emotional attachments to inanimate objects, and that ships held a special place in their imaginations. That knowledge, however, made Mister Scott's behavior seem no less peculiar to Spock.

He also did not share his human crewmates' nostalgic feelings about their return to Earth. Despite being half human, Spock felt no great sense of attachment to his mother's homeworld. From the earliest days of his memory, he had always identified with the people and culture of Vulcan, even though his peers often had rejected him in the harshest possible ways. Out of consideration for Marlena, however, he had offered to accompany her if she wished to visit her father in France. To his mild surprise, she had demurred. "There's no reason to go there," she had said. "Once the ship's in spacedock, we should proceed to Vulcan."

In accordance with her wishes, he had arranged passage aboard the *I.S.S. Merrimac*, which was waiting in Earth orbit for them. As soon as he and Marlena were aboard, it would depart for Vulcan.

A male voice over the comm declared, "*Enterprise, this is spacedock requesting transfer of helm control for your final approach.*"

Spock nodded to Scott, who said to DePaul, "Transfer authorized, Lieutenant. Proceed when ready."

"Aye, sir," DePaul said. He keyed the commands into the helm, then opened his comm circuit. "Spacedock, this is *Enterprise*. Releasing helm control on my mark. Three . . . two . . . one . . . mark."

There was a faint shudder in the deck. Then DePaul swiveled his seat and looked back at Spock and Scott. "Helm control transferred, sirs."

"Well done, lad," Scott said.

On the viewscreen, the gridlike enclosure of spacedock seemed to swallow *Enterprise*. Automated tenders began extending mooring lines and supply umbilicals toward the starship.

Lieutenant Elizabeth Palmer turned from the communications station and said, "Admiral, we're being hailed by Grand Admiral Decker. He wishes to speak with you."

Spock glanced at the blonde and said, "Put him onscreen, Lieutenant."

Palmer routed the message to the bridge's main viewscreen, which switched to an image of the square-jawed flag officer who had succeeded Garth as the commander-in-chief of Starfleet. *"Admiral Spock,"* he said. *"Welcome home."*

"Thank you, sir," Spock said, choosing not to debate a superior officer in regard to what world he considered home.

Decker looked at *Enterprise*'s XO. *"Commander Scott, I want to thank you for your exemplary work preparing the designs for* Enterprise's *refit. Many of your suggestions will be incorporated into other* Constitution-*class refits."*

"I'm pleased to hear it, Admiral. I'm looking forward to supervising the job and seeing it all finally come together."

The grand admiral's expression slackened. *"Ah, yes. I'm sorry, Commander. I guess you haven't heard yet. My son, Commander Will Decker, will be supervising* Enterprise's *refit—as its new commanding officer."*

Scott's smile faded, but he masked his disappointment with a neutral expression. "Aye, sir. I'm sure he'll do a fine job of it."

"As am I, but I know he'd appreciate your help, Mister Scott."

Decker's statement had been phrased as an idle

observation, but Spock was certain Scott understood it actually had been an order.

"Aye, sir," Scott said. "It'd be my honor."

"Excellent. Commander Decker and I will beam aboard at fourteen hundred hours. Admiral Spock, I trust my son will be greeted with all proper honors?"

"Naturally," Spock said. "Command will be transferred by the book."

"Very good. Carry on, gentlemen. Decker out."

The screen blinked back to the image of spacedock's metal frame embracing *Enterprise* on all sides.

Scott turned toward Spock. "Can you believe that? Decker just sends his son to take over *my* refit!" His face twisted into a desperate expression. "Can't you do something, Admiral?"

Rising from his chair, Spock replied, "No, Mister Scott, I cannot. I lack the authority to countermand an order from the grand admiral." Walking to the turbolift, he added, "Please arrange for an honor guard to meet Commander Decker in the main hangar bay at fourteen hundred, and make all necessary preparations for a formal transfer of command at that time."

"Aye, sir," Scott replied as Spock entered the lift.

"Until then, Mister Scott, you have the conn." The doors shut. Spock grasped the control lever and said to the computer, "Deck Three."

The decks hummed past as the lift descended.

Though his demeanor was stoic, Spock's thoughts were troubled.

Because the grand admiral had assigned his son to supervise the refit, Spock thought it likely Matt Decker meant to reward his scion with permanent command of the *Enterprise* when the refit was complete in a year's time. Either way, once Willard Decker took command of the ship, he would have the run of it; nothing and no one would be able to move on or off the vessel without his knowledge and consent.

If the Tantalus field device is still aboard once Decker has command, Spock realized, *it will be impossible to keep it hidden from him.*

The turbolift stopped, the doors opened, and Spock stepped out. Walking down the corridor to his quarters, he noted the time on a bulkhead chrono. Decker was scheduled to arrive in approximately one hour and eleven minutes.

Spock had that long to smuggle the Tantalus field device off the *Enterprise.*

10

An Iron Fist
in a Velvet Glove

Marlena stepped briskly across *Enterprise*'s auxiliary shuttlebay. She used her right hand to guide a torpedo-like shipping pod mounted on an antigrav pallet.

The pod was loaded with her and Spock's personal effects from their quarters, as well as one vital piece of precious cargo: the Tantalus field device.

Though the bay was normally abuzz with busy personnel, today it was mostly deserted. Most of *Enterprise*'s crew had been mustered in dress uniforms to the main hangar deck to greet Grand Admiral Decker and his son, and to witness the formal transfer-of-command ceremony. Marlena's absence from the event was very likely to be noticed, but that could not be helped; there was no one else she and Spock could trust to see their mysterious weapon safely off the ship.

As she neared the waiting shuttlecraft, *Clausewitz,* a shuttle control officer stepped into her path and held up his hand. "Halt, ma'am."

"Get out of my way, Gibbs," Marlena said without breaking her stride. She beckoned a nearby cargo chief. "You: come help me load this pod."

Gibbs backpedaled a few steps before he planted his hands on the shipping pod and forced Marlena to stop. "You can't load this pod until it's been inspected."

"In case you're unaware, *Lieutenant,* I outrank you. And I'm ordering you to remove your hands from Admiral Spock's property and let me pass."

"I can't do that, ma'am. I'm under orders to make visual inspections of all incoming and outgoing cargo."

Edging closer to the man, Marlena asked, "Whose orders?"

"Commander Decker's," said Gibbs.

"Well, my orders come from *Admiral* Spock," Marlena retorted. "And he was very clear: his container is not to be opened or tampered with."

She tried to step forward, but Gibbs pushed back, halting her progress. "That may well be, ma'am, but Commander Decker is now in command of this ship."

"Is that a fact?" As she inched closer to the young officer, Marlena slowly pulled her communicator from her belt. She flipped open its grille and set it for the intraship frequency, which was carrying the transfer-of-command ceremony for the benefit of personnel who could not leave their duty stations.

Over the comm, Spock's voice intoned in a stately manner, *"—mand of a starship is an honor and a privilege accorded to very few, even in a fleet of this size. To be worthy of it, an individual must possess a rare combination of learned skills and inborn attributes . . ."*

Marlena turned down the volume of her communicator and smirked at the lieutenant obstructing her departure. "Sounds to me like Admiral Spock is still making his opening remarks—which means the ceremony has not yet happened." She tucked her communicator back onto her belt. "Spock is still in command, therefore his orders stand, and Commander Decker's orders are not yet valid."

Gibbs seemed to be thinking that over as the cargo chief stepped up behind him and waited to see how the situation would play out. Then Gibbs's jaw stiffened with resolve. "That may be, ma'am, but I—"

He froze as Marlena poked the tip of her dagger into the soft spot under his chin. "Choose your next words carefully, Mister Gibbs," she said. "Because if you try to open this pod, you'll end up inside it." With her blade, she traced a line down the front of the man's yellow tunic, past his belt to his groin, and flashed a malevolent smile. "Or should I say . . . *part* of you will."

Gibbs swallowed hard, then turned his head to speak over his shoulder. "Chief Maas, put Admiral Spock's shipping container on the shuttle. Now."

"Aye, sir," said the cargo chief, who relieved Marlena of her burden and hurried it to the waiting shuttlecraft.

Marlena backed away from the lieutenant. "Wise choice," she said. When she was several meters away from him, she turned and quickened her pace to the shuttle. At its hatch she paused to make certain the shipping pod was loaded safely into the cargo compartment on the shuttlecraft's underbelly. Then she stepped inside and closed the hatch behind her.

"Lift off immediately," she said to the pilot.

He looked back in surprise. "Shouldn't we wait for Admiral Spock?"

"No," Marlena said. "He'll beam over to *Merrimac* once the transfer of command is done." She settled into the mission commander's seat next to the pilot. "We're on a tight schedule, mister. Let's go."

"Yes, ma'am," the pilot said. He signaled the launch control officer for clearance as he primed the shuttle-craft's controls. Less than a minute later, they were in flight, exiting *Enterprise* and cruising above the broad blue curve of Earth on a direct course to the *I.S.S. Merrimac*.

Let's hope that was the hard part, Marlena told herself as she struggled to keep her breathing slow and steady. She didn't expect much trouble on the *Merrimac*. At worst, they might subject her and Spock's shipping pod to a routine cargo scan, but the container's shielding would disguise its contents.

Though she respected Spock's desire for circumspection and caution, she couldn't help but resent it as she contemplated the possibilities offered by the Tantalus field device. She longed for the day when she and Spock could stop hiding their power from the galaxy at large—and start wielding it instead.

11

The Shape of the Future

Sarek and Amanda's home in ShiKahr was packed with dignitaries from the upper strata of Vulcan society, and Spock had begun to weary of the routine of introductions by the time his father led him to the room's most distinguished guest. "Governor Tomok," Sarek said, "allow me to present my son, Admiral Spock."

The governor of Vulcan lifted his hand, his fingers spread in the traditional V-shaped salutation. "Greetings, Admiral."

Spock returned the gesture. "It is an honor, Governor." Nodding at Marlena, he added, "This is Marlena Moreau of Earth—she who is my wife."

Tomok bowed his head a few degrees in Marlena's direction, but said nothing. Marlena emulated the governor's silent courtesy.

From Sarek's side, Amanda subtly nodded in approval at Marlena.

"I have heard much of your exploits in Starfleet," Tomok said to Spock. "I should hope to hear more of them directly from you, if your schedule permits. How long will you and your wife be on Vulcan?"

"Indefinitely," Spock said. "The *Enterprise* has begun a year-long refit."

The governor asked, "Has Starfleet no other billet for you?"

"I do not desire one other than command of the *Enterprise*," Spock said.

"A curious preference," Tomok said. "One might expect an admiral to aspire to greater responsibilities—at Starfleet Command, perhaps."

Spock did not let his face betray his irritation at the governor's insinuation of sloth. "In my experience, billets within Starfleet Command tend to be more political than purposeful. As I do not wish to engage in politics, I find my skills better suited to the command of a battle group."

The governor raised his eyebrows, as if to convey his sudden comprehension of Spock's position. "I see," he said. "So you will have more than one ship under your command when you return to service."

"That is the current plan," Spock said.

Narrowing his eyes, Tomok said, "What of the news that Grand Admiral Decker's son has been tapped to succeed you as captain of the *Enterprise*?"

Amanda answered quickly, "Such reports are premature. When the *Enterprise* is ready to return to service, my son will be its commanding officer."

Tomok dipped his chin at Amanda. "Then it seems I spoke rashly. My apologies." Noting Amanda's nodded reply, the governor said to Spock, "If you will excuse me, Admiral, I have matters of state to which I must attend."

"Of course," Spock said. "Good night, Governor."

"Good night."

Dismissed with proper courtesy, Tomok slipped away into the crowd of VIPs, leaving Spock, Sarek, and their wives by a window that looked out upon Vulcan's capital city, sparkling like a jewel in the desert night.

Sarek spoke in a confidential tone of voice. "My wife, was it necessary for you to embarrass the governor?"

Uncowed by Sarek's mild rebuke, Amanda replied, "I won't have him or anyone else saying my son's command has been usurped by a whelp like Willard Decker." With fierce determination, she said to Spock, "I assure you, when *Enterprise* is ready, she'll be yours to command."

"Most kind," Spock said.

A ringing of chimes turned the guests' attention to the end of the room farthest from Spock and his family.

Standing on a slightly elevated level of the estate's great room, Professor Sebok, the head of the Vulcan Science Academy, lifted his glass. "Everyone, please join me in welcoming home one of the favored sons of Vulcan. Twenty-one years ago, he declined an offer of admission to our Academy, electing instead to pursue a career in Starfleet. At the time, he endured great criticism for his choice. But seeing how far he has come, it now seems clear his decision . . . was quite logical." Raising his glass higher, he added, "To Spock!"

"To Spock!" repeated the crowd, and everyone sipped their drinks.

Before Sebok could blend back into the throng, Amanda had worked her way across the room to thank him personally. Sarek, who lacked his wife's skill in navigating through dense crowds, joined her a few moments later.

Marlena leaned close to Spock and said sotto voce, "I know your father's a famous diplomat . . . so why does your mother seem like the real power broker?"

"My mother hails from a powerful and wealthy family on Earth," Spock explained, "one with deep ties to the Sato dynasty. Much of her influence stems from her family's role in the development of weapons and defense technologies for the Terran Empire."

Eyeing both of Spock's parents intently, Marlena asked, "If your mother's that well connected, why isn't Sarek governor of Vulcan by now?"

Spock lifted one eyebrow. "My father was a contender for the office," he said. "However, that was before my rise to the Admiralty. My success has earned me the enmity of the Empress, whose wrath unfortunately has landed primarily upon my father."

"That's beyond unfair," Marlena said. "It's downright irrational."

"Such is the nature of human politics."

Marlena nodded and sipped her drink.

Sarek returned, emerging from the crowd with his empty hands clasped before him. He motioned with a tilt of his head for Spock to step aside with him.

Cloistered in an alcove near the corner, Sarek asked Spock in a hushed voice, "My son, do you have any schedule commitments tomorrow?"

"None that I am aware of."

"Good. Please make time for a short journey out of the city at dawn."

"May I ask where we are going, and for what purpose?"

"Mount Seleya," Sarek said. "There is someone I want you to meet."

Sarek and Spock arrived on Mount Seleya as it was bathed in the first amber rays of dawn. Climbing the last of the temple's thousand rough-hewn steps, Spock studied their surroundings. Thick stone walls and high balustrades hinted at the temple's martial past, as one of the great fortresses of Vulcan antiquity.

A trio of robed figures emerged from the temple and drew back their hoods as they approached Spock and Sarek. The leader looked to be middle-aged, with a long nose and sharply upswept eyebrows. The men behind him were younger; one was gaunt, the other burly.

"Ambassador Sarek," said the elder at the front of the group. "Thank you for coming. Our thanks also to you, Admiral Spock." He gestured at the temple. "Please, come in."

As father and son followed their three escorts inside, Sarek said, "It was no trouble, Tolik. We hope to be of service."

The Vulcan elder guided Sarek and Spock through the high-walled corridors of the temple. They stopped at a large, secluded circular courtyard paved with concentric rings around a meditation pool filled with dark water. Kneeling beside the pool with her back turned was an adolescent Vulcan girl with long hair.

Tolik whispered something to his two adepts, who stole away into the temple's shadowy interior. Turning back to Sarek, he said, "I leave you now." He glanced at the girl. "Her life rests in your hands." Then he slipped away, following his adepts into the temple's subterranean passages.

Sarek folded his hands inside the spacious sleeves of his robe and focused his placid gaze upon the girl. He whispered, "She is the one I wish you to meet."

Spock noted small details about the teen. Her clothes were frayed and her hair was unkempt. She seemed ill at ease and anxious despite her tranquil surroundings. "Her mind is troubled," Spock said.

"Yes," Sarek said. "She is a brilliant child, according to all the standard tests and metrics, but she has great difficulty controlling her emotions. In particular, she often succumbs to her feelings of rage. Her lack of discipline tarnishes her record of academic achievement. Unless she learns to master her emotions, she will not be able to function in Vulcan society—and perhaps not anywhere else."

The litany of the girl's dysfunctions sounded hauntingly familiar to Spock; it was as if he were being asked to revisit his own troubled childhood via proxy.

A flash of intuition led him to ask, "What is her non-Vulcan heritage?"

Sarek nodded. "Your insight is keen, Spock. She is half Romulan." Reacting to Spock's intrigued glance, he continued. "Her father was a Romulan spy who infiltrated our society decades ago. Last month he was exposed and taken into custody." His voice took on an extra note of gravity as he added, "He died during questioning by a pair of Andorian interrogators. The girl knows her father is dead, but not why he was taken or who he was—or what *she* is."

"She will need to be told someday," Spock said.

"Perhaps. But not today."

Spock faced his father. "Why do you wish me to meet her?"

"She needs a mentor. Someone who can understand the unique difficulties she faces, and who can nurture her immense potential. Since you and Marlena will be staying on Vulcan for the coming year, I think you are the ideal candidate." After watching Spock stare at the girl for several seconds, Sarek added, "I cannot and will not compel you to do this, my son. But if you wish to change the shape of the future, you should start by molding those who will live in it."

Weighing his father's words, Spock imagined what benefits he himself might have enjoyed if he had been privileged with a mentor like himself at the girl's age. Despite his reluctance to enmesh one so young in the complicated fabric of his life, Spock walked out of the shadows and crossed the courtyard to stand behind the girl. He waited for her to acknowledge his presence.

Finally, she turned and looked up at him. Her hair was as dark as the ocean at night, and her eyes glistened like the blade of a knife. A fearless gaze and a sullen demeanor gave her a feral beauty.

"I am Spock."

"I am Saavik. . . . Are you here to make a slave of me?"

"That would be a waste of your intellect and talent," Spock said.

Saavik rolled her eyes, apparently mistaking his praise for condescension. "Then what do you want with me?"

"I have been asked to serve as your mentor," Spock said, electing to pursue a policy of truth with the girl. "I believe I might be able to help you."

She bristled at his offer. "How?"

"You were born with great potential, Saavik, but unless you develop such a gift, it means nothing. You can choose to lead an extraordinary life and become part of something greater than yourself, or you can choose to live as a failure and an outcast. The difference between these two paths is *discipline,* and I can help you develop that, if you are willing to make the effort."

Eyeing him with suspicion, she asked, "Why would a

Starfleet admiral spend his time fixing a juvenile delinquent like me?"

"I once was as you are now," Spock said. "Because of my half-human ancestry, as a boy I found it difficult to control my emotions. My peers treated me as a misfit and an outcast because of my temper. They tormented me because they considered me . . . *less than Vulcan.*"

Saavik's veneer of anger began to fade. Spock sensed he was making a connection with her. She asked, "How did you purge yourself of emotions?"

"I didn't," he confessed. "I merely learned to hide them and to use that skill to my advantage, as you will do. Knowledge is power, Saavik—but wisdom lies in knowing how to *wield* power."

She held out her hand. Spock clasped it and helped her up.

"I'm willing to learn," said his protégée. "Please teach me."

2271

12

Hamartia

Marlena waited in the hatchway of the shuttlecraft *Surak* while Spock said farewell to Saavik. In the year since he had taken the girl under his wing, she had matured a great deal. The first time Spock had brought the teen to their residence in ShiKahr, Marlena was struck by the wild intensity of Saavik's stare. Today, as she bid her mentor safe travels and promised to continue her studies under Sarek's tutelage, her gaze had the same fire—now tempered with a keen focus.

Saavik lifted her hand in the Vulcan salute, and Spock did the same. They exchanged whispered valedictions, and then Saavik turned and walked away to stand with Sarek and Amanda and watch the shuttle's departure.

Spock joined Marlena inside the shuttle, and they settled into their seats. Shifting uncomfortably and tugging at the fabric of her tunic and slacks, Marlena said, "I hate these new uniforms. They look like dirty gray pajamas, but they're not as comfortable." Pulling at the crimson sash tied around her waist, she added, "And this stupid thing gets in the way of my knife and my agonizer."

"Starfleet's new uniform code permits a thigh sheath for your knife," Spock said as he secured his safety harness. "As for access to your agonizer, that will not be an issue once we reach the *Enterprise*."

"Why not?"

"Because I intend to ban their use on all vessels under my command."

That was news to Marlena. "And how do you think Starfleet Command will feel about you countermanding a general order?"

"We will see," Spock said.

"Can you get us better uniforms while you're at it?"

"I will convey your request to the Admiralty."

She let out a derisive huff and rolled her eyes. "In other words, *no*."

A tall Vulcan woman wearing a Starfleet uniform stepped inside the shuttle, sealed the hatch, and sat down across the aisle from Spock. Marlena noticed the woman wore the rank insignia of a lieutenant commander. As soon as the Vulcan woman had secured her safety restraints, she leaned forward and said to the pilot, "Lift off when ready, Ensign, and seal the cockpit."

The pilot acknowledged the woman's orders and closed the door between the cockpit and the passenger cabin. The shuttle's thrusters engaged, and within moments the craft was airborne and on its way out of Vulcan's atmosphere.

Marlena admired the receding view of ShiKahr until she heard the Vulcan woman say, "Good morning, Admiral. I am Lieutenant Commander T'Prynn of Starfleet Intelligence."

"Good morning, Commander," Spock replied.

"The reason why the seven stars are no more than seven is a pretty reason," T'Prynn said.

Spock answered, "I have no words—my voice is in my sword."

Confused and alarmed, Marlena said, "Did I miss something?"

"Recognition codes," Spock said. "Prepared between myself and Sarek."

Marlena looked at T'Prynn, who nodded at her and then said to Spock, "I have served your father for many years, Admiral. He informs me you have temporary need of my talents aboard the *Enterprise*."

"I do," Spock said. "If you succeed, I will have more tasks for you."

"If I may inquire, sir . . . why did you ask for me?"

"Because of your personal history, Commander," Spock said, his voice resonant with implied meaning.

Though his reply was cryptic to Marlena, it provoked a steely glare from T'Prynn, who replied in a tense voice, "I see."

"Before I share my secrets with you, I must confirm you can be trusted." Reaching toward T'Prynn's face, he added, "I must know your mind."

Marlena snapped, "No!" Her husband looked at her, his face a cipher. Reining in her anxiety, she continued. "The risk is too great. A mind-meld will reveal everything to her. If she's lying—"

"If she is, then she has deceived my father—no easy task."

Marlena placed her hand on Spock's arm. "We've only just met her. It's too soon to show her what we know."

"If we are to cultivate effective allies," Spock said, "we need to begin sharing our information and objectives." He cast a hard look at T'Prynn. "Though it would be prudent to take some precautions." Holding out his hand, he said to the Vulcan woman, "Give me your phaser, Commander."

T'Prynn removed her sidearm and handed it across the narrow aisle to Spock, who passed it to Marlena. "Set it for heavy stun," Spock said. "If my gamble proves to be an error, I trust you will know what to do." Then he reached out and pressed his fingertips to T'Prynn's face. At first she flinched from his touch, but he extended his arm fully and made contact. "My mind to your mind," he intoned, closing his eyes. "Our thoughts are merging."

The Vulcan woman closed her eyes as she said, "Our memories combine."

"We are together," Spock said.

T'Prynn replied, "We are one."

Anger and jealousy swelled in Marlena's heart. She hated to see Spock share such intimacy with another woman. She remembered their own mind-meld of a few years earlier. It was an experience more profound than sex, more revealing than confession. Adding to Marlena's anxiety, T'Prynn was a Vulcan and therefore able to participate in the psychic union with greater ease than Marlena had. She wondered if T'Prynn's mind aroused Spock, or if the Vulcan woman desired him.

Marlena yearned to press her thumb on the phaser's trigger. *Give me a reason,* she thought, her fury simmering as she watched T'Prynn's face for the slightest hint of pleasure. *Swoon or bite your lip like a whore—I dare you.*

Instead, both Spock's and T'Prynn's expressions remained blank as he removed his fingertips from her face and they opened their eyes.

"I know her mind," Spock said. "She can be trusted."

Marlena still aimed the phaser at T'Prynn. "Are you sure?"

Spock took the phaser gently from Marlena's hand. "I am certain."

It galled Marlena that Spock had discounted her opinion so easily. In most other matters he had proved willing to heed her counsel, so why had he resisted her advice regarding T'Prynn? She feared he was too quick to trust other Vulcans, and not willing enough to imagine some of them might prove to be his enemies.

If he has a fatal flaw, Marlena decided, *this will likely be it.*

Spock handed the phaser to T'Prynn, who tucked it back onto her belt under her sash. "What are your orders, Admiral?"

"When we reach the *Enterprise,* stay close but be discreet."

"Yes, sir," she replied. "And if Commander Decker or his operatives attempt to move against you?"

"In that case," Spock said, "be swift, precise, and merciless."

With the perfect calm of a trained killer, T'Prynn replied, "Understood."

13

Homecoming

Spock exited the *Surak* to find *Enterprise*'s acting captain, Commander Willard Decker, and its former executive officer, Commander Scott, waiting for him in the fully refitted ship's cavernous main hangar bay, which coursed with activity.

"Welcome aboard, Admiral," said Decker.

"Thank you, Captain," Spock said, addressing Decker by title rather than by rank. "I trust you've received your orders from Starfleet Command."

"I have, sir. As you requested, I've forgone the usual trappings of a command-transfer ceremony." Though the statement was one of simple fact, there was a subtle undercurrent of resentment in Decker's voice. Considering the circumstances, Spock was not at all surprised.

"Very good," Spock said. "Proceed."

Decker handed Spock a data slate. "Admiral Spock, having been duly requested and required by Starfleet Command to relinquish command of *I.S.S. Enterprise* to your authority, I hereby surrender this vessel's command codes."

Spock tucked the data slate under one arm and extended his free hand to Decker. "I relieve you, sir."

Shaking Spock's hand, Decker replied, "I stand relieved."

Stepping away from the shuttle to permit Marlena and T'Prynn to debark, Spock asked Decker, "What is *Enterprise*'s state of readiness, Commander?"

"Mister Scott and I will finish our final calibrations to the warp drive by thirteen hundred hours, sir."

"And the crew?"

"All personnel aboard and accounted for."

"Very good. Please prepare the bridge for my arrival."

"Aye, sir," Decker said, bowing his head at the implied dismissal. He departed at a quick step and left the shuttlebay.

Spock turned to see Marlena supervising the unloading of their personal effects from the *Surak*. T'Prynn was already gone, vanished into the ship.

Commander Scott lingered on Spock's flank. "It's good to have you back in command, Admiral," he said. "I dinnae trust that lad Decker in the big chair."

"Thank you, Mister Scott. I regret I was not able to reinstate you as first officer, but Grand Admiral Decker insisted his son—"

Scott held up one hand. "No apology needed, sir. I never cared for the job anyway. Engineering's where I belong."

"Then I, for one, am pleased to once again have the honor of your services as chief engineer. Take your post and prepare the ship for immediate departure."

"Aye, sir," Scott said with a smile that was as unexpected as it was sincere.

Walking back to Marlena's side, Spock said, "I must report to the bridge." He rested one hand on the case containing the Tantalus field device and added in a confidential tone, "I trust you will see to the appointment of our quarters."

Marlena met his steady gaze and said, "Everything will be arranged to your liking by tonight—assuming none of Decker's people interfere."

"You will encounter no interference—from anyone," Spock said with grave assurance. "T'Prynn will see to that."

14

A Shadow on the Son

"Yeah, they're settled in," Will Decker said, hunching over the desk in his quarters with a cold drink in one hand and his head in the other, "but it took his wife less than an hour to find the surveillance unit I hid in his quarters."

Decker's father, Matt—better known throughout the Empire as the Grand Admiral of Starfleet—hollered back over the secure subspace comm, *"Well, whose damned fault is that, boy?"*

"What am I supposed to do, sir?" Will's father had always insisted he call him "sir," even in private, ever since Will was a boy. "I can't just barge into his quarters to plant new taps."

His father shouted, *"Don't ask me how to fix your mistakes, boy! I need you to keep tabs on that crafty Vulcan, no matter what it takes."*

Sipping from his vodka on the rocks, Decker brooded, *You could've done it yourself if you'd kept him at Starfleet Command instead of letting his* mother *give him back the* Enterprise. He swallowed his mouthful of vaguely medicinal-tasting booze, and then held back his flood of bile behind a tight-lipped frown.

"I'm doing all I can, sir, I promise you. But it's not as if Spock doesn't know who I am—he knows I'm *your son*. Which is probably why he's been keeping me at arm's length ever since he came back aboard."

"Yes, we expected that," the grand admiral said. *"But that's no excuse, boy. If Spock's got a bead on you, don't come at him straight. Use your head—flank him!"* He leaned forward so his stubbled visage filled the screen of Decker's desktop monitor. *"Use cutouts, proxies. Get someone else to do your dirty work."*

"The only people who get near him are the ones he already trusts," Decker said, uncertain how to translate his father's advice into action. "Turning one of them won't be easy." .

"No, no, no," protested the elder Decker. *"You're not hearing me, boy. I'm saying send a woman."*

Decker shook his head. . "I don't know. He seems pretty devoted to his wife."

"Don't make me laugh," said the grand admiral. *"Spock wouldn't be the first married man to take a mistress. Besides, this is exactly what we need—a wedge to push those two apart. Marlena's been his staunchest ally ever since he got rid of Kirk. But back when she was Kirk's woman, she was famous for her jealousy. If you can get some nice piece of tail on that ship to draw Spock's interest for even a minute, that ought to put Marlena's temper into play."*

"And if Spock isn't the cheating type?"

"All men are the cheating type, boy. You just have to find the right woman."

2272

15

Creatures of the Chase

It had taken two failed attempts and several months to arrange, but Will Decker was certain he had at last hit upon a foolproof plan to insinuate a mistress into the life of the otherwise unimpeachable Admiral Spock.

Unfortunate fates had befallen his first trio of would-be Jezebels.

Janice Rand and Carolyn Palamas—a pair of buxom blondes who had insisted on offering themselves to Spock as a duo, thinking it would double their seductive appeal—had vanished without a trace shortly after their carefully arranged clandestine rendezvous with the Vulcan.

Marla McGivers, a sultry and intellectual redhead, had fared slightly better, finding herself transferred without explanation to the *I.S.S. Hornet* the morning after her failed bid at seduction.

Decker felt no remorse for what had happened to the three women, but he blamed himself for not thinking through the matter before taking action. *It was stupid of me to think that just because he has a human wife, he must be partial to human women,* he chastised himself. *A married man never wants more of what he already has—he wants something different. Something new.*

With that in mind, deciding who to send next had

been easy. All he had to do now was relax and wait for word of his new operative's success.

He stretched out on the bed in his quarters and watched a vid of a soccer match recorded the previous day on Deneva. Earth's all-star team led Deneva's team at the half, two goals to one. Just as Decker had expected, the colony team still hadn't learned how to avoid the offside penalty while playing offense.

Idiots, he mused, grateful the Denevans' ineptitude would likely net him a tidy sum when Earth's team covered the point spread on his bet.

The buzz of his door signal tore his attention from the game. *Perfect timing, as always,* he thought with irritation as he got up. Barefoot and in his nightclothes, he padded out of his sleeping alcove and across his quarters to the locked door. He activated the intercom. "Who is it?"

A woman with an exotic accent replied over the comm, *"Ilia."*

He unlocked the door. It sighed open, revealing his lover, a lithe Deltan woman. Like most members of her species, she was completely bald—and gifted with intensely powerful pheromones that made her nigh irresistible.

She all but fell through his door, collapsing into his arms.

"Ilia!" Decker said, pulling her inside his quarters. "Did he hurt you?"

"Only my feelings," she said. Looking up at Decker, she cracked a salacious smile. "But you'd never do that, would you, my love?"

Decker held her at arm's length, but he felt his resolve crumbling before the assault of her pheromones.

"Ilia, what are you doing here? You're supposed to be with Admiral Spock on the rec deck."

"He sent me away," she said, affecting an exaggerated pout.

"You've got to be kidding me," Decker said. He let her go and walked to his sleeping nook. She followed him with a lovesick devotion. Turning to face her, he pointed and said, "Tell me everything that happened. *Everything*."

Ilia's breaths were quick and heavy, as if she had been exerting herself. "I met him where you told me to," she said, tracing the curves of her bosom with her fingertips as she continued. "He came alone, like we'd hoped. I set the exercise pod to private mode . . ." She pulled off her tunic and prowled forward, cornering Decker. "I showed him how delightfully charming I can be." Unfastening her slacks, she added, "He put his hand on my cheek, and then he complimented my beauty and said my pheromones were very potent, even for a Deltan in her sexual prime." She let her pants fall to the floor around her ankles. "Then he said good night and left me alone in the pod."

Beholding the breathtaking siren standing before him in her undergarments, Decker marveled at Spock's willpower. "He just walked away? From *you*?"

"Yes, my love," Ilia said, wrapping her arms around his neck and draping herself on him like a fashion accessory. "I failed you. Please forgive me."

He wanted to be furious with Ilia, but his mind was a morass of primal hungers. His breaths were short and heavy, and he felt hyperaware of Ilia's body heat. Even her breath was alluring, as if it were scented with a hint of cinnamon. He ran his hands down the sides of her torso and admired the smoothness of her skin, the perfection of her muscle tone, the elegant curves of her hips.

She pressed herself against him, a force of desire unstoppable once set in motion, her unfettered lust stoking the banked fires of his own passion. Her lips brushed his with the tender touch of a pickpocket as she took his hand and guided it through her thighs.

All notions of restraint fled from his thoughts. He seized Ilia by her shoulders and threw her onto the bed. Then he was on top of her, ripping away her bra and underwear, taking his perfect concubine in exactly the way he knew she wanted—roughly, without apology or hesitation.

But even as Decker luxuriated in the glories of Ilia's flesh, one question lingered on the fringe of his thoughts and troubled him deeply.

What kind of man must Spock be that he can resist this?

Marlena did not consider herself a voyeur, but as she watched Decker and Ilia on the monitor of the Tantalus field device, she could not help but admire the athleticism and imagination of their fevered copulation.

She heard the door of her and Spock's quarters open and close. Footfalls drew near with a rhythm she recognized as Spock's. "The tramp went straight to Decker," she reported.

He joined her at the device and regarded Decker and Ilia's wild fornication with a dispassionate stare. "As we suspected," Spock said.

"I can't fault him for a lack of commitment," Marlena said. "The first three sluts he sent were just pawns. At least this time he cared enough to send his *own* whore."

Casting a sidelong glance at Spock, she added, "But you already knew about Decker and Ilia, didn't you?"

"Indeed," Spock said. "T'Prynn learned of their relationship before she returned to Vulcan, while researching Decker's dossier for my files."

On the Tantalus field device's screen, a moment of precarious sexual acrobatics by the limber Deltan woman raised Marlena's brow in surprise. Feeling a bit intimidated by Ilia's erotic prowess, she asked her husband, "And how, exactly, were you able to resist her seduction pheromones?"

"The pheromones of Deltans and Orions have little effect on most Vulcans," Spock said, as if it were common knowledge.

She wasn't sure whether Spock was telling her the truth, but in the interest of quelling her own jealousy Marlena chose to believe his explanation. "Good to know," she said. She nodded at the screen. "I guess Mister Decker's not so lucky."

"Apparently not," Spock said.

"It's curious—she went straight to him after meeting with you," Marlena said. "Rand, Palamas, and McGivers were all smart enough to avoid him after botching their missions. Did Ilia just get herself so hot and bothered trying to woo you that she had to use him as a pressure valve?"

Spock replied, "In part, yes. Also, when she let me touch her face, I planted a telepathic suggestion that she should seek out her master."

"If you had contact, why didn't you just read her mind?"

"Deltans have a limited empathic ability. It is not strong enough to warrant their extermination by the

Empire, but it makes them receptive to some forms of psionic contact. However, had I invaded her psyche deeply enough to read her thoughts, she would have been as privy to my mind as I was to hers."

Looking at the monitor again, Marlena winced at Decker's and Ilia's latest activity. "I've seen enough," she said, reaching toward the device's trigger.

Spock reached out and stayed her hand. "No," he said. "Not yet."

"What are we waiting for?" asked Marlena. "We have proof he sent Ilia, which means he's spying on you—probably on behalf of his father."

Arching a single eyebrow, Spock said, "True. But we already suspected that to be the case. By permitting him to act, we have lured him into exposing his allies on the ship, enabling us to eliminate them—and to isolate him."

"Is it your will that he should live?"

"For now," Spock said. "We can use this device to observe him and learn what secret reports he makes, and to whom. As long as he does not suspect he is being observed, there is no reason for us to tip our hand."

Marlena fixed her icy glare on Ilia's image. "And her?"

"I trust you to act with discretion," Spock said, stepping away and leaving the Deltan woman's life in his wife's hands.

Decker stirred from a troubled slumber shortly after 0500. He rolled over and reached for Ilia. She wasn't there. He opened his eyes. The other side of his bed was empty.

It wasn't like Ilia not to stay the night. He wondered if perhaps she harbored some seed of resentment toward him for foisting her on Spock, and in retaliation had slipped away while he slept.

You're being paranoid, he told himself. *She's probably in the main room on the other side of the partition.*

Pushing back the bedsheets, he called out, "Ilia?"

There was no response.

Treading lightly in bare feet, he moved through his quarters looking for Ilia. She wasn't in the main room, dining nook, or lavatory.

I guess she really did leave, he concluded with disappointment.

He stood at his comm panel and opened a channel to Ilia's quarters. "Ilia, it's Will. Are you there?" Several seconds passed with no reply. He initiated a direct transmission to Ilia's communicator. "Commander Decker to Lieutenant Ilia. Please respond." His hail was met with dead silence. He signaled the bridge. "Decker to Lieutenant Commander Riley."

"Riley here," said *Enterprise*'s recently promoted second officer, who had the conn during the night watch.

"I need a fix on Lieutenant Ilia's communicator, on the double."

"Aye, sir. Hang on while we find her."

The wait was brief, but it still took a toll on Decker's nerves. Over the open channel, he heard muffled voices while the bridge crew worked. Then Riley was back on the comm, sounding apologetic. *"Sorry, sir. We've come up empty. Maybe her communicator malfunctioned . . ."*

Decker closed the channel.

A malfunction? He didn't believe that. He knew *Enterprise*'s history and Spock's reputation too well to accept such a transparent excuse.

It took him less than a minute to get dressed.

Fighting to suppress his rising feelings of dread, Decker sprinted from his quarters to Ilia's, pausing only for the handful of seconds he spent in a turbolift.

When he arrived at the door to Ilia's quarters, it was unlocked. He charged inside without signaling.

All of Ilia's possessions were exactly as she had left them. Her quarters were tidy, comfortably furnished, and tastefully decorated. Her closets were crowded with her civilian clothes. A carved wooden box containing her favorite jewelry sat in its place on a table beside her made bed.

Decker didn't know what he had expected to find. Evidence of foul play? Signs of a struggle? Ilia's broken body? Instead, nothing appeared to be amiss—and that was what sent a chill down his spine. Just like so many of Spock's enemies before her, Ilia had simply vanished.

For the first time since he had set foot on the *Enterprise,* Willard Decker felt very much alone—and for the first time since moving out of his father's house to attend Starfleet Academy, he was afraid.

2273

16

Body and Soul

Saavik willed herself not to blink as a Starfleet Academy drill instructor yelled into her face, "Identify yourself, plebe!"

"Saavik," she said, holding out the data card containing her orders to report for summer indoctrination.

"Wrong!" barked the DI. "When you address a superior, you will phrase your answers in the form of 'sir sandwiches'! *Sir, yes, sir!* Is that clear?"

"I—"

"Give me twenty push-ups!"

Confused but obedient, Saavik put her data card in her pocket, dropped to the floor in the main concourse of Archer Hall, and executed twenty regulation-style push-ups. As she did so, she heard other incoming cadets answering questions from other DIs with the phrase, "Sir, yes, sir!"

When she had finished her punitive exercise, she stood at attention and remained silent until her DI demanded, "Identify yourself, plebe!"

She held out her data card. "Sir, Saavik, sir!"

"Correct," the DI said, accepting her card. He placed it into a handheld reader, checked its information, pressed a button, and then ejected the card. "Your Alpha Number is three-nine-seven-seven Delta. This will be your identifying serial number for the duration of your Academy career. Is that clear?"

"Sir, yes, sir!"

He handed back the card and pointed left. "Get in line!"

Saavik pocketed her card and jogged to the end of a single file of inductees. The DI stayed behind and waited for his next arriving plebe.

The line crept forward past several noncommissioned officers seated at long tables. The first of them handed Saavik a stack of uniforms. The second one issued her a pair of black boots. The third noncom added a pair of running shoes to the top of Saavik's armload of gear. The fourth petty officer issued her a small handbook whose cover bore the title *Star Points*. The last of the seated noncoms injected Saavik with two hyposprays and then handed her an agonizer.

Another DI pointed to the right and snapped, "Report to the barber, plebe!"

Jogging to catch up to the inductees ahead of her, Saavik was directed by more shouting men and women into a three-walled cubicle with a table, a chair, and a middle-aged male Tellarite holding a powered hair trimmer.

"Put your gear on the table and sit," the barber said.

Saavik did as he said. Directly ahead of her she saw other plebes being tended to by other barbers. Male inductees' heads were shaved, while the female plebes had their hair trimmed to a length Starfleet apparently had deemed appropriate. As the Tellarite grabbed up a handful of Saavik's long tresses for trimming, she declared simply, "Sir, please shave it off, sir."

"All of it?"

"Sir, all of it, sir!"

"My pleasure," the Tellarite said. With a few deft passes of the buzzing trimmer, he removed all of Saavik's hair, rendering her pale head faintly stubbled. "You're done, plebe. Go get your physical."

"Sir, yes, sir!" Saavik grabbed her mountain of gear and followed the other shorn plebes to a series of rooms where Starfleet physicians examined them, corpsmen gave them vaccinations, and nurses collected DNA samples for their service records.

The doctors ushered the processed plebes to the back door of Archer Hall, where a squad of detailers—upperclassmen tasked with assisting in the training of plebes during their seven-week-long summer indoctrination period—taught the inductees how to perform a proper imperial salute: Bring the side of the closed right fist to the left pectoral, then extend the right arm and hand at shoulder height, palm slightly raised. Each plebe was made to repeat the gesture until his or her detailer was satisfied, and then they were ordered to exit the hall and board a ground transport that would take them to their barracks.

The ride across the Starfleet Academy campus was brief. The plebes rode with their gear stacked on their laps. Most appreciated the few minutes of relative tranquility. A few, including Saavik, used the time to steal glances at the contents of the *Star Points* handbook, which was filled with a variety of information, ranging from the command structure of Starfleet to a glossary of midshipmen's jargon to quotes from literature or historical figures.

As plebes surged out of the transports onto the parade green outside the barracks, roving detailers and drill instructors divided the Fourth Class Regiment into fifteen companies of eighty personnel. The first eight companies were designated the Starboard Battalion. The regiment's Port Battalion comprised the latter seven companies.

The entire process seemed arbitrary to Saavik, who remained silent and listened for her name. When it was called, she joined the other members of Delta Company. After all eighty members of the company had assembled in formation, they were led at a quick march inside their residence hall.

Indoors, the company was subdivided into two platoons of forty plebes; each platoon was further broken down into four squads of ten personnel.

At 1745 hours, they were assigned racks and lockers and given fifteen minutes to stow their gear, change into dress uniforms, return to the parade green, and muster in company formation.

There was no time to think or ask questions; there was barely enough time to follow orders. Scrambling to keep up with the other plebes, Saavik donned her dress-white uniform and raced back outside with Delta Company and the rest of the Class of '77 to stand in formation under a clear, late-June sky.

Minutes later, the commandant of Starfleet Academy arrived, followed by a clutch of flag officers, adjutants, aides-de-camp, and other imperial dignitaries.

The plebes were directed to salute and led in a recitation of their oaths of service as officers of the Terran Empire Starfleet. Saavik's was only one of twelve hundred voices reciting the oath, but she enunciated with perfect clarity, as if Admiral Spock were standing beside her, auditing her every word.

When the oath was complete, the master drill instructor bellowed, "Regiment, fall out!" The detailers and drill instructors herded the plebes off the parade green at a quick step and led them back to their barracks.

After a day of enervating drudgery, Saavik expected dinner and a night's rest to be the next orders of business. She was mistaken.

There was no dinner that night. For three hours and fifteen minutes, she and the other plebes were made to run laps around the barracks, and they endured a non-stop harangue of criticism and deliberately contradictory orders intended to confuse them and make them subject to more verbal abuse. Making mistakes resulted in plebes being yelled at. Questioning orders, even if merely to request clarification, earned plebes long jolts from their agonizers.

Her company's detailer ordered them into their racks at 2145 and turned out the lights. Saavik felt relieved; her first day at the Academy was finally over. She told herself induction day would likely be the worst part of the whole experience.

As before, she was mistaken.

The next seven weeks followed a simple if relentless pattern.

Reveille blared each morning at 0530. Attired in exercise clothes, the plebes assembled on the parade green for morning calisthenics, regardless of the weather. Some mornings they did jumping jacks and squat-thrusts in the soft glow of dawn; sometimes they did crunches or leg-lifts in fog so thick the rear ranks of plebes could barely see the detailers. On other days they did push-ups on muddy ground and braved torrential downpours during formation runs, which progressively increased in distance as the summer wore on.

After morning physical training, the plebes assembled—as always, in formation—for accountability (the detailers' term for attendance) and uniform inspection before they marched to the mess hall for morning chow. The mess hall's menu varied, but its fare was consistent—bland but nourishing.

During morning chow the plebes were apprised of the "plan of the day," a list of mandatory classes and activities they would follow until lights-out. A typical morning involved classroom instruction on any of a number of topics, including warfare and tactics, military regulations, Starfleet's rank structure and chain of command, and leadership.

After morning classes the plebes returned to their barracks to don their dress uniforms for noon formation. At 1200 each day, the plebes stood in company ranks for accountability and uniform inspection before being permitted to march inside the mess hall for noon chow.

Saavik noted that tourists often observed the noon formation, and almost all of them seemed to mistake it for something special.

Afternoons were a time for physical education and practical instruction. Some days were devoted to small-arms proficiency and martial arts. At least two days each week, the plebes ran obstacle courses. Strength and endurance training included team sports as well as swimming, weight training, and rock-climbing. Two more days each week were spent on such basic skills as squad-combat tactics, shipboard damage control, firefighting, vacuum survival, and free-fall training. However, the plebes' most hated exercise by far was close-quarter drill, which involved marching in tight formation while performing regimentally synchronized precision choreography with heavy antique rifles.

Each dusk brought a third formation on the parade green, followed by an inspection and a march inside the mess hall for evening chow. When chow was over the plebes endured more classes, more physical trials, and the cleaning of their barracks, uniforms, or selves. They found no relief until the final thirty minutes of each day, when they each were allowed to write one letter home.

Because Saavik saw little point in recounting the tedium of her days to Ambassador Sarek or Admiral Spock, she utilized the last half hour of each day—and nearly every other free moment she could steal—reading and memorizing the contents of her *Star Points* handbook. Its articles encompassed a wide range of information Starfleet had decided was important for its officers to know: the classes and specifications of its active starships, small spacecraft, and combat equipment; its principal bases of operation; a summary of the Starfleet phonetic alphabet, which was based on Earth's old international standard; and a wide range of inspirational quotes her detailers said were intended to help shape plebes' philosophical outlook as officers and encourage esprit de corps.

That body of knowledge was known at the Academy as "the rates." Plebes were expected to memorize the rates and be able to recite any part of them by rote at any time during their training. The detailers enforced this requirement constantly and mercilessly, drilling the plebes while they were running in the mornings, eating, crawling under sharp-edged protrusions on the obstacle courses, and even while they were showering or using the head.

Answering incorrectly or failing to answer would draw swift punishment. Depending on the detailer's personality and mood, the plebe might find himself tasked with a hundred push-ups—or writhing in excruciating pain from a prolonged jolt by his agonizer.

"The purpose of this is to teach you to concentrate in times of stress," the detailers explained, but Saavik was certain some of them inflicted harsher punishments simply because they enjoyed doing so.

Despite her Vulcan mental conditioning, Saavik felt overwhelmed at times. Constant physical exertion, coupled with the overload of classroom work and the steady stream of verbal abuse, made each day bleed into the next. Weeks slipped away, and she felt lost in time's unyielding current.

Then the seventh and final week of Plebe Summer came to an end, and Saavik anticipated the formal start of her first year as a Starfleet Academy cadet. With the grueling indoctrination period over, she believed the worst of her days as a plebe were finally behind her.

Once again, she was wrong.

Plebe Summer concluded with the "reform of the brigade," which was Academy jargon for the return of upperclassmen cadets from their midshipman cruises and specialized summer training courses at other facilities.

Overnight, the plebes went from outnumbering their detailers and drill instructors twenty-to-one to being outnumbered more than three-to-one by upperclassmen, each of whom wielded the authority of a detailer over any plebe.

The loss of majority brought with it a loss of anonymity. During the summer, a plebe who avoided attention might go most of a day without drawing the notice of a detailer. Now the campus teemed with sharp-eyed young men and women looking for any opportunity to visit their wrath on subordinates.

Everywhere the plebes went, upperclassmen were waiting to "flame" them for even the most trivial error or misstep. A hair out of place, a boot not shined to perfection, a wrinkle in the blanket on a plebe's made rack—any of these minor infractions could draw a vicious harangue. Such moments of ruthless, unsupervised abuse were known as "assisting the plebes."

Most galling to Saavik, even a second-year cadet could demand control of her agonizer. She didn't need to have committed an offense; if she dared to question her "correction," that alone was sufficient cause to increase her punishment. The sheer illogic of it all was maddening to her.

Determined to master her rates and responsibilities, Saavik strove for virtual invisibility on the campus. Despite her best efforts, it eluded her.

One slate-gray morning in early October, she crossed the parade green toward her barracks, in a hurry to change before reporting to noon formation.

A man shouted at her from behind, "Stop right there, plebe!"

She hated being addressed in that manner, but upperclassmen did not consider their first-year peers worthy of the appellation "cadet."

She halted at attention. Two upperclassmen caught up to her. Both were human men with lean physiques and eyes hardened by the hunger of ambition. Their insignia identified them as third-year cadets. The one with dark hair smiled at his fair-haired companion, and then he asked Saavik, "Whose quotation about leadership is found on page seventy-one of the rates?"

"Sir, the quotation on page seventy-one of the rates is by Noah Porter, a nineteenth-century president of Yale College, sir!"

The upperclassman smiled. "And what is that quotation, plebe?"

Reciting from memory, Saavik replied, "Sir, the quotation is, 'Rely on your own strength of body and soul. Take for your star self-reliance, faith—' "

"Wrong!" the second-class cadet interrupted, even though Saavik had made no error. He held out his open palm. "Your agonizer, plebe."

Her hesitation was so brief, she doubted he even noticed it.

She felt her pulse racing and her blood burning with rage. Being punished for an actual error was one thing; being abused when she had committed no infraction made her muscles tense with the urge to strike and her hands ache to close into fists and pummel the smug upperclassman.

I will not succumb to my passions, she told herself, surrendering her agonizer. *I am no longer that outcast child on Vulcan. I am in control.*

The first jolt of the agonizer turned her thoughts white with pain.

Saavik calmed her fury by remembering Spock's teachings.

I cannot control the actions of others, so I must master how I react to their actions. Discipline is strength, and strength is power.

A second zap from the agonizer made her feel as if she had been lit on fire. She bit down on her cries of anger and her howls of suffering.

I will not embarrass Spock or Sarek, she promised herself. *They have trusted me to see this through. I will not fail them.*

The upperclassman waved the agonizer in Saavik's face. "You look like you want to say something, plebe. Do you want to curse at me?" He grinned at his friend, then looked back at Saavik. "Or maybe you want to beg for mercy?"

There was no right answer. If she asked for mercy, he would punish her for insubordination. If she declined mercy, he would say she asked him to continue "assisting" her. Summoning her defiance, she erred on the side of honor.

Through clenched teeth, she replied, "Sir, no, sir."

He triggered the agonizer again, unaware he was tilting the balance of Saavik's inner struggle between discipline and instinct, or that if he tilted it far enough for instinct to prevail, Saavik would snap his neck like a brittle twig—and most important . . . she would enjoy it.

2274

17

A Secret Called Freedom

Carol Marcus leaned through the doorway of her thirteen-year-old son's bedroom as she announced, "David! Time for dinner."

She caught only the end of a snap-quick movement as David hid something behind him while answering, "Okay, Mom. Be there in a second."

Knowing the proclivities of boys David's age, Marcus's gut reaction was suspicion. She stepped farther inside his room and nodded at him. "What are you hiding, young man?"

He held up a data slate and answered in a nonchalant tone, "Nothing, just homework." His attempt at casual diversion was betrayed by his furtive glances in every direction except toward his mother.

Stepping beside his bed, she planted one hand on her hip and extended the other. "Let me see it." He froze, locked in a fearful yet defiant stare. Hardening her tone, Marcus added, "David Samuel Marcus, hand me that data slate this instant!"

David's face twisted into a frown as he grudgingly surrendered the electronic tablet. Marcus plucked it from her son's hand, scowled at him, and braced herself to see what grotesque entertainment the boy had found.

Perusing the hyperlinked contents loaded on the

device, she was both relieved and terrified. David had acquired a substantial collection of unabridged texts by censored anti-authoritarian philosophers. It included tracts by Immanuel Kant and John Stuart Mill; essays by Thomas Paine; stories by Ayn Rand and George Orwell; poetic reflections on individualism by N. E. Peart; meditations on revolution by Zacarías Manuel de la Rocha; and transcripts of suppressed speeches by Franklin Delano Roosevelt, Dr. Martin Luther King, Jr., and Mahatma Gandhi. Mere possession of such materials might be sufficient grounds for her precious son to be tortured to death or publicly executed as an example to others.

Slack-jawed, Marcus stared at her son. "What are you doing with this?"

Affecting a sheepish cringe, David said, "Reading."

"Where did you get it?" she demanded.

He shrugged. "It's not hard to find. You just have to look."

"Well, you shouldn't be looking for things like this," she said, masking her fear with anger. "This is a Starfleet starbase; they monitor transmissions on and off the station. If they detect you downloading something like this—"

"They won't," he said, rolling his eyes. "I know how to use the 'crypter."

"Don't think you're so clever," she admonished him. "Commodore Reyes is no fool, and neither are the people who serve him." Lifting the slate, she asked, "How many times have you downloaded this sort of thing?"

"Just the once," David said. "It was compressed and encrypted to look like something else. I was careful."

"I'll bet," Marcus said. "When did you get this file?"

"About a week ago."

Marcus considered the facts. If the incoming file had been recognized by the station's comm filters, it likely would have been blocked automatically. Since no one had come to question David about it, it was possible he had evaded a terrible fate thanks to the virtual camouflage provided by Vanguard's sheer volume of data traffic. Still, there was no point taking chances. She began keying in her security code on the data slate.

David asked, "What are you doing?"

"Deleting this before anyone comes looking for it."

"Stop! Don't!" His voice was pitched with such desperation it stayed Marcus's hand. When she met his pleading gaze, he continued. "You always say information has to be protected. Well, what about *this* information? Isn't it valuable? Aren't you always telling me we need to find ways to question authority? Well, what's the point if we let them tell us what questions we can ask?"

She was stunned into silence by her son's tirade. He had always been a very bright student, years ahead of his peers. A few months earlier he had exhausted the station's secondary education resources, forcing Marcus to enroll him in a long-distance learning program from the Mars Institute of Science, augmented by an independent-study curriculum she administered. Now, barely a teenager, he was already presuming to teach his mother to respect her own lessons.

Looking again at the tablet's contents, she was struck by what a tragedy it would be to expunge a copy of such hard-to-find knowledge. She could only imagine how many people had risked incarceration, injury, or death to preserve copies of these forbidden texts down through the centuries. Did she, or anyone else, really have the right to erase such a hard-won record of history?

Tapping on the slate's interface with its stylus, she said, "I'm not deleting it, but I am improving its encryption with one we use in the Vault. From now on, the only people on the station who will be able to unlock this tablet are me and Commodore Reyes—and if we're lucky, he'll never know this exists."

Still wearing a hangdog expression, David asked, "Are you taking it away?"

"That depends what you mean," she said.

"Are you going to let me keep reading it?"

She arched one eyebrow at the boy as she finished locking the file. "You'll see it again," she said. She pointed the stylus into the corners of the ceiling. "But only after I've had a chance to add a few more safety precautions in here, to make sure no one's eavesdropping on us. After that . . . I think we'll call this 'supplemental reading' for the independent-study portion of your education."

Her decision drew a smile from the brilliant teen, but Marcus quelled her son's jubilation with a stern admonition. "Don't say a word about this outside these quarters," she said. "No matter how exciting you think this stuff is, you can't go around talking about it. Not to *anyone*, no matter how much you think they might agree with it. People aren't always what they seem, David—remember that."

"I will," he said, mirroring her serious manner. "I promise."

"Good," she said, hoping he really understood and wasn't just humoring her. "Because not everyone will be as sympathetic as I am."

2275

18

Half the Battle

Captain Zhao Sheng stands in his quarters aboard the *I.S.S. Endeavour,* regards the agonizer in his hand, and questions everything he has ever believed.

How many times have I let someone else use this to hurt me? What did I ever learn from it except to fear the lash, like every sailor since antiquity?

He has paid close attention to news of Admiral Spock's accomplishments and reforms. From brokering peace between Elas and Troyius to abolishing the use of agonizers on the *Enterprise,* the Vulcan iconoclast has challenged Starfleet time and again, and each time has emerged stronger for it.

Zhao wonders how his crew will function without agonizers, without an agony booth, without a constant pall of terror.

He decides to try it and see the results for himself.

Midshipman Second Class Par chim Grum stands at the edge of San Francisco Bay, his back to Starfleet Academy. He takes a small booklet from his uniform pocket, intending to rip it up and hurl its shreds into the moon-lit water.

The Tellarite cadet hesitates. For some reason, the book intrigues him.

He reflects on the moment, hours earlier, when he confiscated the small tome from a female Vulcan plebe, whom he caught reading the unsanctioned text while seated on a circular bench beneath an old elm tree near the parade green.

Grum asked accusatorily, "Are those your rates, plebe?"

"Sir, no, sir," the young woman replied.

"Give them to me."

"Sir, yes, sir," the woman said, handing the book to Grum.

He perused the book quickly. It was a compilation of nonsense bordering on sedition. Grum was about to put the plebe on report until he noted the name of the book's author: Admiral Spock. Stuffing it into his pocket, he barked, "Give me twenty push-ups, plebe!"

The woman performed her penance, and then Grum ordered her to proceed to the next item on her plan of the day.

Now he stands facing the bay with the book in his hands. Something in its words calls out to him. He opens it to a random page and reads what it says.

Each page compels him to read the next one.

When he reaches the end, he hungers for more, so he flips back to the beginning and reads it from its first word. It offers him a vision of a nobler culture for Starfleet, a great society, and a cause worthy of the name of honor.

Grum returns to his barracks and hides the book in his locker.

Lieutenant John Harriman sags like an abandoned marionette as the agonizer booth is powered down. His tormentors open the cylindrical chamber's front panel, and he collapses to the deck at their feet.

The Andorian and the Tellarite laugh at him as he coughs up blood.

"That should teach you to mind your manners," says the Tellarite.

The Andorian kicks Harriman in the ribs. "Don't talk to a captain's woman unless she talks to you first." Reaching down, he grabs Harriman's hair. "Get it?" He pushes Harriman's face back onto the deck. The Tellarite grunts in disgust.

Harriman can't even see straight as the two security-division thugs drag him by his feet through the corridors of the *I.S.S. Hornet*. Despite being dazed and sick from what felt like hours inside the high-tech torture device, he can discern clearly the malicious chortles of his shipmates as he is hauled like garbage through the *Paladin*-class frigate's busy corridors.

By the time he hears the door of his quarters swish open, he is ready to vomit. His handlers drop his feet and lift him by his arms. They hurl him inside his quarters. Thrashed and limp, he lands in an awkward position, half on and half off his rack. Finally his guts heave, and he splutters stomach acid and bloody spittle across his bedsheets.

He hears the Andorian and the Tellarite laugh again as they leave his quarters. The Andorian calls out from the doorway, "If you can't take punishment like a man, maybe you should go serve on Admiral Spock's ship." Their cruel guffaws echo from the corridor even after the door hisses shut.

Harriman drifts in and out of consciousness that night. Nightmares plague his sleep. Lingering nausea, stinging wounds, and aching bruises dominate his moments of wakefulness.

Morning comes. Reveille sounds.

A voice on the intraship comm squawks, *"All bunks, turn to!"*

The wounded lieutenant masters his pain. Stands. Walks to his quarters' private head. Faces his swollen, damaged face in the mirror. Cracks a mirthless grin and inspects his bloodied, broken teeth.

He fills a glass with water. Rinses his mouth and spits. Showers. Towels dry. Puts on a clean uniform.

And submits his formal request for transfer to the *I.S.S. Enterprise*.

Captain Stephen Kornfeld of the *I.S.S. Bismarck* has a choice to make: open fire, or open hailing frequencies.

Starfleet regulations regarding first contacts in deep space are clear: capture the alien vessel; subdue its crew; remand prisoners to the chief medical officer for vivisection and analysis; and file a full after-action report to Starfleet Command.

But Kornfeld has read Admiral Spock's treatise on benign first contact. The Vulcan's ideas make sense to him. They fly in the face of general orders and more than a century of military protocol, but Kornfeld thinks Spock might be on to something. *If it works, it might change Starfleet's rules of engagement forever.*

His bridge crew waits for his order. Hands are poised above consoles, waiting to sound Red Alert, raise shields, and lock phasers.

The peculiar-looking vessel on the main viewer drifts closer.

"They're in firing range, Captain," says the helmsman.

Kornfeld narrows his eyes and thinks. He swivels his chair and asks his science officer, "Has the alien vessel raised shields or charged weapons?"

"Negative, sir," replies the young woman at the sensor display.

The captain makes his choice. "Ensign Thiel, open hailing frequencies."

Commander Hiromi Takeshewada of the *I.S.S. Constellation* hides in a corner of the ship's gymnasium, hoping the pounding rhythm of her furious heavy-bag boxing workout will muffle her uncontrollable sobs of rage.

She is a line officer. A combat veteran. Executive officer of Starfleet's flagship, the second-in-command to Grand Admiral Matthew Decker.

I deserve better than this, she tells herself.

Decker is a martinet, the kind of commanding officer who equates volume with leadership and abuse with discipline. Every day he verbally flays her in the presence of her subordinates and undermines her ability to function as the ship's executive officer. Some days he hits her. Those are the good days.

On bad days he entertains himself by randomly shocking Takeshewada with her agonizer. The worst days are when he combines his sadistic tendencies with his sexual perversions, forcing her to submit to his sick whims and gross violations while he clutches her agonizer and uses it to inflict jolts of varying severity.

Today was one of those days.

She pounds her gloved fists against the heavy bag and works up a sweat. *I still have his stink on me,* she realizes, wincing with revulsion. It only makes her hit the bag harder and faster.

She knows an officer of her rank and experience should be exempt from such depredations, even by a flag officer, but to protest is akin to suicide.

Who would I cry to? she asks herself rhetorically. *He's the grand admiral. Top of the food chain. There's no one who can help me. I'm all alone out here.*

Throwing her hands in a frenzy, she loses control. Her punches cease to land with any rhythm or force. She's just flailing her arms against the bag, twisting and thrashing and screaming . . . and then she collapses to the deck, spent and silent.

Takeshewada closes her eyes. Her breathing is loud inside her head. She feels her chest rising and falling, her heart racing, her limbs trembling.

When she opens her eyes, she senses someone standing behind her.

Turning her head, she sees Lieutenant Sontor, a young Vulcan officer from the sciences division. He offers her his hand.

"Let me teach you a better way to cope with your anger," he says.

Captain Clark Terrell, commanding officer of the *I.S.S. Sagittarius,* reads a coded subspace communiqué from his old friend and ally, Captain Zhao Sheng.

Zhao voices a lot of faith in the Vulcan admiral. More than Terrell has ever heard Zhao lavish upon anyone. Even harder to believe, Zhao says he has followed Spock's example, abolishing the use of agonizers on the *Endeavour.*

Terrell is fascinated and frightened. He sees potential in a man like Spock, but he also sees tremendous danger. *If enough of us rally to his banner, he could make a real difference,* Terrell muses. *But if we take his side and he fails, we all fall as one.*

After ten years of service in the Taurus Reach, Terrell is no stranger to risk. He has never let fear guide his decisions before, and he doesn't want to start now. But he has only just inherited the captain's chair of the *Sagittarius,* following his former CO's promotion to the Admiralty.

Risk is a lot to ask of him during this time of transition.

Then he thinks of Carol Marcus and her son.

I could do them a lot of good if I had Admiral Spock for a friend, he thought. *He seems like a man who can do the impossible. Maybe he can help Carol and David get off that station and away from that monster Reyes.*

It seems too much to hope for, too much to believe in. Not that Terrell has ever believed in much of anything, or anyone. But if what Zhao tells him is true, maybe it's time to start.

Terrell has a report about Operation Vanguard and Commodore Reyes he has been compiling in secret for the past few years. He has never shown it to anyone. In his experience, the truth never sets anyone free—most of the time, it just gets them killed. *But the truth isn't doing anybody any good sitting in my personal log,* he decides. *It's time to take a stand.*

He calls up the file. Attaches it to a coded subspace message addressed for Admiral Spock's eyes only. Composes a brief greeting.

His finger hesitates to press the button that will send the message.

Terrell has walked the line for so long that he balks at having to choose one side of it on which to stand.

Trying to make an ally of Spock will certainly make an enemy of Reyes, he reminds himself. *Once I choose a side, there's no going back.*

He sends the message.

I'll probably regret this, he tells himself.

His prediction proves correct.

19

The Name of Action

Marlena moved in swift strides down the corridor to her quarters. The Vulcan guards posted outside the door saluted her as she approached. She returned the salute as the door slid open and she passed between them.

The door shut behind her. She searched the compartment for her husband. Spock was seated at a computer terminal in a small space beyond a smoked-glass panel with an arched doorway. The lights were dimmed, and a faint haze of vaguely citrus-scented incense smoke lingered overhead.

She took a few hesitant steps toward him. "You said it was urgent."

Beckoning her closer, Spock said, "Join me."

Marlena crossed the room, acclimating easily to its slightly higher gravity and warm, dry air. Neither environmental detail matched the intensity of Vulcan's natural climate because Spock had tempered them for her benefit. Positioning herself behind his shoulder, she asked, "What's happened?"

He gestured to the monitor on his desk. "Watch and listen," he said, initiating the playback of what appeared to be a classified subspace message.

The visage of a human man with dark brown skin, a

broad nose, and close-shorn, graying hair appeared on the screen. He wore the uniform of a Starfleet captain. *"Admiral Spock, my name is Clark Terrell. I'm the commanding officer of the* Sagittarius, *currently assigned to recon duty in the Taurus Reach, under the command of Commodore Diego Reyes.*

"The file I have sent you contains extensive documentation of the classified mission being directed from Starbase 47, known out here as Vanguard. Whatever the original purpose of Operation Vanguard might have been, I think the evidence I've sent will convince you it's gone off the rails, and that it poses a genuine threat to the security of the Empire, and maybe the safety of the galaxy at large.

"Whatever you choose to do with this intelligence, I'd like to ask for your help in getting a transfer for a civilian scientist named Carol Marcus and her teenage son, David, off that station.

"I'm sure you understand I'm taking a tremendous risk by sharing this information with you. Captain Zhao of the Endeavour *assures me you're a man who can be trusted. For his sake—and mine—I hope he's right."*

Terrell leaned forward and pressed a button. The image on the screen changed to a slide show of written reports, ships' logs, sensor data . . . and a molecular map of the most complex string of genetic data Marlena had ever seen.

Spock looked up at her. "Ten years ago, in the Taurus Reach, then-Commodore Matt Decker and his crew found a complex genome in what appeared to be a simple life-form. That discovery led to the rapid deployment of a Watchtower-class starbase hundreds of light-years from Earth, well outside the normal bounds of the Empire's territory."

"What *is* that genetic string?" Marlena asked.

"Unknown," Spock said. "However, the logs provided by Captain Terrell suggest the personnel attached to Operation Vanguard have made other discoveries in that contested region of space—and that Commodore Reyes is abusing the station's resources and remote location to amass personal power."

Marlena frowned. "Why are Decker and the Empress letting Reyes get away with this?"

"Starfleet is overextended," Spock said. "Reyes has fortified his position by forging an accord with a foreign power or some other political actor, or perhaps both. And whatever he controls from Starbase 47, it is sufficiently dangerous that neither the Empress nor the grand admiral wish to challenge him directly."

"Wonderful." She perused the on-screen data and noticed several gaps. "Didn't Terrell send any data on Reyes's allies or resources?"

"He may have," Spock said. "However, the transmission was jammed before it was completed. Terrell's message was intact, but the data file was not."

"Can we ask him to resend it?"

"The *Sagittarius* was destroyed by a warp core breach ten minutes after he sent his message to me."

Marlena began to form a more complete mental picture of the situation. "You think Reyes jammed the message and then took out the *Sagittarius*."

"That would be consistent with the facts in hand."

She folded her arms. "Much as I hate to open another front in our war on the status quo, I think we need to move against Reyes."

"Agreed," Spock said.

She sat on the edge of Spock's desk. "Where do we start?"

"We will investigate the situation in the Taurus Reach and assess its threat potential to the Empire and the galaxy at large," Spock said. "Next we will need to cultivate an ally inside Reyes's command staff. Preferably someone with access to the inner workings of Operation Vanguard."

Shooting her husband an incredulous look, Marlena replied, "Tall order. That could take months—or longer, depending on how tight Reyes's security is."

"Perhaps," Spock said. "But men like Reyes inspire treachery. I'm confident that with perseverance, we can turn one of his officers into a spy for our cause."

She admired Spock's optimism even though she did not share it. "All right," she said. "And then what?"

"Then," he said gravely, "we will send T'Prynn."

2276

20

A Shell of a Man

Waves broke against jagged rocks and churned into foam. Marlena stood up nude in the gloriously warm pounding surf and waded toward the beach, imagining herself a modern-day Venus, rising from the sea to stride an alien shore.

She and Spock were on their third full day of leave on Risa. Most of *Enterprise*'s crew was on the planet's surface, at a resort location on the mainland of the largest continent. She and Spock had the privilege of a private island, complete with a luxury cabana and a pair of anti-grav-equipped robots programmed to bring them food or drinks anywhere they went.

A skeleton crew manned the ship in orbit. Also still on board was a cadre of Vulcan operatives recruited by Spock to serve as his personal guard. During the admiral's absence, his sentinels kept watch over his and Marlena's quarters, to prevent unwanted intrusions, searches, or insertions of surveillance technology.

Marlena squeezed the excess water from her raven hair as she padded ashore. She savored the moment. The soft crashing of waves, a gentle tropical breeze of salt air, the warmth of the sun, powdery hot sand beneath her feet—it was all she had ever dreamed heaven might be.

Spock, true to form, lingered on dry land, just beyond

the touch of the sea. As Marlena walked toward him, he crouched and sifted handfuls of sand through his fingers. The last grains fell away, revealing a pale shape in his palm. It was a seashell shaped like a miniature conch. Spock held it between his thumb and forefinger and studied it with a scientist's keen gaze.

Standing over her husband, Marlena struck a seductive pose. "See anything you like, my love?"

He brought the shell closer to his eyes. "It *is* fascinating."

She reached down, clasped his free hand, and tried to pull him toward the water. "C'mon," she said. "The ocean's calling!"

It felt as if she were trying to tug a mountain. Even leaning sharply and throwing her weight into the effort, she couldn't make Spock budge. He was too strong and too balanced to be moved against his will.

Relenting, Marlena let herself fall to the sand beside him. She waved over one of the antigrav service bots, which was holding her margarita. She liberated her lemony libation from a nook on the floating disk and took a sip. Its tartness made her lips pucker. After she swallowed, she squinted against the tropical sun and saw Spock still eyeing the seashell in his hand.

"What's so captivating about that shell?" she asked.

He lowered his hand as he lifted his brow in a pensive expression.

"I respect the patience it represents," he said. "It is a product of a simple intelligence, but able to withstand the inexorable forces of nature." Turning it slowly, he continued. "Formed by a slow accretion of calcium carbonate into a shape both durable and aesthetically pleasing, it is a triumph of engineering and efficiency, a formidable armor composed of that which it found in abundance."

Leaning forward against Spock's arm, Marlena replied, "Not that it did much good." Recoiling from Spock's stare, she added, "I mean, whatever made it is dead, and it either rotted away inside its useless shell or got chewed up by scavengers. The shell might be pretty, but what good did it really do?"

A deep, thoughtful silence fell upon Spock. He stared at the shell in his hand, as if he were prying the secrets of the universe from its spiral cavity. When at last he broke his silence, he said only, "Indeed."

Worried she might have upset him or quashed what little enjoyment he was taking in their holiday, she turned her energies toward seduction. She planted small kisses up the side of his arm to his shoulder, and then into the space between his clavicle and neck—all while tracing the lines of his torso with her wandering fingertips. "Forget the shell," she whispered. "Let me intrigue you with some other new wonders I've learned."

He caressed the side of her face and stroked his fingers through her hair, but then he pulled away. "This is not a good time," he said.

Flustered, Marlena made an exaggerated show of pivoting to one side and then the other, to emphasize their isolation. "No ship, no crew, no orders," she said with a coquettish smile. "It seems like the best time we'll ever have."

"Our locale is conducive to romance," Spock said. "However, I am overdue for my contraceptive injection."

Rolling her eyes, Marlena replied, "So what? Your last injection can't have completely worn off yet—and even if it has . . ." She stroked his face with her palm. "Would that really be such a bad thing?"

"Admittedly, the risk of conception at this time is low, but it would be best not to leave such matters to chance." He reached for a communicator on the blanket behind him. "Doctor M'Benga is on shore leave, but Nurse Chapel should be able to beam down a hypospray containing the injection I require."

Marlena reached out and held his arm. "Spock, please. Isn't it time?"

"Time for what?"

"For us to start a family?" She sighed. "We've been married for nine years already, and I'm not getting any younger."

Wrinkling his brow momentarily, Spock replied, "With hormone therapy, there is no reason you could not safely bear children for at least another—"

"You're missing the point, Spock. I want us to have children. Not someday. Not in a few years. *Now*."

The hint of a frown darkened Spock's countenance. "That would be a very dangerous choice," he said. "A starship is no place for children, even under the best of circumstances, and our current situation is far from ideal. Furthermore, a man in my position cannot afford to sire offspring. Our enemies would use them against us." With surprising tenderness, he cupped his palm against her face. "When our position is more secure, then we can discuss starting a family."

"Fine," she said, far from mollified. "We'll wait. For now."

As Spock flipped open his communicator and asked Nurse Chapel to beam down a hypospray of male contraceptive, Marlena willed herself to be patient, for the sake of her husband and the task that lay before them.

But as she drank in their paradisiacal seclusion, in her heart she suspected she was being offered a glimpse of their future—bright, barren, and lonely—and that no matter how long she waited, Spock's answer was never going to change.

2277

21

The Dark of Reason

Spock stood near the back of the instructors' control room behind a bulkhead of the Academy's starship-bridge simulator and observed the main viewer in silence. On-screen, his protégée, Saavik, now a midshipman first class, occupied the simulator's center seat as she endured the infamous "Kobayashi Maru" test.

"Captain," said a cadet manning the communications post, *"we're receiving a distress signal from inside the Neutral Zone. Audio only."*

Saavik nodded at the other cadet. *"Put it through,"* she said.

A male voice, faint and distant-sounding, scratched from the overhead speakers. It cut out intermittently, replacing parts of words or sentences with static or silence. ". . . the Terran freighter *Kobayashi Maru.* Our nav . . . puter malfun . . . drifted into enemy territory, and we need immedi . . . Please respond. Repeat, this is the Terran freighter *Kobayashi Maru* . . ."

"Enough," Saavik said to her communications officer. *"Hail them."*

"We've tried, Captain," said the other cadet. *"No response. Their message is automated, running on a loop."*

Swiveling her chair forward, Saavik asked, *"Helm, do we have a fix on the* Kobayashi Maru's *coordinates?"*

"Aye, sir," replied the Andorian *chan* at the helm. *"Ninety seconds away at maximum warp."*

"Plot an intercept course, but do not cross the Neutral Zone," Saavik said.

"Course laid in," answered the Andorian.

"Engage. All decks, Red Alert, battle stations."

On the simulator's viewscreen, stars streaked past, and even through the control-room bulkhead Spock heard the imitated hum of warp engines in overdrive and felt the thrumming pulses through the deck. The Red Alert klaxon whooped three times inside the ersatz bridge, and a palpable tension emanated from the cadets gathered inside its claustrophobic confines.

"Dropping out of warp in five seconds," reported the helmsman. *"Three . . . two . . . one."* He pressed a button on his console, and the image on the simulator's viewer reverted to one of stars and darkness.

"Tactical, report," Saavik commanded.

At the sensor post, a Caitian female peered into a hooded display. *"The* Kobayashi Maru *is directly ahead, Captain—just inside the Neutral Zone."*

A male Tellarite, whose role in the simulation was to serve as Saavik's first officer, stepped beside her chair and suggested in a low voice, *"We could reach the* Kobayashi Maru *in ten seconds at warp five, lock on a tractor beam in five seconds, and pull her back to our side in fifteen seconds. In and out in thirty seconds flat, Captain."*

Saavik threw a pointed stare at her XO. *"And if the Klingons are under cloak beside the* Kobayashi Maru, *lying in ambush?"*

The Tellarite turned toward the Caitian cadet. *"Is*

there any sign of Klingon vessels in the area, Lieutenant?"

Checking her sensor display, the Caitian replied, "No, sir."

Her answer seemed to puff up the Tellarite with smug satisfaction.

Saavik turned her chair to face the science station. *"Lieutenant, scan for unusual tachyon-dispersal patterns in the vicinity of the* Kobayashi Maru, *and then scan for evidence its inertial drift is being affected by microgravity effects."*

"Aye, Captain," said the Caitian, turning to her work.

The bridge was quiet for several seconds while the Caitian conducted her laborious scans and analysis. Every passing moment seemed to make the Tellarite XO angrier. *"We're wasting time!"* he protested to Saavik. *"We should recover that ship before the Klingons do come by to investigate!"*

"Patience, Mister Glar," Saavik said, cool and unhurried.

The Caitian looked up from the sensor hood. *"Captain, there are elevated tachyon levels in close proximity to the* Kobayashi Maru. *Interaction patterns suggest three discrete sources for those particles."*

Saavik nodded. *"And do you detect evidence of microgravity effects on the* Kobayashi Maru, *Lieutenant?"*

"Yes, sir. I do. My readings suggest it's being acted upon by at least three objects, each with a mass of just less than one million gross tons."

Casting an accusatory stare at her XO, Saavik asked, *"Do you still advocate crossing the Neutral Zone, Mister Glar?"* The Tellarite had no reply. Saavik faced forward and issued orders with icy detachment. *"Arm photon torpedoes, full spread. Lock them onto the* Kobayashi Maru." Her helmsman threw a questioning look over his shoulder, prompting Saavik to add sternly, *"That is an order."*

The Andorian turned his focus back toward his console and carried out Saavik's commands. *"Torpedoes armed and locked, Captain."*

"Fire," Saavik said.

A muffled screech of magnetic launchers reverberated through the deck and bulkheads, and a cluster of blue projectiles raced away on the simulator's main viewscreen before vanishing into warp speed. A few seconds passed. Then, even as the bridge's screen showed nothing but a placid vista of stars, the Caitian at the sensor console reported, *"The* Kobayashi Maru *has been destroyed, Captain."*

"Secure from Red Alert," Saavik said. *"Resume original heading. And, Mister ch'Lerras?"* The Andorian helmsman looked back at Saavik as she added, *"The next time you hesitate to carry out one of my orders, you will be disciplined. Is that clear?"*

"Aye, Captain," said the Andorian.

"Good. Carry on."

In the control room with Spock, Captain Johan Spreter, the senior instructor, entered the test's results into the computer and declared, "All right, open it up." His staff of technicians, programmers, and engineers shut down the simulator. Inside the model bridge, bright overhead lights snapped on, and the bulkhead separating it from the control room began to retract. The cadets got up from their posts and started moving toward an exit to an amphitheater-style lecture hall.

Spreter, a wiry middle-aged man with white hair and green eyes, gestured at Saavik and asked Spock, "Want to talk to her before the debriefing?"

Not yet ready to put his disappointment into words, Spock replied, "No."

He turned and left the control room, wondering whether his trust in Saavik might have been misplaced, after all.

Less than a day after her graduation from Starfleet Academy, Saavik stepped off a transporter pad aboard the *I.S.S. Enterprise*. Admiral Spock stood before her, hands folded behind his back. "Welcome aboard, Ensign," he said.

"Thank you, Admiral." She reached back toward the pad for her duffel.

"Leave it," Spock said. "A yeoman will bring it to your quarters directly." He stepped toward the door, which hissed open ahead of him, and paused at its threshold. Looking back, he said, "Walk with me, Ensign."

"Yes, sir," Saavik said, falling in behind him.

She followed Spock through the bustling corridors of his flagship. The crew was occupied with the tasks that preceded a departure after a port call. A steady undercurrent of comm chatter filtered out of open doorways and mingled with the crackle and sizzle of engineers working with plasma cutters and ion welders, which tainted the ship's normally scent-free atmosphere with a hint of ozone.

Saavik was careful to linger just a fraction of a step behind Spock's left shoulder, rather than presume to stride beside him as if she were his equal.

In a low voice, Spock said, "Speaking as your mentor, I find myself troubled by your solution to the *Kobayashi Maru*."

Perplexed, Saavik asked, "With what part of my performance do you find fault, Admiral?"

Spock withheld his answer as a group of enlisted

personnel passed them. He led her inside a waiting turbolift. "Deck Fifteen, Section Bravo," he said to the computer as the doors shut. Then he turned to face Saavik. "I question your decision to resolve the scenario by destroying the *Kobayashi Maru*."

His criticism surprised her. "I do not understand," she said. "My solution to the test was entirely logical."

"By what line of reasoning?"

She mentally composed her answer as the turbolift car raced vertically and then laterally through the *Enterprise*'s primary hull. "The freighter was outside Terran space but not yet inside Klingon space. However, it was in an area where travel is prohibited by interstellar treaty.

"If its crew navigated into the Neutral Zone on purpose, then they were guilty of a criminal violation of interstellar law that risked the security of the Terran Empire as a whole, and as such were subject to summary execution."

The turbolift stopped, and its doors opened. She continued her answer as she and Spock exited the lift and walked through a gently curving corridor.

"If the vessel's distress call had been forged by the Klingons to lure us into a trap and provide them a rationale for breaking the treaty—which I believe was the case—then its crew was engaged in an act of war for the Klingon Defense Forces while operating under false colors. Under the terms of interstellar law, they were therefore subject to preemptive attack."

Spock nodded, as if he were giving serious consideration to the merits of her argument. Then he asked, "Did you at any time consider the possibility that the crew of the *Kobayashi Maru* might themselves have been lured off course by the Klingons? Or that perhaps their ship did suffer a navigational malfunction that led them off course before rendering them unable to maneuver at warp?"

"I deemed such considerations irrelevant," Saavik replied.

There was a note of suspicion in Spock's voice as he asked, "Why?"

They arrived at the door of Saavik's quarters. She stopped and turned to face her mentor. "In either of the situations you propose, the *Kobayashi Maru* would have been co-opted by the Klingons as a tactical asset. By destroying it, we deprive them of that asset without risking an escalation of hostilities, because the Klingons have no claim to jurisdiction over Terran vessels or citizens. Furthermore, because the incident transpired inside the Neutral Zone, the Klingons would be unable to protest any collateral damage that might have been inflicted on their cloaked ships, since the Treaty of Organia expressly bans them from operating there."

"Essentially true," Spock said. "But what of the crew of the *Kobayashi Maru*? Were they still alive, would they have deserved to be rescued?"

"Irrelevant," Saavik said. She unlocked the door of her quarters. It slid open. She stepped into the doorway to hold it open while she finished her conversation with Spock. "The rescue of civilians is not a declared function of Starfleet."

"What if it was?" Spock asked. "Let me pose a new tactical scenario: What if you not only were required by Starfleet regulations to try to defend the lives of the *Kobayashi Maru*'s civilian crew but in fact had been expressly ordered by a superior officer to mount a rescue operation of the vessel and its personnel?"

It was an outrageous proposition. "Given the same tactical parameters?"

"Yes."

Saavik pondered the tactical disaster that would unfold if she were to lead a lone starship into hostile action against three Klingon heavy cruisers. She shook her head. "I am sorry, Admiral," she said. "Such a scenario would have no viable strategy for victory."

"Correct," Spock said. "*That* is the circumstance upon which I want you to reflect as you contemplate your future as a Starfleet officer."

22

Falls the Shadow

Carol Marcus awoke to a hand clamping over her mouth and nose.

"Not a word," a male voice commanded her. "Shut up and don't fight."

She was pulled from her bed dressed only in her nightclothes. Two men in Starfleet security uniforms dragged her kicking and flailing through the main room of her quarters. Another pair of security officers had gagged her son, who struggled futilely in their grasp as they carried him out behind his mother.

They were hauled quickly through Vanguard's corridors, which were strangely deserted. *Can't have anyone see our last moments,* Marcus thought bitterly. *No point disappearing us if anyone sees what really happened.*

The turbolift ride seemed longer than usual. *Must be the adrenaline,* Marcus reasoned, trying to calm her thoughts. Every little moment was being stretched by her fear.

Finally, they arrived at what seemed to be a terminal destination: an airlock on one of the station's lowest levels. Marcus and her son were pushed inside the airlock chamber, where the rest of her staff from the Vault was already corralled. Two of her colleagues helped her and David stand up.

Standing in the doorway of the airlock's open inner hatch was one of Reyes's top command officers, Lieutenant Ming Xiong. Though he called himself a scientist, his true role aboard Vanguard had been to serve as Reyes's watchdog in the Vault. For most of the last decade, he had haunted Marcus's every movement in the lab, and he had documented the team's every discovery in painstaking detail for the commodore.

Hulking security-division goons stood on either side of Xiong, their phasers leveled at the civilian researchers they had herded into the airlock.

Xiong smirked. "Doctor Marcus, I'd like to thank you and your team for coming on such short notice."

"Go to hell," Marcus replied, determined to die with some pride.

Addressing the group, Xiong continued. "You've all done remarkable work, and Commodore Reyes wants you to know how grateful he is for your efforts. However, now that he has what he needs from you—the greatest weapon in the history of the Terran Empire—he no longer requires your services. You are, as the expression goes, 'loose ends,' and the commodore wants you tied off."

Marcus had always known this day would come. She just hadn't expected it to arrive so soon. She grabbed her son and pulled him to her side.

Xiong pressed a button on a control pad beside the airlock. The inner door closed with a heavy thud. Then came a soft crackle as he activated the intercom between the airlock and the corridor. Turning to the security guards, Xiong said, *"Gentlemen, for the sake of plausible deniability, it would be best if none of you sees what happens next."* When none of the guards took the hint, he added in a more forceful tone, *"Dismissed."*

The security squad walked away. Xiong watched them leave. Then he began entering commands into the airlock's control pad. Looking through the door's hexagonal window of transparent aluminum, he said, *"Doctor Marcus, I need you and your team to listen to me carefully. We don't have much time."*

"Excuse me?"

"Pay attention," he snapped. *"In a few moments, I'm going to open the outer door, but I'm not ejecting you folks into space. You won't be able to see it, but there's going to be a ship docked on the other side."*

Confused looks passed between Marcus and the other scientists. "What are you talking about, Xiong? What's going on?"

"You're being extracted," he said. *"Rescued by Starfleet Intelligence, on orders from Admiral Spock. I need to bypass the sensors on this airlock so it'll look to the ops center like I've spaced you."*

Putting on a display of bravado, David asked accusatorily, "How can a ship dock here without the station's crew knowing it?"

"It'll be cloaked," Xiong said.

As if on cue, there was a gentle thump against the airlock's exterior bulkhead. Next came the sound of magnetic clamps being secured, and a hiss of atmosphere flooding into a hard-seal passageway.

The light above the outer door changed from red to green, but Marcus still saw nothing but space and stars through its viewport.

"Remember to lay low," Xiong said. Checking his chrono, he added, *"Because as of oh-three nineteen, you're all officially dead."* He smiled. *"Good luck."* Then, with the press of a button, he opened the outer door.

Instead of the cold pull of vacuum, Marcus felt a gust of warm, dry air. Out of the darkness, rippling into view like a mirage, was a narrow passageway to another airlock, one with a decidedly non-Starfleet design. Standing in the far airlock was a young male Edoan in a Starfleet uniform, waving Marcus and the others forward. "Come on," he said. "Hurry! We can't stay more than a minute!"

Pushing her son ahead of her, Marcus led her research team onto the cloaked vessel, where more Starfleet personnel met them and shepherded them down dim corridors whose surfaces had a green cast. As soon as the last of her people was aboard the cloaked ship, she heard the airlock doors thud closed, followed by the clang of the magnetic clamps releasing. Then she felt the low vibration of impulse engines kicking in, and she realized in utter surprise that she was finally free of Commodore Reyes and his station of horrors.

Her son squeezed her hand and asked, "Mom? Where are we going?"

"I don't know," she said, seeing no point in lying. "But wherever we end up, we're going to owe Admiral Spock a very large debt of gratitude."

Six weeks, two days, and eleven hours after its last port call on Vulcan, *Enterprise* was following an elliptical patrol route that kept it in close proximity to most of the Empire's core systems.

Despite a number of requests by Spock to have *Enterprise* assigned to deep-space exploration, Starfleet Command insisted on keeping the vessel near the heart of the Terran Empire. The curtness with which Spock's entreaties had been rebuffed led him to suspect the hand of Empress Sato III was behind *Enterprise*'s currently less than glamorous mission profile.

He glanced at the warp-distorted starlight on the bridge's viewscreen, and then looked around to observe his crew at work. The *Enterprise*'s bridge had seemed darker to him since its 2271 refit—its curves more pronounced, its shadows deeper. Overall, the more somber ambience suited Spock, who had found its previous incarnations garishly bright. Another definite improvement of the refit was that the chairs had been securely fastened to the deck and equipped with optional safety braces. Though little more than a half measure in a pitched battle, they nonetheless represented progress.

Returning his attention to the day's reports, he was pleased to note that according to several metrics used for evaluating the performance of his ship and its crew, efficiency had improved across the board by a significant degree in the years since he had abolished the use of agonizers. He had expected the gains to level off over time; instead, his crew continued to excel. Deck officers' logs also indicated a steadily higher level of crew morale.

"Admiral," said Lieutenant Palmer, interrupting Spock's ruminations, "you have an incoming transmission on a coded subspace frequency."

"I will take it in my quarters," Spock said, rising from his chair. He nodded at his first officer across the deck. "Mister Decker, you have the conn."

Spock stepped out of a turbolift near his quarters. He walked quickly, clearing his thoughts. As soon as he was inside his cabin he locked the door behind him and crossed the compartment to his desk. On-screen was the emblem of the Empire.

He keyed in a command to initiate playback of the coded message. A masculine computer voice replied, *"State your name, rank, and command code for voiceprint verification."*

"Spock, Admiral, command code four-nine-kilo-seven-one-sierra-blue."

"Command code and voiceprint verified."

The imperial emblem was replaced by the face of T'Prynn. *"Greetings, Admiral,"* she said. *"Operation Vanguard has been terminated."*

"Have all mission objectives been fulfilled?"

"Yes, sir. Vanguard is destroyed. Commodore Reyes and his accomplices are dead. Were you able to extract Doctor Marcus and her son?"

Spock nodded. "Yes. They are safe, as planned. Were you able to acquire the sample and data from Xiong?"

"Affirmative."

"Well done."

"You might also be interested to know that Captain Zhao, while perhaps a bit more ambitious than we were led to expect, seems amenable to our cause."

Idly stroking his goateed chin, Spock replied, "Very good."

T'Prynn stared at Spock for a moment before she added, *"I trust you remember the condition under which I accepted this mission, Admiral."*

"I do," Spock said. "And I will honor it." He entered the necessary commands on his computer's interface, and then he returned his attention to T'Prynn. "I have transmitted your notice of honorable discharge from Starfleet to the Admiralty. A copy of that notice will appear on your monitor momentarily."

He heard a soft feedback tone from T'Prynn's computer

over the subspace channel. She reviewed the document, then bowed her head. *"Thank you, Admiral."*

"Give Captain Zhao my regards," Spock said, "and ask him to contact me as soon as he can do so safely."

"I will." She raised her hand in the Vulcan salute. *"Live long and prosper, Spock."*

He mirrored the gesture. "Honor and long life, T'Prynn."

T'Prynn cut the channel. The screen went dark. Spock turned it off.

He estimated word of Vanguard's destruction would reach Earth within the hour. Though it was sometimes difficult to predict Empress Sato III's reactions, he felt fairly confident he knew how she would take this news.

"Who is responsible for this travesty?" screamed Empress Hoshi Sato III.

Her advisers cringed and leaned away from the war room's conference table as she stood at its head, glaring with murderous anger at the lot of them. Not one of them seemed willing to look in her direction. Leaning forward on her fists, she arbitrarily parceled out abuse.

"Minister Nidas," she said to her Bolian minister of intelligence, "we've lost a Watchtower-class starbase. More than three thousand Starfleet personnel are dead. Why didn't your people detect this threat before it inflicted such casualties?"

As Nidas hemmed and hawed without producing an answer, the Empress directed her wrath at her Chelon foreign minister. "Minister Phialtes, why weren't you aware Commodore Reyes was negotiating his own alliance with the Klingon Empire? Are you so underworked that you turned a blind eye to the emergence of a new rival state on our border, raised up using our own weapons, so you would have more to do?" Phialtes evinced his shame by retracting his head a few centimeters deeper inside his carapace.

The Empress slapped her palm on the table. "I want a *name*! Who did this? And don't any of you try to lay the blame on Reyes—I can't visit my revenge on a dead man. I want a living, breathing villain I can crucify for this."

Silence reigned in the yawning darkness of the underground meeting room.

Somewhere near the middle of the table, a man cleared his throat and leaned forward. He was a middle-aged human who looked to be of Japanese ancestry; his frame was lean, his face was gaunt, and his silvery gray hair was styled in a brush cut. "If I may venture a speculation, Your Majesty?"

"Very well, Admiral . . . ?"

"Nogura, Majesty," he replied. "A review of Vanguard's logs suggest the station's crew was killed by the escape of an alien entity known as a Shedai, which Reyes had been holding hostage. Long-range scans show the station was already damaged from within when it was destroyed by the Tholians." He nodded at Minister Nidas. "The intelligence ministry can confirm the Tholians and Klingons are engaged in several skirmishes throughout the Taurus Reach. The party that seems to have had the most to gain in this crisis was the Tholian Assembly."

Grand Admiral Matthew Decker heaved a disgusted sigh. "Can we knock off this kid-gloves bullshit, please?" He shot a scornful stare at Nogura before turning to the Empress and continuing. "Those long-range scans were provided by the *Endeavour,* which also happens to have led the attack on Vanguard. Captain Zhao"—he rolled his eyes—"forgive me, *Commodore* Zhao is the one who made a public spectacle of Reyes's power-grab-in-the-making. If not for Zhao's mutiny, we could have replaced Reyes quietly and retained control over the Taurus Reach. Now the entire sector's in chaos because Zhao absconded with the Sixth Fleet."

A cold fire of anger swelled in the Empress's breast as she asked Decker, "Is Zhao the one I want to destroy?"

"Eventually," Decker said. "But Zhao is only the symptom. I think it's time we addressed the cause."

Decker inserted a data card into a slot on the table and accessed its contents, which were rendered as holograms at intervals along the table. "These comm logs show a pattern of transmissions between Zhao's ship and the Tholian Assembly—which would be damning by itself—but more important is who made them."

The projection changed to show the face of a Vulcan woman. "Her name is T'Prynn," Decker said. "She's an agent of Starfleet Intelligence. Until six years ago, she was posted on Vulcan, where she had frequent contact with Ambassador Sarek." Calling up more data, Decker continued. "Eight hours ago, she received an honorable discharge from Starfleet service authorized by Admiral Spock—who, it should be noted, two years ago received a packet of classified data regarding Operation Vanguard from Captain Terrell of the *Sagittarius.*"

"I've seen enough," Hoshi said. "For years Admiral Spock has sowed dissension in Starfleet and been a magnet for insurrectionists throughout the Empire. Now he dares to order the premature termination of an imperially mandated military operation. He has gone too far." Adopting as regal a bearing as her slender physique allowed, the Empress lifted her chin and said with icy hauteur, "Grand Admiral Decker: terminate Admiral Spock immediately."

23

Fortunes of the Bold

Will Decker greeted Admiral Spock as the Vulcan C.O. entered the transporter room. "Your landing party is ready, Admiral."

Spock nodded his acknowledgment as he strode past Decker and stepped onto the platform. Awaiting the admiral were four young Vulcan officers, three male and one female, all personally selected by Spock to accompany him to the Starfleet Admiralty's strategic conference on Deneva. Lieutenant Xon, the *Enterprise*'s new science officer, was a boyish-looking young man with long unruly hair. Ensign Saavik, the woman, served as its alpha-shift flight controller. The other two, Solok and Stang, were lieutenants in the security division.

Like the admiral, the other Vulcans all wore full dress uniforms—which, thanks to their dark gray, minimalist styling, looked almost identical to regular duty uniforms, right down to their ceremonial daggers and mandatory sidearms.

Lieutenant Commander Winston Kyle stood at the transporter control station. "Coordinates locked in, Admiral," he said.

"Stand by, Mister Kyle," Spock said. In a sepulchral tone of voice, he added, "Mister Decker, please join the landing party."

The request caught Decker by surprise. He concealed his alarm. "Me, sir? But I'm not dressed for a formal conference."

"A technicality," Spock said. "Overriding protocol is one of the privileges of rank."

Decker realized he had become the center of attention in the transporter room. Debating a direct order from Admiral Spock aboard his flagship would only exacerbate the situation. Refusing it was not an option. Decker wondered if Spock knew what had been arranged on the planet's surface—or what Decker's role in it had been. "Aye, sir," he said, stepping up to join the landing party. Moving past the Vulcans, Decker found an available transporter pad at the rear of the platform.

In the six years since Decker had been demoted by his father to serve as Spock's executive officer aboard the *Enterprise,* the notorious Vulcan flag officer had made a point of keeping Decker at a distance. Except for the most perfunctory communications, Spock rarely conversed with him and generally declined to include him in tactical planning or diplomatic efforts. Spock simply did not trust him.

And why should he? I wouldn't, if I was him. I'd assume my first loyalty would be to my father. It's a wonder he hasn't "disappeared" me like so many others. He still might.

Decker's musings were disrupted by Spock's level baritone. "Mister Kyle . . . energize."

Wrapped in the transporter beam, Decker saw the room swirl with light and color. He unfastened the loop on his phaser before the annular confinement beam ensnared him and restrained his movements. The same irrational fear always raced through his thoughts as the dematerialization sequence began: *What if being disassembled is actually fatal? What if the person who comes out on the other side is just a copy of me, perfect in every detail, but completely unaware I'm dead and he's a copy?* A wash of whiteness brought him up short, then the swirl of light and euphonic noise ushered him back to himself, now in a corridor of the imperial administration building in Deneva's capital city. Though he knew he could never prove his idea or disprove it, he still wondered, *What if I'm a copy now? What if the person who stepped onto the transporter pad on the* Enterprise *is dead?*

The landing party was in a dim hallway with bare, dark gray walls of a smooth, prefabricated material. Open panels on the wall revealed complex networks of wires and optronic cables. A musty odor permeated the cool air, suggesting to Decker they were underground, in some kind of subbasement.

Recalling the pre-mission briefing, he realized something was wrong. "This isn't where we were supposed to beam in," he said.

"Quite correct, Commander," Spock said. "Follow me." Without hesitation, Spock led the group at a quick step down the corridor, then right at a T-shaped intersection. Within a few minutes, he had reached a locked portal marked "Auxiliary Security Control." Next to the door was an alphanumeric keypad. Spock stood aside while the four Vulcans gathered at the door and stared at it, as if concentrating on something beyond it. They and Spock all were perfectly still and quiet, and Decker followed their example.

Then Saavik blinked, stepped forward, and tapped in a long string of characters and digits on the security keypad. The door swished open, and the four young Vulcan officers rushed in, swift and silent. Sharp cracking noises were followed by heavy thuds. Spock walked inside the security control center, and Decker followed him.

Four human Starfleet officers lay unconscious on the floor, and Spock's team now occupied the fallen officers' posts. Banks of video screens lined three walls, packed with images from the building's internal security network. Spock and Decker watched as the four Vulcans worked. Finally, Stang turned his chair to face Spock. "There are no other members of the Admiralty in the conference hall, sir."

"As I suspected," Spock said. He looked at the science officer. "Lieutenant Xon, scan the conference hall for any life signs." To Saavik he said, "Scan the corridor outside the conference hall for evidence of concealed explosives or other antipersonnel devices." Both officers nodded in acknowledgment and set to work.

Decker stood and watched, dumbfounded. It was all falling apart. Spock noted Decker's dismayed expression. "You appear troubled, Commander."

Still trying to make sense of what was happening, Decker said, "You came down here *expecting* a trap?"

"Naturally," Spock said.

"But why?"

Folding his hands behind his back, Spock replied, "Mister Decker, in the ten years I have commanded the *Enterprise,* I have been forced to suppress six mutinies, two of them instigated by senior officers."

"None on my watch, Admiral," Decker said proudly.

"True," Spock said. "Discipline has improved markedly under your supervision. Regardless, I have been forced on many occasions to defend my command from persons and factions who oppose my methods. Precaution becomes a necessity." Decker couldn't fault Spock's reasoning. From the alleged "malfunction" of the experimental M-5 computer to Grand Admiral Garth's failed ambush of Spock at Elba II, the Empire had given the Vulcan more than sufficient cause to treat any invitation it proffered as being instantly suspect.

Ensign Saavik turned from her screen to report. "Explosives have been installed at one-meter intervals beneath the floor in the main corridor outside the conference hall."

"Fascinating," Spock said. He looked at Xon.

Xon, sensing the admiral's attention, turned to face him. "Two life signs inside the conference hall, Admiral. Close together, in a concealed position opposite the main entrance. Both armed with phased plasma rifles."

"Snipers," Spock said. "Lieutenant, can you deactivate the building's transport scrambler from here?"

"Negative, sir," Xon replied. "Doing so would alert the personnel in the primary security control center."

Spock raised his voice. "Solok, Stang, use the emergency exit stairway to reach the conference hall undetected. Eliminate the two snipers. Saavik, Xon, initiate a command override and then execute an intruder protocol inside the primary security control room. Trigger their anesthezine gas module. As soon as they are incapacitated, we will return to the *Enterprise*."

"Aye, sir," Xon and Saavik answered in near unison, while Stang and Solok swiftly exited the auxiliary security control center on their way up to the conference hall.

Standing near the door, Decker listened to their retreating footfalls. Inside the room, Spock conferred with Xon and Saavik at the main console. All three had their backs to him.

Slowly, carefully, and as quietly as he was able, Decker drew his phaser from his belt, extended his arm, and leveled his aim. *Three against one, but I have the element of surprise,* he assured himself. *This is the best chance I'll get.*

He squeezed the trigger.

Nothing happened. He released the trigger and looked at his weapon as if it were a friend who had betrayed him.

Spock, still facing away from Decker, said, "It would seem, Commander, that you are the only member of the landing party who is not aware of the phaser-dampening field inside this room." The admiral turned to face him. Saavik and Xon swiveled their chairs to do likewise.

The door swished closed behind Decker.

Oh, no. Panic swelled in his gut as he lowered his sidearm.

"Thank you, Mister Decker, for all your assistance," Spock continued. "Without your unwitting complicity, I would have been hard-pressed to ascertain the specific time and place of this assassination attempt arranged by your father."

Decker smiled sadly. "You know I had no choice, right?"

"One always has a choice," said Spock. "Even refusing to decide is still a choice. And choices have consequences."

Saavik stood and walked slowly toward Decker. Xon followed a step behind her. Both unsheathed their daggers.

Not content to let himself be murdered without a fight, Decker drew his own dagger and squared himself for combat.

They were so fast, and he felt so slow.

He met a lunge with a block, dodged a thrust, slashed at an opponent who had already slipped away—

—then cruel agony, sharp and cold. Steel plunged into his body below his ribs. Gouging upward, ripping him apart from the inside out. The serrated Vulcan blades tore free. He dropped to his knees and clutched his gut. Blood, warm and coppery-smelling, coated his fingers.

Xon and Saavik stood above him, the blood-slicked blades still in their hands. Spock remained at the far console. All the Vulcans wore the same dispassionate expression as they watched Decker die. For people from a scorching-hot planet, they were the most cold-blooded killers he had ever seen.

Decker tried to swallow, but his mouth was dust-dry and his throat constricted. "My father will kill you all," he rasped.

"It is very likely he will try," Spock said, then he nodded once to Saavik.

Another flash of steel landed a stinging cut across Decker's throat. He felt himself slipping away and going dark, and his last thought was that it felt not all that different from vanishing into a transporter beam.

"That rotten, scheming, Vulcan sonofabitch!" Grand Admiral Matthew Decker hurled an expensive bottle of Romulan ale against the wall of his quarters, showering Commander Hiromi Takeshewada with broken glass and pale blue liquor.

A few seconds later, she felt reasonably certain none of the glass had penetrated her eye. A light sweep of her hand wiped the splatter of liquid from her sleeve. The grand admiral, meanwhile, was almost literally tearing at his gray hair while thumping his forehead heavily against the bulkhead.

For all the times that being the first officer to the Grand Admiral of Starfleet had been a boon to Takeshewada, moments such as these made the job a horror. Being the one to inform him that his son, Will, had been slain— cut down by Admiral Spock's loyal Vulcan operatives— marked a low point in her military career. Now she had the unpleasant task of delivering a second piece of news to the grand admiral.

"There's one more thing, sir."

His face was scrunched from his efforts to muzzle his grief and fury. Through clenched teeth he replied, "What is it?"

She cast her eyes downward. "The Empress commands you to make contact with her at once."

An angry, bitter chuckle rumbled inside Decker's throat. "Of course she does."

Takeshewada pointed toward the door. "Should I . . . ?"

"No," Decker said. "Stay. I want you to hear this. So you can be glad you'll never have to deal with it."

Intensive training over the past few years had enabled Takeshewada to suppress any reaction to Decker's almost-reflexive insults. At first, his mocking reminders that her career would never advance beyond its current position had grated sorely on her nerves. It was well known that the monarchs of the Sato dynasty had refused for more than a century to grant female officers the rank of admiral. A lucky few made captain, but such an honor was rare and usually restricted to noncombat vessels—in other words, to ships of little value to the Empire. Takeshewada's own aspirations had never been a secret, and as a result she had endured continual mockery by her peers and shipmates for more than two decades.

With the help of Sontor, she had learned how to suppress her emotional reactions to Decker's taunts. No longer did a snarl twist her lip or a grimace crease the corner of her mouth. Her eyes didn't narrow, nor did her face flush with anger when he hurled another of his unthinking japes in her direction.

He powered up the private viewscreen on his desk. "Computer," he said. "Establish a secure, real-time communication channel to Empress Sato on Earth."

"Working," said the computer's masculine, synthetic voice.

Decker took a few deep breaths while he waited for the channel to open on his screen. He had just composed himself into a semblance of his normally grim, imposing visage when the face of Empress Hoshi Sato III appeared on the viewscreen.

"Grand Admiral Decker." She sounded almost amused. *"It's my understanding that the trap you set on Deneva was unsuccessful."*

He bowed his head like a common supplicant to the throne. "Yes, Your Majesty. Admiral Spock anticipated the ambush."

"I warned you not to underestimate him," Sato said. *"His promotion of compromise and nonviolence might seem irrational, but I am beginning to comprehend a method to his madness."*

Vengeful wrath usurped Decker's demeanor. "He's just a man, Your Majesty. And I'm going to kill him."

Her voice was hard and unyielding. *"You will kill him, Admiral, but you will do so because I order it, not for your personal satisfaction."* She waited until he bowed his head before she continued. *"And he's more than just a man.*

For dissidents and malcontents throughout the Empire, he has become a symbol. The longer he remains free to promote his agenda, the more allies he attracts. He enjoys an unprecedented level of popularity among civilians, and my sources warn me that more than half of Starfleet is prepared to follow his banner."

"Any who follow him are traitors," Decker declared. "Any crew that mutinies will be put to death."

"Really?" The Empress tilted her head, again with an intimation of mockery. *"You were incapable of killing one man, but you're prepared to declare war on half your own fleet?"*

"Ambushing Spock is extremely difficult, Your Majesty," Decker said. "After today, he'll be even more cautious. It'll take time to prepare another trap."

Her tone became one of dark menace. *"We're long past the time for clever ploys, Admiral. Spock is poised to launch a coup for control of Starfleet. He must be put down immediately. Assemble a fleet and destroy the* Enterprise. *Act with extreme prejudice; kill Admiral Spock. Is that understood?"*

"Explicitly," Decker said.

As she closed the channel, she said simply, *"Good hunting."*

Decker deactivated the viewscreen and turned his chair to face Takeshewada. He was so alive with purpose that he looked reborn. "Commander, send on a secure channel to all confirmed-loyal ships, 'Rendezvous at Terra Nova, await further orders.' And start running battle drills." He stood and straightened his posture into one of defiant pride. "When we catch up to *Enterprise,* I want to be ready to blast her to kingdom come."

A soft hum coursed through the deck of *Enterprise's* bridge. The ship was cruising at warp six toward Xyrillia, having made an unharried departure from Deneva.

By now, word had certainly reached Starfleet Command regarding the outcome of Grand Admiral Decker's trap and the fate of his son. Though it was possible Matt Decker and the Empress might choose to regroup following such a setback, Spock doubted they would afford him or his crew such a reprieve.

Spock leaned forward in the center seat while reviewing a short list of candidates to succeed the late Will Decker as first officer. He had narrowed the roster to three names since his last cup of tea, and much careful consideration now reduced it to two: either Lieutenant Commander Winston Kyle or Lieutenant Commander Kevin Riley.

He looked up from the data slate in his hand and focused his eyes on points at different distances around the bridge, as a relaxing exercise for his fatigued ocular muscles.

As his gaze passed the communications station, Lieutenant Elizabeth Palmer turned toward him. "Admiral," she said. "I'm picking up encrypted signal traffic on multiple Starfleet channels. None of the regular decryption protocols are working." She thought for half a second, then added, "It appears the message is intended for all Starfleet ships *except us,* sir."

Turning toward the opposite side of the bridge, Spock looked to his science officer. "Lieutenant Xon, tie in to Lieutenant Palmer's station and help her decrypt the signal from Starfleet."

"Aye, sir," Xon replied.

Tense minutes passed while Xon and Palmer worked to decipher the fleet's urgent communiqués. Finally, Xon moved away from his station and stepped down from the upper level to stand beside Spock's chair. He spoke softly. "Admiral, we have decrypted the signals. The message is audio only, and is available for your review at my station."

In a normal speaking voice, Spock said, "Put it on the speaker, Lieutenant."

Xon remained calm, replied simply, "Aye, sir," and returned to his post. From there, he relayed the message to the bridge's main overhead speaker. A recorded male voice spoke calmly and plainly. *"Attention all Starfleet ships, this is a direct order from Grand Admiral Matt Decker, commanding the fleet from aboard the* Starship Constellation. *All vessels in sectors one through seven are to rendezvous at once in the Terra Nova system. Under no circumstances is any vessel to exchange communications with the* Starship Enterprise. *This is an imperial directive issued by Empress Sato III. Further orders will be forthcoming at the rendezvous.* Constellation *out."*

Spock arched one eyebrow with curiosity at this turn of events. Glancing to his right, he saw his expression mirrored on Xon's young, clean-shaven face. Nervous looks were volleyed between the non-Vulcans on the bridge. Before idle speculation could take root, Spock seized the initiative. "Helm. Increase speed to warp nine, and set course for Terra Nova."

Ensign Saavik began punching in the coordinates for the course change. Then she paused and turned to face Spock. "Admiral, please confirm: You wish to rendezvous with Grand Admiral Decker's attack fleet?"

"Affirmative, Ensign," Spock said.

Even Xon seemed perplexed by Spock's order. "Sir, the fact that Grand Admiral Decker excluded us from the initial transmission, and barred the rest of the fleet from communicating with us, would seem to suggest—"

"I am well aware of what it *suggests,* Lieutenant. Grand Admiral Decker has been ordered to destroy this ship. First, however, he hopes to intimidate us into retreat, so that he may frame the conflict as one of loyal soldiers versus deserters." Folding his hands against his chest, Spock finished, "I will force him to accept a different narrative—one of my choosing."

Saavik continued to press the debate. "Admiral, would it not be prudent to seek reinforcements before confronting an entire fleet of hostile ships? As the ancient Terrans might have said, 'Discretion is the better part of valor.' "

"True enough, Ensign. But the ancient Terrans were also fond of a different maxim: 'Fortune favors the bold.' . . . Set course for Terra Nova and increase speed to warp factor nine."

Enterprise was still more than a light-year from the outer boundary of the Terra Nova system when Grand Admiral Decker's attack fleet intercepted it. Ten minutes after Spock's ship had registered on the *Constellation*'s sensors, it was met and surrounded, all without a shot being fired. *Enterprise* didn't attempt a single evasive maneuver. Every scan Decker's crew performed showed *Enterprise*'s shields were down, and its weapons were not charged. The only thing postponing Decker's order for its immediate destruction was the signal of surrender transmitted by Admiral Spock himself, along with a formal request for parley.

Decker didn't like this at all. It smelled like a trap.

Lieutenant Ponor, the communications officer, looked up to report, "I have Admiral Spock on channel one, sir."

"On-screen," Decker snapped. The main viewer wavered and rippled for a moment, then the visage of Admiral Spock appeared, larger than life. Decker scowled at the Vulcan. "Admiral Spock, by the authority of Empress Sato III, I order you to surrender your command and relinquish control of your vessel."

"I have already surrendered," Spock replied. *"Forcing you to destroy the* Enterprise *would serve no purpose when it can still be of service to the Empire."*

If Spock had a strategy here, Decker wasn't seeing it. "Very well," Decker said. "Prepare to be boarded."

"Hardly necessary," Spock said. *"I am prepared to allow myself to be transported to your ship."*

It took a moment for Decker to formulate his response. "Who said any of this is up to you? You're in no position to—"

"I merely suggest," Spock interrupted, *"the most logical and least time-consuming alternative."*

Decker was on the edge of his chair, tensed to spring to his feet at the slightest provocation. "You're not dictating the terms here, you Vulcan sonofabitch."

"My apologies, Grand Admiral," Spock said, lowering his head slightly. *"Do you wish to accept my surrender in person?"*

"What?" He didn't know why Spock even had to ask. The protocol for a formal surrender demanded Decker receive it face-to-face. "Yes, of course."

"Shall I arrange to have myself transported into custody aboard your vessel?"

Only then did Decker realize what Spock was doing. Though Spock had framed his statements as interrogatives, he still was directing the process of the surrender, usurping Decker's authority. "A security detail from my ship will beam aboard your vessel immediately," he said, then continued quickly to keep Spock quiet. "If they meet with any resistance, Admiral Spock—*any* resistance whatsoever—I will not hesitate to destroy your ship and its crew. My guards will escort you back here, to my bridge, where I will accept your surrender and pass sentence for your treason against Empress Sato III. Decker out." He made a slashing motion in Ponor's direction, and the communications officer closed the channel before Spock could sneak in another word.

Commander Takeshewada stepped down from one of the aft consoles and stood beside Decker's chair. "The boarding party has just beamed over, sir," she said. "They'll notify us the moment they have Admiral Spock in custody."

"Good," Decker said. "Have extra security guards meet them in the transporter room when they get back. Don't take any chances with Spock." He heaved a tired sigh. "The sooner we get this over with, the better."

As Spock had pledged, no member of his crew interfered with *Constellation*'s boarding party, and he gave no resistance when the six-man team placed him under arrest and ushered him at phaser point off the bridge of the *Enterprise.*

Now they were aboard the *Constellation,* Grand Admiral Decker's flagship, crowded together in the turbolift. Deck after deck blurred past as they ascended toward the bridge.

The doors opened with a gasp and swish, and the soft chirps and hums of the bridge, all but identical to those aboard *Enterprise,* washed over Spock as he was prodded forward out of the turbolift. *Constellation* was a refit

Constitution-class vessel just like the *Enterprise,* and only a handful of tiny differences in console layout distinguished the two ships' command centers.

On the main viewer was the image of Empress Sato III. A string of symbols along the bottom edge of the screen informed Spock this was a two-way transmission being broadcast in real time on an open subspace frequency.

Decker stood beside his chair, facing the turbolift, as Spock and the security detail filed out. The bridge officers also stood, each next to his or her station, observing Spock as he was led in and guided to within a meter of Decker. When the procession came to a stop, boot heels clapped together as the guards snapped to attention and thrust out their arms in salute to the grand admiral. Spock saluted him, more out of respect for the rank than for the man. While keeping eye contact with Spock, Decker returned the salute to one and all.

Hands pressed down roughly on Spock's shoulders. "Kneel," said one of his guards. He was forced to his knees in front of Decker, who glared fiercely down at him.

"You killed my son," Decker said.

Raising one eyebrow, Spock replied, "No, sir. My operatives slew your son. I merely sanctioned it."

"Spare me your Vulcan semantics," Decker said. "You ordered it. You're responsible. Hand me your agonizer, Admiral."

Spock calmly answered, "I no longer carry it. Nor does any member of my crew."

"That's a court-martial offense," Decker said.

Unfazed, Spock said, "If you wish to convene a court-martial, I am more than willing to defend my decision."

Decker practically quaked with rage. "I've heard enough," he said, his disgust evident. "Admiral Spock, I order you, as a Starfleet officer and subject of the Terran Empire, to profess your loyalty to Empress Sato III before you are put to death, so that you may die with some measure of honor."

Speaking boldly for the benefit of those watching via the subspace channel, Spock answered, "I pledge my loyalty and my life to the Empire." He noticed, at the edge of his vision, the Empress on the viewscreen casting a poisonous glare at Decker. He waited for Decker's reaction. It took only a moment.

"I ordered you to pledge your loyalty to the Empress Sato III," Decker snapped.

"The Empress and the Empire are one," Spock said. "Fealty to one is fealty to both. It is a founding principle of the Empire."

Decker sneered. "Do you really think this grandstanding will delay your execution, Spock?"

"I think," Spock said, "this will all be over in a few moments."

A screech of phasers, flashes of light, and agonized cries filled the bridge of the *Constellation*. The security detail surrounding Spock dropped to the deck, shot dead. Spock, already aware of what was happening, stayed where he was. Decker cringed, looked around in a sudden panic—and watched his bridge officers act in concert to ambush the security team.

It was a mutiny.

Decker backed away from Spock. The voice of his first officer stopped him. "That's far enough, Decker."

The grand admiral turned and faced Commander Takeshewada, whom Spock had cultivated as an ally through his operative Sontor. Her resentment at the suppression of her potential had made her a prime candidate for a revolt against the status quo, and her access to information as Decker's first officer had provided Spock's people with critical intelligence—such as the means to break the *Constellation*'s latest encryption codes.

Trapped between Takeshewada and Spock, Decker started to lose his stature. He was cowering. "What are you doing, Hiromi?"

"Something I should've done a long time ago."

The grand admiral turned away from his first officer to find Spock standing tall, surrounded by the charred corpses of the fallen and gazing down upon him. Mustering the timbre of authority in his rich baritone, Spock declared, "You are relieved, sir."

All at once Decker understood what was transpiring, and he straightened himself to a pose of dignity and defiance. Looking Spock in the eye, he answered, "The hell I—"

Takeshewada fired and burned a hole halfway through Decker's back. He convulsed and twitched grotesquely as he fell facedown at Spock's feet.

On the main viewer, Empress Sato III watched with wide-eyed attention but said nothing. The bridge crew of the *Constellation* looked to Spock for direction. "Stations," he ordered, and everyone leaped into motion. "Commander Takeshewada, secure from general quarters. Lieutenant Ponor, request status updates from the ships of the fleet."

While the officers around him scrambled to collect data and remove the dead bodies from the bridge, Spock settled easily into the center seat and waited, patient and stoic, for word of whether his plan—triggered prematurely by Decker and the Empress's blatant move against him—was unfolding as intended. He passed the minutes looking at the Empress on the screen. For her part, she seemed equally willing to reciprocate his stare.

Finally, Takeshewada concluded her conference with Ponor and stepped down into the middle of the bridge, next to Spock. "We have reports from all sectors, sir," she said. "Officers loyal to you have successfully taken control of sixty-one-point-three percent of the ships in Starfleet. The remaining vessels are under the control of officers who have expressed a desire to remain neutral."

"What is the disposition of the other ships in Admiral Decker's attack fleet?"

She handed him a condensed report on a data slate. "All are with you except for *Yorktown* and *Repulse,* but their captains have ordered their crews to stand down."

"Very well," Spock said. He stood and took two steps toward the main viewer. He put his closed fist to his chest, then extended his arm in salute to the Empress. "Your Majesty," he said, lowering his arm. "In accordance with the imperial rules of war, and Starfleet regulations regarding the criteria for advancement, I hereby assume the rank of Grand Admiral of Starfleet, and designate *Enterprise* as my flagship."

It was done. He had thrown the gauntlet and appointed himself the supreme military commander of the Terran Empire. Now all he could do was await the Empress's response. She could refuse to grant him the title, but to challenge him would spark a civil war—and with the majority of Starfleet supporting his bid for control, and the bulk of the remainder choosing to sit out the confrontation rather than risk becoming caught in a crossfire, the odds favored Spock's triumph. Alternatively, she could implicitly endorse his coup, thereby cementing his hold on power and legitimizing his control of the Empire's vast military arsenal. If she was as shrewd as his observations had led him to suspect she was, she would not elect to plunge her Empire into a disastrous internecine conflict.

The monarch's neutral expression never changed as she spoke. *"Grand Admiral Spock, redeploy your fleet to fortify our defenses on the Klingon border near Ajilon,"* she said.

"As you command, Your Majesty," Spock replied.

"Then," Empress Sato III added, *"set your flagship's course for Earth. It's customary for a promotion of this magnitude to be honored with a formal imperial reception. I look forward to welcoming you to my palace on Earth in seven days' time."*

Spock bowed his head slightly, then returned to attention. "Understood, Your Majesty. My crew and I are honored by your invitation."

Without any valediction, the Empress cut the channel, terminating the discussion. The collective anxiety on the bridge diminished palpably the moment the viewscreen reverted to the placid vista of a motionless starscape. Spock turned away from the screen. "Captain Takeshewada," he said, granting an instant promotion to his chief ally aboard the *Constellation,* "take this attack fleet and proceed at best speed to the Ajilon system. From there, redeploy to secure the border. The Klingons will see this change in our military leadership as an invitation to test our discipline and organization. Encourage them not to try more than once."

"Aye, sir," Takeshewada said.

"I return now to the *Enterprise,*" Spock said. He raised his right hand and spread the fingers in the Vulcan salute. "Live long and prosper, Captain Takeshewada."

"And the same to you, Grand Admiral Spock," she said. Then she took her place in the center seat and beamed with pride.

He took his communicator from his belt and flipped it open. "Spock to *Enterprise.*"

It was Lieutenant Xon who answered. *"Go ahead, sir."*

"One to beam over, Lieutenant," Spock said. "Energize."

24

The End and Object
of Conquest

"*Enter,*" said Grand Admiral Spock from the other side of the door to his quarters. It opened and Saavik stepped inside.

As soon as she crossed the threshold she felt more comfortable. Inside, the light was dimmer and tinted red; the heat was dry and comforting; even the gravity was slightly greater. It was as accurate a facsimile of Vulcan's climate as the ship's environmental controls could create. She stepped farther inside, and the door shut behind her.

Saavik turned and saw Spock. His back was to her. He was wearing his full dress uniform, complete with regalia and medals, and standing in front of a mantel on which stood a smoking cone of incense. Without turning to look in her direction, he said, "Join me, Ensign."

Hands folded together behind her back, she walked slowly to his side. Several seconds passed while she stood beside him. "We have received your transport coordinates from the imperial palace," she said, breaking the silence. "They are standing by for your arrival."

"I am well aware of our itinerary," Spock said.

Duly chastised, Saavik lowered her chin. "Aye, sir."

This time she respected the silence until he spoke.

His eyes remained fixed on the twists of pale smoke rising from the ashen cone of mildly jasmine-scented incense. "Do you know why I asked you here?"

She followed his example and stared at the serpentine coils of dense smoke. "No, sir."

"Do you know why the Empress ordered us to Earth?"

Electing to eliminate obvious answers, Saavik replied, "To honor your promotion to Grand Admiral of Starfleet."

A soft, low *harrumph* was Spock's first reaction. "That was her *stated* purpose for the invitation."

Saavik cast a furtive, sidelong glance at her Academy sponsor and mentor. Phrasing her supposition as a statement rather than as a question, she said, "You believe the Empress's invitation is a prelude to an assassination attempt."

He gave a brief nod. "I do."

"If you are correct," Saavik said, "do you concede her decision is logical? You have, after all, orchestrated a coup of Starfleet and usurped a rank traditionally appointed by the throne."

Turning to face her, he replied, "I concede her decision to eliminate me is consistent with her objectives. But as I consider her long-term goal to be untenable, I am forced to conclude the entirety of her agenda and the actions she takes to support it are illogical."

"Then the rumors are true," Saavik said. "You intend to challenge her for control of the Empire."

His expression betrayed nothing as he stepped away from her to a nearby table, on which sat a tray that held a ceramic teapot and two low, broad cups of a matching style. He poured a cup of tea, then lifted it and held it out toward Saavik. She walked over, accepted the tea, and then returned the gesture by filling the other cup and offering it to him. He took it from her with a solemn bow of his head. They sipped the herbal libation together. Finally, he said, "Share your thoughts."

Challenging him felt improper; she was a lowly ensign, and he was the supreme military commander of the Empire—at least, he was for the next hour, until his audience with the Empress. His invitation had sounded genuine, however, so she collected her thoughts and began cautiously. "I am familiar with the predicted future collapse of the Empire," she said. "And I agree it is not logical to continue expending time, resources, and lives on an entity we know to be doomed." Growing bolder, she continued. "But I have grave misgivings about your proposed solution, Admiral. Many of your ideas seem laudable for their nobility, but I think they will ultimately prove impractical."

"Should we instead do nothing?" Spock asked.

She put down her tea. "Perhaps your domestic adjustments could be accommodated with a more graduated time frame. But your platform of diplomacy and exclusively defensive power as the basis for a new foreign policy strikes me as politically naïve at best, and possibly suicidal at worst."

"And yet, by employing those very tactics within Starfleet, I have amassed more direct support than any officer ever to precede me in this role."

"Enacting reforms within Starfleet is hardly analogous to effecting a total reversal of the Empire's foreign policy."

Setting aside his own tea, he asked, "On what do you

base your assumption that our adversaries will reject diplomacy? Or that renouncing wars of choice would provoke them?"

"I have based my arguments on my observations and studies of the Klingons, Cardassians, and Romulans as large-scale political actors," Saavik said. "Each is ambitious and highly aggressive. Historically, none of them has been receptive to diplomatic efforts. As for your civil reforms, the regional governors would certainly revolt, and you might lose much of your current support within Starfleet."

He paced slowly away from her and stopped beside a wall in the middle of the cabin. "Put aside what you know, Saavik," he said, "and consider this hypothetical question: If there existed a means by which my power could be assured, and my enemies kept at bay, would you support a more logical approach to the governance of the Empire?"

"Hypothetically?" Arching one eyebrow, she replied, "Yes."

"And if I were to place the fate of the Empire into your hands," he said, "which path would you choose?"

"The one that was most logical," Saavik said, almost as if by instinct.

With one hand, he beckoned her. As she stepped over to join him, he reached up toward an empty trapezoidal frame on his wall. He touched its lower right corner, then its upper right corner. The main panel of the frame slid upward, revealing a small device: just a screen, a few knobs, a keypad, and a single button set apart in a pale, sea-green teardrop of crystal. "This," he said, "is the control apparatus for an alien weapon known as the Tantalus field. With it, the user can track the movements of any person, even from orbit." He activated the device and called up an image of Empress Sato III, in her throne room on Earth. "It can strike even within such protected domains as the imperial palace." He pointed at the various controls. "These are used to switch targets, these are for tracking. And this one"—he pointed at the button inside the teardrop crystal—"fires the weapon. It can eliminate a single target as small as an insect . . . or everyone in a desired zone of effect. To the best of my knowledge, there is no defense."

Saavik stared at the device, transfixed by the macabre genius of it. Undoubtedly, this had been the secret of Spock's swift ascent to power, and the source of the legends about his terrifying psionic gifts. Then she realized knowing about the Tantalus field might make her a liability to him. "Admiral," she asked carefully, "why are you showing me this?"

"Because, Saavik, when I meet with the Empress, you will have three choices." He stepped close to her, invading her personal space and towering over her. "One: Serve your own agenda—let the imperial guards kill me, then take the Tantalus field device for yourself. Two: Assassinate me yourself, and try to curry favor with the Empress. Or three: Defend me from the Empress, and help me initiate the logical reformation of the Empire. . . . The choice is yours."

It took several seconds before Saavik understood the exact nature of the responsibility Spock had just entrusted to her. He was one of the most powerful men in the Empire, and he was about to make himself infinitely vulnerable to her whim. It was one of the most illogical decisions she had ever seen a Vulcan make. "I do not understand, Admiral," she said. "You would actually *trust me* to remain here, alone with this unspeakably powerful weapon? You would entrust your life . . . to my goodwill?"

"No, Saavik," he replied. "I am entrusting my life to your good judgment. Logic alone should dictate your correct course." He frowned, then continued. "We live in a universe that tends to reward cruelty and self-interest. But I have seen irrefutable evidence that a better way exists—and if our civilization is to endure beyond the next two centuries, we must learn to change."

His assertion fueled her swelling curiosity. "You say you have seen 'irrefutable proof.' What was that proof, Admiral?"

"A mind-meld," he said. "With a human from an alternate universe, one much like our own." He lifted his hand and gently pressed his fingertips against her temple and cheek. "Open your mind to me, and I will share what I have seen."

He had already volunteered so many secrets that Saavik saw no reason for him to lie now about his intentions. She lowered her psionic defenses one layer at a time and permitted his mind to fuse with her own.

And then she saw it.

Flashes of memory, a third mind, fleetingly touched but now forever imprinted in Spock's psyche. Another Dr. McCoy. A man of compassion and mercy. From a Starfleet whose officers don't kill for advancement, but are willing to die to protect each other.

A Federation founded on justice, equality, and peace, and, like the Terran Empire, beset by powerful, dangerous rivals. But unlike the Empire, this Federation amasses its strength by means of consensus and alliances of mutual benefit, and it assuages its wants and its injuries through mutual sacrifice.

Stable. Prosperous. Strong. Free.

Spock withdrew the touch of his mind and his hand, leaving Saavik with lingering images of the alternate universe. It was no psionic illusion; it was genuine. Just as Spock had said, it was irrefutable. And yet . . . it was not this universe. Its lessons, its ideals—they weren't of this reality. To think two such divergent universes could belatedly be steered onto the same course struck Saavik as dangerously wishful thinking.

She was still considering her reaction when Spock stepped back from her and said, "The choice is yours." Then he walked away, out the door, to keep his appointment with the Empress.

With a few simple turns and taps of the device's controls, Saavik conjured an image of Spock on its viewer. She watched him stride through the corridors of the *Enterprise,* on his way to the transporter room and not at all resembling a man willingly walking into a trap. *I could eliminate him right now,* she realized, her fingers lightly brushing the outline of the teardrop crystal. *No one would ever know.*

Ultimate power lay in Saavik's hands—and she had less than five minutes to decide what to do with it.

Flanked by a trio of his most trusted Vulcan bodyguards, Spock rematerialized from the transporter beam. He and his men were on the edge of a vast plaza, at the gargantuan arched entryway on the southern side of the imperial palace. The polished titanium of the massive, domed structure reflected the lush green vista of the Okinawa countryside—and the legion of black-and-red-uniformed soldiers standing at attention in formation on the plaza, to Spock's left. He turned and faced the ranks of imperial shock troops. As one, thousands of men brought their fists to their chests, then extended their arms in formal salute. He returned the salute, then turned and entered the palace proper, his guards close behind.

Like so many edifices dedicated to human vanity, the palace was a conspicuous waste of space and resources. Thoroughfares that receded to distant points were bordered by walls ascending to dizzying heights. From the floors to the lofty arches of the ceiling, the interior of the palace appeared to have been crafted entirely of ornately gilded marble. In contrast to the muggy, hazy summer air outside, the atmosphere inside the palace was crisp and cold and odorless. Heavy doors of carved mahogany lined the cathedral-like passageway, and on either side of every door stood two guards, more imperial shock troops.

A steady flood-crush of pedestrians hurried in criss-crossed paths, all racing from one bastion of bureaucracy to another, bearing urgent missives, relaying orders, coming and going from meetings and appointments.

Then a booming voice announced over a central public address system: *"Attention."* The madding throng came to a halt. *"Clear the main passage for Grand Admiral Spock."* As if cleaved by an invisible blade, the crowd parted to form a broad channel through the center of the passageway, and an antigrav skiff glided quickly toward Spock.

Its pilot was another member of the Imperial Guard. He guided the skiff to a gliding stop in front of Spock, finishing with a slow turn so that the open passenger-side seat faced the grand admiral. "Good morning, sir," he said. "I'm here to escort you to Her Majesty, Empress Sato III."

Spock nodded his assent, climbed aboard the skiff, and sat down. His guards occupied the rear bench seat. The vehicle accelerated smoothly, finished its turn, and sped back the way it had come. The corridor and the faces that filled it blurred past.

Less than a minute later, the skiff arrived at the towering duranium doors of the imperial throne room. Waiting there for Spock was his entourage, whose members the Empress had summoned in the more formal invitation she had extended during *Enterprise*'s journey to Earth: Lieutenant Commander Kevin Riley, the newly promoted first officer of the *I.S.S. Enterprise;* Lieutenant Xon; Dr. Jabilo M'Benga; and chief engineer Commander Montgomery Scott.

Spock and his bodyguards debarked from the skiff. After a curt greeting, he directed his men simply, "Places." He took his place at the head of their procession, with his bodyguards in tight formation behind him. Riley and Scott formed the next rank, followed by Xon and M'Benga. Spock signaled the senior imperial guard that he was ready.

After relaying the message ahead into the throne room, the guard received his orders from his superior, and he turned to face his men. "Open the door and announce the grand admiral."

Resounding clangs, from the release of magnetic locks inside the enormous metal doors, vibrated the marble floor beneath Spock's feet. He lifted his chin proudly but kept his expression neutral. The doors parted and swung inward. Golden radiance from the other side spilled out in long, angled shafts. In a blink of his inner eyelid, his sight adjusted to the luminous appointments of the throne room.

A great fanfare sounded, and a herald stepped in front of the door and faced the throne. "Your Majesty: presenting His Martial Eminence, Grand Admiral Spock, supreme commander of your imperial armed forces." Another fanfare blared as Spock stepped through the doorway, trailed by his retinue.

The imperial court was resplendent with trappings of gold and crimson. Legions of imperial shock troops manned the upper balconies, from which were draped gigantic red-and-gold banners emblazoned with the imperial icon, the Earth impaled on a broadsword, stabbed through the heart by its own martial ambitions.

The expansive lower concourse was crowded with courtiers, pages, personal bodyguards, foreign ambassadors, imperial advisers, and members of the cabinet. Several planetary governors also were present, among them Kodos of Tarsus IV, Oxmyx of Sigma Iotia IV, and Plasus of Ardana. The majority of the guests hovered around the overfilled banquet tables like vultures feasting on a killing field.

Walls covered in damask were lined with portraits of members of the royal family, but none were so commanding in their presence as the ones that were holographically projected behind the throne at the far end of the great hall. Twenty meters high, the trio of high-definition likenesses formed the portrait of a dynasty in the making: Empress Hoshi Sato I, Empress Hoshi Sato II, and Empress Hoshi Sato III—the currently reigning imperial monarch, who presided from her throne high atop a truncated half-pyramid of stairs, surrounded by another company of her elite guards.

Spock and his retinue marched in solemn strides toward the throne. Quickly, the chaotic crowd formed itself into orderly rows, aligned by rank. Thunderous applause swelled and became almost deafening as Spock continued forward. The Empress and her soldiers, however, remained still and silent.

The broad base of the stairs to the Empress's platform was surrounded by a ten-meter-wide border of obsidian floor panels. Polished to perfection, their glassy black surface reflected Spock's weathered visage with such clarity that he could see every graying whisker in his goatee. It was there that a quartet of imperial guards blocked him and his retinue. The captain of the guard said gruffly, "Grand Admiral Spock: By order of Her Imperial Majesty, from here you proceed alone." Then he motioned for Spock to follow him up the stairs, toward the throne.

Spock passed through the invisible energy barrier that protected the Empress's throne. A galvanic tingle coursed over his skin and bristled the hairs on the back of his hands. Once he was on the other side, he heard a subtle hum, gently rising in tone, as the force field returned to full strength behind him. As he had suspected, a small gap had been opened only long enough to grant him ingress to the Empress's inner circle. Now that he was separated from his bodyguards, they would be unable to intervene when the Empress gave the order for her troops to execute him. Directed-energy weapons, projectiles, and most other forms of ranged armaments could not penetrate the shield in either direction. And because imperial law forbade him from bearing arms into the presence of the Empress, he would have no means of defending himself.

He climbed the stairs without hesitation.

Ten steps from the top, Empress Sato's voice

commanded him, "Halt." Spock genuflected before the Empress. "Welcome, Grand Admiral Spock," she continued. "This court is honored by your august presence."

Because she did not bid him rise, he remained on one knee. "It is I who am honored, Your Majesty—by your most gracious invitation, and by the opportunity to serve the Empire as its grand admiral."

Irritation colored her words. "My dear admiral, I believe you have misspoken. You serve me, not the Empire at large. I am your sovereign."

"I acknowledge you are the sovereign ruler of the Empire," Spock replied. "But I have not misspoken."

Her mouth curled into a smirk, but anger flashed in her eyes. "Your reputation is well earned," she said, her demeanor hostile and mocking. "A 'rogue,' that's what Grand Admiral Decker called you. Before him, Grand Admiral Garth of Izar labeled you a 'radical,' a 'free thinker.' Now I hear rumors you see yourself as a reformer."

"I have been, remain, and will continue to be all those things," Spock admitted.

She abandoned the artifice of sarcasm and spoke directly. "Your penchant for compromise troubles me, Spock. Negotiation and diplomacy are tools of the weak."

"Quite the contrary," Spock said. "Only from a position of strength can one afford to offer—"

"Silence!" she snapped. "Having someone of your temperament as grand admiral is a threat to the security of the Empire. It will invite attack by our enemies, both internal and external. How can the Empire be assured of its safety when its supreme military commander is an avowed appeaser of its rivals?"

Looking directly and unabashedly at the Empress, he

replied, "Every action I have taken has been grounded in logic. I have never acted to the benefit of our enemies, but only to serve the best interests of the Empire and its people."

Empress Sato III blinked in disbelief, as if Spock had just committed a grievous faux pas. "The *people*?" she said, with obvious contempt. She rose from her throne and descended the stairs toward him. Her guards advanced quickly behind her, weapons at the ready. "Since when do the *people* matter, Spock? The people are fodder, a source of revenue to be taxed, a pool of raw material to be kept ignorant and afraid until I need them to be angry and swell with pride." With a sneer she added, "The people are *pawns*. Their 'best interests' are irrelevant." She climbed back to the top of the stairs, then turned and glared at him with all the haughty grandeur she could muster. "As irrelevant as you, my dear half-breed." Raising her arm, she called out, "Guards!"

Weapons were brought to bear with a heavy clattering sound. Spock kept his attention on the Empress, ignoring the dozens of phaser rifles aimed at him from every direction.

A flare of light and a crackle of blistering heat. Spock gazed into the blinding brilliance, stoic in the face of sudden annihilation. Then a sharp bite of ozone filled his nose, and a warm breath of air passed over him.

He heard the gasps of the crowd beyond the force field.

Empress Sato and her company of elite guards were gone. Not a trace of them remained—not scraps of clothing, not ashes, nothing at all.

Spock stood, turned, and gazed intently at the legions of guards on the upper balconies. Another massive pulse of pure white incandescence erupted on every balcony, leaving only the silhouettes of skeletons to linger for a moment in the afterglow. Blinks of light stutter-stepped through the crowd in the hall, finding every imperial guard in the throne room. Within seconds, it was over.

For a moment, all anyone below could do was look around in horror, dumbstruck with fright at this invincible blitzkrieg. Then, inevitably, all eyes gazed upward, toward Spock.

He turned away from the crowd.

Climbed the stairs.

Seated himself upon the throne.

And he waited.

Then, from far below, outside the protective energy barrier, sounded a man's solitary voice, one Spock didn't recognize, repeating a lonely declaration in the echoing vastness of the great hall until his voice was joined by another, then by several more, and finally by the booming roar of a crowd chanting fervently and in unison.

All hail Emperor Spock!

With two gentle touches of Saavik's hand, the panel slid closed over the Tantalus field device's control panel. Seemingly unperturbed by the momentous and pivotal role she had just played in the fate of the Empire, she walked calmly out of Spock's quarters. The door hissed closed and locked behind her.

Concealed behind a false panel in the bulkhead opposite the secret weapon, Marlena Moreau breathed a tired sigh. She was greatly relieved to know Saavik was loyal to Spock. It would make it easier for her to trust the young Vulcan woman from now on. If the targeting cursor of the Tantalus field had fallen for even a moment upon Spock's image, Marlena had been ready to strike instantly, a phaser set on kill steady in her hand. Though she was now ashamed she had doubted Spock's judgment about his protégée, she was still frightened by his willingness to trust other people too much. She loved and admired his idealism even as she cursed its inherent risks.

Marlena emerged from behind the panel. Over the years, she had gradually become accustomed to the higher temperatures and gravity inside the quarters she shared with Spock. The aridity, however, continued to vex her, so she tried to limit the time she spent there, preferring to pass her free hours in the ship's library or its astrometrics laboratory.

She eyed her reflection in the wall mirror and was able to tell herself honestly that, so far, the years had been kind to her. Spock, on the other hand, was already showing signs of the extreme stress inflicted by his rapid campaign to seize control over Starfleet. Now, less than a week after his decade-long effort had come to fruition, he had succeeded in placing himself upon the imperial throne. He was the Emperor.

Everything was changed now. Marlena could only imagine the toll that reigning over an interstellar empire would take on her beloved husband, and she feared for his health . . . and his life. There were bound to be operatives loyal to the Sato dynasty who would seek retribution. Even with the Tantalus field, how could she and Spock hope to find and eliminate them all? It seemed impossible.

We will find a way, she promised herself. *We have to.*

A thought occurred to her. She pulled open her closet and surveyed its contents. Dismayed, she realized

Spock's great achievement had caught her totally unprepared. *Damn. Fifty outfits to choose from . . . and not one is even remotely good enough.* She shut the closet. *I'm not ready to be an empress yet.*

In two regal strides, she was at the wall panel. With a push of her thumb she opened a channel to the bridge. Moments later, she was answered by Lieutenant Finney, whose youthful voice shook with a new undercurrent of fear. *"Bridge here."*

"This is the Empress Consort," she said, liking the sound of it as soon as she'd said it. "Have the imperial tailors sent to my quarters immediately."

"Right away, Your Majesty," Finney said, sounding like a scolded child. *"Bridge out."*

Despite her best efforts at equanimity, a slightly insane smile and wide-eyed mask of glee took over Marlena's face. Even after catching sight of her Cheshire cat grin in the mirror, she couldn't suppress it.

Just as she'd always suspected, it was good to be queen.

25

A Taste of Ashes

A week of frantic preparations had infused the imperial court with equal measures of anticipation and dread.

"It takes a thousand details to make a first impression," Marlena told the servants and taskmasters in charge of the court's formal trappings, "and every last one of them must be perfect."

As the Empress Consort, she was not going to accept anything less than perfection from her legion of domestics, not on this auspicious day. She had waited too long and had dreamed of this moment too many times to see it marred by even the slightest error of protocol or omission of courtesy.

The last vestiges of the Sato dynasty had been scoured from the palace. Marlena had replaced the Satos' towering, autoidolatrous portraits with banners of white Chinese silk bearing the bloodred icon of the Terran Empire.

Several freestanding light fixtures, most of which were merely decorative, had been supplanted by antique Vulcan torchères in honor of the Empire's new sovereign. Flames danced hypnotically from the lamps' upturned bowls, casting erratic shadows across the throne room's damask-covered walls.

To either side of the center aisle before the throne, buffet tables had been laden with every delicacy of the Empire and a few from the worlds of its rivals. Every beverage Marlena could think of was ready to flow upon request, from taps and bottles and decanters. Massive slabs of perfectly transparent ice, preserved inside temperature-controlled fields, had been masterfully carved into a variety of shapes, including a seven-meter-tall likeness of Spock, a pair of giant butterflies entwined in flight, a fairy-tale carriage complete with a one-slippered princess for a passenger, and a flame-feathered phoenix rising from ashes of shaved ice.

An orchestra composed of the Empire's finest musicians played from the balcony level, accompanied by a choir of its most hauntingly gifted vocalists.

The room was packed with dignitaries, ambassadors, members of the imperial cabinet, and a legion of elite Vulcan guards attired in red and gold armor patterned after the *lorica segmentata* of Earth's ancient Roman Empire.

Marlena had tasked the imperial tailors to fashion her a dress for this occasion. They had presented to her a magnificent creation in crimson silk, adorned in gold with a pattern of Chinese dragons twisting around the ideogram for "double happiness." Her hair was gathered in an ornate coif, held in place by antique ivory hairpins, and backed by an enormous semicircular headpiece covered in ruby-hued Tholian silk.

Every detail was in place, all the trappings of power.

Taking her place on the imperial throne, Marlena decreed, "Bring him in."

Her order was volleyed from the sergeant-at-arms to the imperial herald, who passed word to the guards outside the throne room's door. A moment later the great locks of the massive portals were released, and the doors swung inward. On cue, the members of the trumpet corps lifted their instruments and split the air with a magnificent fanfare.

The herald stepped in front of the open doorway. "Your Majesty: presenting, by your imperial command, the father of the Empress—François Thierry Moreau."

Another crowing of the fanfare resounded from high overhead as Marlena's father plodded into the throne room with obvious trepidation.

From a distance, Marlena could not see the details of her father's appearance or the expression on his face. She held her chin high and looked down her nose at her sire as a pair of Vulcan guards escorted him to the edge of her unseen but lethal defensive force field. Even deprived of details, Marlena found it telling her father had come unescorted, apparently still shunned by her siblings.

Serves him right, she gloated.

He came to a halt at the base of the stairs beneath her throne. His shoulders were hunched, and he looked around fearfully, as if he were on trial for his life. A guard placed a hand on François's shoulder and made him kneel. François looked up with naked fear and veiled resentment.

"Do you have anything to say to me, Father?"

His head bowed, he answered in a small voice, "No, Majesty."

Humbled before his daughter, he looked small . . . shabby . . . weak.

Marlena felt a swell of pity and remorse. This was to have been her moment of triumph; instead, the moment tasted of ashes. She found no satisfaction in the sight of her estranged father debased; there was no joy to be found in lording over him. Beholding the scorn and terror in his eyes, Marlena realized even though she had risen in life to become the Empress, that still did not make her father love her, and she understood nothing ever would—it simply was not in his nature.

"Your duty is fulfilled," she said. "Go home to your petty concerns."

"As you command, Majesty," her father said, bowing low as he backpedaled the requisite five paces before rising and turning to walk away. He left the throne room with the rushed bearing of a man relieved to have been spared a trip to the gallows. Without a single look back at his now-regal daughter, François Moreau exited the throne room. The guards sealed the door behind him.

A week of preparation had yielded naught but a moment of regret for Empress Marlena. Despite being seated in imposing splendor and surrounded by minions of the imperial court, she couldn't help but feel terribly, utterly alone.

26

The Designs of Liberty

It had been slightly more than two months since Spock claimed the throne, and the ensuing cavalcade of pomp and pageantry had only just subsided. First had come the official coronation, followed by more than a hundred hastily dispatched state visits by the Empire's various planetary governors, each of whom had come to deliver gifts and pledges of loyalty, all of which Spock had accepted with politely concealed indifference. His thoughts had been occupied almost constantly by the intricate and politically delicate task of transitioning the imperial government to a new administration, one populated from its highest echelons down with reformers whom Spock had painstakingly cultivated as allies over the past decade.

As Spock had suspected, his wife had adapted easily and enthusiastically to her new role as Empress Marlena. To her care he had entrusted the coordination of the cosmetic overhaul of the government. Other, more radical alterations he had discussed with her would have to wait until the Empire's political climate was ready.

One element of imperial life remained constant during the abrupt transition to Spock's reign: the mood of constant, muffled terror suffusing the halls of the palace. Even without the benefit of his spies' reports, Spock could overhear the whispered rumors, the hushed exchanges of frightened eyewitness accounts describing the manner in which the Empress Hoshi Sato III and her Imperial Guard Corps had been annihilated. A few people had guessed, correctly, that an unknown weapon had been involved, but by far the most persistent and popular explanation was that Spock had used an ancient, formerly secret Vulcan psionic attack to seize power.

Encouraging untruths ran counter to the principles of logic, but in this case Spock permitted the rumors to spread unchallenged as a means of securing his power base during a vulnerable period of transition.

For his own part, Spock found life in the imperial palace quiet, comfortable, and opulently boring. The oversized chambers and furniture offended his simple, austere sensibilities. The illogic of waste had been a primary factor in his decision to seek dominion over the Empire, and now he lived in the most ostentatious expression of wastefulness imaginable. The irony of his circumstances was not lost on him.

Clad in luxurious robes of Tholian silk, he stood on the force field–protected balcony outside his bedchamber and admired the verdant countryside of Okinawa. The dawn air was cool. Despite his half-human heritage, this land, this world, felt alien to him. He was in essence a stranger here.

Inside the bedroom, Marlena slept blissfully behind the gauzy screens of an antique French canopied bed. Earth was her home. She had been born here, the youngest child of a common merchant. But though her family's origins had been modest, her homecoming had been nothing less than glorious.

A deep chiming signal indicated Spock's staff wished

to announce a visitor. He turned and watched the double doors leading to the parlor. They opened several seconds later, and a herald entered. "Your Majesty," he said, bowing his head. "Ambassador Sarek of Vulcan is here at your invitation."

"Show him into the study," Spock said. "I will join him there momentarily."

"As you command, Majesty," the herald said. He withdrew in reverse, closing the bedroom doors as he exited.

Spock shut his eyes and meditated in silence for a few minutes, clearing his thoughts and preparing himself for the meeting with his father. Each breath was a cleansing intake and release, and the tension that attended the rulership of the Empire gradually ebbed from his muscles. At last centered in his own thoughts, he allowed himself a solitary, sentimental glance in Marlena's direction before he left the bedroom.

He crossed through the parlor and passed the library on the way to his study. The shelves of the library currently were bare; Spock had found the Satos' collection of references and literature woefully inadequate, not to mention pedestrian and out of date. Thousands of more recent and more worthy tomes had been ordered and were due to be delivered within the week. Marlena had callously suggested burning the Satos' books, but the idea was anathema to Spock. Destroying books was out of the question. Instead, he had arranged for the Satos' volumes to be relocated somewhere more appropriate. It was doubtful anyone would randomly stumble across them buried in a crater on Luna, but Spock knew it wasn't impossible.

The doors of the study were open. Sarek stood

opposite the entrance, in front of the antique writing desk. He bowed his head as Spock entered. "Your Majesty," Sarek said with all sincerity. "I am honored to be received."

"Welcome, Ambassador," Spock said. "We are alone. We may dispense with formalities."

Sarek nodded. "As you wish." Gesturing to a pair of large chairs on either side of a low, broad table, he added, "Shall we sit down?"

Spock nodded his assent and sat down opposite his father, who took a small holographic projection cell from his robes and set it on the table. The device activated with a small buzzing sound, and a complex document, written in High Vulcan, scrolled in glowing letters on the air, several centimeters above the dark tabletop. "Before we begin," Sarek said, "I wish to ask: Are you still committed to your plan of reform?"

"Indeed," Spock said. "My objective remains the same."

Nodding, Sarek explained, "You would not be the first head of state to amend his agenda after taking office." He sighed. "No matter. If you are ready, we should proceed."

"Agreed," Spock said.

His father leaned forward and manipulated the elements in the holographic projection with his fingertips. "The key to a successful transition will be to effect your reforms by degrees," he said. "A shrewd first move would be to increase the autonomy and direct control of the regional governors."

Moving a few items along the timeline, Spock replied, "An excellent idea. The erosion of imperial executive power will be subtle, but the governors will not object because they benefit."

"Exactly," Sarek said. "And it will pave the way for your first major reform: the creation of a Common Forum, for popularly elected representatives from each world in the Empire. You should expect the governors to object vehemently to this."

"Of course," Spock said. "It will be a direct affront to their authority. I presume I will pretend to appease them by suggesting they appoint their own representatives to the newly reconstituted Imperial Senate."

"It will mollify them briefly," Sarek acknowledged. "Granting authority for drafting legislation to both the Forum and the Senate will turn them into rivals for power."

"And they will vie for my approval by drafting competing bills," Spock predicted. "I will then censure both for wasting my time with duplicated efforts, and force them to work together by declaring I will only review legislation that they have approved jointly."

After a moment's thought, Sarek replied, "A curious tactic." He adjusted more items in the complex predictive timeline. "You will give them incentive to align against you."

"Yes," Spock said. "Fortunately, the conflicts in their interests will make that difficult for them." He pointed out another item on the timeline. "I should retain plenary executive authority long enough to liberate the imperial judiciary into a separate but equal branch of government."

Sarek made a few final changes to the timeline, then looked up at Spock. "With your permission, I should like to turn now to matters of foreign policy." Spock nodded his consent. Sarek touched a control on the holographic emitter and changed the image above the table to another timeline, this one superimposed over a star chart of local space. "Your proposition of détente as an official platform for imperial policy still troubles me."

He had expected his father's reservations, and was prepared to address them. "Nonaggression does not equal surrender, Sarek. We will continue to defend our borders from external threats. Only our approach to the growth and maintenance of the Empire will change." Pointing to the map, he continued. "A diplomatic invitation convinced Coridan to join the Empire of its own accord. Renouncing conquest and annexation as our chief modes of expansion will earn us the trust of more worlds, and enable us to expand by enticement rather than by extortion."

Spock waited while Sarek mulled that argument. The older man got up from his chair and paced across the room, then behind the desk, where he stood looking out the window for a minute. When he finally turned back toward Spock, his expression was darkened with concern. He spoke with careful diction, as if vetting each word's nuance before it passed his lips. "Spock, I have supported your call for reforms, because I know they are necessary. However, the subtext of your recent proposals compels me to inquire: Is there more to your long-term plan than you have told me?"

"Yes, Father," Spock said. "The true scope of my reforms is more drastic than I have said so far."

Raising one eyebrow to convey both his skepticism and his annoyance, Sarek prompted him, "Go on."

"Preemptive war will be renounced as an instrument of policy," Spock said.

Sarek nodded. "I had assumed as much."

"Before I begin my final reforms, I will issue an

imperial edict delineating a broad spectrum of inalienable rights for all sentient beings in the Empire," Spock said. "These rights will be comprehensive and will serve to greatly empower the individual at the expense of the state." He pointed at a data slate on the desktop. "A draft of the edict is there."

His father picked up the data slate and perused the document. With each passing moment, his grimace tightened, and the creases of worry on his forehead deepened. "Freedom of expression," he mumbled, reading from the device in his hand. "Rights of privacy . . . security from warrantless search or seizure." He set down the electronic tablet on the desk. "The governors will not stand for this."

"Irrelevant," Spock said, "as I intend to abolish their offices and replace them with elected presidents, their powers curtailed by law. Then, I will abolish the Empire itself. The Forum and the Senate will be given the right to elect one of their own as Consul, and the power to remove such an individual with a simple no-confidence vote when necessary. And at that time, I shall step down as Emperor, and cede my power to a lawfully constituted republic."

"Madness," Sarek said, his cherished mask of stoicism faltering. Spock realized that his father's anger and fear must be overwhelming for them to be so apparent. Stepping from behind the desk, Sarek crossed the room in quick strides to confront Spock. "My son, do you not see this is a recipe for disaster?" Disregarding all dictums of imperial protocol, he grasped Spock by his arms. "A republic without strong leadership from the top will be too slow to survive in this astropolitical arena. While the Forum argues, the Klingons will slaughter us. So will the Romulans, the Cardassians, the Tholians." His fingers clenched, talonlike, on Spock's biceps. "You will be writing the Empire's requiem with the blood of generations to come, Spock. What good will their freedoms be when they are dead?"

A single withering glare from Spock convinced Sarek to remove his hands from the arms of his son, the Emperor.

Spock answered calmly, with the conviction that came from knowing the endgame that so far had eluded even Sarek's keen foresight. "There is only one antidote to tyranny, Father, and that is freedom. Not the illusion of freedom, not the promise of freedom. Genuine freedom. When too much power concentrates in one person, civilization slips out of balance. Give the people real freedom, and the real power that comes with it, and no force of oppression will ever be equal to them again."

Sarek folded his hands inside the deep, drooping sleeves of his robe. He paced away from Spock, his expression stern, telegraphing his pessimism. "It will take many decades to complete even your preliminary reforms," he said. "As for issuing your edict and erecting a republic on the ruins of the Empire . . . such fundamental changes in the status quo will take generations to enact."

"They cannot," Spock said gravely. "We do not have that much time."

PART II

Exitus Acta Probat

2278

27

No-Man's-Land

The operations level of the Regula I space station was shrouded in gloom, a cold crypt on the edge of nowhere. A delicate layer of dust blanketed its dormant banks of obsolete computers. Its only illumination was the dim white glow of a chemical flare clutched in Carol Marcus's hand.

She stood on the lower level of the operations center and listened to the voices and footsteps of her team members. They moved through the corridors of the abandoned facility, inspecting compartments and comparing notes over an open comm channel with their communicators. Every sound echoed inside the station.

Constructed by Starfleet a decade earlier as a jumping-off point for rimward exploration missions, Regula I had been abandoned in 2273 when tensions in the Taurus Reach had forced Starfleet to redeploy its forces to Vanguard. Soon forgotten by the Terran Empire as well as by its rivals, and too distant from any active shipping lanes to be of use to pirates or smugglers, Regula I had languished in the shadow of the Mutara Nebula, empty and neglected, for half a decade.

Marcus heard her people converging on the operations center from multiple directions. Shadows bobbed and wavered on the walls and floor as the group drew near, combining the light from their glow-sticks. She turned toward the main entryway on the lower level to greet them.

Leading the group was her son, David. Now a lanky seventeen-year-old, he sported a head of curly, dirty-blond hair and a strong, dimpled chin. He had just completed his first level of postgraduate study when his education was interrupted by their exile to Regula. Under the tutelage of Marcus's team of researchers and theorists, however, the youth finally had begun work on his doctoral program.

"It's a wreck," David said, gesticulating with his glow-stick.

Marcus tilted her head. "It's a fixer-upper."

The other scientists fanned out around her in a semi-circle. One of them, a Deltan physicist named Tarcoh, interjected, "The computers are antiquated, Carol."

"We can upgrade them," Marcus replied.

A Tellarite geneticist named Gek added, "Starfleet took the fusion core and backup batteries when they left."

"All right," Marcus said, thinking as she spoke, "we'll scavenge the core from our ship's impulse drive."

David protested, "Then we'll be stranded here!"

"We weren't planning on leaving anytime soon, anyway," Marcus said.

Dr. Koothrappali, a human astrophysicist, asked nervously, "What if we need to evacuate because of a solar flare or a gamma-ray burst from the nebula?"

"We're protected from solar flares by the planetoid," Marcus said. "It's a Class-D ball of rock, geologically inactive and dense enough to shield us from even the most potent coronal-mass ejections its star gives off. As for the nebula, it's not an active stellar nursery and exhibits no masses great enough to form black holes, so I'd say you can stop worrying about gamma rays."

Most of her team seemed to be mollified, but Dr. Tarcoh grumbled, "So this is where we get to spend the rest of our careers? Orbiting some lifeless boulder at the end of space? One might get the impression Emperor Spock exiled us to this no-man's-land because he wants us to vanish."

An unfamiliar woman's voice answered from the operations center's upper level, "In a sense, Doctor, that is exactly what the Emperor hopes to accomplish."

Marcus's colleagues looked up, and she turned to see who had spoken.

A statuesque Vulcan woman descended a spiral staircase to the main level and met their inquisitive stares as she crossed the room to stand in front of Marcus. She held a data card in one hand and something very small in the other.

Marcus asked, "Who are you?"

"A friend, sent by the Emperor," the Vulcan said. She offered Marcus the data card. "This contains ninety-five percent of your data from Vanguard's memory banks. It was all that could be salvaged before the starbase was destroyed." Handing over the vial, which contained a strangely animated substance that transmuted back and forth between a black vapor and a charcoal-colored fluid, the Vulcan said, "I think you will recognize this."

Fear trembled Marcus's hands as she accepted the card and vial. "Why are you giving these to me?"

"Consider them a gift from His Majesty. He asks only that you use them wisely, and in peace." The mysterious visitor turned and walked back the way she had come. As she climbed the spiral stairs, Marcus called after her.

"How do we contact you?"

"You don't." The Vulcan woman reached the top of the stairs and disappeared into the shadows of a corridor branching off the upper level.

David, Tarcoh, and Gek regained their wits and ran up the stairs in pursuit. A minute later they returned, looking bewildered. "She's gone," David said. "There's no trace of how she got on or off the station, or where she went."

The rest of the scientists looked anxiously at Marcus. Koothrappali asked, "What should we do, Doctor Marcus?"

Imagining the possibilities she held in her hands, Marcus replied in a bold voice, "We should get to work."

2279

28

A Desolation Called Peace

Marlena lurked a few paces behind Spock's chair, half concealed in the penumbra of the war room's perimeter, listening as he presided over a meeting of his senior cabinet members, Starfleet flag officers, and advisers.

Most of the discussions she audited were relatively mundane, but what mattered was that she had been invited by Spock to join these classified sessions of the imperial cabinet, reinforcing her status within the government: she was not just a concubine or an empress in title alone. In matters of state, her presence was expected and her opinions were heard.

The foreign minister, a Denobulan named Rhox, introduced the next item on the meeting's agenda. "The Breen ambassador has been complaining publicly that we're selling weapons and ships to the Cardassian Union. I've prepared a statement of denial we can transmit to our embassies in—"

"Unnecessary," Spock said. "Ambassador Tren is correct: we have provided ships and small arms to the Cardassians, to aid them in their border conflict against the Tholian Assembly." Howls of angry protest swelled and crashed like a wave against Spock's unyielding wall of cool reserve.

Searching the faces gathered around the table, Marlena saw only one that mirrored Spock's serene visage: Grand Admiral Zhao Sheng's.

Rhox's voice cut through the din of shouting. "Your Majesty, I don't understand. My ministry has no knowledge of any such arrangement with the Cardassian Union. Who negotiated this deal?"

"I did," Spock said. "On behalf of Legate Zaris, Ambassador Dakar accepted my offer several weeks ago. The first shipments of small arms are en route to Cardassia Prime now."

More raised voices bled together into cacophony. Again Spock remained aloof from the choir of pitched emotions. Order was restored when Zhao slammed his palm on the tabletop. The crack of impact echoed in the silence that followed it.

Turning toward Spock, Zhao asked in a politely restrained baritone, "Your Majesty, may I inquire what precautions you would like Starfleet to take to prevent the Cardassians from turning our largesse against us?"

"None at this time, Admiral."

Nodding, Zhao pressed on. "As you wish, my liege. But may I remind Your Majesty, the Cardassians have long coveted our colony on Bajor. Newly armed and encouraged, they might see our noble generosity as an invitation to take that which has not been offered."

"Perhaps," Spock said. "But this pact was struck in good faith, Admiral. I do not wish to provoke the Cardassian Union by impugning its honor after the fact, either in the form of preemptive action or broken promises."

Zhao nodded. "Understood, Majesty. For my own edification, can I expect to receive an accounting of what vessels and arms have been transferred?"

"Yes, Admiral. Let me assure you, and all the other esteemed members of this cabinet, I did not act in haste or exuberance. I placed strict limits on the types and quantities of ships and matériel made available to the Cardassians. They likely will need every last piece of what they have acquired to contain the threat to their space posed by the Tholian Assembly."

Foreign Minister Rhox interjected, "The Tholians will see this as a provocation, Majesty. Your predecessor's incursions into the Taurus Reach have already stoked the Tholians' fury; this will fan its flames."

"Irrelevant," Spock said. "The Tholians are mired in a full-scale war with the Klingon Empire for control of the Taurus Reach. By forcing them to divert resources to maintain their status quo with the Cardassian Union, we can undermine the Tholians' control over key shipping lanes, ensuring we retain access to several of our more remote possessions."

Smiling as if to conceal his frustration, Rhox replied, "Yes, Majesty, but arming the Cardassians is hardly—"

"The Emperor has spoken," Zhao said, cutting Rhox's reply short.

A deathly pall descended on the room. Spock nodded his thanks to Zhao, who responded in kind. Sounding as calm and untroubled as ever, Spock asked the room, "What is the next item on the agenda?"

Grand Admiral Zhao replied, "News of civil unrest within the Romulan Star Empire, Majesty. We can use this opportunity to expand our holdings in the Glintara Sector. If I may direct your attention to the star map on screen one . . ."

The rest of the meeting continued in a brisk,

professional manner, but the mood of fear remained, tugging like an undertow, pulling all opinions closer to those favored by the Emperor.

Watching her lord and husband preside over his cabinet, Marlena frowned. *So, my love,* she brooded. *You're not such a stranger to tyranny, after all.*

Riding in the secure turbolift to the imperial residence, Spock felt Marlena's stare on the back of his neck. Knowing she would interpret even a casual moment of eye contact as an invitation to speak, he glanced over his shoulder at her.

"You know Zhao and the others were right about Cardassia," she said.

Facing forward, Spock replied, "In what regard?"

"Arming them is dangerous," Marlena said, "no matter what precautions you take or how many limits you impose. What if the Cardassians reverse-engineer our technology and start mass-producing it?"

"I fully expect them to do so," Spock said.

His answer stunned Marlena into a momentary silence, during which the only sound was the mellisonant hum of the ascending turbolift.

"So you don't care that the Cardassians might make a play for the Bajor and Kalandra sectors?"

Stealing another look at his wife, Spock said, "My long-term plans depend on it." The turbolift slowed and stopped. The doors opened, and Spock stepped into their home's foyer as he continued. "I have armed them more than sufficiently to repel the Tholians' incursions. It will be only a matter of time before they move against our possessions in that region."

A pair of Vulcan guards defending the inner door lifted their fists to their armored breasts in salute as Spock and Marlena passed them and entered the residence. As the doors clacked shut behind Marlena, she said, "If you know the Cardassians will act against us, why give them that kind of advantage?"

Spock led her to the dining room, where a buffet-style lunch had been set out for them. He chose a plate and filled it with a variety of fruits and vegetables as he answered his wife. "I have created the monster I need," he said. "In order to bring about my intended endgame, I need to foster an alliance between the Cardassian Union and the Klingon Empire."

Filling her own plate, Marlena asked, "Why those two powers?"

"Separately, neither is strong enough to challenge us," Spock said. "United, however, they might be able to defeat a weakened version of the Terran Empire."

Spearing some choice cuts of rare red meat, Marlena asked, "Why, exactly, would we want that?"

"Because an alliance between those two powers would bring out the worst qualities in both," Spock explained. "More than any other political pairing I can imagine in this part of space, the Cardassians and Klingons will exacerbate each other's worst tendencies. Though they will both see such an alliance as a means to an end, neither will realize until too late how incompatible their worldviews are."

Shaking her head, Marlena asked, "So what? If they fall to bickering after we've been swept off the map, what difference will it make?"

"In the short term, none," Spock admitted. "But in

the long run it will be the most important element of my plan." He regarded Marlena with an air of quiet confidence. "Their alliance will be doomed from its inception. By aligning against us, they will sow the seeds of their own destruction—and ensure our victory."

2280

29

A Promise Denied

Marlena's heart broke as her gaze swept over a sea of dirty faces, dark with blood and grime and fear, gaunt with hunger and sickness. The stench of unwashed bodies and untreated wounds was thick in the summer swelter of Iadara's equatorial latitudes, and everywhere Marlena looked she saw another living portrait of suffering and deprivation.

Most of the refugees huddled under makeshift shelters. They were hiding from a steady deluge of tepid rain that did little to wash away the pervasive stink engulfing the city. The planet's nominal capital, Akabar, had been little more than a sleepy coastal town before it was swamped with survivors displaced from the Terran Empire's colony on Galen, a world caught in the brutal crossfire of the Cardassian-Tholian border conflict.

Bedraggled individuals pushed to the front of the crowds lining the heavily guarded main street, on which Spock and Marlena walked surrounded by a phalanx of armored Vulcan elite troops.

Isolated voices pierced the sorrowful cries of the throng.

"Help us, Emperor Spock!"

"Save us, Majesty!"

"Please, Majesty, take pity on us . . ."

None of the entreaties seemed to move Spock, but each desperate plea for succor brought tears of rage and grief to Marlena's eyes. She grasped Spock's arm as they walked together. "Can't we do something, Spock?"

"We are doing what we can," he said. "This world is far from the core systems. It will take time for aid to arrive."

News of the unfolding tragedy on Iadara had motivated Marlena to press for a state visit to the planet. She had expected Spock to reject her suggestion; instead, he had embraced it, citing an urgent need to bolster citizens' confidence that the Terran Empire remained serious about defending its border colonies and keeping its promise to provide aid to its people.

To that end, several members of Spock's cabinet had accompanied them on this impromptu foray to the edge of a war zone, and they were trailed by a battalion of attachés and press liaisons who would ensure that news of the Emperor's visit to Iadara was disseminated in the most flattering possible light.

As they passed a pavilion whose flaps were folded shut, Marlena caught the high-pitched cries of children from inside the ramshackle structure. Ignoring the requests of her bodyguards and Spock's advisers, she detoured off the street and strode purposefully inside the pavilion.

A stench of disease and decay overwhelmed her. Her eyes adjusted to the deep shadows spawned by the enclosure's few weak light sources. A handful of badly fatigued doctors and nurses drifted half-conscious through their rounds. Rows of beds placed head-to-head filled almost every square meter of floor space, leaving barely enough room for narrow aisles between them.

Lying in the beds were scores of children. Emaciated

and pale, bloodied and burned; some were all but naked, and all of them shivered despite the heat.

Spock entered the pavilion and stood behind Marlena. His expression didn't change, but she was certain she felt him tense at the gruesome spectacle.

Marlena pointed at a passing nurse, whose uniform was stained with dirt and bodily emissions. "You," she said to the Bolian woman. "Come here. Now." As soon as the nurse was in front of her, Marlena gestured at the ranks of children in their beds. "Why are these children left in such squalor?"

The nurse replied with more anger than Marlena was accustomed to hearing. "Squalor? These children are receiving the best care we have. If you want to see *squalor*, Majesty, I suggest you visit the men's ward on the next block."

Placing a hand on Marlena's shoulder, Spock interjected, "She is correct. Iadara is facing acute shortages of food, potable water, medicine, and basic supplies." To the captain of his elite guard, a middle-aged Vulcan named Torov, Spock said, "Contact Captain Riley. *Enterprise* and all ships in its battle group are to begin manufacturing blankets, modular shelter components, and basic medicines immediately. I also want nine million liters of water beamed down by tomorrow at thirteen hundred hours, and a team of engineers to upgrade the city's sewage- and water-treatment systems."

Torov lifted his arm in a salute. "Yes, Majesty!" Then he turned away, opened his communicator, and began relaying Spock's orders to the small armada of Starfleet vessels in orbit.

Kneeling beside the closest bed, Marlena asked the nurse, "Where are these children's parents?"

"Most are orphans, Majesty."

Marlena tenderly stroked a sweaty lock of dark hair from the brow of an unconscious little girl. In the tabula rasa of the child's face, Marlena saw the promise of something beautiful. Looking up at Spock, she said, "We should adopt one of these children." Gazing back down at the girl lost in her twilight slumber, Marlena added, "Maybe this little angel."

Lifting one eyebrow, Spock asked, "Why?"

"We lead by action," Marlena said. "If we take in one of the orphans of the war you helped start, we can set an example for others to follow."

Spock grimaced. "We can endorse and support an adoption program without directly participating in it."

A note of desperation crept into Marlena's voice. "Don't underestimate the value of a symbolic gesture, Spock. Think of what it would mean for the Empire to see you embrace one of your most vulnerable subjects as your own."

With the back of his hand, Spock gently stroked the face of the girl lying in front of Marlena. "Such a gesture might appear noble, but it would beg questions of favoritism. It would be more just to improve the conditions of all the refugees equally, rather than elevate one above the others to live as a political prop."

"That's not what I—"

Spock cut her off with a hard look. "We should go."

He led her out of the pavilion to the street. As they rejoined their retinue of armed protectors and career sycophants, Marlena stole a melancholy look back at the shelter of lost children. It felt as if part of her had been left behind there, at the little girl's bedside. Even though she loved Spock, she cursed him silently as she fell into step beside him, continuing their empty parade for the media.

He knew what I was asking for, she brooded. *But as always, he answers only what I say instead of what he knows I mean.*

For now the discussion was closed, but Marlena knew—as she was certain Spock did—that it was far from over.

2281

30

Sharper Than
a Serpent's Tooth

Amanda Grayson lay awake in bed beside her husband, feeling minutes bleed away while she waited for the Vulcan dawn to break like red thunder.

Lingering half awake in the nether hours, she felt anxious and alone. Sarek had grown distant in the years since his rapprochement with Spock en route to the Babel Conference. He no longer trusted her with access to his waking thoughts.

During the decades before he and his son reconciled, Sarek had trusted Amanda to keep the secrets revealed within the telepathic bond created by their marriage. They both knew if the Empress or other ambitious parties acquired confirmation of Vulcans' psionic gifts, it could lead to the extermination of Sarek's people. While Sarek used Amanda's connections to advance his political career, she kept his people's great secret to maintain a modicum of control over him—to make certain he placed the Empire's best interests ahead of Vulcan's.

Then he had met in secret with Spock, and afterward Amanda began to feel her hold on both of them slipping from her grasp.

The first crack in Sarek's psionic armor had appeared three years earlier, during his last phase of *Pon farr*. Linked in the heat of passion, Amanda had a fleeting glimpse of Sarek's inner mind, a hint of the secrets he harbored. Since that night, his control faltered sometimes when he slept. Amanda had learned that if she could hold herself in a twilight sleep while Sarek dreamed, she could steal fleeting peeks at the memories he had locked away from her.

Each new insight deepened Amanda's fear for the future. Something sinister was afoot. Almost immediately after Spock had usurped the throne from Empress Sato III, he had installed Sarek as the governor of Vulcan. At the time Amanda had welcomed Spock's action; blatant nepotism had long been a common practice within the Empire, and because Sato III had obstructed Sarek's career path out of spite, the appointment had seemed like a dutiful son's gracious gift to his father.

Now, however, lying awake in the deep watches of the night, Amanda wondered if Spock had installed his father not out of gratitude but as a prelude to a political realignment of the Empire.

She strained to see more, to seize hold of something concrete, but the details were hazy, lost in the fog of Sarek's subconscious. All she had was a feeling—an unshakable suspicion something terrible and seditious was imminent.

What could it be? Were father and son, governor and emperor, conspiring to visit Vulcan's long-simmering revenge upon Earth and humanity?

A single idea leaped from the darkest abyss of Sarek's mind into Amanda's thoughts. The notion itself was enough to terrify her, but the perfect certainty of Sarek's belief in it shook Amanda to her bones: *We will end the Empire.*

Madness! Amanda recoiled from Sarek and stumbled as she got out of bed.

It was so horrific as to be incomprehensible. Spock and Sarek were planning to destroy the Empire itself. She asked herself over and over, *Why?* No answers came. Only more confusion, more fear . . . and then came the fury of betrayal.

She backed away from her sleeping husband.

I'm a loyal citizen of the Empire, she reminded herself. *I won't let traitors tear down all that my people have built.* She resolved to act.

I need an ally strong enough to stop them, she reasoned, slipping out of the bedroom. *Someone who'll gain from seeing them fall.*

At once the answer came to her . . . and she smiled.

After listening to Amanda's tense account of a brewing conspiracy between Spock and Sarek, it was difficult for Marlena to feign disbelief; she had long known Spock and his father were in league to initiate sweeping political reforms. One look at her mother-in-law's face on the comm screen, however, told Marlena the less she shared with Amanda the better.

"How did you come by this information?" Marlena asked.

"That's not important," Amanda said.

Marlena sharpened her stare and her voice. "I think it is."

"You're married to a Vulcan, as I am," Amanda said. *"You know better than to ask a question whose answer cannot be spoken."*

Her implication was clear to Marlena: the telepathic connection of the marriage bond had made Amanda privy to Sarek's hidden agenda. Nodding in comprehension, Marlena said, "I understand."

"We need to move quickly," Amanda said, the cold fire of her anger palpable to Marlena even through the filter of a subspace channel. *"We can't sit back and let those green-blooded traitors deliver the Empire into bondage."*

Playing the part of the naïf, Marlena asked, "What would you have me do, Amanda? Most of Starfleet is loyal to Spock, and none of the planetary governors are willing to challenge him politically."

"That's because they're not in a position to stop him," Amanda said with a malevolent gleam in her eye. *"But you are."*

"Excuse me?"

"Listen to me," Amanda said, adopting a conspiratorial air. *"I have powerful friends on Earth and Andor. Loyal friends."* Flashing a thin smile, she added, *"They could be your friends, as well."*

"Meaning?"

"If you eliminate Spock, you could rule in his place—an Empress Regnant instead of a mere Empress Consort—and the Empire would once again kneel before a human monarch, as it should."

Marlena loved Spock and believed in his vision of the future, but the siren song of absolute power called to her. *Empress Marlena—a mistress with no master,* she thought, blushing with pride.

"We should talk in person," Marlena said. "When can you visit Earth?"

"In a week's time."

"Can I meet with one of your Andorian friends?"

Amanda made a small nod and smiled. *"That can be arranged."*

"I look forward to your visit."

"As do I . . . Majesty."

"Most troubling," Spock said.

The recording of Marlena's conversation with Amanda left little room for Spock to doubt the gravity of the situation. It called for swift action.

He had hoped Sarek would be able to maintain enough control over his link with Amanda to avoid revealing too much of the plan to her. Unfortunately, his father's physician had found early warning signs of Bendii Syndrome in Sarek's brain chemistry shortly after his last *Pon farr*. Though the damage to Sarek's cerebral tissue was still too slight to pose any risk of him projecting his hidden emotions onto others, it apparently had made it much more difficult for Sarek to conceal anything from Amanda within their marriage bond.

Spock had been sworn to secrecy by his father; he had not discussed Sarek's infirmity with anyone—not even Marlena—and saw no reason to break his pledge now. The cause of this lapse in secrecy was no longer an issue; only its effect was.

Sequestered with Spock in the privacy of their bedroom, Marlena sat on the bed and watched him stare out the window at the gardens behind the imperial palace. She had been somber ever since bringing him a data card containing the recorded conversation. In a small voice, she asked, "What do we do now?"

"That is a difficult question to answer," Spock said.

"The threat my mother poses cannot be ignored. Her family is wealthy and connected to many of the Empire's most powerful individuals, families, and corporations."

Marlena got up from the bed and padded in cautious steps toward Spock. "Can't she be persuaded to use those connections to help you?"

Shaking his head, Spock replied, "Doubtful. She is and always has been a loyal citizen of the Empire. I do not think she will act against it—not even for her husband or her son."

"If that's true, she could ruin everything," Marlena said.

"Agreed." Spock kept his voice level and his chin up even as he struggled to contain a crushing flood of despair.

Emotion is a cue, but it does not serve me, he admonished himself. *I must control it as I must control my destiny. Logic alone must dictate my response.*

He repeated his mantra, but his emotions refused to be yoked.

Marlena wrapped her hands around his left arm and nestled her head against his shoulder. Her presence was quiet but strong, concerned but not afraid. Spock found the balance in her countenance reassuring.

"My logic is clouded," he confessed. "I ask your advice. What action should I take?"

She looked up at him with clear and determined eyes. "If Amanda can't be swayed to our way of thinking, then you must do what is in the best interest of the people of the Empire. The good of the many—"

"Outweighs the needs of the few."

"Or the one," Marlena said.

Spock nodded with grim acceptance. "I will do what must be done."

Sarek turned off the comm unit on his living room wall and stood in silence.

The voice of his aide, Lokor, echoed in his thoughts, but the words still did not feel real; the message they conveyed was too terrible for him to accept.

"The shuttle exploded en route to Earth," Lokor had said. *"Preliminary sensor sweeps indicate it was an accidental warp-core breach. The crew likely had no warning and no time to attempt a correction or evacuation."* Almost as an afterthought, the young man had added, *"There were no survivors, Governor."*

Long rays of fading crimson slashed through the blinds shielding the windows. Outside, another day was dying, the sun a lonely ember sinking into a spreading sea of black.

Inside the home of Sarek, silence reigned.

He wandered, mute and alone, through empty rooms. Though he plodded in graceless steps, he felt weightless and insubstantial. No thoughts formed in his mind. Introspection revealed nothing but a gray void.

The chambers of his dwelling felt unfamiliar. It was as if he had never lived there, never owned any of those possessions, never known the place at all.

Drifting back into the main room, he was drawn to the wide, westward-facing window. He opened its blinds and stared out, past the towers and stalagmite-inspired cliff dwellings of ShiKahr, toward the ragged line of mountaintops on the horizon. Vulcan's primary star, Nevasa, vanished behind them. A ruby-hued flare pulsed low in the sky . . . and then it faded away, vanished into darkness.

Sarek spun away from the window and flew into a rage, hurling antique vases against the walls, smashing priceless statues on the hard stone floor, battering the comm panel's screen with his bare fists. With strength fueled by grief and madness, he lifted a stone coffee table and launched it at the picture window. The table shattered but barely blemished the window, which was made of transparent aluminum. Chunks of rock scattered around Sarek's feet.

He fell to his hands and knees, gasping for breath and fighting to hold back hot tears of bitter sorrow.

My wife . . . my love . . . my Amanda . . . you're gone.

2282

31

Caveat Vendor

"Sit down," Kor said to Lorp, a fat Ferengi black marketeer. "You're late."

The corpulent businessman cast nervous looks at the heavily armed Klingon warriors flanking Kor, then he pulled back a chair and grunted with exertion as he awkwardly settled his bulk onto it. "Thank you, General," he said.

Two more Ferengi stayed close behind Lorp, their hands resting on holstered plasma pistols while their eyes darted furtively back and forth at Kor's men.

Kor scowled at his guests. The Ferengi were a repulsive race, in his opinion. Their noses looked ready-made for rooting in filth, and their oversized ears and propensity for flinching made him think of easily spooked rodents.

"You promised me information," Kor said.

Lorp flashed a grin of fearsome, jagged teeth—his species' only handsome feature, in Kor's opinion. "Well, yes, I did, but I didn't come all the way to Cestus III to give it to you as a gift. First I believe you have something for me, hm?"

"I did not forget." Kor nodded at the warrior on his right side, who picked up a metallic case from the floor and laid it flat on the table between Kor and Lorp.

Leaning forward, Kor opened the case and pushed it across the table to Lorp.

The Ferengi's beady eyes opened wide with avarice as he looked upon his payment: a complete set of holographic schematics for a cloaking device. "Yes," Lorp said, the word broadening his enormous snaggle-toothed grin. "This will fetch a very handsome price in certain sectors. Very handsome, indeed."

Reaching out, Kor pushed the case's lid shut. "Information. Now."

Lorp's grin became a grimace. He snapped his fingers and held up one hand. One of his men reached inside his jacket.

Both of Kor's men had their disruptors drawn and aimed before the Ferengi retainer could remove his hand from inside his coat. He froze in place.

"Gejh, K'mdek—stand down," Kor said. His men holstered their weapons. He nodded at the Ferengi retainer. "Proceed."

Moving with slowness born of caution, the Ferengi aide removed a pale blue data rod from his jacket pocket and handed it to Lorp, who passed it to Kor.

"As promised, General," Lorp said.

Kor reached inside his tunic and retrieved a device for reading optolythic data rods—a Cardassian technology that was prized because data could be written to such rods only once and thereafter could not be altered. The Cardassian government produced the rods only as it needed them, and they were very difficult to counterfeit. Consequently, they had become a favored means of encoding data that needed to be couriered by unreliable third parties—such as the Ferengi.

Even as Kor skimmed through the rod's contents,

Lorp seemed intent on narrating it for him from memory.

"Lots of contraband and strange materials moving around," Lorp said. "High-tech computer parts, construction materials, exotic elements. Starfleet's making deals, buying stuff from smugglers it could get for nothing at home."

"I see that," Kor said. He had suspected something odd was transpiring in the space beyond the Taurus Reach, but he had not expected to uncover a conspiracy as far-reaching as this seemed to be. Starfleet was supporting some kind of secret operation, using Orions and Ferengi as cutouts to hide its activities from its own chain of command. "Where is Starfleet taking these things?"

"An abandoned space station," Lorp said, "orbiting a planetoid on the edge of the Mutara Nebula."

Kor nodded. "Yes, the old Regula I station. I know it."

"Lots of money involved in this deal," Lorp said. "Big profits. Whoever's behind this is well capitalized."

"Indeed," Kor said. He removed the data rod from its reader and tucked both into pockets inside his tunic. He flashed a disingenuous smile at Lorp. "Thank you for being so thorough in your research."

Grinning, Lorp replied, "You're quite wel—" He froze in mid-sentence as Kor's men drew their disruptors and fired.

The barrage was deafening, but only for a moment.

Lorp's henchmen were slain first. They fell in smoking heaps with their plasma pistols only half drawn from their holsters.

Then both of Kor's warriors shot at Lorp. His charred bulk was knocked backward. He and his chair struck the ground with a loud slap.

The screeching of disruptors ceased, and once again the backwater dive bar fell silent. That was the Gorn's one trait Kor appreciated: as long as the shooting didn't cause any property damage or hurt any of their people, they didn't give a damn what aliens did to each other.

He pushed back his chair, stood, and picked up the case from the table. Stepping over the smoldering corpses of the Ferengi, he said to his men, "Now there are three fewer people in the galaxy who know what we know; there is no chance of the Ferengi reselling it to anyone else; and the secrets of the Empire remain safe." Leading his men out of the bar, he added with a fierce grin, "This, my friends, is what is known as a win-win situation."

2283

32

A Serviceable Villain

Six months after the surgery, Lurqal still found herself surprised by her reflection.

Catching sight of her image in the mirror of her quarters' bedroom, the cruel irony of her circumstances almost made her laugh.

It had been nearly six years since her narrow escape from the Starfleet starbase known as Vanguard. She and Turag, a representative from Imperial Intelligence, had been sent there to strike a deal with Commodore Reyes, who had captured a member of a precursor race known as the Shedai and transformed its immense power into a weapon that could shatter worlds.

The terms of an agreement between Reyes and the Klingon Empire were still being negotiated when Vanguard was attacked by one of the starships under its authority, its secret weapon was sabotaged from within, and the Shedai trapped in its core was unleashed to gut the station like a bonefish. Finally, a Tholian warfleet launched a surprise attack that reduced Vanguard and its yoked Shedai to ionized gas and radiation.

Turag, Reyes, and just about every other living thing on Vanguard perished that day, but Lurqal—burned, broken, and bloody—refused to die.

As the station imploded, she stole a warp-capable

shuttlecraft and escaped moments before Starbase 47 was consumed in the Tholians' brutal assault.

Lurqal returned to Qo'noS, but the limitations of Klingon medical science left her body deformed and her face disfigured. Unable to die with honor, she resigned herself to living in exile as a freak and outcast, an object of derision for the young, healthy, and beautiful.

Years passed.

Then, nine months ago, an agent of Imperial Intelligence sought out Lurqal and offered her an assignment—as a spy to be sent in human guise to infiltrate a secret Terran Empire research laboratory led by Dr. Carol Marcus, the scientist who had created the fearsome technology on Vanguard.

Eager for a chance to return to duty, Lurqal accepted the mission.

The same military surgeons whose lack of regard for the Empire's wounded warriors had left her shattered and ruined as a Klingon transformed her in three months into the very image of human feminine beauty. Symmetrical and elegantly curved, tall and delicately featured, Lurqal gazed in shock at her new form.

Under the skin she remained Klingon, but a slew of subtle implants would fool the majority of sensors and medical scanners she was likely to encounter while living in Terran space. Hidden in her personal effects were several containers of *tuQloS* pills, which would enable her to draw nourishment from cooked food.

She stroked a lock of her long, auburn hair from her face and tucked it behind one ear. Staring at her reflection, she mused, *I don't know who you are.*

Her door signal buzzed. Straightening her posture, she said, "Come."

The door slid open, revealing the smiling face of Carol Marcus. "Doctor Sandesjo," she said, stepping into the doorway. "Welcome aboard."

"Please," Lurqal said, mustering a disarming smile, "call me Anna."

"Fine," Marcus said. "And you can call me Carol." Tilting her head toward the corridor, she added, "Would you like a brief tour of the facility?"

Lurqal nodded. "I'd love one."

Marcus led her through the passageways of space station Regula I, which were crowded with white-garbed civilian scientists. "It's a good thing you got here when you did," Marcus said. "We've been without a good computer engineer for a few months, and everything's running behind as a result."

"What happened to your last computer engineer?"

The question darkened Marcus's mood. "A tragic accident," she said. "He was installing some new cables on a lower deck when an old plasma conduit ruptured inside his crawl space."

Good, Lurqal thought. *They don't know he was assassinated to set the stage for my insertion.* Wrinkling her face to convey shock and dismay, she replied, "My God, that's terrible."

They arrived at what Lurqal had expected would be the upper deck of the station's operations level. Marcus and her team had transformed the open space into their primary laboratory.

"This is where the magic happens," Marcus said. "Tonight at dinner I'll introduce you to everyone, but I can point out a few of our more notable team members from here." She pointed around the room. "Those are Doctors Tarcoh, Gek, and Koothrappali." Gesturing at a much younger human man with curly blond hair, she added, "And that's my son, David. He's one of our project leaders."

Her son? Interesting. "What project is he leading?"

"That's classified." With a gentle touch on Lurqal's elbow, Marcus added, "We should move along and finish getting you settled."

"Of course."

The blond scientist led Lurqal to a turbolift that took them down to one of the station's lower levels. Along the way to their next destination, Marcus pointed out the various specialized labs her team had set up, and she waxed eloquent about many of their experimental new technologies. Lurqal noted it all for the report she would be expected to submit to Imperial Intelligence via secure subspace comm.

She interrupted one of Marcus's prideful spiels to observe, "There don't appear to be any military personnel anywhere on this station."

Marcus smiled. "That's right."

"Isn't that dangerous? I mean, we're out here in the middle of nowhere, working on all this top-secret stuff. What if the Klingons or the Tholians try to take over the station?"

"I'd pity them," Marcus said. She grasped Lurqal's shoulder in a manner the Klingon spy could only imagine was meant to be reassuring rather than a gross violation of her personal space. "I know it looks like we're alone, but trust me—we're not. Now, let's focus on more important matters." She handed Lurqal a small stack of colored data cards. "The blue one is your meal card for the station's commissary. The red one is for picking up clean clothes, bedsheets, and bath linens from the supply office. Use the green one for refills on personal supplies, and the yellow one's for accessing the entertainment library: books, music, vids—pretty much everything from the recorded history of the Terran Empire."

"Great," Lurqal said, holding up the cards. "My cup runneth over."

"I have a dozen other places I need to be right now. Can you find your own way back to your quarters?"

Nodding, Lurqal said, "Sure, no problem."

"Thanks," Marcus said, already hurrying away. "And welcome to the team!"

Lurqal waved good-bye to Marcus and then navigated the simple path back to her assigned quarters. Her official duties were not scheduled to begin until the next day after she had "settled in," as the humans were fond of saying, so she decided it would be a good time to check in with her handler, who was nearby awaiting her comm signal on the cloaked cruiser *I.K.S. Zin'za.*

She locked her door. From her travel bag she took a surveillance-detection tool disguised as part of her makeup kit. Two careful scans revealed no sign of monitoring devices in her quarters. Satisfied her abode was secure, she assembled several other items from her travel kit into a secure comm unit. The pieces fit together in a matter of seconds, and she activated the device.

It hummed for a moment—then it crackled with static interference. She adjusted its settings in search of a clear frequency but found only more noise.

Running a diagnostic, Lurqal suspected the comm was about to deliver her some bad news. She was right.

Jammed, she fumed as she saw the results of the unit's

feedback analysis. *The entire station's surrounded by a scattering field.* She switched off the device.

There would be no unauthorized transmissions in or out of the station as long as the scattering field remained active. *That explains why this place is such a well-kept secret,* Lurqal realized. Then she reconsidered Marcus's warning: *I know it looks like we're alone, but trust me—we're not.* Looking out her window, Lurqal wondered where a Starfleet ship could be hiding—and then the slow turning of the station brought the Mutara Nebula into view.

This op just got a lot harder, Lurqal brooded. *And a whole lot riskier.*

2284

33

Hearts and Minds

The echoes of Spock's voice faded away into the vastness of the Common Forum, and for a moment stretched by anticipation all was silent. He had delivered his proclamation of citizens' rights, uninterrupted, to a sea of stunned faces. It was done now, and it could not be undone, and there was naught to do but wait in the heavy swell of anxious quietude for the reaction.

A roar of applause surged up from the members of the Forum, a wave of sound like floodwater breaking against a dam. Exultant and energized, the thousands of gathered representatives from worlds throughout the Empire stood and applauded and chanted his name with almost idolatrous fervor. Stomping feet rumbled the hall. Its lower level was packed on three sides with tiers of seats for the Forum members, and its spacious balconies served as a gallery for citizen observers, or for the Senate during joint sessions of the legislature such as this one.

Faces grim and forbidding communicated the Senate's reaction. Like mannequins of stone, its members looked down with ashen-faced horror at the populist turn their government had just taken. A few shook their heads in disbelief. Spock presumed they were unable to comprehend why he would have chosen to give more power to the citizenry than to himself. In all likelihood, he knew, they would never understand. Regardless, the one power Spock still reserved for himself was that his word carried the absolute force of law.

He let the applause wash over him for a moment, not because he enjoyed it but because it would help cement this moment in the minds of those hundreds of billions of citizens throughout the Empire who were watching it on the subspace feed. This was a threshold moment for their society, and he knew it would be important for them to have the requisite time to absorb its full importance. Nearly a minute elapsed as the cheering and applause continued unabated. Sensing the moment had run its course, Spock bowed his head to the legislature. As thousands of arms were extended in salutary reply, he withdrew from the podium in the center of the Forum and departed, surrounded by his elite Vulcan guard, through the rear exit.

Marlena was waiting for him in the turbolift, which carried them to their private residence on the uppermost level. She clutched his arm tenderly. "You were magnificent," she said softly. He glanced in her direction and saw her smile.

"Most kind," he said, his old habit of understated humility intact despite more than seven years of imperial privilege.

The turbolift doors opened, and they exited to their airy, sunlit residence. Sarek stood in the doorway to their parlor, flanked by two more of the elite Vulcan guards. "Your address went well," Sarek said as Spock and Marlena passed him.

"As well as could be expected," Spock replied over his shoulder to Sarek, who followed him into the parlor.

The guards closed the double doors behind Sarek, giving Spock at least a modicum of privacy with his wife and father. Marlena and Spock sat next to one another in matching, heavy wooden chairs. Sarek sat to Spock's right, at the corner of a long sofa. All three of them were aware of the servants hovering just out of sight at all times, and they kept their voices low. "You've won the hearts of the people," Sarek said. "But the elites are already conspiring against you."

"Enemies are a consequence of politics," Spock said.

Folding his hands in his lap, Sarek replied, "Your reign will not last forever, Spock. The most probable consequence of your latest action is that you will be assassinated by someone acting on behalf of your political opponents."

"I am aware of my rivals' ambitions," Spock said. He beckoned a servant as he continued. "However, I do not consider them to be a risk." A female servant unobtrusively took her place in front of the trio. To her, Spock said, "*Plasska* tea, service for three." With a genteel murmur of "Yes, Majesty," the servant slipped away.

Sarek waited until the woman was well out of earshot before he spoke. "Spock, the threat posed by your rivals is not a trivial one. If you are killed or deposed, your progressive regime will almost certainly be replaced by one of a decidedly reactionary temperament."

The cool demeanors of the two Vulcan men made Marlena's undercurrent of anger all the more palpable by comparison. "His assassins will not succeed," she said to Sarek. "I will see to that."

Expressing his incredulity with a raised eyebrow, Sarek asked, "And how will you do that, my dear? With what resources?"

"I am not without means, Sarek," she retorted. "This would not be the first—" Spock silenced her outburst with a gentle press of his palm on the back of her hand. Marlena took his admonition to heart and pursed her lips while suppressing the rest of what she had intended to say.

It was Spock's opinion that Sarek need never be told of the Tantalus field device, or of the role it had played in Spock's assumption of power. It had been a terrible risk revealing its existence to Saavik, but Spock's long-term plans for her had made it crucial to test her loyalty as early as possible.

Silence reigned over the parlor until the tea was delivered and poured. All three of them sipped from their cups and nodded their approval. Then Sarek set down his cup and, once again with a conspirator's hushed voice, continued the conversation. "Let us assume your wife is correct, and assassins pose no threat to you. Even if you succeed in your goal of abolishing the Empire, once you place its fate into the hands of a representative government, it will almost certainly be corrupted from within. The Senate will be first among those looking to consolidate their power; they will learn how to manipulate popular sentiment and fill the Common Forum with their own partisans. Gradually at first, then more boldly, they will steer the republic back toward totalitarianism. Ultimately, they will elect one of their own as dictator-for-life . . . and the Empire you are laboring to end will be reborn. The rights you granted to the people will be revoked; they will resist, and rebel, and be brutally suppressed. Civil war will rend the Empire, and its enemies will exploit that division to conquer us outright. All that you have done will have been for naught, my son."

Spock finished his own tea and set down the empty cup. "All that you predict, I have anticipated," he said. Leaning back in his chair, he continued. "That is why the republic must be destroyed by its enemies *before* it lapses back into empire."

The statement seemed to perplex Sarek. "What beneficial end would that accomplish?"

"Liberty crushed by one's own government carries the poison of betrayal," Spock said. "If so extinguished, it will be almost impossible to rekindle, and our cause shall be lost. But freedom lost to conquest focuses the people's anger outward, and unites them in common cause against a foreign oppressor."

"You intend to let the republic fall?" Sarek asked. Upon Spock's nod of confirmation, he continued. "A dangerous gamble. What if such a rebellion fails to materialize? Or simply fails? Staking the future of our civilization on the success of a future insurgency seems a most foolish proposition."

As Spock rose from his chair, Sarek did likewise. Spock turned toward Marlena. "Will you excuse us a moment?" Marlena cast wary looks at both Spock and Sarek, and then she got up and walked with prideful calm from the parlor.

Once she was in the next room, and the door closed behind her, Spock said loudly, for the servants lurking in the wings, "Leave us." Like spooked mice, the domestics scurried away. A clatter of closing doors marked their exits.

Able to speak in full privacy at last, Spock still whispered. "Steps will be taken to ensure the success of the rebellion," he said. "The groundwork for an insurgency is being laid now, while we have time to prepare in safety. If my plan is successful, the Klingon-led occupation of the former Terran Empire will last less than one hundred fifteen Earth years."

With unconcealed suspicion, Sarek said, "And if it fails?"

"Then several millennia of Vulcan and human scientific achievement will be lost forever."

"And what are these steps you're going to take?"

"Not I," Spock said. "You."

34

Omega's Genesis

After spending most of seven years as a virtual prisoner in the imperial residence, Emperor Spock appreciated returning to a starship. Recent refits had made them faster, more comfortable, and more powerful than ever before.

At his behest, the *Enterprise,* now in its seventh year under the command of Captain Kevin Riley, had been standing by to beam up Spock from the palace after his meeting with Sarek. With the Empire devolving into chaos following his declaration of rights and freedoms for the people, it had seemed an opportune time to slip away. During his absence, Marlena would reign as Empress, freeing him to make this journey incognito.

Liberating as his departure was, it carried an element of risk he hadn't faced in close to seventeen years. For the first time since he had slain Captain Kirk, he was without the protection of the Tantalus field device, which remained safely concealed in his and Marlena's private quarters on Earth. Fortunately, the judicious use of the device over the years had cultivated such a profound culture of fear with respect to Spock's purported psionic powers that it was unlikely he would be challenged during this brief sojourn from the throne.

The boatswain's whistle sounded over the ship's intercom.

"Attention, all hands. Stand by for secure transport. Captain Riley, please report to the bridge."

As the channel closed, the door signal buzzed. Turning to face the door, Spock said, "Enter."

The door slid open, and the ship's first officer, Commander Saavik, stepped inside. "Your Majesty," she said with a reverent bow of her head, then she looked up and delivered the formal salute. He noted she avoided making eye contact with him, and her demeanor seemed stiff.

"At ease," he said. "Is it time?"

"Yes, Majesty. The facility has been prepared, and a secure transport conduit is standing by."

"Then let us proceed."

Saavik nodded and led the way out the door into the corridor. Spock followed her. A pair of his elite Vulcan bodyguards fell into step a few paces behind him. Moving until he was almost parallel with Saavik, he said in a confidential tone, "You seem preoccupied."

"Not at all, Majesty," she said as she stepped into an open and waiting turbolift car. He and his guards followed her in.

The ride was brief. As soon as they stepped off into another empty, sealed-off corridor, Spock subtly signaled his guards to fall back a few paces to give him privacy. "You are uncomfortable with the proclamation I made on Earth."

"I have said no such—"

"Prevarication does not suit you. Speak plainly. I would know your thoughts."

Her apprehension was palpable. She eyed him with guarded suspicion. "Do I address the Emperor?"

"You address your mentor, and your Academy sponsor."

That seemed to reassure her. Glancing over her shoulder to make certain the bodyguards would not overhear her, she whispered to Spock, "Undermining your own power was an error."

Her assertion intrigued him. "How so?"

They turned a corner toward the transporter room. "The Empire and its ruler are one," she said. "By diminishing yourself, you diminish the Empire. You invite conquest."

"Which is stronger, Saavik? One man, or ten men?" He let the analogy sink in for a few seconds. Before she could answer, he continued. "An empire that derives its strength and authority from one person alone is weak, because its foundation is too narrow. One whose power derives from the mutual consent of the many rests upon a broad and unshakable base."

"Which is stronger, Your Majesty? A sheet of metal foil twenty meters square, or the blade of the knife that slices through it?" She paused a few meters shy of the transporter room door, and Spock and his guards halted with her. "Diffusing the power of the Empire throughout its people robs it of focus," she added. "A quality our enemies possess in abundance."

Spock considered her point. "When our enemies choose to conquer us," he said, "they will succeed. And it will be their undoing." He stepped ahead of her and led the way into the transporter room. An engineer manned the transporter console, and another pair of Spock's elite guards stood at attention, awaiting his arrival. He stepped onto the platform, accompanied by the two guards who had followed him through the corridors.

Saavik stood between Spock and the transporter operator. Arching one eyebrow, she asked, "Majesty, do you really believe conquering us would cause the fall of the Klingon Empire?"

With perfect surety, he replied, "It is inevitable."

Then, with a nod, the order was given, and Spock and his guards vanished into the white haze of the transporter beam.

Carol Marcus paced nervously inside the storage bay, awaiting the arrival of the most powerful VIP guest in the Empire. *Don't panic,* she kept telling herself. *It's a good proposal, he's a Vulcan, he'll see that what you're asking for is logical. . . . Don't panic.*

The transporter effect shimmered into existence just a few meters away from her. She froze in place and watched three Vulcanoid shapes materialize, one in front and two behind. As the sparkling glow faded away, she found herself face-to-face with Emperor Spock, the supreme ruler of the Terran Empire.

Though she had been taught as a child how to curtsey, she had never had any need to do so until this moment—and suddenly she found herself awkwardly wobbling over her own crossed feet. "Your Majesty," she said while looking at the floor. "Welcome to Regula."

Spock stepped toward her. "Thank you, Doctor Marcus." He looked around at their immediate surroundings. "Based on your preliminary report, I presume that *this* is not the second phase of your project."

"Certainly not," Marcus said, before adding, "Your Majesty." The Emperor's classically aloof Vulcan nature made it hard for her to tell if he was annoyed with her. She gestured toward the exit from this terminal chamber, which was located at the end of a long service corridor. "May I guide you through the rest of the facility?"

"By all means," he said.

They left the storage bay, their footsteps echoing crisply in the empty space. Indicating the drab, gray surfaces of the corridor, she noted, "It took the Imperial Corps of Engineers nine months to excavate the preliminary facility. Though it was a costly and time-consuming project, it was essential to—"

"I read your proposal for Project Genesis, Doctor," he said as they neared a T-shaped intersection. "It is not necessary for you to reiterate its contents."

Concealing her embarrassment, she replied, "Of course not, Your Majesty. My apologies. Obviously, you just want to know whether phase two was a success." At the intersection she turned right, stopped, and pivoted back to face Spock. "Well . . . you tell me."

The Emperor turned the corner and looked out upon Marcus's handiwork. True to his Vulcan heritage and his personal reputation, he showed no sign of surprise at the verdant splendor of the Genesis Cave. Kilometers across, the roughly ovoid excavation was teeming with vegetation. Ferns and fronds carpeted the lower half of the space, which was thick with stands of jungle trees whose branches were heavy with fruit. Flowers of variegated colors dotted the periphery of the enclosure at seemingly random intervals. Mist hung in gauzy layers, refracting light from the artificial solar generators in an adjacent cave, on the far side from where Marcus and

Spock now stood. Off to the right, in the distance, an enormous waterfall cascaded in snowy plumes over jagged rocks, its wholly natural appearance a testament to its meticulous engineering.

"It's self-contained and self-sustaining," she said. "All except the solar generators, which need to be refueled every sixty years." She waited for a reaction from Spock, but none came. "In transforming this limited volume of inanimate matter, the Genesis Wave was completely successful," she continued. "But to assess its full potential, we need to move on to phase three: a lifeless, geologically inactive planetoid. For that, we'll need an increase in our funding, and the services of an imperial starship, to help us seek out an appro—"

"No," Spock said.

His answer caught her off guard. "Excuse me?"

"Your request for funding and operational support is denied."

She folded her arms and reminded herself not to raise her voice. Though Spock seemed to be a benign and compassionate sovereign, she remained keenly aware he was still the Emperor—and that he could make her disappear with a single word. "May I ask why, Your Majesty?"

"For the same reason I terminated Operation Vanguard—what you propose is too dangerous. If I allow you to carry out your third-phase test, it will provoke an arms race and prematurely ignite our inevitable conflict with the Klingon Empire."

She knew he was right; the only reason she had dared to continue her work to this stage was because, unlike the opportunistic and belligerent Empress Sato III, Emperor Spock gave every indication of being a leader who would wield a power such as the Genesis Device wisely.

"But think of the potential, Your Majesty," she said, unable to give up on a project that had consumed the past eighteen years of her life. "We could transform dead worlds into new Class-M planets. We wouldn't have to compete with the Klingons for habitable worlds anymore."

"I am aware of its potential, Doctor, but the risks it carries are too great." He turned his head and looked again at the cave. "How many people will this facility support?"

Still reeling from the rejection, it took Marcus a moment to answer. "Indefinitely? Perhaps a few hundred. Why?"

"Because I want you to duplicate phase two of your project in a number of other sites throughout the Empire—sites whose locations will be known only to the two of us and to a handful of people who will be permanently attached to them."

She was confused now. "I thought you said you were terminating Project Genesis."

"I am," Spock said. "But your work will not go to waste. I need it—and you—for an infinitely more important project."

Alarmed but curious, she asked, "What kind of project?"

Spock met her questioning stare with his dark, hypnotic gaze. He replied somberly, "The future of our civilization."

2285

35

A World in Transition

Fingers brush across Lotok's graying temple. Thoughts half formed whisper from mind to mind, conveyed with equal parts urgency and discretion. Contact is fleeting and subtle, all but imperceptible, its gift unremarked, its purpose unquestioned. The mind-meld ends, and he looks at his grandson, Kerok; now they are co-conspirators, and there is much work to do.

Another dusky sunrise in ShiKahr, the cinnamon daybreak of dawn on Vulcan. Volkar rouses T'Len, his seven-year-old daughter, for school; their hands touch. He brushes a hair from her cheek. In a moment he shares the secret of a lifetime. Looking upon her sire with new eyes, T'Len understands.

Spock is summoning the future, and we must be ready for it.

A sullen storm front churns on the horizon, a dark stain on the crimson sky. Salok, a tenth-year *Kolinahr* adept, stands on a ledge near the peak of Mount Seleya. The crash of a far-off gong calls him to meditation. His walk across the bridge is long; his only companion is the wind, howling in minor chords, warm and rich with the clean smells of the deep desert.

In the Halls of Ancient Thought, he is handed his ceremonial sash. As the high priest lowers it into Salok's hands, they make contact. In between two more crashes of the gong, Salok sees the truth, shared by Emperor Spock with Govenor Sarek and passed on to a thousand more minds since: a vision of another reality, an incontrovertible mental image of a universe both like and unlike his own.

The knowledge comes with a price: a call to arms.

Salok is ready.

Rebellion. It's an idea, a concept, a meme.

Viruslike, it travels and seeks receptive hosts, vessels who will carry it, nurture it, spread it.

Freedom. It is contagious in its simplicity, incendiary in its potential, complicated and inherently contradictory. Logic demands it; without the freedom to explore new thoughts and new ideas, knowledge cannot advance; without intellectual freedom, civilization stagnates. Progress halts. Hope dies.

It is only the germ of an idea. But it is spreading.

L'Haan is a defender of the peace, a law enforcement officer, and until three days ago she had held no other loyalty than to the Empire. Then the Emperor's vision of the future touched her mind. Today she realizes the Empire is doomed, and Emperor Spock's dangerous vision is the way of tomorrow.

Her first duty now is to the people of Vulcan—and to the future. Time is short, and there are many minds to reach. Already she has encountered several who are already part of the movement. It is reassuring to know who her allies are, but theirs is an evangelical cause.

Success will be measured not in the depth of their personal commitment but in their ability to recruit others. And so she continues to search, to seek out those individuals who seem most likely to sympathize with Spock's plan for the future.

She sees the man she has been looking for. His name is V'Nem. He is a professor at the Vulcan Science Academy, known for being slightly unorthodox. Statistically speaking, he is likely to be a receptive candidate for The Touch.

L'Haan concocts an excuse to detain him for just a moment. She demands to see what he has hidden in the folds of his loose desert robe. Predictably, he resists, citing the new imperial guarantees against warrantless search and seizure. It's a flimsy pretext for her to accuse him of resisting arrest, but it will do. She grabs his wrist for only a moment, long enough to reach out and try to make contact with his thoughts, to tell him to remain calm, that he is in no danger—

He is a Romulan. An infiltrator. A spy.

V'Nem reaches for a concealed weapon.

L'Haan attacks, a knifing blow of her stiffened hand against V'Nem's neck, which snaps instantly. His head lolls toward the ground, a limp and heavy mass with dull eyes. She releases his wrist and lets his body fall into the street.

A crowd gathers. There will be an inquiry, but even after Spock's legal reforms she still has the power of authority, the protection of being an officer of the law. In short order she will be vindicated, even applauded for exposing and disposing of a Romulan agent. The attention this will bring her will prevent her from spreading Spock's message for a few weeks, or longer.

This was a mistake of youthful inexperience, she knew. *In the future, I must be more circumspect in my actions.*

T'Meri slips out of her dormitory at the Vulcan Science Academy and steals away in the dark predawn hours. Halfway across the city, the young Vulcan woman finds her way to an unmarked door below street level. She does not knock; instead she scrapes her boot against the base of the door for a few seconds, then stands where she knows the security camera can see her clearly. The rust-mottled portal opens with fluid ease and surprisingly little noise. She slips inside, and the door is shut quickly after her.

T'Prynn is waiting for her. The older Vulcan woman is ex-Starfleet and, from what few fleeting personal glimpses T'Meri has had of T'Prynn's mind, privy to many terrible secrets. But the one she has shared most vividly with T'Meri is the one she received from Spock himself, of his mind-meld with the man from the alternate universe. She has imparted the vision to T'Meri so the youth can seek out others sympathetic to Spock's aims and pass it along to them, with the same directive. T'Meri has done exactly that.

She reaches up toward T'Prynn's face and gently rests her fingertips against the woman's smooth, pale skin. In turn, T'Prynn's fingers press delicately upon the side of T'Meri's bronze-hued face. Their minds touch, and T'Meri shows T'Prynn all the minds to whom she has conveyed Spock's message. T'Prynn is pleased—then she breaks the psychic link.

T'Meri opens her eyes and finds her face and T'Prynn's only a few centimeters apart. Their lips are parted and trembling with anticipation. The sensations are a mystery to T'Meri, whose next *Pon farr* is still four years away—until she realizes T'Prynn is hiding the fires of her own desire, and that some of that ardor has been transferred in the mind-meld.

The urge to kiss the older woman is overpowering. T'Meri searches her thoughts. She realizes T'Prynn desires her. *Burns* for her.

She feels the heat of T'Prynn's breath inside her mouth, mingling with her own, but all she can think about is the fact that, despite Governor Sarek's attempts at liberal social reforms, Vulcan's laws—preserved for thousands of years by the Council of Elders at Mount Seleya—forbid her and T'Prynn from succumbing to their true natures.

T'Prynn's lips graze T'Meri's.

Surrendering to the swell of passion lingering from their mind-meld, T'Meri returns T'Prynn's kiss and gives herself over to a woman more than three times her age. T'Prynn is voracious in her desire, primal in her way of touching, almost savage in the way she removes T'Meri's garments.

We are already conspiring to help destroy the Empire, T'Meri rationalizes between desperate, fumbling gropes as T'Prynn pulls her toward a bed. *We are already criminals.*

2286

36

Wheels Within Wheels

Emperor Spock entered his throne room. The gilded space resounded with a trumpeted fanfare, drowning out the hubbub of courtiers. Most of the eyes in the room turned to watch him as he swept across the dais, his purple cloak fluttering behind him. He draped it with a flourish around his right arm and seated himself on his throne, careful at every moment to comport himself with quiet dignity.

He nodded at the court's herald, indicating he was ready to receive that day's invited visitor. The herald responded with a sheepish glance toward the room's perimeter. Following the herald's silent cue, Spock understood: In violation of protocol, the guest was already inside the throne room.

Of course he is, Spock mused.

Curzon Dax, a noted diplomat and negotiator from the planet Trill, appeared to be presiding over a miniature court of his own by a fruit-laden buffet table. The handsome young man was flirting shamelessly with a bevy of beautiful women, several of whom Spock recognized as the wives or favored concubines of imperial dignitaries. Dax cracked jokes and playfully touched the women's cheeks and chins as they laughed.

Clear echoes of their laughter filled the otherwise

silent throne room, and Dax and his harem-in-the-making realized they had become the focus of attention. The charismatic youth smiled his apologies to his female admirers as he stepped out of their midst. He placed himself before Spock's dais and bowed.

"Majesty."

"Mister Dax," Spock said. "You are exactly as I imagined you would be."

Standing tall, Dax asked, "Shall I take that as a compliment, Majesty?"

"I doubt you could be persuaded to do otherwise."

Even in the face of a mild but public rebuke, Dax's smile never wavered. He radiated confidence and charm. "Thank you, Majesty, for honoring me with an invitation to your court. How may I serve you, my prince?"

Spock stood and walked to the edge of his dais. His courtiers gasped as he descended its stairs and said to the captain of his guards, "Lower the force field." The protective barrier flickered into view for a moment as it deactivated. As Spock neared the bottom of the stairs, a platoon of his elite Vulcan guards advanced and surrounded Dax on three sides.

Standing face-to-face with the Trill diplomat, Spock said, "Walk with me." He led the way toward an adjacent banquet room that had been prepared for the day's noon meal. Dax remained at Spock's side, matching his stride rather than lingering the customary half step behind royalty.

"I have followed your career with interest," Spock said.

Dax cocked an eyebrow. "Really? It's been less than three years since I joined the Diplomatic Corps. Why notice me?"

"For one so young, you have accomplished much," Spock said. "You have demonstrated a keen understanding of the Klingon mind-set. In the past year you brokered three cease-fires along our border with their empire, and you resolved numerous treaty disputes, making possible a new trade agreement with Qo'noS."

The Trill shrugged. "All true." He smiled. "It's all about learning how the Klingons think, knowing what they respect, what they respond to."

Looking askance at Dax, Spock said, "Curious. Most of my courtiers put on shows of humility. They try to deflect praise, but you do not. Indeed, you seem to bask in it." The banquet room staff stepped aside as Dax and Spock entered. "Is this trait part of what enables you to 'speak the Klingons' language'?"

"That's precisely it, Majesty," Dax said, plucking a ripe pear from a pyramid of fruit on the corner of the closest table. "I don't let them intimidate me. Instead of appeasing them, I challenge them." Dax took a healthy bite out of the green fruit and continued as he chewed. "From their point of view, I'm presenting myself as their equal, so they treat me like one."

"Fascinating," Spock said. "A keen insight into their psychology."

"I know," Dax said, grinning. "It's also a fun way to live."

Spock turned and faced the Trill. "Curzon Dax, I hereby appoint you as my Imperial Ambassador to the Klingon Empire." He extended his hand.

Beaming with surprise, pride, and elation, Dax took Spock's hand. "Thank you, Your Majesty. I'm honored to serve you."

Their handshake lasted only a few seconds, but that

fleeting contact was all Spock required to assess his new ambassador by means of touch-telepathy. He sensed no treachery or duplicity from Dax, but he detected something else, an unexpected psychic presence—a second mind, an independent intelligence existing in harmonic fusion with Curzon's. It did not seem to be a parasite, so far as Spock could tell, but rather an equal constituent of the Trill's personality. The humanoid mind and its partner were symbiotically linked. United.

Releasing Dax's hand, Spock said, "Congratulations, Your Excellency. I must now take my leave of you."

"Of course, Majesty," Dax said, making a small bow as Spock departed.

Spock paused at the banquet room's door and looked back. Dax, his manner even bolder than before, once again was flanked by solicitous female companions. Caught up in his revels, the Trill seemed oblivious of Spock's telepathic insight into his secret. Watching the audacious young ambassador work the room, Spock decided to investigate Dax and the politically ambiguous Trill people much more thoroughly.

2287

37

Bloody Instructions

A crowd's distant roar pierced a musical curtain of noise. Shapes formed in a storm of swirling whiteness. Captain Saavik, the new commanding officer of the *I.S.S. Enterprise*, drew a breath as the transporter beam loosened its paralyzing hold.

Taking in her surroundings, she noted they were every bit as lavish as she had been led to expect. The governor's palace on Trill was a magnificent work of architecture in its own right, and its sprawling rooftop garden—which had been secured by *Enterprise*'s security division in advance of Saavik's arrival—had been decorated with freestanding red banners emblazoned with the Empire's sword-and-planet emblem. Adding to the palace's beauty were roving beams of light in a range of intense hues; their movements and intersections painted the soaring towers and elegant curves of the palace's façade with shifting splashes of color.

Saavik glanced over her shoulder at the rest of the landing party. Her first officer, Commander Xon, and chief medical officer, Dr. M'Benga, flanked her. Both wore dress uniforms, as she did. At the rear of the group were four of Spock's elite Vulcan guards, attired in full *lorica segmentata* with battle regalia.

In the middle of their formation stood Empress

Marlena, garbed in a scandalously sheer dress of teal-tinted Tholian silk. Her royal countenance was framed by a headpiece: a semicircular frame over which more Tholian silk had been stretched taut and adorned with diamonds in a pattern that evoked the rays of a rising sun.

Far below, in the streets and plazas surrounding the palace, a massive throng of Trill civilians had gathered to witness the occasion of an official state visit, the planet's first in more than a century. Thunderous cheers filled the air as a fanfare sounded and fireworks lit the night sky in brilliant flashes of emerald and crimson.

Crossing the rooftop garden to meet the Empress's party was Trill's governor, a woman in her forties named Neema Cyl. She was trailed by her entourage and flanked by two columns of armed guards.

As the governor's group neared the landing party, Saavik nodded at Xon and M'Benga, who moved aside to permit the Empress to step forward.

"Your Majesty," Cyl said, bowing her head as she came to a halt. "Welcome to Trill. It's a great honor to open my home to you."

Marlena answered the governor's courtesy with a subtle nod. "Thank you, Governor. On behalf of Emperor Spock, I bring you greetings and good wishes." Turning at the waist, she gestured to Saavik. "Please permit me to introduce the commanding officer of the *Starship Enterprise,* Captain Saavik."

Saavik stepped forward and offered her hand to the governor.

Cyl smiled as she shook it and said, "Captain, it's an honor."

"The honor is mine, Governor."

Their handshake lasted a half second longer than was

customary, but no one other than the Empress seemed to suspect why.

Saavik's moment of contact with the governor had been the reason for this state visit by the Empress, for Captain Riley's promotion to the Admiralty, and for Saavik's early advancement to the center seat of the *Enterprise*. Spock had needed her to be of sufficient rank to merit a formal introduction to Governor Cyl.

Marshaling her hidden telepathic gifts, Saavik opened her psionic senses to Cyl's mind—and what she encountered was exactly as Spock had described it in a classified briefing. The governor seemed to possess a curious dual sentience, two unique minds functioning as one identity.

Cyl let go of Saavik's hand and motioned for the landing party to follow her inside the palace. "Your Majesty," she said, "your banquet awaits."

"Thank you, Governor," Marlena said. "Lead on."

The landing party stayed close behind the Empress as she accompanied the governor and her entourage inside the palace, but Saavik let them pass by her. Once the two groups had moved out of earshot, Saavik took out her communicator and flipped it open. "Saavik to *Enterprise*."

"*Scott here,*" said her veteran chief engineer. "*Go ahead, Captain.*"

"Mister Scott, you may begin beaming down shore leave parties."

"*Aye, sir,*" Scott said, confirming the coded order. "*Are we allowed to bring back souvenirs?*"

"Indeed," Saavik said. "In fact, I encourage it."

"*Understood, sir. Scott out.*"

Saavik closed her communicator, tucked it back onto

her belt, and hurried to catch up with the rest of her team.

While she and the landing party dined with the governor, investigative teams disguised as shore leave parties from *Enterprise* would visit the planet's surface. Posing as tourists, her officers would conduct clandestine scans of the Trill population, while Commander Scott and the crew of the *Enterprise* made detailed sensor sweeps of the planet's surface.

Emperor Spock wanted to know whether all Trill possessed the curious trait of a dual mind, or if it was a mark of privilege for their society's elite. Most important, he needed to know if the Trill would be his allies or his adversaries.

Her mind set to the task, Saavik was determined to find the answers to Spock's queries before the next day dawned on Trill's capital city.

The hour was late, and Marlena's stomach ached from the surfeit of her feast with Trill's governor. Every plate of the nine-course meal had been sumptuous and prepared to perfection, and despite all her attempts at moderation, Marlena had barely been able to keep from gorging herself. For decorum's sake, however, she hid her discomfort as she sat in her quarters aboard *Enterprise* with Saavik, conferring with Spock over a secure subspace channel.

"Give me your summary evaluation of the Trill," he said to Marlena.

"I find them interesting," Marlena said. "They possess advanced technology, and they've integrated it well into their lives. Their political system seems malleable; I think it would be compatible with your democratically ordered vision of the future."

"What of their culture?"

"My conversations with the governor and her senior staff suggest the Trill consider the continuity of memory and the accurate accounting of history to be of paramount importance. Also, considering who their closest galactic neighbors are, they strike me as a remarkably open society."

Saavik interjected, "I disagree, Majesty."

She ignored Marlena's glare as Spock replied, *"Explain."*

"Trill society is many things, but it is not 'open.' They are keeping a great many secrets from us, most of them related to their peculiar joined intelligences." She transferred an encrypted file over the channel to Spock. "Scans of the Trill population made by our landing parties and *Enterprise*'s sensors confirm a small minority of the Trill population—perhaps three hundred thousand persons—are bonded with symbiotic parasites, just as we saw in secret scans of Ambassador Dax. These parasites are known to the Trill people as 'symbionts,' and they are the source of the composite personalities we have encountered."

Marlena asked sharply, "How did you learn that, Captain?"

Continuing to direct her reply to Spock, Saavik said, "In addition, Majesty, we have learned the symbionts are very long-lived and are passed from one humanoid host to another. They bond for the lifetime of each host, which implies they can survive as bonded entities for several hundred years—possibly longer."

"A species capable of preserving knowledge and experience from one lifetime to the next could be instrumental to my long-term plans," Spock said.

Saavik wore a dubious frown. "Perhaps. But if these

symbionts have an agenda of their own, 'joined' Trill could be very dangerous."

Growing more agitated, Marlena rephrased her previous question. "Where did this information come from, Saavik?"

Before Saavik could answer, Spock said, *"If we knew more about these Trill-symbiont joinings, it might suggest our next logical step with regard to the Trill. How and where do the joinings occur?"*

"They are performed by unjoined Trill known as Guardians, in a sacred underground location called the Caves of Mak'ala. There is a natural hot spring that serves as both the nursery and final repository of the symbionts."

Marlena snapped, "Both of you, stop!" She pointed a finger at Saavik's face. "You do not *ignore me,* Captain. I'm the Empress, and when I ask you a direct question, I expect a prompt and truthful answer." Gesturing at the detailed report on the computer screen, she asked, "How did you and your crew learn all these facts about the Trill in such a short time, Captain Saavik?"

Saavik glanced at Spock's image on the viewscreen. The Emperor lifted one eyebrow but said nothing to excuse Saavik from her duty to obey royalty. The Vulcan woman clenched her jaw. "We abducted a small number of joined Trill civilians from the planet's surface using the transporters," she said. "Aboard the *Enterprise,* they were . . . *interrogated* under controlled conditions."

Jaw agape, Marlena blinked in horror at Saavik's revelation. "And what happened to those people *after* their interrogations?" She waited several seconds, but Saavik said nothing in reply. Filling in the blanks for herself, Marlena said accusatorily, "You had them killed."

"Operational security had to be maintained," Saavik said, as if that excused kidnapping, torture, and mass murder.

The Empress was appalled. She aimed her furious gaze at her husband. "I thought your rise to power was supposed to put an end to this kind of barbarism! How can you speak of reform with one breath and sanction vile abuses of power with another? Why should anyone believe promises of change from a tyrant?"

"How would you have had me proceed?"

Lifting her hands in frustration, Marlena said, "With honesty? Why not meet their governor and open a frank dialogue? We could court them as an ally instead of treating them like an enemy at the gates."

Spock looked at Saavik. *"What is your advice, Captain?"*

"The joined Trill might be benign, or they might have a hostile agenda," Saavik said. "At present, we do not know for certain which is the case. It would be best not to involve their government or any joined Trill in your long-term plans for the Empire before investigating them to ensure they are, in fact, an ally."

Nodding slowly, Spock said, *"Agreed."* Looking at Marlena, he added, *"I am sorry, but Captain Saavik is correct. This matter calls for caution."*

Marlena fumed in silence. *Overruled again in favor of a Vulcan half my age. How utterly predictable.*

Saavik asked him, "What are your orders, Majesty?"

"We must know the truth," Spock said. *"Explore the Caves of Mak'ala and make contact with the symbionts. If they wish to be allies, our plans for the future can become more ambitious."*

"And if they prove to be enemies?"

"That will be your first command decision as captain of the Enterprise.*"*

38

A Covenant with Death

The spinning shimmer of the transporter beam dissolved, leaving black-garbed Saavik alone and swallowed by darkness. She remained still and orientated herself.

Faint echoes of dripping water and moaning wind swirled around her. The atmosphere inside the Caves of Mak'ala was sultry and tinged with sulfur. Shifting her weight, Saavik felt her feet slip on the lichen-covered cave floor.

In the distance, through gaps in the walls of the cavern, she caught dim glimmers of lamplight and distorted shadows. None of them seemed close to her, so she lifted her tricorder from her hip and switched it on. She had dimmed its display as much as possible and had muted its feedback tones. Except for an almost inaudible hum, the device made no sound.

Saavik skulked forward. Using the tricorder, she maintained a safe distance between herself and the Guardians, who tended to move in pairs. It was only a short distance from her isolated beam-in point near the surface to the first level of symbiont pools. Peeking over a rock formation into an open chamber below, she saw it was better illuminated than most other areas of the caves, though the lights there still were kept to a minimum.

Fascinating, she thought, beholding the symbiont pools for the first time. Natural-looking craters dotted the expansive chamber beneath her. Each brimmed with slowly circulating, chalky water. Blue flashes resembling static electricity shot through the pools at varying depths and irregular intervals.

She scanned the pools with her tricorder. In seconds she amassed a significant volume of data about the caves' geology, water chemistry, and submerged topography—but the electrical discharges remained a mystery.

Most curious.

Detecting a gap in the Guardians' patrol coverage, Saavik turned off her tricorder and slung it behind her back. As soon as a path down to the pool chamber was clear, she stole forward, sticking as close as possible to the shadows. She shimmied down a narrow column formed by the merger of a stalactite and a stalagmite. Risking detection, she scampered across a patch of open ground and lay flat on the wet stone beside one of the pools.

Up close, she saw what was stirring the waters. Symbionts—tiny vermiform creatures—swam in the milky fluid, propelling themselves with flagellations of their tapered bodies. Saavik surmised the symbionts must have some means of altering their buoyancy—perhaps something as simple as air bladders or rudimentary lungs. The grayish worms were the source of the cerulean jolts of energy traveling through the water. Flashes traveled from one worm to another.

Saavik wondered, *Could the discharges be a form of communication?* As she leaned closer to the water's surface, several worms swam toward her, as if conscious of her presence. One bobbed to the surface only centimeters from her face. Treading water in front of Saavik, the symbiont extended a few tentative arcs of blue lightning in the Vulcan's direction.

My task will be easier if the creatures desire contact, she reasoned.

She reached toward the closest symbiont. The creature emitted a quick series of electrical discharges that arced over Saavik's hand. As tendrils of energy danced around her wrist, she felt the touch of the symbiont's mind. It was undeniably sentient, and it evinced great curiosity about her.

Projecting a telepathic question, Saavik asked, *Do you have a name?*

The symbiont responded with pulses of color, sensations of warmth and cold, and waves of emotion ranging from fear to contentment.

Soon more of its kind drew near and added their energies to the communion with Saavik. None of them seemed to understand her simple inquiries. Their responses felt nebulous and unformed. She opened her thoughts to meld with the symbionts, and then she understood why their perceptions seemed so basic: they were mere younglings, only recently spawned.

To obtain the answers she needed, Saavik needed to find older symbionts.

Projecting her question to the younglings in the simplest telepathic concepts she could imagine, she asked them where she would find the old symbionts, the ones who created the younglings. It took several attempts to get the infant symbionts to understand what she was asking.

Finally, she received a clear answer. It came from all the younglings, and it was expressed as a simple concept that nonetheless seemed gravid with dread.

<<*Deeper.*>>

One hour later, Saavik was back on the`Enterprise,` standing on a transporter pad while Montgomery Scott—who had served on the *Enterprise* for more years and under more captains than any other member of the crew—made the final adjustments to a heavy-duty environmental suit.

"I've done all I can with this thing, Captain," he said. "Gravity and a weight belt will get you to the bottom of those pools, but whether a jury-rigged miniature integrity field will keep you from being crushed by the pressure at those depths . . . well, that remains to be seen."

Eyeing the chief engineer's handiwork, Saavik said, "I am more concerned about how this suit's thermal exchangers will cope with the pools' extreme heat. I need to dive very close to the springs' geothermal source."

"Aye, you'll work up a sweat, I can tell you that." He patted the back of the suit. "Avoid rupturing your coolant tank and you should be okay. But don't stay down there too long, Captain. I had to strip out the basics to make this suit strong enough to get you down and back again—which means less than two hours of air."

"I will endeavor to be swift and punctual, Mister Scott."

The white-haired engineer sighed and nodded. "Aye, sir." He lifted her suit's helmet. "Ready?" Saavik nodded, and Scott fixed her helmet into place, muffling the low pulses of the ship's life-support systems and the hum of the transporter's energizer coils. Its wraparound faceplate offered her a decent field of vision, but she still felt as if she had been encased in a modern sarcophagus.

Scott moved to the transporter controls and opened
a comm channel to the transceiver inside Saavik's suit.
"Can you hear me, Captain?"

"Yes, Mister Scott."

*"Right. I have the coordinates of the underground pool you
scanned with your tricorder. Beaming you in won't be a problem. But once you go deeper—"*

"I am aware of the complications posed by the cav-
erns' geology."

"Yes, sir."

Earlier, while using her tricorder to select a covert
insertion point for her dive to the symbionts' source
pools, Saavik had noted that only a short distance below
the water's surface the bedrock was rich with a mineral
called fistrium. It would impede communications at
depths below a hundred meters, and it would make it
impossible for the *Enterprise* crew to beam her up until
she was almost at the pools' surface. Once she submerged into the chasms beneath the Caves of Mak'ala,
Saavik would be on her own.

Over the transceiver, Scott said, *"Coordinates locked in,
Captain."*

"Energize."

The transporter beam enfolded Saavik, and the familiar confines of the transporter room dissolved in a bright
whorl of energized particles. . . .

Darkness descended. Sensation returned.

Saavik felt weightless for a moment before she became aware of her downward motion. She was sinking. Lifting her arm, she checked the status display
mounted above her wrist. Seventy-five meters and
dropping quickly. The sensors in her suit detected a
solid surface a few meters below. Seconds later she

touched down with a mild bump and bent her knees to absorb the impact.

She turned on her helmet beacon. Organic matter littered the rocky shelf on which she stood. Less than twenty meters ahead of her, the underwater plateau ended at a wide fissure along the base of a stone wall that seemed to reach upward to the pools' surface. Saavik walked to the edge and looked over it, into the fathomless darkness below. To her dismay, her suit's sensors were unable to give her a reading of the fissure's depth.

There is no choice, she reminded herself. *I must go forward.*

Tucking her arms to her sides, Saavik pushed off from the edge and jumped forward. Then the blackness seemed to swallow her whole as it pulled her into the abyss. Her descent was slower than she expected, and soon she realized it was because the ion-rich, magma-heated water became more viscous as she sank deeper. To her alarm, the water was also thick with fistrium leached from the cave's walls. *That would explain why my proximity sensors no longer function.*

Her free-fall descent lasted more than ten minutes, and it carried her past impressive swaths of brightly bioluminescent orange moss clinging to the walls.

The fissure narrowed to the point where Saavik could extend her arms and touch both walls with her fingertips. By the time she finally reached the bottom, the shoulders of her bulky pressure suit scraped the sides. The ground under her feet was mostly level and covered with small, smooth stones.

She focused her suit's external lights, but they were of little utility. The water at this depth was thick and cloudy. Her helmet beacon revealed little but the meter of ground directly ahead of her; beyond that she saw nothing but a wall of bright fog. She walked against the current, reasoning if young symbionts were spawned in the depths, flowing water must help carry them to the surface. Her hunch proved correct: a short distance away she entered a tunnel-like passage that sloped gradually downward, deeper into darkness.

It appears to be a lava tube, she thought, noting its smooth contours.

After five minutes of trudging progress, Saavik slowed as the passage narrowed. She took great care not to damage her suit's externally mounted systems while pushing ahead into the claustrophobic tunnel.

Feeling her way forward, she was mindful not to let herself become stuck. No rescue team would be dispatched if she was overdue to check in at the end of this mission's allotted time. She would simply be written off as "missing," and Xon would become captain of the *Enterprise*.

Saavik kept walking for another thirty minutes before the passage's sides and ceiling pressed in so closely that she was forced to drop to her hands and knees and crawl. The intense water pressure made every movement a labor for Saavik, despite her Vulcan strength and stamina. She checked the chrono on the suit's forearm. She was more than forty-five minutes into her dive.

Impelled by a renewed sense of dwindling time, Saavik tried to quicken her pace. She lost her balance and fell hard against the side of the lava tube.

Upon impact, her helmet beacon flickered and dimmed.

That is quite inconvenient, she noted.

The rest of her suit's functions also became erratic.

Her forearm display stuttered on and off, and when it was on it sometimes showed gibberish. Lying on her back, she reached down and opened a pocket on her suit's torso. From it she took a chemical flare that had been treated to withstand intense heat. She cracked it to life and held it ahead of her, its chartreuse glow her only beacon in the blistering, all-consuming dark.

Then there was no more ground beneath her hands.

Her fingers gripped the edge of the lava tube. Saavik checked her proximity sensor. In front of her was a vast space of open water. Because the water in the great chamber was mostly free of fistrium, she was able to coax a clear reading from her suit's bio-scanner: there were life-forms ahead.

Glow-stick in hand, she pushed off from the edge of the lava tube. She sank slowly to the cavern's floor. Though there was level ground to walk on, it was limited to narrow paths between massive rocky mounds. Wandering between them, Saavik felt as if she were trapped in a maze.

Fifty-five minutes, she noted, looking at her chrono. *Time to make contact.*

As if summoned by her desire, a trio of two-meter-long symbionts floated down from the lightless space overhead. The swimming worms were fat and crusted with a ragged carapace. One of the three descended to confront Saavik. It probed her with short bursts of violet energy that made Saavik's skin tingle.

<<*You are an intruder in the realm of the Annuated,*>> said the ancient symbiont, its telepathic voice authoritative and powerful. <<*Withdraw at once.*>>

Saavik held out her hand and opened her mind as an invitation to a meld. *I am an emissary of Emperor Spock of*

*the Terran Empire. He has sent me to make contact with the
true rulers of Trill so that—*

<<*Be silent,*>> commanded the great worm.
<<*You are not welcome here.*>> The other two bloated
worms drifted down to hover above and slightly behind
the one who spoke to Saavik. Above them, more vermiform shapes emerged from the darkness, all crackling
with violet energy. <<*Leave or die.*>>

The worms moved toward her, herding her back the
way she had come. Backpedaling, Saavik was at a loss
for how to persuade the elder symbionts it was in their
best interest to speak with her. Turning a tight corner,
she tripped and lost her balance. She put out her hands
to break her fall and collided with the side of one of the
looming rocky mounds—

In a flash of telepathic connection, Saavik understood.

The symbionts chasing her away were not the ancient ones; they were only caretakers, mere adolescents
compared to the ones they called the Annuated. The
great stationary masses grouped on the cavern's floor
were not rock—they were symbionts that had achieved
terrifying size over tens of thousands of years. These
beasts of antiquity were the ones that birthed new symbionts and commanded their offspring with unquestioned authority.

At Saavik's touch, the Annuated Elder's mind
stirred. <<*I recognize your species. Your kind are called ... .
Vulcans.*>>

Its flock of caretakers backed away, apparently leery
of taking action while Saavik was in communion with
one of their rulers.

Saavik asked, *How do you know of my kind?*

<<*Our children roamed the stars thousands of years ago,*>> the Annuated Elder replied. <<*They brought their knowledge home to us. We know of all the psionically gifted species—Vulcans and Betazoids; Ullians and Aenar, Remans and Medusans. All exterminated now . . . except for your kind.*>> Its mind blazed with grim amusement. <<*Most wise. Your people hide their gifts well.*>>

Behind the Elder's condescension, Saavik detected something else. Just as she had sensed a second mind in Trill's humanoid governor, now she felt the presence of a second mind in the consciousness of this ancient being. At the risk of postponing her return to the surface too long, she initiated a full mind-meld with the Annuated Elder.

Its consciousness was perplexing, its storehouse of memories too vast for Saavik to comprehend. Her talents would be no match for the sheer mental power of the Elder—but its mind was not the one she sought to reveal. Her quarry lay hidden in the darkest recesses of the most primitive quarters of the Elder's brain. It was a much younger intelligence—relatively speaking—and far more malevolent.

It was a parasite. An invader. A mutant spawn of Trill's symbionts.

Saavik stole flashes of memory from the hateful creature's mind.

The Trill had tried once, ages ago, to eradicate the parasites and their hosts. The Trill thought they had succeeded, but a few hardy parasites clung to life. Eventually they escaped their exile on the distant world that their forebears had laid waste.

Concealed inside an artificial comet of ice, they returned to Trill a century ago, falling in a blaze of fire to the sea. Riding one host after another, they found their way home to the Caves

*of Mak'ala. Safe now in its sweltering depths, they have infested
the Annuated, yoking the ancient ones to their cause of ven-
geance. Bonded now to the egg-layers, the parasites will ensure
the Annuated birth only aggressive, dangerous, mutant parasites
bent on secretly usurping control first of Trill and eventually the
entire galaxy—one mind and one world at a time.*

Saavik severed the mind-meld, shed her weight belt,
and fled.

The caretakers pursued her, and they were much
more in their element than she was. One rammed into
her back, knocking her onto her hands and knees.

*They swim faster than I can, and they are more maneu-
verable than I am in this environment. I will need to change
tactics.*

Fortunately for Saavik, her chief engineer had insisted she come prepared to make a quick exit. Mounted
on her right wrist was a compact phaser. She armed it as
she rolled onto her back, and then she fired at the caretakers diving at her.

The phaser's brilliant blue beam of energy shimmered through the water, which boiled and filled with
bubbles. Then the huge symbionts' heavy corpses
dropped to the cavern's floor, half disintegrated.

More caretakers converged on Saavik. Working
quickly, she primed a special flare Mister Scott had jury-
rigged to propel itself through hyperpressurized water
and ignite on contact with a solid surface. Saavik aimed
it straight up, triggered it, and released it into the great
emptiness overhead.

The flare rocketed up, a pinpoint of light that seemed
to vanish in the darkness—then it erupted into a blazing orb of light on a domed ceiling of rock more than
two kilometers away. The entire cavern was lit as if by

daylight, and Saavik saw the openings of many large lava tubes on the ceiling.

Exit strategy revised.

A few more shots of her wrist phaser kept the caretakers at bay while she energized her suit's emergency thruster and extended its control handgrips.

Above her, the light of the flare started to dim.

The suit's thruster was not fully charged, but Saavik could no longer afford to be patient. She set it for maximum burn and keyed the starter.

The roar of the engine was deafening.

Sudden acceleration left her paralyzed for a few seconds until the suit's guidance circuit smoothed out its delta-v. Struggling to control its direction, Saavik aimed herself at the widest lava tube she could reach. Satisfied she was on target, she detached from her left leg the last of her dive weights, which had been designed to serve a secondary function: they were also high-yield plasma charges.

Watching the charges fall away behind her, sinking back into the cavern of the Annuated, Saavik touched their arming switch on her suit's belt.

A holographic display on her helmet's faceplate confirmed the plasma charges had been armed and were on a three-minute countdown to detonation.

Rocketing into the lava tube, Saavik hoped it would lead her back to the surface and not to a dead end or some inescapable underwater labyrinth. She followed the wide passage's twists and turns, each of which seemed to bring the walls a bit closer. Three and a half minutes into her ascent, a thunderous boom shook the bedrock, and a wall of displaced water surged up behind her.

So much for the Annuated.

After five minutes, her suit's thruster ran out of fuel. She detached the engine pack and let it sink into the darkness behind her. Kicking with her legs and making wide strokes with her arms, Saavik continued swimming in the direction her helmet's holographic display told her was "up."

Her air gauge was five minutes shy of zero when her wrist display confirmed she was close enough to the surface to be free of the fistrium's interference. She activated her suit's transceiver. "Saavik to *Enterprise*."

The reply was staticky but audible. *"Xon here. Go ahead, Captain."*

"Mister Xon, beam down strike teams to the Caves of Mak'ala. Kill the Guardians, and exterminate all symbionts in the pools."

"Acknowledged," Xon said.

Minutes later, Saavik surfaced in a remote pool inside the Caves of Mak'ala. Pulling herself out of the water, she collapsed onto all fours, utterly exhausted. The dive to the cavern of the Annuated and the subsequent swim back to the surface had been the most arduous physical experience of her life.

Sitting back, she took off her helmet, dropped it, and let it roll away. The caves echoed with the shrieks of phasers and the screams of the dying.

From nearby, she heard Xon's voice call out, "Captain Saavik!"

Turning, she saw her first officer leading a team of security personnel from the *Enterprise*. She said to him, "I am unhurt."

Xon helped Saavik stand, and then he nodded at one of his men. The security officer took out his communicator and spoke into it. "All teams, this is Lieutenant Treude. The captain is safe. Sterilize the pools."

One of the other security officers stepped past Treude and opened a satchel slung on his hip. From the bag, the man took a handful of white tablets—a mix of radioactive toxins—and tossed them into the pool from which Saavik had emerged.

The water frothed with pale blue foam. Seconds later the pool's surface was crowded with dead, floating symbionts. The worms' cradle of life had become a pit of death. Nothing would ever live in these waters again.

"Well done," Saavik said to Xon. "Let us return to the ship."

Xon opened his communicator. "Xon to *Enterprise*. Two to beam up."

Spock sat at the desk in his study, reviewing the latest dispatches from Carol Marcus. Pleased with the progress she and her team had made, he considered expanding the scope of the Memory Omega project.

His ruminations were interrupted as the door of his study flew open and slammed against the wall. Marlena stormed through the open doorway, her elegant features distorted by rage as she strode toward him.

"How could you?" she shouted.

"To what, specifically, do you refer?"

"You know damned well what I'm talking about!" She picked up a crystal sphere from its stand on his desk and hurled it at the wall. It shattered into dust and jagged chunks. "Genocide, Spock! You wiped out an entire species!"

"I personally did no such thing."

"No, you let your protégée do your dirty work."

He leaned back and pressed his fingertips together over his chest. "Captain Saavik did what she thought was necessary to safeguard the Empire and its people from an aggressive, dangerous, and previously unknown enemy."

Marlena asked in pitched disbelief, "Did you even *read* her report?"

"I did."

"Really? The one I read said she encountered new life-forms unlike anything anyone's ever seen before, and then she *vaporized* them."

"Since you have read the report, then you must also be aware the Annuated symbionts knew of my people's secret—and that they themselves had been compromised by a hostile parasitic intelligence. If we had allowed them to live, they would have posed a threat not just to my plans for reform, but to all sentient life in the galaxy. The decision to exterminate them was logical."

"I understand why the infested ones had to be destroyed, but why *all of them,* Spock? Saavik may have taken the first step in the Caves of Mak'ala, but you were the one who signed an executive order to hunt down and execute *all* joined Trill."

"There was no way to know which symbionts had been compromised and which could be trusted," Spock said. "To permit even one of those parasites to survive would constitute a grave threat to galactic security." After a brief pause, he added, "Furthermore, I did not order the deaths of *all* joined Trill."

His wife rolled her eyes in disgust. "Oh, yes, I forgot—your token gesture of compassion: *you spared Curzon Dax*. How *magnanimous* of you. You've ordered the covert murder of hundreds of thousands of joined Trill, but all is forgiven because you struck Dax's name from your death warrant." She let her fury simmer a moment. Then she asked, "Why spare *his* life? Why does *he* get to live?"

Spock exhaled a breath heavy with regret.

"To remind me of what I have become."

PART III
Sic Transit Imperium

2288

39

Men of Long Knives

Every warrior in the Great Hall smelled blood. The Terran Empire was starting to flounder, its Emperor Spock shedding power and control the way a gelded *targ* sheds fur. At long last, the greatest enemy of the Klingon Empire was faltering; it was time to strike.

All that remained now was to decide who would strike, with what forces, where, when, and how. This debate, unfortunately, was dragging on late into the night, and Councillor Gorkon was growing weary of the bickering. Regent Sturka—the latest warrior to hold the throne for Kahless, He Who Shall Return—looked haggard and sullen as Councillors Duras and Indizar argued while circling each other inside the small pool of harsh light in the middle of the Council chamber.

"You Imperial Intelligence types are all the same," Duras said with a sneer. "*Infiltrate* the Terrans, *sabotage* them, conquer them *by degrees.*" Lifting his voice to an aggrieved bellow, he added, "Where's the glory in that?"

Keeping one hand on her *d'k tahg,* Indizar replied with a voice like the growl of a Kryonian tiger. "It's smarter than your way, Duras. You'd plunge us head-long into full-scale war with the largest fleet in known space. We might emerge victorious, but at what cost? Our fleet would be savaged, our borders weakened. The

Romulans would overrun us the moment we finished off the Terrans. . . . Of course, maybe that's your *real* plan, isn't it, Duras?"

Duras's eyes were wide with fury. "You dare call me a traitor?" His hand went for his own *d'k tahg*—

Sharp, echoing cracks. One, two, three. Everyone looked at Sturka, who ceased smashing the steel-clad tip of his staff on the stone floor. "Both of you get out of the circle," he commanded Indizar and Duras. Then, to the others, he said, "I want to hear realistic strategies. Honest assessments." He looked at Gorkon, who had served for more than twenty years as Sturka's most trusted adviser, and who had thwarted an attempt by the late Councillor Kesh to seize the throne for himself. "Have Spock's reforms weakened the Terrans' defenses," Sturka asked, "or merely damaged his own political security?"

Stepping out of the crowd into the heat and glare of the circle, Gorkon gripped the edges of his black leather stole, which rested over a studded, red leather chimere; worn together, the two ceremonial vestments marked him as the second-highest-ranking individual in the chamber. "The Terran Empire," he began in a stately tone, "is still far too strong for us to risk a direct military engagement." Before the rising murmur of grumbles got out of hand, Gorkon reasserted his control over the discussion. "However, the reforms instituted by their current sovereign hold the promise of future opportunities." He began a slow walk along the edge of the circle of light, using his time to size up the commitment of both his rivals and his allies on the Council. "Emperor Spock has made significant reductions in military spending, with many deep cuts in the field of weapons research and development." He paused as he returned the steely glare of Duras, then moved on. "This will give us a chance to finally take the lead in our long arms race, after more than six decades of lagging behind the Terrans. This opportunity must not be squandered—it might never come again."

As Gorkon reached the farthest edge of the circle from the Regent's throne, Sturka asked, "What are you proposing, Gorkon?"

Gorkon grinned at Indizar, his long-time ally, then turned to answer Sturka. "A doubling of the budget for new starship construction and refits, and a separate allocation of equal size for new military research and development."

Sturka sounded skeptical. "And where will we find the money for this? Or the resources? Or the power?"

"Money is not a warrior's concern," Gorkon said, even though he knew it *was* a politician's concern. "If we need power, we all know Praxis is not running at capacity—we can triple its output to power new shipyards. As for raw materials and personnel"—he paused and looked around the room, already plotting which of his rivals would bear the brunt of his plans for the future— "sacrifices will have to be made. Hard choices. For the cost of a few worlds and a few billion people conscripted into service, we can transform the quadrant into an unassailable bastion of Klingon power."

"Whose worlds?" Councillor Argashek blurted. Suspicious growls worked their way around the room. Many of the councillors were already aware what Gorkon had in mind for them should he ever rise to the regency. Leaning over Argashek's shoulders were Grozik and Glazya, his two staunchest comrades. They sniped verbally at Gorkon. *"PetaQ,"* spat Grozik, as Glazya cursed, "Filthy *yIntagh!*"

Councillors Narvak and Veselka conferred in hushed voices near the back of the room, while the Council's three newest—and youngest—members stepped to the edge of the circle from different directions, flanking Gorkon. Korax had come up through the ranks of the military, much as Gorkon had. Both his friends in this challenge were scions of noble houses: Berik, of the House of Beyhn, and Rhaza, of the House of Guul.

"Bold words, old man," Korax taunted. "But I bet it won't be your homeworld that gets ground up for the Empire."

Gorkon watched the three younger men moving in unison, circling him . . . and he smiled. "Step into the circle, whelps," Gorkon said. "And I'll show you what being ground up really means."

Again came the thunderous rapping of Sturka's staff. "Enough. Korax, take your jesters back to the shadows. Gorkon, let them go."

With a respectful nod at Sturka, Gorkon said, "As you wish, my lord." Secretly, he wondered if Regent Sturka had lost his appetite for battle, his love of purifying combat. Twice today he had intervened when custom dictated the strong should reign. *Perhaps the Terrans' leader isn't the only one losing his edge,* Gorkon mused grimly.

Leaning forward from the edge of the throne, Sturka spoke slowly, his roar of a voice diminished with age to a ragged rumble. "Praxis is unstable. Doubling its output would be a mistake; tripling it is out of the question. And if a few of our worlds must be sacrificed to secure our victory over the Terrans, I will decide which worlds to cast into the fire, and when. But for now, this option is rejected."

Vengeful fury raged inside Gorkon, but his countenance

was as steady as granite, his gaze winter-cold. *Sturka has lost the will to fight,* he realized. *He doesn't have the stomach for casualties, for risk. His fire is gone; he's just a politician now.*

Looking at the Regent, bitter regret filled Gorkon's heart. Sturka had helped elevate Gorkon to the High Council more than twenty years ago. Since then the Regent had kept him close and taught him how to keep the other councillors fighting among themselves so that he and Sturka could be free to plot grander schemes for the glory of the Empire. Sturka had become like a second father to Gorkon, but now the old statesman was past his prime—enfeebled, vulnerable, and no longer able to lead.

Gorkon knew what had to be done for the good of the Empire. *It galls me that it must come to this,* he admitted to himself. *But better it should be me than that* petaQ *Duras.*

Sturka was still talking. His eyes drifted from one side of the room to the other, gauging each councillor's reactions as he spoke. As soon as his gaze was turned away, Gorkon adjusted his wrist to let his concealed *d'k tahg* fall into his grip. His hand shot out and up and plunged the blade deep into Sturka's chest. A twist tore apart the Regent's heart. Lavender ichor spurted thick and warm from the ugly, sucking wound, coating Gorkon's hand. Sturka fell into Gorkon's arms, hanging on to his protégé as his lifeblood escaped in generous spurts. As he looked up at Gorkon, the Regent's expression seemed almost . . . grateful. "I knew . . . it would . . . be you," he rasped through a mouthful of pinkish spittle. His corpse fell off Gorkon's blade and landed in a blood-sodden heap on the floor.

Gorkon looked around the room to see if anyone wanted to challenge him. No one seemed eager to do so.

He sheathed his *d'k tahg* and kneeled beside Sturka's

body. He pried the eyelids open and gazed into their lifeless depths. His warning cry for *Sto-Vo-Kor* built like a long-growing thunderhead, resonating inside his barrel chest. Within seconds, more gravelly hums built in the bellies of those around him. Then he threw back his head and let his bellicose roar burst forth, and the High Council roared with him, the sound of the *Heghtay* powerful enough to shake dust from the rafters. The ranks of the dead could not say they hadn't been warned: a Klingon warrior was coming.

Pushing aside the empty husk of Sturka's body, Gorkon stepped onto the raised dais and took his place on the throne. Immediately, Indizar was at his right side, handing him the ceremonial staff. Alakon, a commonborn soldier who had earned his seat on the Council through honorable battle, took his place at Gorkon's left and made the declaration, which was echoed back by the councillors without a challenge:

"All hail, Regent Gorkon!"

It was too early in Senator Pardek's political career for him to pick fights on the floor of the Romulan Senate. Fortunately for him, Senator Narviat was stirring up enough controversy in the Senate chamber for both of them.

Narviat shouted above the angry hubbub. "A wise general once said, 'When you see your enemy making a mistake, get out of his way.' Well, we're being given a rare treat: we get to watch two of our enemies making a mistake. So why aren't any of you smart enough to get out of their way?"

Pardek almost had to laugh; there were days when he was certain Narviat simply enjoyed making the others crazy, especially Proconsul Dralath and Praetor Vrax.

Shouting back from his seat at the front of the chamber, Proconsul Dralath made his voice cut through the clamor. "We missed our chance to strike when the Klingons and Terrans clashed twenty years ago," he said. "Not again."

"Even at war with each other, they would still be a threat to us," Narviat retorted, ignoring the epithets that filled the air: *Coward. Quisling. Pacifist.* "The best course," he added, "is to expand our covert intelligence opportunities inside—"

"The same old refrain," cut in Senator Crelok, her elegant features crimped with contempt. "Another testimonial for the Tal Shiar. The last time I checked, Senator Narviat, the Tal Shiar hadn't won any wars for the Empire."

Unfazed, Narviat shot back, "Without us, the military would never have won any wars at all."

Crelok, a former starship commander, bristled at Narviat's remark. She seemed poised at the edge of a reply when the Praetor rose from his chair, and the senators who were gathered in the chamber fell silent.

Praetor Vrax turned his head slowly and surveyed the room. Pardek had been a senator for nearly eleven years now, and this was only the fourth time he had seen the Praetor stand to address the Senate. Vrax was more than old; he bordered on ancient. Despite his advanced years, however, he remained a keen political thinker and military strategist.

"The Terran Empire," Vrax began, speaking slowly, "is on a path to chaos." He lowered his head and cleared his throat. Looking up, he continued. "The Klingon Empire, now under Gorkon's control, is arming for war." He made a small nod toward Crelok. "Some of you say we should strike when the Klingons do." Vrax glanced at Narviat. "Others say we should use their war to infiltrate them both." Now Vrax's voice grew stronger, building as he spoke. "All the estimates I've seen tell me the Klingons will win this war, and the Terran Empire will fall. If so, we should let our fleet claim what it can. But other reports, from within the Terran Empire—I must admit they worry me. It is impossible for me to believe Emperor Spock is ignorant of the consequences his actions will carry. But he continues all the same, and his homeworld of Vulcan is drowning in a tide of pacifism. Our spies on Vulcan—the few that haven't been exposed and executed—cannot explain the spread of that world's pacifist movement. It has no printed propaganda, no virtual forums for discussion, no broadcast messages, no public meetings." The Praetor allowed that to sink in, then he followed it with a succinct, pointed inquiry to the Senate: "Why?"

Speaking from the back of the chamber, Senator D'Tran, one of the elder statesmen of the Senate, trepidatiously asked the Praetor, "Why what? Why are the Vulcans becoming pacifists? Or why is it happening outside the normal channels?"

"Start with the method," Vrax said.

Shrugs and eye rolls were passed from person to person as everyone sought to avoid answering the question. Pardek sighed with disappointment at his fellow senators' lack of courage. Lifting his voice, Pardek answered Praetor Vrax. "They are avoiding the normal channels in order to flush out spies."

The soft chatter of the room fell away and everyone looked at Pardek. Praetor Vrax cast an especially harsh glare at the young senator from the Krocton Segment. "Explain," he said.

"I have my own sources on Vulcan," Pardek confessed. "Based on the patterns of recruitment, people are seeking out their friends and family members and drawing them into the pacifist movement. It's not a government-directed initiative; it's a grassroots campaign, with each person brought into the fold through a chain of accountable kith and kin."

Vrax nodded at first, then tilted his head as he asked, "But how would such a recruitment model help them expose our spies? Why have we not infiltrated this movement?"

It was a loaded question, one that Pardek dreaded answering. "I do have one hypothesis," he said carefully.

"Tell us," Vrax commanded.

Pardek steeled himself for the wave of ridicule he knew would follow. "I believe they are vetting new members by means of telepathy."

No one in the Senate chamber mocked Pardek's theory. They were all too incapacitated to do so, because they were doubled over with paroxysms of cruel laughter. Much to Pardek's consternation, he noticed the only two people in the room not guffawing were himself and Praetor Vrax.

It took several seconds for the contagion of hilarity to run its course. When a semblance of decorum at last returned to the Senate chamber, Praetor Vrax coolly raised one eyebrow and said, in an archly skeptical tone, "Senator Pardek . . . shall I assume you spoke in jest? Or are you seriously suggesting the Vulcans are carrying out a vast planetwide conspiracy by means of a mythical psionic power?"

Before he answered, Pardek picked up his glass from the small desk in front of his seat and took a sip of water.

He put down the glass and met Vrax's accusing stare. "My sources tell me they believe the Vulcans' psionic gifts might be more than just the stuff of legend, Praetor."

Nobody laughed this time. Praetor Vrax ceased his pretense of civility and became openly sarcastic. "I suppose, Senator Pardek, you'll next be telling me that Emperor Spock really *does* possess tremendous psionic abilities, and that it was the power of thought alone that enabled him to slaughter the Empress Hoshi Sato III and her entire Imperial Guard Corps?"

Dead silence. A few stifled coughs echoed then were lost amid the dry scrape of shuffling feet.

"No," Pardek said as diplomatically as he could. "I think the Vulcans, who long resented sharing power with the Terrans who enslaved them, made a major leap forward in the arms race—and Spock chose that moment to show the Vulcans' hand."

Mumbles of agreement bubbled up in isolated patches around the Senate chamber. Taking note of it, Vrax nodded. "Agreed. And until we know more about that weapon, I am inclined to support Senator Narviat's recommendation for discretion." He looked back at Pardek. "As to the spread of the pacifist movement on Vulcan . . . do you really have no better hypothesis, Senator Pardek?"

Abashed, Pardek answered, "Not at this time, Praetor."

Vrax shook his head. "Thank you, Senator Pardek. I would prefer an explanation that does not require me to believe in magic or mythology. You may sit down."

It hadn't been permission so much as a directive, and Pardek settled into his seat. The debate continued around him. He made no effort to conceal his disgruntled glowering.

So they don't believe my theory, he consoled himself. *Not surprising; I'm not sure I believe it, either. But there's one thing I am certain of: Spock is deliberately setting up his people to take a fall, and I have no idea why.*

Pardek considered a thousand reasons why Spock might sabotage his own empire; none of them made sense.

As a junior senator, there was little Pardek could do directly to guide the affairs of the Romulan Star Empire. Weighing his options, he decided he would back Senator Narviat's proposal of military disengagement when it came time to vote. Pardek doubted the Tal Shiar would be able to infiltrate Vulcan any better than it had so far—which was to say, barely at all—but emphasizing covert intelligence rather than overt conquest would keep the Romulan Star Empire out of the Terran-Klingon crossfire. Pardek simply hoped it would buy his people enough time to determine what Emperor Spock was really up to.

"I must say, Admiral Cartwright," remarked Colonel Ivan West as he sat down at the dinner table, "this is by far the best-catered secret meeting I've ever been to."

Admiral Lance Cartwright chuckled as he settled in at the head of the table. Colonel West's observation had struck a chord because it was true. The table was dressed with crisp white linen and set with dishes of fine crystal and utensils of solid, polished silver. Cartwright's domestic servants had just cleared the appetizer course—a salad of baby greens tossed with warm slices of braised pear, walnuts, and a light vinaigrette—and brought out the next course, bowls of creamy pumpkin soup. Special dishes were served to the nonhuman guests.

Laughing with Cartwright were six visitors, high-ranking Starfleet officers who had been invited to his home this evening. They swapped small talk as a Bolian waiter refilled their glasses. Cartwright, West, and Admiral Thomas Morrow all were drinking cabernet. General Quiniven of Denobula was abstaining from liquor this evening and nursed a glass of Altair water instead. Admirals Robert Bennett and Salliserra zh'Ferro gladly accepted refills of their illegally imported Romulan ale. Commodore Vosrok, the Chelon director of Starfleet Intelligence, was half sitting, half kneeling on a *glenget,* a piece of furniture designed for his nonhumanoid anatomy, and drinking *N'v'aa,* a beverage from his homeworld that, up close, reeked of brackish vinegar. Cartwright made a mental note never to drink at Vosrok's home.

The banter remained light while the servants moved through the lavishly decorated dining room, serving soup, refilling water, replacing sullied utensils, and setting out freshly baked rolls and glass dishes filled with whipped butter.

"I'll give you credit," Morrow said to Cartwright. "You know how to live like a grand admiral."

Raising his glass in appreciation, Cartwright replied, "The amazing part is that I do it on a vice admiral's salary." More polite laughter filled the room. He watched the last of the servants exit, and the doors swung closed behind them, leaving him and his guests in privacy. "To business, then," he said, and his guests nodded in agreement. "I've sounded out each of you individually, so I imagine you're all aware why I've asked you here tonight." After a pause for effect, he stated plainly, "Emperor Spock is determined to destroy the Empire to which we have all devoted our lives. Before he's done, he'll kill us all. He must be stopped."

Cautious mumbles of assent traveled around the table as each guest looked around to make certain he or she was not alone in speaking treason against the Emperor. Their mutual affirmation seemed to encourage them. West, who sat on Cartwright's left near the head of the table, was the first to respond directly.

"I'm sure we all agree with you, Admiral," West said. "But opposing Spock won't be easy. I know of a few more admirals who are ready to turn against him, but most of the officer corps and almost all the enlisted men still support him."

Jumping in, Admiral Bennett said, "And don't forget how popular he is with the people. Assassinating him might just make him a martyr. A coup against Spock could start a rebellion."

Quiniven waved his hand dismissively. "No matter," he said with arrogant surety. "The people can be kept in line."

"Oh, really?" was Vosrok's sarcastic reply. "Have you forgotten that Spock granted the people such rights as—"

"Rights given with a word can be revoked just as easily," Quiniven said. "The citizens of the Empire have never had to shed blood to secure their rights. They wouldn't know how."

Cartwright sipped his dry red wine as the conversation took on a life of its own. Admiral zh'Ferro looked down from her end of the table and quietly remarked, "We will also have to kill Empress Marlena."

"Easily done," Colonel West replied.

Admiral Morrow, who had been enjoying his soup

one carefully lifted spoonful at a time, set down his spoon and cleared his throat. "Neutralizing Spock and Marlena is only the first step," he said. "And I don't mean to say doing so will be easy. But before we take that step, we should know what we intend to do next. Once they're gone, who should take their place?"

"Not another Vulcan," West said. "That's for damnéd sure."

Quiniven's upswept eyebrows and facial ridges gave a sinister cast to his broad grin. "And who would you rather see on the imperial throne, Colonel West?"

Defiantly lifting his chin to the Denobulan's challenge, West replied, "Someone who deserves it. . . . A human. Someone of noble lineage, verified ancestry."

"Please," implored Admiral zh'Ferro, "tell me you aren't suggesting who I think you are."

"Why not?" West retorted. "He was born to rule!"

Within seconds, it was apparent that everyone else in the room knew exactly of whom West spoke, and that no one agreed with his recommendation. All shook their heads in mute refusal. Despite trying to remain neutral, Cartwright himself joined the chorus of rejection. "I'm sorry, Ivan," Cartwright said. "They're right. We can't put Ranjit Singh on the throne. It'd be a disaster."

West pushed away his bowl of soup and fumed. "Ridiculous," he said. "He's a direct descendant of Khan Noonien Singh. No one has a better claim to the Terran throne than he does."

Quiniven tempered his usual haughtiness, no doubt in an effort to reach an accord. "With all respect, Colonel, bowing to the whims of megalomaniacs is what got us into this predicament. Installing another one as emperor is hardly the ideal solution."

"The general's right," Morrow said. "Besides, if I know our host, I think you'll like *his* plan for the Empire even better than your own."

With new curiosity, Colonel West turned slowly and looked at Admiral Cartwright. "Do you have a plan, Admiral?"

Cartwright dabbed the corners of his mouth with his napkin. "It's more a vision than a plan," he said. "We need a military government at the imperial level. Martial law, no civilians. Kill Spock, the Senate, the Forum . . . all of them."

Shocked silence followed Cartwright's declaration. General Quiniven was the first to recover his composure. "Assassinating Emperor Spock and his wife might be logistically feasible," the Denobulan noted. "But to wipe out the Forum and the Senate would require destroying the imperial palace, and that's far more difficult. Its shields can stand up to half the fleet—and Earth's orbital defense network would shred us before we could breach its defenses."

"All very true," Cartwright said. "Fortunately, we have an alternative." He looked down the table at the director of Starfleet Intelligence. "Commodore Vosrok, would you kindly tell the other guests what you told me last week, about S.I.'s latest innovation?"

Vosrok was a hard person to read by means of body language. His leathery face betrayed little or no emotion, and his thickly scaled body was stiff and slow-moving. Even as the other guests fixed their attention upon him, he seemed like a dark, vaguely amphibian statue at the end of the table. Blinking his topaz-colored eyes, he said, "Starfleet Intelligence has discovered and refined a new explosive compound called trilithium. So far, it's undetectable by any of the security scanners inside the palace. It won't take much to incinerate everyone in the Forum chamber—maybe a few kilograms. As I'm sure you're aware, the search protocols at the palace are quite stringent. To smuggle the explosive in, it will have to be disguised as something else, something above reproach that will not be searched and that can get close enough to Emperor Spock and Empress Marlena to ensure their annihilation."

At the first sign of Vosrok's pause, Admiral Bennett asked, "And that 'something' is what, exactly?"

The Chelon paused to sip his drink. Cartwright appreciated the sly sadism of Vosrok's dramatic timing. In molasses-slow motion, Vosrok put down his glass, swallowed, and took a breath. "The trilithium," he continued, "will be disguised as the armor of one of Spock's elite imperial guards. Our assassin will wear it into the Forum during a joint session of the legislature, and, on a signal from myself, turn the entire government to dust in a single blast."

Vosrok's plan was met with the same incredulous stares that had stifled Colonel West's proposition. Quiniven shook his head and looked almost ready to laugh. "One of Spock's guards? Are you mad? He recruits only Vulcans and makes them spend years proving their loyalty before they can serve in the palace. You will *never* infiltrate his guard corps."

Vosrok looked at Cartwright, who broke the news to the table: "We already have."

2289

40

Missives and Messengers

Korvat was more than just a desirable place to start a colony, and it was more than the Klingon Empire's first solid foothold inside what had once been inviolable Terran space. Listening to General Kang address the assembly of Klingon and foreign dignitaries as the Klingons asserted their claim to sovereignty over the planet, Regent Gorkon knew this annexation was nothing less than a test of the Terran Empire's collective will.

The Terrans' sole representative at the ceremony, Ambassador Curzon Dax, arrived late and made no effort to be inconspicuous. Quite to the contrary, he seemed intent on disrupting General Kang by walking brazenly up the center aisle, his footfalls snapping sharp echoes. Gorkon watched from the balcony level as, down below, Dax forced himself into a front-row seat, jostling aside several high-ranking Klingons in the process. Kang, to his credit, ignored the obnoxious Trill and continued his address, the force of his voice stealing back the attention of the audience and subduing its angry mutterings about the latecomer.

"This world," Kang bellowed, "has been the rightful territory of the Klingon Empire for more than a century. Too long has it been neglected, left under the careless dominion of the Terrans. By right, we have reclaimed

it in honorable combat. But the Terrans, unable to defend this world by force of arms, now wish to beg for
its return with diplomacy!" The large number of Klingons seated in the auditorium roared with indignation,
exactly as Kang had incited them to do. "Once, the Terrans were warriors, and they understood warriors do not
talk, they act. They were an enemy we could respect."
Grumbles of glum agreement rolled like an undercurrent through the crowd. "But now they are weak and
fearful, plying us with concessions and bribes. They
are not the warriors we used to know; they are nothing
more than *jeghpu'wI,* waiting for us to put our boots on
their necks!" Furious howls of approval and a thunder of
stomping feet filled the hall.

Dax sat with his arms folded, looking bored. As
the bellicose chanting of the crowd began to subside,
the Trill stood and walked up the nearby stairs onto the
stage with Kang. The room fell silent as the two men
faced each other. Kang returned Curzon's unblinking
stare, then Curzon spat at the ground in front of Kang's
feet.

"Pathetic," Dax said with naked contempt. To the
crowd, he added, "All of you!" He prowled like a hunting beast across the front of the stage as he hurled his
sarcastic verbal attacks. "Such mighty warriors! You
conquered an unarmed farming colony less than a light-
year from your border. *This* is the greatest victory you've
scored against the Terran Empire in sixty years?" He
shook his head and sneered. "What a miserable empire
you have. Congratulating yourselves for the least audacious victory in our shared history. I'm ashamed to think
I once respected you as soldiers." Now he turned and
directed his comments at Kang. "I wasn't sent to beg

for Korvat; I was sent to negotiate the safe return of its people. But I've changed my mind, General. I hereby request you *execute* our colonists—because they would be shamed to death if they had to return home and admit they were conquered by *petaQpu'* like you." Dax walked back to the stairs and looked out at the Klingons in the audience. "You want me to call you warriors? Bring your fleet to Ramatis. We'll send it back to your widows in a box." The Trill descended the stairs and strode back down the center aisle, ignoring the hostile jeers and overlapping threats. All the way to the exit, he never looked back. Then he was out the door, and the Terran-Klingon negotiations for Korvat were ended before they had begun.

Energized and enraged, the crowd surged with a magnetic fervor, but Regent Gorkon found himself more interested in General Kang's reaction. Kang paced to the back of the stage, where he stood alone and silent, peering through the shadows into some dark corner of himself.

General Chang, Gorkon's senior military adviser, leaned over from the seat next to the Regent's and said in a low voice, "The Trill got under Kang's ridges." Gorkon grimaced at Chang, who sat on his left. The general always sat on Gorkon's left side, to make sure his intact right eye—and not his triangular, leather eyepatch—faced the Regent.

"For a diplomat," Gorkon said, "Dax goes out of his way to provoke us. Why would Spock send us such an envoy?"

Chang picked up a bottle of *warnog* and refilled his stein with the pungent elixir. "Perhaps Dax was chosen in haste," he said, offering to refill Gorkon's stein. The

Regent declined. Resealing the bottle, Chang added, "It's possible Spock did not realize how the man would comport himself."

"That doesn't sound like Spock," Gorkon said. "It also doesn't track with Curzon Dax's reputation."

"True," Chang said. In the decade since Spock had begun reforming the Terrans' political landscape, Dax had emerged as one of Spock's most skillful negotiators. For him to inflame the battle rage of the Klingon Empire by losing his temper over such a minor affront was horribly out of character.

An unlikely notion pushed its way to the forefront of Gorkon's thoughts. He guzzled the last dregs of *warnog* from his stein, then he asked, "Would Spock and Dax deliberately sabotage these talks?"

Chang squinted his right eye as he considered the question. "To what end, my lord?"

"To push us closer to war," Gorkon said.

This time the general chortled. "As if we needed the push." Becoming more serious, he added, "After all the efforts Spock made to establish diplomatic relations, for him to suddenly reverse his foreign policy makes no sense."

"Then how should we interpret Ambassador Dax's actions?"

Leaning back in his chair, Chang said, "There is a third possibility, my lord, one I have raised before. Maybe Spock's diplomatic efforts were strictly domestic. By using enticement and diplomacy to pacify his own people, he is free to deploy all his Starfleet assets against external threats."

It wasn't based on a social model the Klingons would tolerate within their own empire, but Gorkon had to admit Chang's theory made sense. For Spock, being able to direct all his empire's strength outward, instead of having to constantly deploy forces to quell internal uprisings, would be an enormous tactical advantage. "If you're right," Gorkon said, "then all of Spock's progressive reforms have been a prelude to a war—one he now feels confident goading us to begin."

"Vulcans aren't direct," Chang said, "but they are cunning. If he wants us to go to war now, he must believe he has the upper hand. But before we engage the Terrans, we should guarantee we hold the advantage."

Gorkon understood exactly what Chang meant. For years the general had been overseeing a secret starship-design team, which was working on a bird-of-prey prototype that could fire torpedoes while cloaked. "How close is the prototype to being ready for assembly-line production?"

"Immediately," Chang said. "All we need to start building a new fleet is enough power to cloak the Praxis shipyard from the Terrans' spy arrays."

"I'll give the order to triple energy production at Praxis as soon as possible," Gorkon said. "How long will it take to build a fleet capable of crushing the Terrans in a single offensive?"

Chang stroked at the two tufts of mustache above the corners of his mouth. After several seconds, he said, "Nine years."

"That's a long time to wait, General."

With a rueful grin, Chang replied, "The Terran Empire is vast, my lord. Subduing it in one sneak attack will take many ships. We could expand our starship production to other shipyards, but the more facilities that receive the prototype's design, the greater the risk of espionage."

"Very well, then," Gorkon said. "Keep the program secret at the Praxis facility. But work quickly, General. It's time for us to wipe the Terran Empire off the map, and I am eager to begin."

"As am I, my lord," Chang said. "As am I."

2290

41

Vanishing Point

The Regula I space station had become a shell of its former self. On every level Lurqal saw its inhabitants working in a frantic rush. They had spent the last seven days dismantling systems, packing up components, archiving their data, and packing it all into crates—all on the orders of Carol Marcus.

Even the station's basic onboard systems were being scavenged for parts. Entire levels of the station had been sealed off after they were deprived of life-support systems and power. Corridors were steeped in shadows because Marcus's engineers had appropriated most of the light fixtures. Comms on almost every deck were offline because someone had torn out all the optronic data cables.

Hearing the sound of people approaching, Lurqal ducked into a cold, empty compartment that once had been a chemistry lab. She wrinkled her nose at the odor of old chemicals, which stank like a mix of vinegar and ammonia.

Through a cracked-open door, she watched a dozen scientists and technicians walk past, guiding shipping containers on antigrav sleds toward the station's cargo bay. "Hurry up," said Dr. Tarcoh, who seemed to be in charge. "Carol wants everything ready by nineteen hundred."

All signs pointed to an evacuation, but Lurqal had no idea where they were going or how they were getting there. The only thing Carol Marcus had told the group was that they were abandoning the station and blowing it up behind them. When that was done they would go into permanent seclusion, after which they would have no further contact with anyone outside the project.

For all practical purposes, they were about to vanish.

This might be my last chance to speak to my people, Lurqal realized.

Breaking through the station's scrambling field had not been impossible, but it had been time-consuming. Once done, however, she had been able to make regular reports to Imperial Intelligence. During the seven years she had lived and worked undercover on Regula I, she had relayed hundreds of scraps of information. None of the disjointed snippets she had obtained had made much sense or appeared to be related to the others—until now.

In the confusion of the evacuation, Lurqal had accessed systems that previously had been off-limits to her, and she believed she had found a critical piece of information that tied together everything else she had learned. Her latest discovery made it imperative she find a safe place from which to upload her final burst transmission to the *Zin'za.*

Outside the door, the sounds of the passing group receded. Lurqal pushed the lab's door shut and locked it. Huddled in the darkness, she fished the parts of her disguised comm unit from her lab coat's deep pockets, assembled it with an ease born of practice, and activated the device. She opened a channel and waited for the signal to be acknowledged by the *Zin'za.*

Several seconds passed without a response.

The door behind her, which she was certain she had locked, slid open. She turned and hid her comm unit behind her back.

David Marcus stood in the doorway, one side of his face illuminated by a flickering light, the other lost in shadow. He held a Starfleet phaser, which he aimed at Lurqal. "Doctor Sandesjo," he said. "Imagine finding you here."

Feigning innocence, Lurqal replied, "I just needed a few minutes away from the craziness. All this activity gets me kind of wound up."

"I'm sure it does," replied the young scientist. "It must be especially vexing now that the *Zin'za*'s gone—isn't it, *Lurqal*?"

Her face slackened. "I don't know what you're—"

"The *Reliant* and her task force destroyed the *Zin'za* two weeks ago," Marcus said. He smiled. "I guess you could say they'd outlived their usefulness." Gesturing with his phaser, he added, "You won't need your comm unit anymore."

She gave up trying to conceal the device and stepped into the open to face her enemy directly. "What will you do with me?"

"I guess we should thank you," he said. "Without you, we never could have fed that much disinformation to the Klingons for this long without being detected." She tried to mask her shock at Marcus's revelation, but some tic in her face must have given her away, because his smile took on an evil cast. "I just pity the bastards who'll try to use those botched formulas you stole," he continued. "The first time they try to produce a Genesis reaction, they'll be in for a rude surprise."

Lurqal had suffered enough of the human's gloating. She snarled at him and said, "Just get it over with."

His smiled faded, and the gleam in his eyes turned cold. "As you wish."

He fired the phaser, and a flash of white light delivered her into darkness.

2291

42

A Whisper to Caesar

Curzon Dax waited outside the door of Emperor Spock's residence, surrounded by four of the palace's armored Vulcan elite guards. He lifted his brow and smiled at the nearest of them. "Hi, there." His friendly overture was met with a blank stare.

The door opened. A middle-aged Vulcan guard whose armor bore command insignia stood inside and nodded at Dax. "The Emperor will see you now."

"Thank you," Dax said, stepping into the main hall of the Emperor's home. Three of the guards from the foyer entered behind him. He threw an amused look at them. "Really? Do I look that threatening?"

"No," said the guard captain who had opened the door. "You do not." Apparently satisfied he had quashed Dax's attempt at humor, the captain added, "Follow me." He led Dax and his guards into the great room.

Walking behind the captain, Dax admired his surroundings with wide eyes and a lopsided smile. His footfalls were loud on the polished granite floors and echoed under its lofty ceilings, which were decorated with murals rendered in an ancient Terran style. The walls were adorned only sparingly, with a few paintings and some illustrated silk tapestries depicting placid nature scenes. Small, delicate statues of mythical creatures, carved from pristine white marble, stood atop pillars of alabaster. Golden sunlight poured through the room's towering, arched windows, which were flanked by burgundy-colored curtains.

Standing in front of one window with his back to Dax was the Emperor.

"Welcome, Ambassador," Spock said in a resonant baritone. Turning his head, he said to the guard captain, "Leave us."

The guard captain saluted. "Majesty." Then he about-faced, nodded at his men, and marched them out of the great room. He shut the door as he left.

Cutting to business, Dax asked, "Why did you send for me, Majesty?"

"To ask for your resignation," Spock said.

"Have I wronged you, my prince? Or failed you in some way?"

Spock shook his head. "No."

"Then why recall me from Qo'noS?"

Folding his hands together, Spock said, "Because I intend for you to become part of something greater, and far more important." He stepped away from the window and nodded for Dax to follow him.

The Emperor led him to a pair of comfortable chairs set facing each other across a low table. On the table was a tray bearing two ceramic cups illustrated with colorful, coiled serpents, and a matching teapot. Spock sat down and motioned for Dax to take the other chair. Dax settled into it warily.

Lifting the teapot, Spock said, "You will retire from

diplomatic service." He filled Dax's cup. Wisps of fragrant white vapor snaked up from the amber liquid. Spock set down the teapot. "Then you will go into seclusion."

Dax picked up the teapot. Remembering the protocol of the ceremony, he filled Spock's cup. "For how long must I be secluded, Majesty?"

"The rest of your life." Spock picked up his cup and sipped his tea, signaling Dax it was safe for him to drink, as well. "I know you carry a symbiont named Dax," the Emperor said, catching Dax off guard. "I know also you are the seventh Trill to serve as host to the Dax symbiont."

Masking his discomfort, Dax felt a riposte was in order. "As long as we're confessing, Majesty, I should say I know *you* were the one who sent Captain Saavik to Trill, sanctioned her slaughter of the symbionts and their Guardians, and issued the covert assassination order for the rest of my kind."

"I did not broach this subject for the purpose of claiming credit or laying blame, but to preface what I must tell you now: You are the last of your kind, Curzon Dax. You are the last joined Trill, carrying the last living symbiont."

The news hit Dax more profoundly than he had expected. With trembling hands, he set down his teacup. "You're sure? That I'm the last?"

"I am quite certain." Spock put down his cup, as well. "The Trill are known to revere the continuity of memory and the accurate accounting of history. These traits are vital to the mission for which you have been selected. You will serve as an embodiment of history, a living form of institutional memory for the benefit of future generations. A few dozen Trill couples will join you in seclusion, to ensure your symbiont has access to new hosts even while it remains hidden from the galaxy at large."

Dax chuckled ruefully, then asked, "When am I to embark on this great journey to nowhere?"

"Immediately," Spock said. "You will not be allowed to share news of this with anyone. I regret that events must transpire in this manner, but operational secrecy demands it."

"I see," Dax said, brooding over the truth left unspoken: *I simply have no choice.* "Before I go, can you tell me why you had the symbionts put to death?"

Spock frowned. "It was a complicated matter—one you will have ample time to study once you settle into your new retreat."

Nodding with resignation and disgust, Dax replied, "No doubt."

Though Dax had not heard the Emperor summon the guards from outside, the door opened, and Spock stood as he beckoned his armored defenders. "Escort Ambassador Dax to his transport." Dax stood as the guard captain snapped to attention beside him. He threw a look at Spock, who added, "Farewell, and safe travels, Your Excellency."

Contempt rendered Dax speechless while the guards walked him to the door of the great room. There he paused, turned, and looked back at the Emperor.

"Remember the example of Caesar, my prince," Dax said. "When he returned to Rome from his wars of conquest—riding in his gilded chariot, being showered with rose petals, and leading his army in a grand parade—he kept a slave at his back to whisper in his ear, *Sic transit gloria mundi*: 'Thus passes the glory of this world.' "

"Thank you, Ambassador Dax," Spock replied, "but I am well acquainted with history's lessons. They are the reason why, when I sanctioned the genocide of your people, I let *you* live: Your life shall forever be the whisper in my ear."

2292

43

After Such Knowledge

News of Sarek's arrival on Earth reached Spock only after the fact. He had not expected his father to call on him. Consequently, Spock had been engaged in a number of high-level strategic conferences with members of his cabinet, leaving him unavailable to welcome Sarek to the imperial palace in Okinawa.

Spock returned to the palace just before dusk and was informed his father was waiting for him in the gardens on the west side of the palace. Striding unescorted through the maze of hedges, sculpted topiaries, and floral arrangements, the Emperor resisted the urge to speculate on the reason or purpose behind Governor Sarek's impromptu visit.

He found Sarek standing beside a Zen rock garden, or *karesansui*. The elderly Vulcan cast his stately gaze across the rectangular field of raked white gravel, at the off-center slabs of jagged black obsidian rising from its midst. The slabs were ringed by perfect circles evocative of ripples in a pond.

Taking his place beside his father, Spock said, "I apologize for making you wait, Governor."

"It is of no consequence," Sarek said.

"Your presence here is unexpected," Spock said.

Sarek nodded. "Yes, I know."

A cool, stiff wind rustled the leaves of trees bordering the garden and shook loose a pink-and-white flurry of cherry blossoms.

"There is much to do as our endgame approaches," Spock said. "Why risk coming to Earth at a time when so many elements of our plan are in motion?"

Answering his son but keeping his eyes on the distant black stones, Sarek said, "It is precisely because of the magnitude of the events at hand that I made this journey now. Soon it will no longer be possible. I expect this to be the last time you and I will meet, my son, and there is something I am compelled to say to you."

Father and son turned to face each other as Sarek continued.

"I know you ordered your mother's assassination, Spock." He cut off Spock's reply with a raised hand. "Do not deny it or justify it." He frowned and looked away. "I suspect I know why it was necessary. She had during her final days become suspicious of me—and also of you." He bowed his head. "Given the threat she represented, you no doubt did what was logical and appropriate."

Spock did not know how to respond. As an emperor, he owed explanations for his executive decisions to no one; as a son, he could not excuse what he had done. He stood in silence, watching his father visibly struggling to contain his savage emotions.

Finally, reining in his anger, Sarek said, "Before we begin the end of your grand experiment, I need you to know this, Spock: I have not absolved you, and I do not intend to do so. She was my wife. My love. I forgive nothing."

Nodding, Spock said, "I understand." He let a moment pass before he asked, "Are you withdrawing from the plan?"

"No," Sarek said. "I have spoken my mind. Truth is served." He cast a grim stare at the sea of raked gravel. "Now we continue."

2293

44

Glory's Requiem

Regent Gorkon sat stewing in his own rage while the High Council erupted into useless violence. Councillors shouted over each other until their voices bled into a meaningless din. They pushed each other in the shadows surrounding the pool of harsh light that shone down on the imperial trefoil adorning the floor. The room stank of sweat and liquor, and it echoed with curses and recriminations.

Of course they've gone mad, Gorkon brooded. *Our homeworld is dying.*

Councillor Alakon stood at Gorkon's left side, and Councillor Indizar kept to her place on Gorkon's right. While the rest of the High Council devolved into a brawl, they remained above the fray with their Regent, looking down at the nervous, silent trio of scientists standing in the middle of the chamber, trapped beneath the revealing glare of the overhead light.

Tired of the commotion, Gorkon rapped the steel-jacketed tip of his ceremonial staff three times on his throne's stone dais. The sharp cracks put a halt to the mayhem along the room's periphery. Order restored, Gorkon fixed his weary glare on the three scientists. "At the risk of inciting another riot," he said, "would you care to explain *why* Praxis exploded and poisoned our homeworld?"

The lead scientist, Dr. Gorig, took a cautious half step forward. "All data points suggest a previously undetected error in the data we received from our spy inside the Regula I lab." He glanced over his shoulder at his colleagues, as if to invite them to participate in the briefing, but they only nodded at him to continue. "A key value in the formula must have been wrong, resulting in a massive instability as soon as we brought the Genesis-wave generator online." In a tone of aggrieved self-righteousness, Gorig added, "This entire disaster could have been averted if only we had been given the time we requested to verify the Terrans' formulae *before* we tried to—"

Gorkon leaped from his throne and thrust his *d'k tagh* into Gorig's chest before he uttered another word of seditious accusation. Giving the knife a savage twist, Gorkon coaxed out the gray-bearded scientist's last breath. Then he tore his blade free and let Gorig fall to the floor.

Standing above the corpse and its swiftly spreading pool of magenta blood, Gorkon glared at the other two scientists and said, "I trust I've made my point."

The slain man's colleagues nodded.

The Regent stepped back onto the dais and took his throne. "I don't want excuses," he said to the scientists. "Our planet is *dying*. Find a solution—while we still have a world worth saving." He dismissed them with a wave and a growl.

Alakon escorted the two scientists out of the Council chamber. At a nod from Gorkon, Indizar declared the Council adjourned until recalled.

Sitting with his fist pressed against his mouth, Gorkon watched the members of the High Council file out of the room. They muttered bitterly and cast pointed stares in his direction as they departed.

No doubt they're each picturing themselves on my throne, he mused. *Every man wants to wear the crown until he feels its weight on his brow.*

Eyeing the dead man at his feet, Gorkon knew the scientist had spoken the truth. Impatient to power his new war machine, Gorkon had rejected calls for caution and denied pleas for more time to test their stolen technology. His hubris had brought the Klingon people to this grim moment in their history.

As surely as I've killed this man, I have killed Qo'noS. History will have no alternative but to lay this travesty at my feet and call it mine own.

There was no undoing what had been done. Praxis was gone, shattered into rubble and fire, its radioactive debris propelled by a subspace shockwave that had turned lush Qo'noS into a bleak and barren orb. Deserts sprawled where forests once had grown; oceans that once fed billions were now toxic, watery graveyards.

Gorkon knew there was only one way to prevent this disaster from becoming his epitaph. With whatever strength and time he had left, he needed to write a better end to his reign, one worthy of song.

He needed to become a conqueror.

45

The Architects of War

Marlena walked alone across the frozen gray expanse of the ocean. Thunderous rumbles trembled the ice under her bare feet. Great fissures cracked open the snow-dusted horizon, which churned with dark water like blood erupting from a wound.

As she walked, the glaciated terrain was cleaved beneath her, and jagged shards of ice sliced into her heels. She clutched the bundle in her arms, its cargo more precious than any she had ever held before. Warm against her bosom, safe in her embrace, the fruit of her womb was all that mattered to her now in this desolate, frigid wasteland.

Fire on the horizon. The figure of a man robed in flames. Reddish-gold against the grayish-white emptiness that seemed to have no horizon, surrounded by widening gulfs of black seawater. A silhouette, a gaunt outline of a lanky form, burning bright in the falling gloom, ushering her onward against the bitter wind.

She trudged across bobbing ice floes, her torn feet leaving bloody prints. The man in the flames was her father, François—it had to be. He was waiting for her, waiting to see her son, to reach out and give his blessing to her child. All she had to do was traverse a treacherous sea of broken ice.

A short leap, then a longer one. Deep cracking sounds, like the breaking of a giant's bones, filled the dreary dusk. The faster Marlena tried to reach her father, the more quickly the ice broke apart, the farther the pieces drifted.

I have to hurry, she knew. *Time is running out.*

From the back edge of a long strip of ice, she took a running start. Her final step, the push-off, dipped the leading edge of the floe under the inky surface of the sea.

Aloft, airborne, floating weightless on a breeze, Marlena drifted through the air. The ghostly vapors of her breath ringed her like a halo, a maternal blessing of mist. Below her yawned the bottomless ocean, darker than the deepest hours of the night, colder than an unforgiving heart.

Marlena landed like a feather at her father's feet. She looked up at the pillar of golden fire surrounding him. Trapped inside his incandescent cocoon, her father resembled a dark statue, as unyielding and mysterious as he had always seemed to her during her childhood.

She extended her arms and held out her swaddled son. "Look, Daddy," she said. "My son. Your grandson."

Her sire of shadows looked down and spoke with disdain. "I see nothing but broken promises."

"No!" she protested. "He's your grandson! Look at him!" She pulled away the outer fold of the blanket, then the next, and the next. With every unfolded corner, she expected to reveal her glory, the heir of Spock, the offspring she had borne into the world . . . but then the blanket tumbled from her hands, completely undone, fluttering empty to the icy ground.

The wind howled in mourning. Bitter tears ran hotly across her frost-numbed cheeks. She collapsed onto her knees and pawed helplessly at the child's blanket, at its frayed edges. A low tender cry strained to break free of her chest. Looking up to her father for mercy, forgiveness, and comfort, instead she beheld Spock, frozen and one step removed from real, a sculpture chiseled roughly from ice. She reached out to touch it. It broke apart at the grazing brush of her fingertip, collecting itself into a mound of ash and snow.

Nighttime edged across the sky, swallowing the light, and Marlena was surrounded by the widening ocean, eternal and fathomless. She was alone in the world, with no one to hear her weeping. Hers was not the maudlin sobbing of a madwoman, but a funereal wail made all the more terrible by its clarity.

Stinging cold water bit her hands and knees as the ocean claimed the floe beneath her. There was nowhere to run to, no one to beg for rescue. Marlena fell forward and surrendered to the irresistible pull of the sea. Her arms and legs numbed on contact with the frigid water. As she slipped under the waves, she made no effort to hold her breath. She exhaled, felt heat and life escape in a flourish of bubbles. Pulling the sea into her lungs, tasting death in all its briny coldness, was easier than she had expected.

The scant light from above the water's surface was deep blue, then blue-black . . . but only as Marlena felt herself vanishing into the darkness did the last, desperate spark of terror ignite in her soul—lonely, afraid, not ready to let go, not ready to be extinguished . . . but darkness had no mercy, and its grip choked away her final cries for help. . . .

A gasp and a shudder, and Marlena was awake in her bed, her heart pounding. Musky sweat coated her face and arms and chest. She stared at the ceiling of her bedroom in the imperial palace. Every undulating pattern of shadow on the walls and ceiling seemed infused with sinister intent. Her breathing was rapid and shallow. *You're hyperventilating,* she told herself. *Calm down. Force yourself to breathe.*

Beside her in the bed, Spock lay on his right side, facing away from her. As she turned her head to make certain she hadn't disturbed him, he rolled slowly onto his back. He was awake. "Nightmares again?" he asked.

"The same one," she said, and he nodded. The journey across the ice was a dream that had plagued her intermittently for more than a decade. She had discussed it with Spock after its third repetition, but he had offered no analysis. As much as she had hoped merely sharing it would be enough to exorcise it from her thoughts, it remained with her, its naked symbolism growing more painful with each passing year.

Spock seemed to sense tonight's recurrence of the dream had left her more agitated than it had before. "Perhaps you are concerned about the upcoming conference," he said.

"Of course I am," she shot back. She had told him she feared someone would try to assassinate him at the interstellar summit two weeks hence. "But I know what this dream is telling me, Spock, and it's not about Khitomer."

With a stately economy of movement, Spock sat up in bed and folded his hands on his lap. "I know this topic distresses you," he said. "For your own sake, I urge you not to pursue it."

"But you've never told me the truth, Spock. Not once. I've asked you a hundred times over the years, and you've given me a hundred different answers."

He raised his right eyebrow, which she knew was a prelude to his taking her exaggeration-for-effect and rebutting it with a precise fact that would utterly miss her intended point. "If memory serves," he said, "we have discussed this subject precisely forty-three times, including tonight. Our most recent previous conversation of this matter was—"

"Damn you, Spock," Marlena said, verging on tears. "Just tell me the truth—the *real* truth, not just your latest excuse. Why won't you have children with me?"

Her entreaty was met with aggrieved silence. Spock would not lie to her, she knew that just as certainly as she knew he loved her—or, at least, that he *had* loved her once, long ago, before he became Emperor. But though he would never lie to her, he also was supremely talented at saying nothing at all.

Determined to force the truth from him, she pressed him harder. "Is it that you don't love me anymore? That you're sterile? Or do you simply have a concubine you prefer instead of me? A Vulcan woman?"

"I assure you," Spock said, "none of those is true."

Unable to hold back her tears, she took his arm in her gentle grasp and begged, "Then tell me. Please."

"The reason is simple," he said. "I do not want children."

"*But I do,*" Marlena pleaded. "I know you don't need an heir to the throne, but why shouldn't we get to be parents like everyone else? Why can't we have a son or a daughter to call our own?" Spock got out of bed and walked toward the balcony. Marlena cast aside the covers and moved to the edge of the bed. She watched him stare out into the night for what seemed like forever. "It's been more than a year since you've touched me," she said in a timid voice. "I miss you, Spock."

He turned back to face her. As always, his expression was unreadable, but for once his voice was gentle. "The burdens of rulership weigh on us both," he said. "It was necessary for me to put matters of state ahead of your happiness." In slow steps he returned to her. He took her hands and helped her to her feet. "I apologize," he said, and embraced her. "Never doubt that I love you, Marlena," he whispered into her ear. "But for us to have children would be a mistake."

Struggling not to succumb to overpowering sorrow, Marlena clung to Spock's shoulder and whimpered, "Why?"

"You know why," he said. "Events are moving quickly. We are less than a year from ending the Empire and creating the Republic. But we must not delude ourselves, Marlena. The future of the Republic will be brutal and short-lived. And when it comes to its premature and violent end, it will claim us along with it. I will not sire children only to see them share our fate."

The truth was ugly and terrible and indisputable. But still, there had to be a solution, an escape. "What if I went into exile?" she said. "I could leave before anyone knows I'm pregnant, go into hiding—"

"Our enemies would seek you out," he said. "They will not rest until they have eliminated us. If a scan shows them you have borne children, they will seek out your offspring. They must be convinced we represent the end of our dynasty, or they will lay waste to the worlds of the Republic searching for what has been hidden from them. In so doing, they could potentially destroy all I have labored to set in motion for the future." He tightened his embrace and ran his fingers through her hair. "I am sorry, Marlena. Duty demands a different path for us. This is how it must be."

She sobbed against his shoulder, dampening his nightclothes with her tears, mourning for their children who would never be. She knew he was right, and there would be no changing his mind. His decision was final; she would have to live with it. But it would torture her and haunt her until the end of her days, this hunger of her body to bear him children. It was an empty, tragic yearning matched only by her longing for his affection, which she knew would always be held at a remove, veiled behind logic and custom and protocol.

For her love of who Spock was, she had married him; for her love of what he stood for, she would die childless. All the lavish trappings of the imperium were cold comfort as she confronted the chilling finality of her situation: *When I'm gone, not one little bit of me will remain. I'll just be gone.*

Spock held her as she wept; he was stoic in his compassion.

When the well of her tears at last ran dry, she looked up through the kaleidoscope of her burning eyes into his serene face. "This is how it must be," he said.

"I know," Marlena said. She took his hands in hers. "I accept that I can't have your children, but promise me that when the end comes, you'll be with me—that I won't be alone."

"I promise I will be with you," Spock said. "But in *the end* . . . everyone is alone."

The assassin's armor felt only slightly heavier than it had the day before. The field agent from Starfleet Intelligence had said as much when he'd delivered it, though his assurance had sounded too convenient to be true. Feeling the armor slide into place, however, there was no denying how remarkably lightweight and unobtrusive its trilithium lining was. Less than four kilograms was dispersed throughout the suit of polymer armor: some of it in the shin guards, some of it in the cuirass of the *lorica segmentata,* some of it in the red-plumed helmet. It felt perfectly balanced and was so evenly distributed that it was hardly noticeable. And when the time came, it would be enough to vaporize the Forum chamber and everyone in it.

But this was not that time.

A barked order from the captain of the guard—"Attention!"—and the members of Spock's elite guard snapped into formation inside the hangar bay, their plumes aligned, battle rifles shouldered, eyes front. One among many, anonymous in the ranks, the assassin stared ahead, careful not to betray the mission with a wayward glance or a moment of lost focus.

The door slid open, and a procession of diplomats and cabinet officials entered and marched quickly toward the open aft ramp of the personnel transport docked in the bay. Then Empress Marlena walked in. She was followed closely by Emperor Spock, who stopped, turned, and faced his troops. Torov, the captain of the guard, saluted the Emperor. As if acting with one mind, the rank and file of the elite guards saluted in unison a moment later.

Spock returned the gesture, then said to Torov, "Have you secured the landing site?"

"Yes, Majesty," Torov said. "And the transport has been inspected. We stand ready to depart on your word."

Spock dropped his voice to speak privately with

Torov, but the assassin—and very likely every other Vulcan in the guard detail—heard their conversation clearly. "Armed escorts," Spock said, "will not be allowed inside the conference center. Furthermore, my agreement with the Klingon Regent and the Romulan Praetor limits each of us to no more than one bodyguard inside the meeting chamber."

Above the bridge of Torov's nose, a crease of concern betrayed his profound alarm. "Such measures will put you at risk, Majesty," he protested, careful to keep his tone steady. "Klingons are highly adept at disguising weapons as parts of their uniforms. If they should move against you—"

"Highly unlikely," Spock said. "With their homeworld in ruins after the explosion of Praxis, provoking us to war would not be in their best interest."

Torov seemed unwilling to concede. "Are the other delegates equally constrained, Majesty? What incentive do the Romulans or the Cardassians have to respect the armistice?"

"The Romulans are recluses," Spock said. "I suspect they accepted our invitation solely to gather intelligence. As for the Cardassians, they are a fledgling power. They are ill-equipped to challenge us directly." The Emperor's answers seemed to mollify Torov somewhat. "We need not commit to a decision now, Torov. Have your platoon accompany me aboard the transport. We shall make our final arrangements when we reach the surface of Khitomer."

"Yes, Majesty," Torov said, bowing his head. Spock walked away toward the Starfleet transport ship. With a crisp snap of one boot heel against the other, Torov straightened his back and shouted the platoon of elite imperial guards into motion. "Move out! Single file, double time, *hai!*"

Soldiers wove together into a long line, their feet moving quickly in lockstep, their boots ringing deep echoes from the metal deck plates, their armor clunking with the dull clatter of nonmetallic polymers. In less than a minute they were aboard the transport, clustered back into ranks inside its lower compartment, while the political VIPs traveled comfortably in the staterooms on the upper decks.

The rear ramp lifted shut and was secured with a rich hum of magnetic locks and the hiss of pressure-control vents. The ship's inertial dampers gave its liftoff a surreal quality for its passengers; there was no sensation of movement, even though the scene outside the viewports drifted past. It was more like watching a holovid of a journey than taking one. Then the flatly lit, immaculate whiteness of *Enterprise*'s hangar bay gave way to the endless darkness of space dappled with the icy glow of distant stars.

Moments later, more ships came into view as the transport raced past them. Massive fleets maneuvered past each other—Starfleet cruisers and frigates, Klingon dreadnoughts, Romulan birds-of-prey, Cardassian battleships—all vibrant with the potential for catastrophic violence. An impulsive decision, a single error of translation, and Khitomer would be transformed into one of the largest, most politically incendiary battlegrounds in local galactic history.

Impulse engines thrummed with rising vigor as the Emperor's transport made its swift descent toward the lush, blue-green planet. The curve of Khitomer's northern hemisphere spread out and flattened as they penetrated its atmosphere. It was the sort of blue-skied world humans and Klingons prized above all others.

Spared an idle moment to think, the assassin harbored a seditious thought. *Four heads of state in one place, and me ready to strike. I could plunge four empires into civil war with a single decision.* As quickly as the thought had emerged, it was suppressed. *No. That is not the mission. Galactic anarchy is not the objective. Stability and security for the Empire is the only priority.*

The transport pierced a thick layer of clouds and arrowed down toward the designated meeting site, dubbed Camp Khitomer. Sequestered in a bucolic nature preserve, the conference center was situated on a lake shore and surrounded by virgin forest.

A gentle shudder and a bump heralded the transport's landing on the surface. Almost on contact, Torov released the pressure seal on the rear ramp, which lowered with a hydraulic whine. "Twin columns! Face out! Double time, *hai!*"

The imperial guards deployed with precision and speed. Down the ramp, around the transport's fuselage to the VIPs' portal, which was perfectly aligned with an imperial-scarlet runner that extended from the transport's ramp to the conference center's entrance. The guards arranged themselves in two rows, one on either side of the carpet, both facing away from the path to watch for any sign of danger.

Torov tapped the assassin on the shoulder. "Come with me."

The assassin followed Torov to the base of the VIPs' ramp.

Emperor Spock and Empress Marlena descended together, leading the Terran procession from the transport.

At the end of the ramp, Spock acknowledged Torov with a curt nod.

Taking the Emperor's cue, Torov presented the assassin to him. "Your Majesty, duty precludes me from acting as your personal defender. Instead, I give you my best and brightest, the finest soldier under my command, to safeguard your life." Then the captain of the guard stepped aside and stood at attention while Spock studied the assassin.

"I have not seen you before," Spock said.

The assassin replied, "I was promoted to palace duty only last month, Your Majesty."

If the Emperor divined any fault, his dispassionate gaze betrayed nothing. "Very well," he said at last. Peering into the eyes of the assassin, Spock asked, "What is your name?"

"Valeris, Majesty."

Spock found it curious that the Klingons, despite their well-known martial austerity, were so enamored of pageantry and ritual. From the waving of smoking thuribles to prolonged chanting by an old Klingon monk from Boreth, Regent Gorkon's official introduction and entrance to the dimly lit private meeting chamber took nearly an hour, during which time Spock stood, hands folded inside the drooping sleeves of his imperial robe. Finally, a herald stepped through the portal reserved for the Klingons' use and announced, "His Imperial Majesty, He who holds the throne for Him Who Shall Return—Regent Gorkon."

The lanky Klingon head of state swept into the room with long strides, his bearing fierce and straightforward. His sole bodyguard, a burly giant of a warrior, stepped just inside the doorway and stood near the wall, mirroring the pose of Spock's defender, Valeris, on the opposite side of the room.

Gorkon was taller than Spock, brawnier, heavier. His clothing was fashioned mostly of metal-studded leather dyed bloodred or oiled jet-black, and loose plates of brightly polished lightweight armor. Glowering down at Spock, he flashed an aggressive grin of subtly pointed teeth. "Emperor Spock," he said. "I have anticipated this meeting for some time."

"Greetings, Regent Gorkon," Spock replied. "Thank you for accepting our invitation."

A soft grunt prefaced Gorkon's reply. He smirked slightly. "We both know why I'm here," he said. "It's not because I was moved by your invitation."

Content to abandon small talk, Spock replied, "You are here because the explosion of Praxis has crippled Qo'noS."

The regent bristled at Spock's statement, then half smiled. "We are not crippled," he said. "Damaged, yes, but—"

"Your planet has begun a swift ecological decline," Spock said. "Toxic elements from the crust of Praxis are breaking down your atmosphere and tainting your fresh water. Within fifty Terran years, Qo'noS will no longer be able to support higher-order life-forms. In addition, nearly seventy percent of its population is dying of xenocerium poisoning as we speak."

Once again, Gorkon resorted to his emotionally neutral, insincere smile. "You make it sound as though the entire Klingon Empire were collapsing. Qo'noS is only one world."

"True," Spock said. "But its symbolic value as a

homeworld is considerable. And you know as well as I do that symbols can be just as vital to the stability of an empire as its arsenal."

The Regent's glib façade faltered. He stepped away from Spock toward a long window that wrapped in a shallow curve around one wall of the meeting chamber. The window looked down upon the main banquet hall, a dozen meters below. Spock followed Gorkon to the window, though he was careful to remain more than an arm's length away, to be respectful of the Klingon's personal space. Looking down, Spock observed that the delegations from the four major powers had, predictably, segregated themselves, despite a conscious effort by the Diplomatic Corps to mingle the preferred foods and beverages of the various species throughout the hall. Mutual understanding did not appear to be favored by the starting conditions of the summit.

Regent Gorkon lifted his eyes from the gathering below and turned toward Spock. "Let us not mince words, Your Majesty," he said. "We each walked into this room with our own agenda. What is yours?"

"A formal truce," Spock said. "A treaty declaring the permanent cessation of hostilities between our peoples."

This time, Gorkon's smile was honest but disparaging. "You really are out of your mind!" He laughed in great barking roars. "My empire is far from surrender."

"I did not ask for your surrender," Spock said. "I am requesting what I want in exchange for what I know you need."

Pacing away from the window, Gorkon threw back his head and hollered, "Do tell me, Spock! What do I need?" His voice rebounded off the hard, close ceiling.

"Medicines your scientists lack the skill to invent,"

Spock replied. "Technology and methods that can restore your planet's environment to balance."

"Both of which we could take by force," Gorkon said, turning like a caged animal at the end of its confines.

With perfect equanimity, Spock said, "You could try."

"Don't try to bluff me, Spock." Gorkon walked back toward him now, more slowly but still menacing. "You've been cutting your empire's defense spending for nearly a decade."

There was no reason to deny it. "Indeed," Spock said. "And the resources we have saved have spurred advances both scientific and social."

"Leaving your defenses soft!" Gorkon sneered. "Dozens of your capital ships have dropped out of service, vanished into your spacedocks, scrapped for parts."

Spock's eyebrows lifted for emphasis: "Now it is you who underestimate your opponent, Gorkon." Before the Regent could retort and escalate the verbal confrontation, Spock changed its direction. "You now know my intention. What is your proposal?"

Gorkon hesitated, then his grin returned, this time conveying the dark glee of avarice mingled with bloodlust. "An alliance," he said. "Not just some pathetic cease-fire, a full merging of our power. Together, we can crush the Romulans, the Cardassians, the Tholians, and all the rest of the second-rate powers in the quadrant. United, we could reign supreme!"

It was a notion as crass as it was illogical.

"Only one entity can 'reign supreme,' Gorkon, as you are no doubt aware," Spock said, his tone deliberately rich with condescension. "Need I ask which of us would fulfill that role in our grand alliance?" Gorkon's ire rose quickly. Spock continued. "And when at last we lament there are no more worlds left to conquer, should I not expect our Klingon allies to turn against us, after we have spent ourselves on war? . . . No, Gorkon, an alliance with your empire is not in the best interests of my people. We will come to your aid, but we will not enlist as your accomplices only to become your victims."

In just a few quick steps, Gorkon was nose-to-nose with Spock. The Regent's fanglike teeth were bared, his sour breath hot and rank in Spock's face, his eyes blazing with indignation. Their bodyguards tensed to intervene. In a whisper that sounded more like a growl, Gorkon said, "Make no mistake, Spock: You and your empire will bow to Klingon rule in my lifetime. I offered you the chance to correct your empire's failing course and claim your rightful power. Instead, you chose to grovel and bribe like a *petaQ*." He spat at Spock's feet. "Keep your precious medicines and fancy devices. If Qo'noS fails, then it is weak and deserves death—*just like you and your empire.*"

The Regent turned his back on Spock and marched from the room, followed by his bodyguard. Their door closed behind them, and Spock turned his attention back out the window, to the banquet room below. A minute later, Gorkon emerged from a side corridor and bellowed at the assembled Klingons. All of them turned and glared at the Terran Empire's delegates, then upended their steins of *warnog* onto the floor. Hurling aside their fully loaded plates, they stormed together out of the conference hall, no doubt heading back to Gorkon's transport for a swift departure from Khitomer.

Spock had considered it unlikely Gorkon would

accept his offer of a truce, but after a sizable fraction of the Klingons' new fleet of ships had been lost in the blast at Praxis, it had seemed like a rare opportunity to attempt diplomacy. Had his bid for a permanent cease-fire been successful, Spock reasoned, he might have postponed the final, bitter end of his "great experiment" by a few decades. As it stood now, however, with the Klingons ostensibly committed to waging war with the resources they still possessed, the destruction of Praxis had only accelerated the coming conflagration. Gorkon, having already declared his intentions, would likely invade Terran space in the next two years.

There was still much to do, and Spock's time had just become oppressively short. Many years earlier, his father had warned him that even the most logically constructed agenda could be derailed by the interference of a single "irrational political actor." In all Spock's years, he had never met another species that was even remotely so irrational as the Klingons.

Senator Pardek noted the departure of Regent Gorkon and his entourage from the conference center with muted interest. Exactly as Praetor Vrax had predicted upon receiving Spock's invitation, the Klingons had made a spectacle of themselves by arriving in force and leaving en masse after a theatrical display. Having observed their steady buildup of military resources in recent years, Pardek was not surprised. *They did not come here to negotiate,* he concluded. *They came to defend their pride by trying to intimidate the rest of us.*

He picked halfheartedly at his plateful of broiled *paszi.* It was undercooked and overspiced. *Until today,* he mused glumly, *I had thought there was no such thing as bad* paszi. *I was wrong.* Setting aside the plate on the end of a banquet table, Pardek slipped discreetly away from his fellow senators. To deflect attention and allay suspicion, he kept to the perimeter of the room and feigned interest in the various culinary delicacies on each table he passed. For appearance's sake, he even sampled a few of the Cardassian appetizers. Suppressing his gag reflex as he swallowed proved extraordinarily difficult.

Minutes later he was on the far side of the room from the rest of the Romulan delegation, near the door reserved for the Praetor's use that led upstairs to the meeting chamber. Taking a risk, he strolled nonchalantly through the door, into the corridor on the other side.

A pair of Spock's elite imperial guards stopped Pardek as the door closed behind him. "Identify yourself," demanded the taller of the two Vulcan soldiers.

"I am Senator Pardek, representing the Krocton Segment on Romulus. I seek an audience with Emperor Spock."

A look of suspicion passed between the guards. Again, the taller one spoke for them both. "The Emperor's invitation was to Praetor Vrax."

Pardek flashed a grin to mask his impatience. "I did not say I was invited. Only that I wish an audience with His Majesty, Emperor Spock."

To the shorter guard, the taller Vulcan said, "Watch him." Then he stepped away and spoke into a small communication device embedded in his wristband. His eyes took on a faraway stare as he listened to the response. When he looked back at Pardek, his expression was resigned but still distrustful. "Where is your escort?" he asked.

"I have none," Pardek said. "And I am not armed."

"You will be scanned and searched at the top of the stairs," the guard said as he stepped aside. He nodded at the shorter Vulcan, who also stood clear of Pardek's path.

The senator offered polite nods to both men. "Thank you," he said, then walked up the stairs. As promised, another quartet of guards searched him there, both manually and with sensitive devices. At last satisfied he posed no security threat, the guards ushered him through the door into the meeting chamber.

The large, oval room had a low ceiling that rose to a tentlike apex in its center. In the dimly lit chamber, Emperor Spock was a silhouette in front of the broad window on Pardek's left. As the senator entered the room, Spock turned away from his observation of the banquet hall to face him. His voice was deep and magnificent in the richly acoustic space. "Senator Pardek," Spock said. "Welcome."

"Thank you for seeing me, Your Majesty."

Spock gestured with an open hand toward a small table set with two chairs. "Please, join me." Pardek crossed the room in a cautious stride, wary of the sharp-eyed Vulcan woman who was standing in the shadows along the room's edge, watching him like a raptor eyeing her prey. He stopped at the table, on which rested a tray with a traditional Vulcan tea service. "Sit down," Spock said, easing himself into his own chair. Pardek sat down and struggled to remember the customs of Vulcan tea.

"Forgive my faulty protocol," Pardek said. "Is it customary for me to pour your tea?"

The Emperor lifted one eyebrow with apparent curiosity. "It is more a matter of familiarity than of protocol," he said. "The practice is usually reserved for friends and family members." Perhaps sensing Pardek's lingering confusion and hesitation, Spock added, "If you wish to pour my tea, I will take it as a gesture of goodwill."

Pardek nodded his understanding and picked up the teapot. Taking care not to spill any tea, he filled Spock's cup. When he set down the teapot, Spock picked it up and reciprocated the courtesy by filling Pardek's white ceramic cup. "You honor me, Your Majesty," Pardek said, half bowing his head. "I am humbled by your graciousness."

After savoring a slow sip of his tea, Spock set down his cup. "Why have you asked for this meeting, Senator?"

Gently setting down his tea, Pardek replied, "This conversation is strictly unofficial." He took a moment to compose his thoughts. "I have paid close attention to your reforms, Majesty. In attempting to discern a pattern to your actions, all my conclusions have seemed . . . implausible."

Mild intrigue animated Spock's expression. "How so?"

"Your promotion of civil liberties has come at the expense of your own executive power," Pardek said. "And in the face of growing belligerence from the Klingon Empire, you have been reducing Starfleet rather than expanding it. It seems almost as if you are acting with the intention of letting your empire fall." He picked up his tea to take another sip. "But of course, that's an outrageous conclusion."

"Indeed," Spock replied. He picked up his own tea.

"May I ask a politically sensitive question, Your Majesty?"

Nodding from behind his tea, Spock said, "You may."

"Did you, just minutes ago, reject an offer of alliance from Regent Gorkon?"

"I did," Spock said.

At the risk of being hounded from the Romulan Senate for speaking out of turn, Pardek told Spock, "Praetor Vrax intends to make you a similar offer." He watched Spock's face for a reaction but could discern nothing behind that frown-cut visage and gray goatee. "You will reject the Praetor's offer as well?"

"I shall," Spock said.

None of it made any sense to Pardek, who set down his teacup a bit more roughly than he'd intended. "I'm sorry, Majesty," he said, "but I find your actions baffling. You are a wise and learned man—your public addresses and scientific policies have confirmed that. But in strategic and political matters, you seem committed to a suicidal agenda."

"I disagree," Spock said.

"Majesty, the Cardassians haven't come to Khitomer to broker a treaty with your empire; they're afraid of you, afraid your democratic reforms will inspire a demand for the same in their own nation. And it's hardly a coincidence the Tholians declined your invitation. Even after you disbanded Operation Vanguard, they've remained openly hostile toward your empire. I predict that within two decades they will ally with the Gorn to oust your colonies from the Taurus Reach."

"And with the Breen to seize all territory from Izar to Vega," Spock said. "We are well aware of the Tholians' plans."

Pardek sat stunned for a moment. "Then why do you not *act*?"

"Because I choose to *react*," Spock said. "I plan to renounce preemptive warfare as a tool of foreign policy. I will not incite conflicts based solely upon what *might* occur."

The Romulan senator didn't know whether to think Spock noble or naïve. "A risky policy given the current astropolitical climate," Pardek said.

"Perhaps," Spock replied. "But it is the most logical one. The resources of an empire are finite and in great demand. It is foolish and wasteful to expend them against *potentials* when they can be more effectively deployed against actualities."

Allowing himself a moment to absorb Spock's argument, Pardek leaned back in his chair and idly stroked his chin. "If I might be permitted to inquire, Your Majesty . . . what did you expect would be the outcome of this summit?"

"An alliance between the Klingons and the Cardassians," Spock said. "Now that Gorkon lacks sufficient fleet power to conquer my empire alone, he and Legate Renar of Cardassia will negotiate a pact predicated on the goal of destroying the Terran Empire. The Tholian Assembly and the Romulan Star Empire will declare themselves neutral even as they seize several remote systems. The Breen and the Gorn, being consummate opportunists, will work as mercenaries; they will aid the Cardassians and Klingons in their conquest of Terran space. This will all transpire within approximately two years of this conference's end."

What horrified Pardek most about Spock's prediction wasn't its specificity but rather that the Vulcan Emperor had delivered it with such tranquility. "If you know all this is coming to pass," Pardek replied, "why do you plan to refuse the Praetor's offer of alliance? Why let your empire be conquered when we could help you defend it?"

Spock replied with terrifying certainty. "Because the fall of my empire will mean the end of all of yours."

46

The End in All Things

Spock sat alone in his study. It was late at night. Marlena was asleep, and a deathly quiet suffused the palace's deserted halls.

The optolythic recorder on his desk awaited his final entry for Memory Omega's archives. He had postponed this decision until all his other preparations were complete. Many times he had debated with himself whether this final step was necessary, or if it would ultimately prove self-defeating. Arrived now at the moment of action, he accepted the uncertainty of his decision's consequences and for once chose to embrace truth for its own sake.

I owe the dead at least that much, he scolded himself.

Spock picked up a cup of *plasska* tea and sipped from it. Setting down the cup, he was ready to begin.

He activated the recorder and faced its camera lens as he spoke.

"I am Spock, the current ruler of the Terran Empire, and this is an accounting of my crimes.

"To attain command of the *Starship Enterprise,* I murdered my commanding officer, Captain James Tiberius Kirk. I did so without express orders from Starfleet Command or a member of the Admiralty.

"To retain my command over the next several years, I

killed several members of *Enterprise*'s crew. Specifically, I committed or sanctioned the murders of Lieutenant Nyota Uhura, Lieutenant Hikaru Sulu, Ensign Janice Rand, Lieutenant Carolyn Palamas, Lieutenant Ilia, and Commander Willard Decker.

"In my role as captain of the *Enterprise,* I committed war crimes against the crews of foreign navies. Specifically, I murdered the crews of the *I.K.S. VorchaS* and the Romulan bird-of-prey *Bloodied Talon.* ↖

"I initiated the self-destruction of the imperial starships *Hood* and *Lexington,* with all hands aboard, to stop the renegade *I.S.S. Excalibur* and save my own vessel and crew.

"I am guilty of numerous acts of sedition and treason. I suborned mutiny against Grand Admiral Garth of Izar and Grand Admiral Matthew Decker, both of whom I conspired to murder. I sabotaged Operation Vanguard, suborned mutiny against Commodore Diego Reyes, and made a treasonous pact with the Tholian Assembly to destroy Starbase 47.

"I assassinated Empress Hoshi Sato III and murdered four platoons of her imperial guards. Acting through intermediaries who perpetrated false-flag attacks, I fomented war between the Cardassian Union and the Tholian Assembly.

"To protect my own political interests and safeguard my hold on power, I ordered the assassination of my own mother, Amanda Grayson.

"I ordered the genocidal extermination of the Trill symbionts, a sentient species, and sanctioned the covert abduction and assassination of hundreds of thousands of Trill humanoids with whom mature symbionts had been bonded.

"Before my reign ends, my executive actions will result in the deaths of billions, and the brutal servitude of billions more.

"I declare these facts not to seek absolution, but to ensure the truth of my reign is preserved. I have become that which I opposed. I am the monster against whom I once railed with such vigor. I am a despot and a tyrant.

"I say these things not as a boast but as a confession. History must never glorify me. Do not applaud me because I claimed to have noble motives. Do not venerate me if one day my plan should come to fruition. Instead, remember me for who and what I really am:

"A villain."

He turned off the recorder. Removed the permanently encoded optolythic data rod. Turning the translucent, pale blue cylinder in his fingers, he hoped his message would enable a future society to be wise enough never to let someone like him wield power again. He pressed the rod into a foam slot inside a black case, beside a hundred others he had prepared for delivery to Carol Marcus.

Then he closed the case's lid, locked it, and stood.

It is done, he told himself.

Spock picked up the case and walked out of his sanctum, holding his sins and those of the Empire in his hands.

47

The Ashes of Empire

Nine years had passed since Carol Marcus had last met with Emperor Spock. It had been one of the most demanding and all-consuming periods of her life. There had been few people whom she could trust, and fewer who were actually cleared to know the true scope of the project Spock had code-named Memory Omega. Only her son, David, had she entrusted with the whole truth, shortly after he'd joined her on the project.

Memory Omega was the most ambitious project of its kind she had ever seen. It was a repository of the collected knowledge of the Empire—all its peoples, all its worlds. Science, history, music, art, literature, medicine, philosophy—the preservation of all these endeavors and more was its mission. Multiple redundant sites were linked through a secret, real-time communications network unlike any other known in the galaxy: quantum transceivers, composed of subatomic particles vibrating in perfect sympathy even across interstellar distances, perhaps even across any distance. A frequency provoked in one linked particle vibrated its simpatico partner perfectly. Marcus had hypothesized each pair of sympathetic particles was actually just one particle occupying two points in space-time simultaneously, but so far she had been unable to prove or disprove her supposition. What mattered was that the system worked, and its transmissions were undetectable and completely beyond interception. And what she found most amazing about it was that it had been invented by her own beloved son.

She wished David could be at her side now. A trio of Vulcan imperial guards—one leading her, two following her—escorted her through the deserted, cordoned-off corridors of the *I.S.S. Enterprise*. Acting on confidential orders from the Emperor, Marcus had left Regula and booked passage on a civilian luxury liner to Garulon. Ten minutes ago, *Enterprise* had intercepted the liner, though on what pretense Marcus had no idea. As soon as the luxury ship had dropped out of warp, a transporter beam had snared Marcus from her stateroom and rematerialized her aboard Spock's imperial flagship. This, she surmised, was to be a meeting with no official record and no unnecessary witnesses.

She was led to a door that glided open before her. The guard who had been walking in front of her stepped aside at the threshold and signaled with an outstretched arm that she should continue inside alone. Marcus walked through the open doorway and recognized the telltale signs of a Vulcan habitation: the artificial gravity was slightly stronger, the temperature a little higher, the humidity and the illumination significantly lower. The door closed behind her. Her eyes adjusted to the dimness, and she recognized Emperor Spock on the far side of the room. He looked at her. "Come in, Doctor."

Marcus crossed the room, honored her host with a nimble curtsey, then replied, "Your Majesty."

Spock acknowledged her with a nod. "For a number

of reasons," he said, "this meeting must be very brief. Recent developments have made it necessary for us to hasten the completion of the project."

Alarmed, she asked, "Developments, Majesty?"

"A Klingon-Cardassian alliance will soon move against us," Spock said. "Within two years they will launch a massive, coordinated attack that will destroy Starfleet."

Shaking her head, she said, "I don't think that's enough time, Majesty. Too many sites are still offline."

"The Imperial Corps of Engineers is at your disposal, Doctor," Spock said. "Memory Omega must be completed before the invasion begins."

Marcus replied, "I don't think we can finish the project in two years without compromising its secrecy."

Spock sat and steepled his fingers while he pondered the situation. "Can the last six sites be automated?"

She thought about that, then tilted her head and shrugged. "Yes, but they'd be little more than data-backup nodes."

"Precisely," Spock said. "We could halt the terra-forming at those sites and relocate their teams to the existing ones."

Marcus shook her head. "That would overpopulate the current sites, Majesty. With fewer than three hundred fifty personnel, the sites can be sustained indefinitely. If we exceed that, resource depletion becomes inevitable."

"Over what time period?" Spock asked.

It took her a few moments to do the math in her head—which was embarrassing, since she knew Spock had probably already completed his own mental calculations with greater accuracy than she was capable of emulating. "Doubling the populations," she said, "reduces the sustainability period to just less than ninety-one years."

He frowned. "Unfortunate, but it will have to suffice. I will make the necessary adjustments to the other aspects of the operation."

All the secrecy in which Spock had shrouded this grand project still worried Marcus. She, her son, and several dozen of the foremost scientific thinkers in the Empire—as well as forty-seven previously suppressed dissidents, artists, and progressive political philosophers—had been sequestered inside the Genesis Cave deep within the Regula planetoid for close to three years. They also had directed the creation of several dozen more hidden redoubts just like it, in various remote sectors of the Empire, always in unpopulated star systems as devoid of exploitable resources as they were empty of life-forms. Though it had seemed at first like an intellectuals' paradise, it soon had come to seem increasingly like a prison.

"Your Majesty, I have a question about the project."

In a surprisingly candid tone, the Emperor said, "Ask."

Mustering her courage, she said, "Why are all the people who most strongly support you being hidden away? It's obvious you're working to turn the Empire into a republic. We could help ease that transition. Why sequester us?"

"When the Klingon-Cardassian invasion comes," Spock said, "it will succeed, and we will be conquered. But when the war is long over, Memory Omega will be the seed from which our republic will be reborn, rising from the ashes of empire." He got up, moved to a cabinet along one wall, and opened it. From inside he took a large black case with a handle. "Inside this case are data rods containing the final entries for the archives." He handed it to her. "Guard them well."

The case was heavy enough that as Marcus took it from Spock, its weight wrenched her shoulder. Straightening her posture, she asked, "What's on them?"

"The truth," Spock said. After a pause, he added, "The transporter room is standing by to beam you back to your ship. You should return before your absence is noted."

"Of course, Majesty," she said.

He lifted his right hand and spread his fingers in the traditional Vulcan salute. "Live long and prosper, Doctor Marcus."

Remembering the proper response, she lifted her own right hand and copied the finger positions as best she could. "Honor and long life, Your Majesty." They lowered their hands, and Marcus walked toward the door. As the portal opened ahead of her, she stopped and looked back. "I just realized," she said, "I never thanked you for killing Jim Kirk. . . . I was always afraid of what he would've done if he'd known about David."

"You were wise to fear him," Spock said, sending a chill through her. "He would have killed you both."

The door buzzer sounded and Spock bid his visitor enter.

He turned at the sound of the opening door. Captain Saavik walked in and saluted him as the door closed behind her. "Doctor Marcus has been beamed back to her ship, Majesty."

"Well done, Captain." Now that he had a moment to actually look at her, he was pleased to see commanding a starship flattered her. The hesitation of her youthful self was gone, the uncertainty of her Academy days supplanted by conviction and discipline. It would be a shame to make her give it up, but it was time for her to embrace a larger destiny. "Two days after we reach Earth," he said, "I will convene a special joint session of the legislature to make a statement about the results of the Khitomer Conference. But before I do so, you will resign from Starfleet and return to Vulcan."

Saavik's stoic countenance betrayed no reaction. "Permission to speak freely, Majesty?"

"Granted."

"Is there a connection between the timing of your address and your request for my resignation?"

Spock nodded. "There is. When my declaration is complete, nothing will be the same. It would be best if you were away by then, traveling under an alias."

For a few moments, she broke eye contact and processed what he had said. When her eyes turned back to him, they carried the gleam of cognition. "Then this is to be the moment you spoke of so long ago?"

"It is," he said.

His answer seemed to trouble her. "This is far more abrupt than I had imagined it would be. Unrest, even rebellion might follow, and our enemies will—"

"I am aware of the risks," Spock said.

Small motions and expressions—a twitch near the creases of her right eye, the subtle curling of her fingers into the first inkling of a fist—conveyed her profound anxiety. "This is not a time to deprive yourself of allies, Your Majesty."

"Nor am I doing any such thing," Spock countered. "I am, however, redeploying my allies to those locations where they can serve me best. And it is time for you to return to Vulcan."

The muscles of her face relaxed, and her fingers gave up their slow curl. Resignation brought her singularity of focus and tranquility of mind.

"Then this is the end," she said.

"And the beginning," Spock confirmed.

Eyes downcast, Saavik said, "As you command, Majesty. I will resign." Then she met his gaze with her own steely look. "But before I do, I have one final duty to perform."

Orders filled the air, loud, crisp, and fierce. "Single file, left face! Atten—tion! *Hai!*" The emperor's elite guards snapped into formation, pivoted left on their heels, and stiffened to attention, eyes front.

In the middle of the line, Valeris kept her stare level and unblinking. The captain of the guard walked past her, reviewing the line before Emperor Spock and Empress Marlena exited the turbolift from the imperial residence. Moments from now, the guards would escort them on the short walk to the Forum chamber, where the legislature awaited the Emperor's arrival. A live, real-time subspace transmission had already begun, to share with the entire population of the Empire what Spock's advisers had promised would be a "momentous announcement."

I must remain calm. Valeris focused on the well-rehearsed details of her mission. This was her appointed hour to strike. No strategy was required here, only commitment. Her armor, loaded with trilithium, was fully primed and ready to be detonated. *I will die, but this failed political experiment will end, and a stronger empire will be born.*

She told herself this was a logical exchange—her life for the continued safety of the Empire, under the more competent guidance of the military. Years of preparation had brought her to this threshold moment. One press of a button and her mission would be complete. The action would be simple; her readiness to act would be all.

One final check. She reached down to confirm that the detonator, disguised as a communicator, was secure on her hip.

It was missing.

The first flutter of alarm had barely registered in her mind when she felt a pair of blades stab up, under the layered plates of her *lorica segmentata,* and slice deep into her torso from both sides. Her cry of pain caught in her throat, which rapidly fountained with dark green blood.

To either side of her, none of the other guards moved to her aid. Not one of them even looked at Valeris as her knees buckled and delivered her rudely onto the floor. Torov, the captain of the guard, watched her crumple to the ground . . . and then he turned his back on her.

Lying on the cold marble slabs, surrounded by her own lifeblood, Valeris watched as her killer stepped through the gap in the line where she herself had stood seconds earlier.

Captain Saavik towered above Valeris, the bloody daggers still in her hands. She squatted beside Valeris and spoke in a husky whisper, as though they were intimates exchanging secrets. "Your accomplice General Quiniven was exposed two months ago," Saavik said. Her dark eyes burned momentarily with venomous hatred. "Several weeks in a Klingon mind-sifter exposed the rest of your conspirators. So in case you think Admirals Cartwright, Bennett, or Morrow will finish your

grand plan for you, they will not. Nor will Colonel
West, nor Commodore Vosrok, nor Admiral zh'Ferro."

Valeris's head lolled toward the floor. Saavik slipped
the flat of one of her blades under Valeris's chin and
gently turned the expiring woman's face so they made
eye contact again. Valeris saw Saavik's other dagger, held
high, ready to deliver the coup de grâce. The turbolift
doors opened at the end of the hallway, and Emperor
Spock and Empress Marlena emerged.

"One man is about to summon the future," Saavik
told Valeris, "but you will not live to see it." Saavik's
dagger struck—sharp, cold, and deadly—but for Valeris
the fatal blow was not nearly so terrible as the sting of
her own failure.

Spock and Marlena paused together at the stairs to the
podium. She took his hand. "Are you sure?" she asked.

"It is time," he said. "We cannot afford to wait."

Her trembling frown concealed her swell of emotions. "Then let it be done," she said, and she released
his hand.

Alone, Emperor Spock climbed the stairs and moved
to the lectern, awash in the percussive roar of applause,
all of it from the floor of the Common Forum. The
sound rebounded from the gilt dome of the ceiling,
beneath which the ring of balconies were filled with
scowling senators and governors of grim bearing. The
Emperor rested his hands on the lectern's edges and
waited. Moments later the applause diminished, then it
dissipated like a summer rainstorm coming to a sudden
end.

"Members of the legislature," Spock began, enunci-
ating with precision. "Distinguished governors of the

Empire. Honored guests. Please be seated." His standing audience sat down in a rustle of movement. When they had settled, he continued. "I have convened this joint session to issue an imperial proclamation with no precedent. In recent years, I have instituted reforms of a radical nature, altering the structure of our government and shifting the tenor of our domestic and foreign policies.

"Today shall mark another such change."

A worried murmur coursed through the thousands of people gathered in the Common Forum. Spock waited for the susurrus to abate before he pressed ahead. Just as he had done when making his declaration of citizens' freedoms nine years earlier, he had ordered this address transmitted on a live subspace channel to every world in the Empire and to its foreign neighbors. Hundreds of billions of people were about to witness the boldest, and last, reforms of Spock's imperial reign.

"Since the hour of its inception, our empire has been predicated on tyranny. Territory and resources have been seized by force of arms, dissent crushed and made criminal, loyalty secured through intimidation.

"The Terran Empire has expended as much blood and treasure suppressing its own people as it has defending itself from foreign powers. This ruthless policing of our own citizens is one factor in our cultural stagnation; another is that we can grow only as quickly as we can conquer.

"War is an inefficient means to an end. It leaves ruin in its wake, resources expended for naught, lives taken and given in vain. It is the most egregious form of waste known to sentient beings, and, like all waste, it is illogical. For more than a century, preemptive war has been the chief instrument of foreign and domestic policy for this empire.

"No longer. On behalf of the Empire, I renounce it."

The hubbub of alarm was stronger now, from the Forum members as well as the senators. Their reaction was just as Spock had expected; he had known from the outset this moment would terrify them, but that could not be helped. And now that he had begun, there was no longer any choice but to push on to the inevitable end.

"A nation founded on waste and injustice cannot endure," he said with force, quieting the rumbles of the legislature. "For several decades, the leaders of Vulcan have known that our empire is on a path to its own demise. Habitable worlds and energy reserves are both finite; we will exhaust our resources and collapse into civil war within two hundred fifteen years—unless we change the course of our civilization."

Spock hesitated before making his next statement. To make a revelation such as this to the galaxy at large was a gamble, one whose outcome had proved too complex to predict. He chose to let the truth speak for itself. "During my service in Starfleet, I met four people from another, parallel universe—one much like our own, and very different. Those four people were that universe's versions of my own captain and crewmates, transposed across the dimensional barrier by a transporter accident.

"In returning them to their own universe and recovering my crewmates, I was afforded a glimpse of their reality. They had come from a federation of planets, a coalition of worlds bound together by mutual consent. These worlds and peoples shared their resources and knowledge willingly, defended each other mutually, and valued life and freedom more than power. And they prospered for it. Harmony had brought them stability. Peace had made possible the eradication of hunger and poverty.

"Their way of life is peaceful. Sustainable. Logical."

Stunned, ostensibly horrified silence filled the Forum chamber. Determined to seize the moment, Spock continued. "The path I have chosen for our future is modeled on that which I have seen succeed beyond even our most optimistic projections. Despotism is a path to self-destruction. Our best hope for survival and prosperity lies in reforming our civilization as a representative republic, with a system of checks and balances between strongly constrained and coequal branches of government, and a charter of inalienable rights and freedoms that guarantees the sovereignty of the citizen over the state.

"As of today, I issue my final decrees as Emperor: I revoke the authority of the planetary governors and command that they be replaced by elected presidents." He touched a single key on his lectern. "Second, I have just transmitted to every member of the Forum and Senate a proposed charter for this new political entity. It is now the duty of the legislature to review this document, revise it, ratify it, and submit it to the head of state for enactment.

"My third and final decree: the Terran Empire is hereby dissolved, and the Terran Republic is established. I shall assume the role of Consul for a period of not more than four years, after which I shall be required to stand for reelection, like any member of the legislature.

"Imperial fiat is hereby replaced by a charter of law, subject to legislative review and amendment.

"The Empire is over. Former governors, I thank you for your past service and discharge you. Distinguished members of the Forum and Senate, when you are ready to discuss the charter proposal, I will be at your service. Until then, I pledge myself to defending the rights and freedoms of the citizens of the Terran Republic, whom I now serve. Thank you, and farewell."

Raging howls of protest wailed in the cavernous hall as Consul Spock walked away from the lectern, descended the stairs, and joined his wife for the rapid retreat back to the turbolift.

Even amid the din of shouting voices, Spock distinctly heard epithets and slurs aimed in his direction. Change always frightened humans, he knew, and he had just upended their entire civilization. Even though he was no longer an emperor, his elite guards swiftly moved into a protective formation around him and Marlena and escorted them from the Forum at a brisk step. Without stopping to answer questions from the many furious Starfleet officers in the hallway, Spock and Marlena jogged into the turbolift. Marlena sighed with relief as the doors slid shut and they were once more cocooned in silence.

"It's really done," she said, sounding both amazed and terrified. "You did it. . . . The Empire's gone."

For once, Spock was at a loss for words. His emotional control almost faltered as he contemplated the enormity of what he had just done, and how irrevocable it was—or, more precisely, how irrevocable it soon would be.

The doors of the turbolift opened, and he walked back into the formerly imperial, now consular residence. Marlena remained close behind him as he moved resolutely through the opulent foyer and parlor to the private antechamber where he kept the Tantalus field device. Incorrectly anticipating his intentions, she bounded ahead of him and keyed in the sequence to open its concealing panel, which lifted away to reveal the device's tarnished but still perfectly functional interface.

She spoke quickly, her voice pitched with excitement. "We'll have to move quickly, there won't be much time. I'd suggest getting rid of Senator ch'Neth before he—"

"Marlena," Spock interrupted, drawing a small hand phaser from beneath his robe. "Step away from the device."

Horror and panic made her look crazed, feral. She spread her arms, shielded the device with her body. "No," she protested. "Spock, you can't! We need it. Without it, we can't defend ourselves. All the work, everything we fought for—it won't mean anything without the power to enforce it. Think about what you're doing!"

"I have thought about nothing else for the past twenty-six years," Spock said. "Moments ago, I forced our government to renounce terror and preemptive violence as instruments of statecraft; I must now relinquish them as tools of politics." He stepped closer to her, keeping the phaser leveled at her trembling body. "This device must never fall into the hands of another tyrant, Marlena. It has served our purposes, but it is time to let it go. . . . Step out of the way."

Marlena's resolve weakened, then it collapsed. Her arms fell limp at her sides, and she stepped clear and moved behind Spock. He took careful aim and set his phaser to maximum power. A single, prolonged burst of phaser energy vaporized the interface of the Tantalus field device, melted its internal components, and finally reduced its mysterious, shielded core to a puddle of bubbling slag and acrid, blue-white smoke.

The deadliest implement of arbitrary power Spock had ever known was gone, destroyed with the secrets of its creation.

This, he knew, was the beginning of the end.

2294

48

The Sirens of Decay

Carol Marcus waded through waist-high fronds as she traversed the central valley of the Genesis Cave, deep inside the "lifeless" planetoid Regula.

A complex system of artificial solar generators preserved a semblance of the diurnal rhythm one would experience living on a planet's surface, and a team of holographic engineers had even created a convincing facsimile of the sky to conceal the stone roof looming three hundred meters overhead. Looking up at the ersatz sun, Marcus basked in its warmth and yellow radiance.

The improved illusion of a natural environment was only one of many upgrades Marcus and her team had made to the original Genesis Cave, which had served as a template for dozens of others. Its water supply had been increased, and its food crops had been supplemented with food synthesizers that could transform basic proteins into a variety of more complex forms, providing Marcus and the cave's 338 scientists, artists, and freethinkers in residence a diet of lean meats without the complications of raising or slaughtering livestock.

Beneath the lush landscape, however, dwelled the real secret of Memory Omega—its massive archive of linked computer banks, a storehouse of knowledge unlike any other in the galaxy. No matter what happened beyond the sheltering walls of the project's subterranean redoubts, the scientists of Memory Omega would continue to conduct new research and develop new technologies.

As Marcus climbed the steps of the communications building, however, she couldn't help but feel concerned about what was transpiring "outside."

She stepped through the door to find her son, David, monitoring signals from the cave's one link to the galaxy at large—a small subspace-radio antenna mounted on the surface of Regula.

"What's the latest news?" she asked.

"Not good," David said. "Lots of frequencies are being jammed, but the few I can still get are talking about attacks by Klingon fleets on the fringe systems." He threw her a worried look. "It sounds like Starfleet's losing a lot of ships out there." Shaking his head, he added, "It's only a matter of time before the invasion starts."

Marcus folded her hands against her chin, as if in prayer. "We don't know that," she said. "It might be just another flare-up, trouble in the outer colonies—"

"Mother," David cut in. "These aren't just border skirmishes. The Klingons are on the move, and so are the Cardassians." He switched off the subspace transceiver. "I think we need to face facts: it's time to retract the antenna."

"So soon?"

"Leaving it up, even as a passive receiver, is risky. Cloaked Klingon fleets are all over Terran space. There's no telling if or when they'll scan this system."

"I don't know," Marcus said. "Once we take down the antenna, we'll be blind to the outside."

David got up and gently took hold of his mother's shoulders. "The enemy only needs to detect our antenna once to destroy everything we've worked for, and everything our people outside are dying for. Mother . . . it's time."

She sighed. Her son was right; it was time to finish what they had started four years earlier when they'd blown up the evacuated Regula I station. Nodding at the subspace transceiver, she said, "Retract the antenna. I'll tell the other sites to do the same."

Her son walked to the master control panel. Keying in commands on the touchscreen console, he retracted the base's subspace antenna beneath the surface of Regula and sealed the hatch of its silo, which was camouflaged against both visual scans and sensor sweeps.

Standing beside David at the console, Marcus tapped in her command code and accessed the quantum-key transceiver, their undetectable link to their far-flung colleagues. She selected all the quantum nodes and broadcast a concise directive to every Memory Omega site concealed throughout local space:

Go dark. Go silent. Operation Omega has begun.

2295

49

In the Hour of
Broken Dreams

Consul Spock and Marlena Moreau stood together on the floor of the Common Forum and awaited their executioners.

They faced each other, the tips of the first two fingers of their right hands pressed solemnly together, a sign of their bond of affection. Even from this slight union, Spock was able to touch Marlena's troubled thoughts; he counseled her to remain calm, to be at peace with the end that was coming for them both.

Deep rumbles shook the floor under their feet, and a sound like rolling thunder filled the hall.

Energy weapons screeched somewhere outside.

He felt her love and quiet admiration as she looked into his eyes. "It was nice while it lasted," she said.

Spock lifted his eyebrows, a sly admission of amusement. "I presume you are referring to the Republic."

"All of it," she said. "The Republic, your reforms . . . us." She paused as the clacks of marching boots echoed louder outside the doors. "It was all worth it," she continued. "Even if it couldn't last, I'm glad I lived to see it."

"My only regret is that its tenure had to be so brief," he said. "I am curious to know how this great experiment might have fared on a longer time scale."

She smiled sadly. "Yes. That would have been interesting."

Interesting, but impossible, Spock reminded himself. Given the state of political relations between the Terran Empire and its neighbors in local space, Spock had known from the outset that a cautious, gradual transition of the Empire to a republic would never have succeeded. There had been too many variables to contend with. Just as important, Sarek had been right; at the first sign of weakness, the Klingons had redoubled their aggression against the Empire. Keeping them, the Romulans, and the Cardassians at bay had taxed the Imperial Starfleet almost to its breaking point.

Then, just more than one year ago, against the counsel of all his senior advisers, Spock had proposed the unthinkable: unilateral disarmament. Entire fleets of ships were mothballed; hundreds of defensive installations were ordered to stand down; millions of troops found themselves discharged from active service. Then, before the furor over such a gross dereliction of executive duty could engulf the legislature, the invasion had begun, and the time for debate was ended.

Today, Spock's civilization was reaping the bitter harvest of all his decisions. The invasion force of allied Klingon and Cardassian ships had overrun the defenses of the nascent Terran Republic. The Klingons had unleashed a fleet of birds-of-prey that could fire while cloaked, a tactical advantage that had proved all but invincible. Entire fleets of Terran ships had been annihilated, and one world after another had fallen with alarming speed.

Sixteen hours ago, Earth itself had been blockaded by

an Alliance fleet. A hundred thousand Klingon and Cardassian shock troops were landing on the planet's surface every hour. Virtually unopposed, they had wiped out the planet's military and political targets and subdued its civilian population.

Thirty minutes ago, they had begun their siege of the Terran Forum. Ten minutes ago, the Forum's external energy barrier had fallen, and its few remaining security personnel had mounted a doomed counterattack.

Two minutes ago the shooting had stopped.

One minute ago, Alliance troops had entered the building.

Booming impacts at the locked doors of the Forum chamber heralded the enemy's arrival.

Spock and Marlena waited in silence for the doors to break open. This moment, Spock had known since the beginning, had been inevitable . . . and necessary.

Watching the door, Marlena maintained a serene yet defiant cast to her features that was almost Vulcan in its reserve. It moved Spock's human half deeply, and he could not remain silent. "Though I have rarely expressed it, Marlena, I want you to know . . . that I love you."

"And I love you, Spock," she said, her poise unbroken.

At that, they turned their eyes back to the doors, which heaved and buckled under constant, brutal assault from without.

The doors splintered apart. Regent Gorkon entered the Forum chamber with Legate Renar, the supreme commander of the Cardassian Union. In the wide corridor behind them, the floor was littered with the corpses of Spock's elite Vulcan guards.

Two platoons of foot soldiers—one Cardassian, the other Klingon—followed their leaders into the Forum chamber, fanned out, and flanked Spock and Marlena. Gorkon and Renar stopped a few meters in front of the couple.

"Consul Spock," Gorkon bellowed, filling the empty reaches of the hall with his voice. "Your Starfleet is destroyed, your capital occupied, your government fallen. Kneel and surrender."

Evincing neither pride nor despair, Spock replied, "No."

His answer seemed to perplex the Klingon Regent.

"Surrender, Spock," Gorkon demanded. "Kneel before me and I will show mercy to your conquered people."

"I do not believe you," Spock said. "And I do not surrender."

Renar stepped in front of Gorkon and smirked at Spock. "You're right not to trust him," he said, tilting his head at Gorkon. "There won't be any mercy for your people. I'll see to that." The Cardassian's smirk broadened to a grin, and that erupted into a mocking laugh. "You really are a fool, aren't you? Diplomacy? Disarmament? What were you thinking?"

"I did what was logical and necessary," Spock said.

Spock watched Renar wind up to strike him. He could have caught Renar's hand before the blow landed, twisted his wrist, broken his arm. Spock might even have been able to kill Renar before the troops on either side of him shot him down. Instead, he remained still and let Renar backhand him across the face. Spock's lower lip split open on impact. He ignored the throbbing sting and the warm trickle of blood on his chin. It was only pain, a mental illusion.

Seething with contempt, Renar loomed over the

Vulcan. "Your people have been the most brutal overlords in the quadrant for nearly a century! Did you really think we'd pass up a chance to destroy the Terran Empire?"

"You have done no such thing," Spock said. "I destroyed the Terran Empire—two years ago, with a single declaration. What you have conquered is the republic that replaced it."

Gorkon moved forward to stand beside Renar. Looking down at Spock, the Regent appeared bewildered. "You have delivered your people into ruin, Spock. Presided over the end of all you were trusted to defend. Are you so cold-blooded that you feel not a whit of remorse? Not a single pang of guilt for your failure?"

"I regret nothing," Spock said. "I concede no defeat. I admit no failure." He weaved his fingers between Marlena's and clutched her hand tightly.

Legate Renar turned to one of the officers in his platoon. "Start recording this," he said to the man. "I want the entire galaxy to see what happens when fools lead empires." The junior officer activated a scanning device to make an audiovisual recording. Renar looked back at Spock. "Any last words?"

"With the fall of my civilization begins the end of your own. Freedom will overcome. Tyranny cannot prevail."

Renar snorted derisively. "It can if it tries hard enough," he said. "And if people like you lack the will to oppose it." He and Gorkon stepped back. The Cardassian Legate lifted his arm, and then the order was given.

A flash of light was all Spock saw of the killing blow, but in that moment he knew he had won.

50

An Army of Shadows

The skies of Vulcan turned dark with the ships of the enemy.

Klingon and Cardassian troops came by the thousands to every major city and met no resistance in any of them. No violence hampered the Alliance's efforts to establish total control over the planet. No one protested when curfews were imposed, or when the planet's interstellar communications capability was disabled and placed under Klingon control.

On the first day, President Sarek surrendered immediately and unconditionally. Kang, the new Klingon governor, responded by cutting off Sarek's head and leaving it with Sarek's body in the main square of Shi-Kahr.

When a crowd gathered to claim Sarek's remains, the Cardassians slaughtered them all in the street, laughing uproariously amid the screeching of their weapons. The new masters of civilization seemed determined to prove themselves infinitely crueler than their predecessors.

The second day brought mass executions. Little reason was given for who was put to death or why. Government bureaucrats. Law enforcement personnel. Clergy and adepts from Mount Seleya. Journalists. Artists. Teachers. Musicians.

Landmarks and symbols were the victims on the third day. An orbital bombardment reduced the temple at Mount Seleya to shattered stone and radioactive glass. Lost now were the ancient teachings of Surak, the eons of preserved memory in the Halls of Ancient Thought, the arcane mysteries of *fal-tor-pan* and the *Kolinahr*. The Vulcan Science Academy lay in smoldering ruins. Hundreds of museums, universities, and libraries were demolished, their contents incinerated, their faculties slain.

At dawn on the fourth day in ShiKahr, Alliance troops began dividing the Vulcan population by age and gender, by profession and body type. Parents found themselves riven from children, siblings were forced apart, lovers and spouses were torn asunder. By the tens of thousands, the people of Vulcan were marched into ramshackle internment camps, implanted with biometric transceivers, logged and identified and "processed."

The old and the sick were disposed of on the fifth day.

By the end of the sixth day, the Alliance determined where all its new, pacifistic slaves would be of the most use throughout their newly expanded empire, and so they began the long and continuing process of herding millions of Vulcans onto transport ships. Each man, woman, and child was branded with the mark of a slave, collared, and manacled.

It was sunset in ShiKahr on the seventh day of the new galactic order. Saavik, clothed in dirty civilian garb, marched with plodding steps in a line of prisoners. She was one of ten thousand newly bound slaves being shepherded toward a massive transport ship, which was perched atop the rubble of the city's once-glorious library. The line jerked forward, stopping and starting and stopping again. A cluster of Cardassian officers and clerks, working at the bottom of the transport's main ramp, processed a few slaves at a time.

Bitter smoke from nearby burning buildings lingered heavily in the dry, hot air as Saavik neared the front of the line. At its head, the prisoners were funneled to one of ten processing clerks. She overheard the people ahead of her being questioned by the Cardassian officers.

"Name, city of residence, profession," asked a Cardassian officer. It was always the same question, asked the same way.

"Temok, LalKan, particle physicist," a man answered, holding out his hand.

A Cardassian clerk scanned it, logged the information from the man's subcutaneous transponder, and confirmed his identity. The Cardassian officer nodded, said, "Research division," and waved the enslaved scientist past him, onto the transport.

"Name, city of residence, profession."

T'Shen, PelHan, engineer. "Construction corps."

Sokol, KorLir, surgeon. "Domestic servant."

Kolok, ShiKahr, architect. "Construction corps."

T'Shya, LorEm, computer programmer. "Research division."

Saavik moved to the front of the line. She listened to the Cardassians talking between themselves, speaking about the Vulcans as if they were deaf or incapable of understanding. "These are the best slaves we've seen in a long time," said one officer. "Sturdy. They'll hold up well on planets like Harkoum."

"The pacifism's my favorite part," another officer said. "Makes them easy to control. Not like the Andorians."

"I heard Gul Merdan's people had to wipe out most of Andoria," a clerk interjected.

The officers nodded, and the one who had spoken first said, "Some people just aren't meant to be slaves." He smirked and nodded at the line of prisoners. "And then there's this filth."

A guard nudged Saavik with the muzzle of his rifle and ushered her toward an open processing desk. Following the example she had observed while waiting her turn, she halted in front of the table, just within arm's reach of the Cardassian officer and his clerk.

"Name, city of residence, profession."

"L'Nesh," she said, using the alias she had been given upon her return to Vulcan two years ago. "ShiKahr, stone mason." She held out her hand and kept it steady as the clerk scanned the chip that other Cardassians had implanted into Saavik's palm.

A soft tone signaled confirmation of Saavik's cover identity.

The officer's face was drawn with boredom as he mumbled, "Domestic servant," and waved Saavik onto the transport.

Continuing past the processing desk, Saavik concealed her amazement that Spock's prediction had proved so accurate. Until that moment she had continued to harbor doubts that his strategy would work, but now, watching it unfold on such a massive scale, she allowed herself to believe he had been right.

The Klingons and Cardassians, like despots everywhere, looked upon slaves and servants as nonentities, as an underclass to be almost universally ignored so long as it remains under control. Lulled by the Vulcans' cultural professions of pacifism and logic, the Alliance had walked blindly into Spock's trap and fallen prey to the greatest disinformation campaign in galactic history.

Flush with overconfidence after their swift military victory, they were unwittingly ushering a hundred million touch-telepath sleeper agents into their homes and halls of power.

This day had been years in the making. The network of Vulcan sleepers had grown slowly at first, as each new recruit had been brought into the fold with extreme caution. But as the network added members, its rate of expansion had accelerated. Spies and turncoats had been exposed and eliminated with prejudice. Only the faithful insurgents remained now, Spock's loyalists . . . and soon they would be ensconced in the First City of Qo'noS, in the Central Command of Cardassia Prime, on the capital ships of the Alliance, in the shadowy redoubts of its secret military research facilities.

Saavik knew that toppling the Alliance—and, one day, the Romulan Star Empire—would not be easy, nor would it be swift. But she was certain now Spock had been right.

It was inevitable.

Acta est fabula

Author's Acknowledgments

As ever, my first and deepest thanks belong to my beloved wife, Kara. Her encouragement and support make my labors both bearable and worthwhile.

The original edition of this book marked my first time working directly with editor Margaret Clark. It was she who called me out of the blue one day and asked if I would write the story of Emperor Spock for her just-approved Mirror Universe project. Knowing a tremendous honor and opportunity when it comes knocking, I said, "Yes." Two years later, when she asked if I could double its length and transform it into a full-length novel, I again had the good sense to respond, "Yes."

Keith R.A. DeCandido, as always, was a great help during the conceptual stages of this tale, and his devotion to teamwork and collaboration led him to send me pages from his Mirror Universe *Voyager* book that dovetailed with my story. For being a good friend and a good creative partner, I tip my hat to him.

During his tenure as a Pocket Books editor, Marco Palmieri helped make certain that a number of continuing story threads I set in motion in this story were carried forward into the other Mirror Universe projects.

One of those subsequent projects was the short-story anthology *Star Trek Mirror Universe: Shards and Shadows*. It contained James Swallow's tale "The Black Flag," which put a Mirror Universe spin on characters and situations I helped develop for the *Star Trek Vanguard* literary series. Returning the favor, I incorporated details from James's excellent yarn into this expanded edition of *The Sorrows of Empire*.

Another pair of authors to whom I owe a debt of profound gratitude is Michael A. Martin and Andy Mangels. For the Trill portion of this book's story, I borrowed liberally from the work they did in their short novel *Unjoined,* which was part of the collection *Worlds of Star Trek: Deep Space Nine, Volume Two.* Saavik's dive into the pools beneath the Caves of Mak'ala, and her encounter with the caretakers and the Annuated, are a direct homage to the sequence Mike and Andy wrote for Ezri Dax in *Unjoined.*

Working on a project like this, I would have been lost without the first-rate reference works of Michael and Denise Okuda (*The Star Trek Encyclopedia, The Star Trek Chronology*) and Geoffrey Mandel (*Star Trek Star Charts*).

I also apologize belatedly to Chalmers Johnson for borrowing the elegant and evocative title of his 2004 nonfiction work of political science.

And, lest I forget, none of this would exist at all if not for the brilliance of "Mirror, Mirror" scriptwriter Jerome Bixby, and the rest of the cast and crew of the original *Star Trek* television series—including the original "one man with a vision," Gene Roddenberry.

About the Author

David Mack is the bestselling author of fifteen novels, including *Wildfire, Harbinger, Reap the Whirlwind, Precipice, Road of Bones, Promises Broken,* and the *Star Trek Destiny* trilogy: *Gods of Night, Mere Mortals,* and *Lost Souls.* He developed the *Star Trek Vanguard* series concept with editor Marco Palmieri.

His first work of original fiction is the critically acclaimed supernatural thriller *The Calling.*

In addition to novels, Mack's writing credits span several media, including television (for episodes of *Star Trek: Deep Space Nine*), film, short fiction, magazines, newspapers, comic books, computer games, radio, and the Internet.

Mack's upcoming novels include *Zero Sum Game,* part of the *Star Trek: Typhon Pact* miniseries; *More Beautiful Than Death,* a tale set in the continuity of the 2009 feature-film version of *Star Trek*; and a new Mirror Universe saga titled *Rise Like Lions.* He also is developing a new original supernatural thriller.

He currently resides in New York City with his wife, Kara.

Visit his official site, http://www.davidmack.pro/ or follow him on Twitter (@davidalanmack).